Praise for *The Medallion* and other novels by Cathy Gohlke

The Medallion

"Cathy Gohlke skillfully weaves true stories of heroism and sacrifice into her novel to create a realistic portrayal of Poland during WWII. *The Medallion* is a stunning story of impossible choices and the enduring power of faith and love."

LYNN AUSTIN, author of *Legacy of Mercy*

"*The Medallion* is a rich story about the deepest of loves, the most impossible of choices, the determination to live and love others in the midst of paralyzing grief. Some stories stick with me for a season, but these characters—and the strength of this beautifully written novel—will cling to my heart for a lifetime."

MELANIE DOBSON, award-winning author of *Hidden Among the Stars*

"Set against a backdrop of our world's darkest time, Cathy Gohlke's *The Medallion* seamlessly weaves heartache with healing. I read the story of these two women valiantly fighting for life in the midst of so much death, and felt myself humbled in the shadow of their strength. With every page, Gohlke reminds us that where there is life, there is hope."

ALLISON PITTMAN, award-winning author of *The Seamstress*

"A master storyteller, Cathy Gohlke has created unforgettable characters in unthinkable circumstances. This story completely undid me, then stitched me back together with hope. A novel that has grabbed my heart—and won't let go—for what I'm sure will be a very long time."

HEIDI CHIAVAROLI, Carol Award–winning author of *The Hidden Side*

"Cathy Gohlke has done it again! *The Medallion* is a beautifully written story with a riveting plot, realistic characters, and moving themes of sacrificial love, redemption, and forgiveness. Highly recommended for readers who are willing to stay up late, because they won't be able to put this book down!"

CARRIE TURANSKY, award-winning author of *No Ocean Too Wide* and *Across the Blue*

"Cathy Gohlke has done it again—woven history with stories of two families that must face the unthinkable. *The Medallion* is timeless and gripping, taking readers on a journey of bravery and hope."

TERRI GILLESPIE, award-winning author of *Cut It Out* and cohost of Proverbs LIVE

"What a wonderful book, filled with characters I loved and cared about. *The Medallion* will grip your heart with its message of the sustaining power of faith in the direst of circumstances. Do not miss this book."

GAYLE ROPER, author of *A Widow's Journey*

Until We Find Home

"Gohlke's powerful historical novel features a suspenseful and heart-wrenching plot and unforgettable characters."

LIBRARY JOURNAL, starred review

"Gohlke's latest takes place in England's lush Lake District during the early days of World War II. Readers will likely smile at appearances from various literary icons, such as Beatrix Potter and C. S. Lewis, among others. The story is well researched and well written."

ROMANTIC TIMES

"Splendid at every turn! *Until We Find Home* is a lushly penned novel about a courageous young woman whose definition of love—and trust—is challenged in every way. A must for fans of WWII and British front history. Not to be missed!"

TAMERA ALEXANDER, *USA Today* bestselling author of *To Whisper Her Name* and *A Note Yet Unsung*

"*Until We Find Home* is a deeply moving war story. . . . Gohlke's well-developed characters, vivid descriptions, and lush setting details immerse readers into the story. All the way to the very last page, readers will be rooting for the unlikely family forged through the hardships of war."

JODY HEDLUND, Christy Award–winning author of *Luther and Katharina*

Secrets She Kept

"Cathy Gohlke's *Secrets She Kept* is a page-turner with great pacing and style. She's a terrific writer."

FRANCINE RIVERS, *New York Times* bestselling author

"This well-researched epic depicts life under the Nazi regime with passionate attention. While the Sterling family story serves as a warning about digging into the past, it is also a touching example of the healing power of forgiveness and the rejuvenating power of faith."

PUBLISHERS WEEKLY

"Gohlke takes the reader on a compelling journey, complete with mystery and drama. She weaves in real stories from Ravensbrück, making this drama one that will be difficult to forget. It is well researched, and the multilayered characters demonstrate the power of love and sacrifice."

ROMANTIC TIMES, Top Pick review

"Gripping . . . emotional . . . masterfully told, this is an unforgettable tale of finding family, faith, and love."

RADIANT LIT

Saving Amelie

"Moving . . . At times both emotional and suspenseful, this is a fantastic novel for those who love both historical fiction and human interest stories."

ROMANTIC TIMES

"In this compelling and tense novel, Gohlke tells a haunting story of the courageous few who worked tirelessly and at great risk to themselves to save people they did not know. . . . Reminiscent of Tatiana de Rosnay's stirring stories of human compassion and hope, this should appeal to fans of both authors as well as to historical fiction readers."

LIBRARY JOURNAL

"Definitely worth the read. Cathy Gohlke is a very talented author, and . . . I recommend *Saving Amelie* for everyone who likes World War II . . . fiction with inspirational tones."

FRESH FICTION

THE MEDALLION

Also by Cathy Gohlke

William Henry Is a Fine Name
I Have Seen Him in the Watchfires
Promise Me This
Band of Sisters
Saving Amelie
Secrets She Kept
Until We Find Home

The Medallion

CATHY GOHLKE

Tyndale House Publishers, Inc.
Carol Stream, Illinois

Visit Tyndale online at www.tyndale.com.

Visit Cathy Gohlke's website at www.cathygohlke.com.

TYNDALE and Tyndale's quill logo are registered trademarks of Tyndale House Publishers, Inc.

The Medallion

Designed by Eva M. Winters

Edited by Sarah Mason Rische

Published in association with the literary agency of Natasha Kern Literary Agency, Inc., P.O. Box 1069, White Salmon, WA 98672.

Scripture quotations are taken from the *Holy Bible*, King James Version.

The Medallion is a work of fiction. Where real people, events, establishments, organizations, or locales appear, they are used fictitiously. All other elements of the novel are drawn from the author's imagination.

For information about special discounts for bulk purchases, please contact Tyndale House Publishers at csresponse@tyndale.com, or call 1-800-323-9400.

ISBN 978-1-4964-2966-7 (hardcover)
ISBN 978-1-4964-2967-4 (softcover)

Printed in the United States of America

25 24 23 22 21 20 19
7   6   5   4   3   2   1

FOR SOPHIA CHARLOTTE

Whose name aptly means Wisdom, Feminine, and Free

You are all these, and Absolute Sunshine to me,

Precious Granddaughter

All my love, forever

Acknowledgments

WITH DEEP GRATITUDE and debt to those whose courageous lives inspired this work:

Irena Sendler, and all those who worked to save 2,500 Jewish children from certain death at the hands of the Nazis. Your determination, great heart, and fortitude amid the most difficult and frightening of circumstances continue to inspire and convict me.

Itzhak Dugin (Isaac Dogim), for not giving up, even when your heart was broken. Because of you and the men who worked with you to escape the horrors in the Ponary Forest, we know what happened and are better equipped to challenge the world in the hope that history does not repeat itself.

Dr. Janusz Korczak, for loving children more than your own life, for your determination and sacrifice as you comforted and sustained others, and for showing us that we can all be stronger than we imagine.

Jan and Antonina Żabiński, for risking all to save the lives of many by hiding them in your zoo. Generations live because you dared to do what you could.

John Evans (Jan Iwaniczko), for living a life of faith and resilience when the world offered you little hope through WWII and

Communism in Poland, and even a family sentence to Siberia. Thank you for sharing your inspiring memoir through your grandson, Matthew Lemanski.

Thank you to all who have encouraged me to write this story:

Sandra Lavelle, dear friend, for alerting me to the discovery of the escape tunnel in the Ponary Forest of Lithuania.

Gloria Delk, dear sister, and all those who sent me links to Irena Sendler's story. I so appreciate that you share with me real-life accounts that move your hearts.

Terri Gillespie and Carrie Turansky, dear friends, authors, and writing retreat partners. You are joys in my life. Thank you, Terri, for answering my questions of Jewish life and culture, for providing new insights, and for reading this manuscript. Thank you both for cheering me on from the moment I first shared this story idea with you.

Natasha Kern, agent extraordinaire, who enthusiastically cheers and blesses me in this writing and life journey. Your insights, love for our Lord, and friendship mean so much.

Stephanie Broene, Sarah Rische, and Elizabeth Jackson, my amazing and insightful editors at Tyndale, who make all the difference in each and every manuscript; Andrea Garcia, marketing manager and Katie Dodillet, PR manager—both extraordinary in bringing news of my books to the world; Eva Winters, who creates stunning book covers, including this one; and all the proofreaders and Tyndale team who tirelessly and creatively work to bring my books to life and readers.

My beloved family—husband, daughter, son-in-law, son, granddaughters, mom, sister and brothers, nieces and nephews, and the generations fast on your heels—you are all so supportive and encouraging. I cannot imagine doing life or writing without each of you. Thank you, Dan, my husband, for our trip to France, Germany, and Poland with our daughter, Elisabeth, and son, Daniel. Exploring those lands together has proven inspirational in every way. Thank you, Dan Lounsbury and Randi Eaton, wonderful brother and sister-in-love, for allowing me to take up residence on your porch to write. It's the perfect spot to "steal away" and create.

Blend Coffee Bar in Ashburn, Virginia, for not minding when I visit my favorite chair for hours to write. Your coffee and cardamom honey cappuccinos keep me going!

Wilbur Goforth, my uncle, whose words of wisdom changed my life when I was uncertain which career path to take in the second half of my life's journey. You reminded me that a sure way to know if I'm working in the will of God is to ask, "Do I have joy? Is this yoke easy? Is this burden light?" So—is writing joy to me? Yes! A thousand times, yes!

Most of all, I thank my heavenly Father and Lord Jesus Christ for the unmerited gifts of salvation, of relationship and unbounded joy in You, for precious gifts of family and story, and for pressing on my heart things that grieve Your heart and things that bring Your heart joy. My heart breaks and sings in response. I pray my pen brings You glory and that this story brings kinship and encouragement to readers. All praise and honor to You, Father, now, and joy for eternity!

I know that my Redeemer lives. In Thy presence is fullness of joy!

Prologue

THE VIOLIN CRIES SOFTLY from the summer garden, weaving its notes among the gathered guests—a lament of the bride's passing youth and the leaving of her father's house.

Itzhak, his breath groom-tight, watches from the kitchen stoop, waiting for his Rosa. The door opens behind him, and he turns. A gasp escapes. Overcome by her beauty, he whispers, "Do you hear, my Rosa, the singing of the violin for us?"

Rosa nestles close, and though her veil obscures her features, he can hear her smile. "Itzhak, my love, I hear only the beating of my heart."

He lifts her veil in this one private moment, revealing her beautiful face. He wants only to run his finger down her silken cheek, to touch her lips with his own, but steps back and quickly winks before lowering the lace once more.

"I saw that! Itzhak, don't make me laugh."

"I cannot help it. It's really you, my beautiful Rosa! Even your papa, who knows I'm not good enough for you—" he makes sure to whisper this—"has not played the trickster like that old Laban."

"Hush, now. Don't say such a thing. Pay attention, Itzhak. Your mama nears."

Itzhak presses her hands in hope and promise, then walks ahead to link arms with his father and mother. Heads high, they approach the chuppah. Ducking beneath the fringes of the grandfathers' prayer shawls, Itzhak's parents step to his right.

The violin still sings, but Itzhak cannot focus on its notes. Instead, he turns and watches his Rosa as she links arms with her parents, though he's not meant to. He cannot breathe as she walks toward him, a white cloud in summer.

They enter the chuppah, and her parents step to her left, now one family beneath the families' prayer shawls. Rosa lifts the edge of her skirt from the ground and begins her ritual. For Itzhak's ears only she whispers, "I circle you seven times, my tall and handsome Jericho. Smile as I do this, but do not dare to laugh. Listen for the cantor."

Forcibly, Itzhak swallows his smile. *If I laugh, I laugh for joy. You broke down every defense, each wall and barrier to my heart, long before today, my Rosa. I am a city captive, surrendered to your love.* As she finishes her final circle, he reaches for her fingers.

Together, they face the rabbi, who prompts them in Hebrew, *"Ani l'dodi v'dod li."*

Itzhak repeats the words to his Rosa. "I am my beloved's, and my beloved is mine."

She responds, "I am my beloved's, and my beloved is mine."

The rabbi encourages, "Itzhak, speak to your bride the words that you've chosen."

"In the words of King Solomon, 'Rise up, my love, my fair one, and come away. For, lo, the winter is past, the rain is over and gone; the flowers appear on the earth; the time of the singing of birds is come, and the voice of the turtle is heard in our land; the fig tree putteth forth her green figs, and the vines with the tender grape give a good smell. Arise, my love, my fair one, and come away.'"

"Now, Rosa," the rabbi intones, "speak to Itzhak the words of our mother Ruth."

Clear and steady, like the deeper, surer strains of the violin, comes Rosa's vow. "'Intreat me not to leave thee, or to return from following after thee: for whither thou goest, I will go; and where thou lodgest, I will lodge: thy people shall be my people, and thy God my God: Where thou diest, will I die, and there will I be buried: the Lord do so to me, and more also, if ought but death part thee and me.'"

Itzhak holds her gaze for a moment, his throat too full to speak, then remembers what he is to do next. He takes the ring from his father and slips it on her finger. "I give you this ring, my wife, with no adornment, its symbol eternal. And I give you this medallion, for you and for our children's children—the best and greatest hope my heart and hands possess."

He places his hand on the small of her back and turns his new wife, gently, firmly, as he would in dance. He clasps the slender golden chain around her neck.

She turns to face him once more, taking the medallion in her hand to examine its intricate and delicate filigree. "The Tree of Life, Itzhak! I vow, my husband, to wear it always."

From the wedding of Itzhak and Rosa Dunovich
August 17, 1938
Warsaw, Poland

PART I

CHAPTER ONE

Warsaw, Poland
September 1939

Plummeting from the ceiling, the library dome's chandelier exploded into a million crystal shards as it crashed to the floor—the floor polished three days before to a high sheen. Sophie Kumiega dove beneath the reading table as the bomb hit, shielding, as best she could, her stack of first editions, and the baby in her womb. A second bomb rocked stonework and shattered the floor-to-ceiling window, despite row upon row of crosshatched tape. Marble busts exploded. Great chunks of plaster crashed to the floor. Acrid flames burst from the shelves.

"Get out! Get out of the building now!" Stefan Gadomski, the library's junior officer, cried.

"Move those books first! We must save the books!" insisted the librarian in charge, shoving a cart at breakneck speed to the far end of the building.

"If we move them, the next bomb is likely to fall there!" Pan Gadomski shouted.

"Then we will move them to the basement," the librarian shouted back.

Sophie could take no more. She'd worked hard to obtain her position in Warsaw's library—a coup for an English foreigner, a greater coup for a woman. But she would not risk their baby—the baby she and Janek had prayed for, saved for, planned for every day of their married lives. Even now, Janek played cat and mouse in his Polish fighter plane, dodging the Luftwaffe in bomb-bursting skies above. The least she could do was save their unborn child.

She dropped the first editions into their designated crate and had nearly made it to the door when the librarian thundered after her, "Pani Kumiega, come back! If we lose our library, we lose everything!"

But Sophie didn't turn. She feared she might relinquish her purpose, as crazy as such hesitancy was. She'd always submitted to authority, but not now. Two children had perished within her in two years. This child must live.

Sophie cowered in the shadow of the library door, uncertain which way to turn, to run. Day after day, more of Warsaw was being reduced to a war zone, and still the relentless bombs fell on new targets or punished old. Low-flying Heinkels strafed men, women, children, without mercy, without discrimination.

Finally she dodged between buildings, crouching beneath overhangs and awnings and in the crevices below steps as far and as long as she could. If they could not see her, would she be safe? Which could be worse? To be crushed by a familiar roof or gunned down in the street by German planes? Block after block she alternately crept and ran through the rubbled city, praying for the safety of her husband, praying for their baby, praying that their apartment building had not been obliterated. She reached their street and had glimpsed her apartment in the block ahead when a brief whistling came from high overhead, a sudden silence, then a brilliant flash of white light and fire before her, opening a chasm without end.

◆ ◆ ◆

"Sophia! Dear girl, you must wake up. Please, please, wake up."

Janek, dearest Janek. Sophie barely heard him through dense fog and a constant rumbling in her ears. She tried to open her eyes, but her lids lay too heavy.

"She's coming round." Another voice—Pani Lisowski, her neighbor from across the hall, surely.

"Thank God! We thought we'd lost you. I thought . . ."

Through slits Sophie did her best to focus, to find her husband's face, but it wasn't there.

"You're alive. That's all that matters." It was her neighbor, her friend, old Pan Bukowski.

Her heart caught. "Janek? Am I bleeding? Am I bleeding?" Fear pushed her up.

"No, no, my dear, lay back—only your forehead and knees."

"I'll find bandages. You musn't get up, not yet." Pani Lisowski again.

"Your Janek is in the skies, still fighting for us." She heard the pride in Pan Bukowski's voice.

Sophie pushed hair from her forehead; her fingers came away sticky and red. "An explosion. I remember an explosion."

"The whole street is gone . . . rubble."

"Our apartment?"

"The front blown off—open, like a doll's house," Pani Lisowski insisted.

Sophie tried to remember if she'd washed the dishes that morning. What Pani Lisowski must think if she'd left a mess upon the table for all the world to see.

"Stay here, stay quiet," ordered Pan Bukowski. "I'm going to get help and then salvage what I can. I'll come back."

"Don't leave. Don't leave me, Janek." Her mind reached for his coat, but her arms refused to obey.

"Your Janek will be back before you know it. I won't be gone long. I promise."

"Bring me—"

"Yes, I'll bring all I can. Whatever is still there, I will place in your hand."

◆

When Sophie opened her eyes, she lay on a pallet in a room smelling of smoke and scorched metal, burned paper and wood, smoldering hair. The only light came from a shielded lantern on a small table in the center of the room. Ash crusted her teeth, her tongue, matted the hair stringing her face. The rumble of explosions came from farther away, as if her hearing had dimmed. A dark form huddled in a chair beside her pallet. It was too slight, too slumped, too round to be Janek.

"Pan Bukowski?" she whispered.

The form stirred, sat up, lost its roundness. She heard the vertebrae pop in his neck. "Ah, you are awake, Sophia Kumiega."

"Pan Gadomski?" She had not expected her coworker, but then, the man was also godfather to her Janek.

"*Tak*, it is I. It's good to see you in the land of the living. You've slept for three days."

"What are you doing here? Where am I?"

"You are in a storeroom in the basement of the library—the safest place I could find at the moment. Though here we're likely to be buried in all the knowledge of the ages if this bombing continues. Still, that is better than the rubble of the meat market. At least, I like to think so."

"But, Pan Bukowski—the last I knew, Pan Bukowski—"

"The radio reports one hundred people have been killed. You won't recognize the city. The zoo is a shambles. Zebras, lions, tigers, wallabies—they're saying all the wilds of Africa, of Australia, of the world have escaped. A pedestrian's nightmare and a hunter's holiday."

"What? They bombed the zoo?" It made no sense.

Pan Gadomski shrugged, as if he could read her mind. "What of reason is found in this? Jan's heart must be broken—he's poured his life into that work—not to mention Antonina's."

"The zookeepers. I know them. Janek and I love to . . ." But she'd heard nothing of Janek since the bombing began. Her eyes must have shown her pleading.

"We've heard only that they're fighting, called back, regrouping, doing all they can. Janek is a good man, a strong pilot. You must trust that, my dear."

Sophie swallowed, her throat thick. She knew Pan Gadomski worried for him too. He loved her Janek, almost like a son. She wanted to trust.

"Mayor Starzyński is pleading with the citizens of Warsaw to dig trenches—there are signs everywhere, calling us to arm ourselves, to cross the Vistula and regroup for a defensive line. Shovels and trenches against German panzers," he chided. "Still, I must go and help."

"Here? Now?"

"Not yet, but they're coming, crawling their way across Poland, preceded only by hundreds—thousands—of refugees pouring into the city. Ironically, they believe themselves safer beneath German bombers than in the countryside. No matter that most of Warsaw is now without running water, many without electricity." He shook his head. "All is chaos, but all is not lost . . . not as long as Władysław Szpilman continues to play Chopin for Radio Poland."

"Pan Bukowski?"

Pan Gadomski looked away. "France and England have declared war on Germany. Between explosions and the rubble of fallen buildings, our citizens rejoice in the streets—they even tossed the French military attaché into the air outside the embassy, all the while singing the *Marseillaise*. Do you know how poorly Poles sing in French?

Thank God in heaven, at least we won't be alone now. But we must wait it out. Victory will take time."

"Pan Gadomski—where is Pan Bukowski?"

A long moment followed. "He had his son bring you back to the library when you passed out, thinking there might be refuge among the stacks. Apparently your apartment building is no more. I'm sorry."

"Janek . . ." Every picture, every book, every memory of Janek and their life together was in that apartment.

"Your friend sent these for you. There is a photograph of your husband." Pan Gadomski pointed to two bags. "After he sent you back, he salvaged all he could for everyone on your floor, before . . ."

"Before what?"

Pan Gadomski moistened his lips, hesitating again.

"Where is Pan Bukowski?" Sophie insisted, while her heart quickened.

"I'm sorry to tell you that your friend was hit, strafed by a plane as he left the apartment for the last time. His son was with him, caught him as he fell. He did not suffer long, so the son said. He brought these things for you yesterday."

"No . . . no!" Sophie's heart stopped. It wasn't possible. Pan Bukowski, her friend, her only real friend besides Janek since coming to Poland.

"He said his father's last words were for you. 'Tell Sophia to fight, to keep faith.' Something about, 'Remember the Red Sea.'"

The Red Sea . . . how Adonai will make a way where there is no way . . . It was what he'd always reminded her of when she was tempted to despair.

The tension and the worry, the anguish Sophie had suppressed ever since Janek left for the battle, ever since the first bombs fell on an unbelieving Warsaw, finally ruptured in her chest. The cry came first as gasping breaths, then deep heaves, bursting from a place she'd known only in the losing of her babies—primitive, naked keening.

Pan Gadomski slipped from the room as the storm played out.

◆ ◆ ◆

When Sophie woke again, the lantern still burned, casting weird shadows on the wall. There was a small loaf of bread and some cheese on the floor beside her pallet, and a cup of water. The smells of burned clothing and hair were still there, but the silence was new. She heard only her own breathing . . . slow, fluid.

And then she remembered. Pan Bukowski. Silent tears escaped her eyes, riveting down her sooted cheeks, dripping down her neck. She swiped them away and sat up, her swallow painful. Had he been hit while saving her treasures? Nothing she owned was worth that.

Sophie had no idea of the day or the time. She must be in an inner room—no windows. No wonder the bombing had sounded far away. Now she heard no bombing. Whatever that meant, it was a relief.

A cramping in her belly brought her wider awake. She felt for the mound of her baby and breathed, relieved again.

She must get up, must find the restroom, must eat something. But when she pushed back the blanket, her pallet was covered in blood.

CHAPTER TWO

Vilna, Lithuania

"Are you mad? Tell her she's mad. Tell her, Itzhak! Your wife is mad."

"Mama, she is not mad; she's grieving. Her father was killed and she wants to go to her mother. Is that so hard to understand? I'm a man, and even I understand this thing." Itzhak shoved his best shirt into the case and slammed the lid.

"It is willfulness to go to Warsaw in such a time. She's not settled, your Rosa, not strong. She's—"

"She is my wife, Mama, and I will thank you not to speak against her." Itzhak could not understand the war that raged between the two women. Did his mother not think Hitler and his allies enough to deal with? Why must there be discord in his house?

"But to travel now—this is *meshugge*! It's too dangerous. Germans everywhere! Stay here, stay in Vilna until the spring, and then see. Perhaps it will be over by then."

"It won't be over by spring, and how can it be worse in Warsaw than here? Germans first, now Russians less than a day away—we'll be occupied yet again, and if you think the Russians are coming to save us, you're *me*—" He stopped before he voiced the unthinkable. "We're Jewish wherever we go."

"Already the roads are blocked, crawling with soldiers. It will be worse in Warsaw; mark my words!"

"Maybe," Itzhak sighed. "Maybe the world will end tomorrow, but before it does, Rosa needs to see her mother. She's lost her *pape*. I should have taken her sooner. I'm done listening. She wants to go, and I will take her. We leave at first light."

◆

"I'm sorry, Itzhak," Rosa whispered as he held her that night, the moon casting its glow through the open window over their arms, their necks and cheeks. "I'm sorry to take you away from your family, but I can't stay, not when Matka is all alone."

"Rosa, stop apologizing. There is nothing to be sorry about except that we did not go sooner, that I did not get you there in time to see your papa before . . . before all this. I never should have listened to Mama. You are my family. We are our family."

"We couldn't travel sooner. I was—we thought—" But she couldn't continue.

He cradled her against his chest, kissing her hair.

"Your mama blames me. She blames me because I have not borne you a son."

"She wants a grandson to carry on the family name, to look like me, and to hold her head up before Ponia Dziedzic, who has five grandsons. She will blame everyone until she gets what she wants. It's not your fault. Things happen, they don't happen. We don't know why. We don't have to know why. We keep going."

"Will we ever be more than two?" Twin tears slid down her cheeks—tears that had become too familiar, constant companions.

Itzhak wiped them away, pushing strands of hair from her eyes, and traced the fine chain from the curve of her neck to her chest, fingering the filigree of the medallion he'd placed there on their wedding day, the symbol of life as it was meant to be in Eden, of wholeness and home eternal, of relationship with Adonai. "We will be all that Adonai has prepared us to be, all that He means us to be." He found her mouth and kissed her deeply, warmly. "You are all the home I will ever need, my Rosa."

◆ ◆ ◆

The bomb-pocked streets of Warsaw were flooded with refugees—so many that Itzhak feared Rosa, petite and light, might be trampled by the handcarts, by the horses and drays pouring in from the countryside. He pulled her onto the curb just before a rope-led goat butted her side.

"Where does he think to house a goat in the city?" Rosa shook her head. "All these people—where will they go? Who can take them in?"

Itzhak didn't answer her questions. Even now, after days of hiding by day and traveling by night through bombed cities and fields and woods, his Rosa did not seem to comprehend the magnitude of Germany's invasion. Who knew what the Russians brought from the east? Everywhere, he knew, people ran for their lives, taking everything of value—to live upon or sell to survive all that would come. "It's not much farther . . . just down this street and turn right at the next, I think."

"Your memory is strong, Itzhak. Oh, I pray our house stands. It would be awful for Matka to lose both Tata and her house in the same month."

Itzhak prayed the same. Yes, it would be hard on her mother to lose the house, but it would be a blow to Rosa, too. And where would they stay? How would they find her mother? He held little hope. Street after street had suffered from Germany's blitzkrieg. And yet, in the middle of a decimated block, one, two, sometimes three houses stood without a scratch, or with perhaps only shattered windows.

"There!" Rosa shouted, pointing. "There it is! Oh, thank You, Adonai, for sparing our house!"

Itzhak no longer needed to pull Rosa along. She dragged him forward in her eagerness to reach her mother's doorstep. She didn't seem to see the overgrown front garden, but Itzhak noticed.

"Matka! Matka! It's your Rosa, come home! Let us in!" Rosa pounded on the locked door, but no one came. "She's never locked the door before—never."

Never in your memory, my love. "I'll check the back door. Wait here with our case." Itzhak jumped from the stoop and rounded the corner of the sturdy stone house before Rosa could object. He'd met his mother-in-law only a few times before the day he and Rosa had married. He'd known her father better, having rented an apartment from the older man while attending classes in Warsaw for his electrician's training. Marya Chlebek was a generous and fastidious woman, a loving and doting mother, but he did not think her strong. From the moment Rosa had received the letter from Pani Dobonowicz, a neighbor, saying that her father had been killed in the first days of the bombing, Itzhak had feared for his wife's mother, fears he would not voice to his beloved.

The back door, leading to the kitchen, was locked, the inner curtains drawn. Though dusk gathered, no light shone. He reached beneath the dusty mat and again beneath the cracked potted geranium, now dry and withered, standing beside the door. His own mother hid keys in similar places. Nothing. He ran long fingers above the door's lintel and finally grasped a rusted skeleton key. How long it had hidden there, he could not imagine. Perhaps from the time Rosa's father had built the house and carried his wife over the threshold.

Itzhak drew a deep breath and unlocked the door. The kitchen was dark and chill, but clean. Each time he'd visited, the air had been filled with fragrances of chicken soup, warm black bread slathered in *powidła śliwkowe*—Polish plum butter—and even cinnamon kugel, a meal ending so sweet that his Lithuanian mouth had salivated. That was the most noticeable thing to Itzhak—the nothingness—and that was what constricted his heart.

"Matka! Matka? Are you here? It's Itzhak and Rosa, come home to you!" he called as he walked quickly from room to room. He wouldn't keep Rosa waiting on the doorstep long, but he wanted to make sure of things first. He wanted to be able to prepare and care for his Rosa, whatever they found.

The downstairs was empty. He'd started up the stairs when Rosa pounded on the door again, her voice near tears. "Matka! Please! Open the door!"

Itzhak took the stairs down two at a time and unlocked the front door, pulling Rosa into his arms.

"Where is she? Why didn't she answer?" He heard the panic in his wife's voice.

"Maybe she stepped out—to the shops. Maybe she's visiting a neighbor, or—" He stopped, not wanting to say *your tata's grave*.

"Yes, that's right. That's right," she said, forced reassurance in every breath. She pulled away and stepped inside the parlor, scanning the room—taking inventory, Itzhak knew. "Everything's the same. Just the same." The relief in Rosa's voice steadied Itzhak's heart.

She ran her fingers over the large oval table in the center of the room—the family heirloom table where they'd cut their tiered wedding cake, baked and intricately decorated by her mother. But Rosa's face contorted as she pulled her fingers away and held them up to Itzhak, almost accusing. "Dust. My matka would never allow dust to settle."

Itzhak knew this was true. "I haven't checked upstairs yet. Wait here, and I'll—"

Before he could finish, Rosa pushed past him, racing up the stairs. "Matka!"

Itzhak followed, his heart in his throat for Rosa's sake. If something ill had befallen her mother, Rosa would be haunted. This he knew beyond doubt.

The hallway abovestairs held three rooms—a small bath with toilet Rosa's father had built when she was small, Rosa's girlhood room, and her parents' bedroom. Each door was closed, shutting out the light. Rosa hesitated long enough at her parents' bedroom door for Itzhak to catch up. He covered her hand as she turned the doorknob and gently pressed his other hand into the small of her back.

The room lay dark, the curtains drawn tight. Contrary to practice, the window must have been locked; not a particle of air stirred. Not a sound.

"Matka?" Rosa's voice came tentative, that of a little girl. "Matka, are you here?"

Itzhak pulled the heavy drapery from the window. Waning light filtered through the sheer curtain beneath.

Rosa gasped, seeing the form of her mother on the bed before he did.

Please, Adonai, don't let her be—

"She's breathing!" Rosa gasped. "Oh, Itzhak! Barely, but she's breathing."

Itzhak pulled aside the sheers and opened the window. Fresh air billowed into the room. He switched on the lamp by the bed, but nothing happened. He found the lamp on the dresser and tried that, too. "No electricity."

"Matka! Matka!" Rosa shook her mother's arm.

"I'll get her water." Itzhak raced down the stairs and into the kitchen. He found a glass, but just as he reached the sink and turned the faucet, he realized there would be no running water. He slammed his palm against the counter. And then he remembered. His father-in-law had installed a pump in the back garden—years ago, Rosa had told him, to water his wife's flowers and the vegetables and fruits he loved to grow.

Itzhak rummaged through the cupboard until he found a sturdy pitcher, then ran to the garden. How long it had been since the pump had been used, he'd no idea. The water was bound to be dirty at first—from disuse, and probably from September's bombing. It took a while to prime, but at last muddy water gushed freely. He let it run, hoping to filter rust and dirt, though it was getting too dark to see.

By the time he returned to the upstairs bedroom, pitcher and tea towel in hand, Rosa had lit a candle. She sat against the bedstead, cradling her mother's head in her lap, crooning over her. Gently, she pushed hair back from her forehead.

Itzhak poured water into a teacup sitting on the bedside table. He dunked the towel into the pitcher, wrung it out, and offered it to Rosa.

For all that he'd expected to see his wife crumple before him, she did not. Gently, she washed her mother's face and the back of her neck. She rolled the towel and lay it across her forehead, all the while speaking softly, as if to a small child. "I'm here, Matka. Your Rosa is home. I love you, my matka. Come back to me. Please, please come back to me."

Itzhak saw the glisten of his wife's tears in the candlelight, but her voice remained steady. The rise and fall of her mother's chest was barely visible. Her eyes remained closed. But at last he saw her swallow and draw a deeper breath.

Rosa lifted her mother's head and whispered, "Hold the cup to her lips. Let her drink."

Itzhak did as he was told. Marya turned away, grimacing, but Rosa persisted. "You must drink, Matka. Just a little, that's all I ask, but you must drink. Now . . . yes, there . . . very good. In a moment we'll have more, but that's good, very good."

Rosa sang, soft and low, a lullaby Itzhak had never heard.

"Oh, sleep, my darling.
If you'd like a star from the sky, I'll give you one."

Something she sang to you as a child? Itzhak didn't know, but he marveled at how easily his wife stepped into this switching of mother/daughter roles.

Marya's chest rose higher, evidence of a deeper breath, but she moaned and turned her head away. Rosa stroked her forehead, leaned down to kiss her brow, and hummed the same tune. "I love you, Matka . . . how I love you. I need you, my dearest matka." Over and over Rosa whispered the words into the room. Again and again, at his wife's instruction, Itzhak lifted the cup to her mother's lips. The feeble light outside the window faded into darkness and the darkness into black night.

When at last, perhaps an hour, perhaps an eternity later, Marya's breathing grew steady and even, deep enough to please Rosa, she slipped from the bed and laid her mother's head upon the pillow, tucking the comforter beneath her chin. "Sleep now, Matka. You've done well. We will have more soon."

She motioned for Itzhak to take the candle from the room and into the hallway. Softly, she pulled the door closed and, turning to him, showed the first signs of weariness and resignation since she'd found her mother. He pulled her to his chest with his free arm, stroked her hair, and let her cry.

CHAPTER THREE

SOPHIE HELPED TERRI FOLD the last of the towels and bed linens, hand-washed in the river and dried on the line outside the Gadomskis' home. There was still no electricity in much of Warsaw, and water pressure ran low. Hand pumps in the streets provided the only source of water for many in the city. Helping with laundry and cooking was the least she could do since Pan Gadomski and his daughter had taken her in—over a month and a half now, weeks longer since she'd heard anything from Janek, and weeks enough since she'd lost their baby. That loss, above all, wore heavy on Sophie's heart.

"There's a new decree." Terri—Tereza—less than a year older than Sophie, shook out the last towel. "No more Glenn Miller. No more radios—we're to turn them in. But of course, we won't."

"Is there a penalty?" Sophie hardly cared. Caring took such energy. She did her best to feign interest, though she knew she wouldn't fool Terri, who had become her new and only confidante. Since the bombing Sophie had not returned to her work at the library. Pan Gadomski had insisted she remain at home to recover and that she give him time to work things out with the Germans. Libraries had been closed immediately. Pan Gadomski hoped to negotiate the reopening of their building but had, as yet, made no progress.

Terri grunted. "There's a penalty for breathing through the wrong nostril. Penalty for possession of a radio is imprisonment. Penalty for possession of a radio transmitter is death."

Sophie shuddered. Earlier in the month a dusk-to-dawn curfew had been decreed for everyone. Violators were shot. But the Gadomskis seemed to live on another plane, taking risks, ignoring laws they did not care for. They weren't fearless, weren't careless, but sometimes acted as if the new laws didn't apply to them.

"Fear is an ungainly enemy. Give it a foothold and it will control your life." Pan Gadomski had said it on more than one occasion. His daughter repeated it often, as creed.

"Still," Terri continued, "we're not so badly off as some."

As Jewish citizens—that's what she means. Sophie knew that was true. From the beginning of the German occupation, the Jewish population had been under attack. Right away all Jewish businesses were transferred to German "trustees." Those trustees were not allowed to retain Jewish employees—not even the original owners. Landlords were deprived of their properties and could not administrate in their own buildings. Pension rights were revoked. Only those able to prove pure "Aryan" lineage could obtain new business licenses.

Polish youths applauded one another for tripping old men in the street or for stealing a needed cane from an elderly Jewish woman. Jewish peddlers were robbed in plain sight. Wehrmacht soldiers, supposedly patrolling Warsaw's streets, were no help at all. Not only did they dare anyone to come to the aid of the persecuted, but they helped themselves just as freely to retail goods, openly persecuted the Orthodox by cutting beards and sidelocks, humiliated old women, and forced young girls into back alleys. No one stopped them, and few reprimanded them. Those brave enough to do so found themselves on the brutal end of truncheons or deported to labor camps or shot in the street.

Sophie had known Poland as an old-world country of manners and polite behaviors. She'd teased Janek that Warsaw was the land of "finger kissing and pleased-to-meet-you flowers." But it was only teasing, for she'd loved that very cultured and romantic nature of Poland. Now, with Wehrmacht soldiers and SS crawling the streets and crossroads, she would not feel safe to walk to and from the library alone, even if its doors had been open. Pan Gadomski insisted on escorting both Sophie and his daughter whenever they left the house. Perhaps he was overprotective, but in her heart, Sophie was grateful.

That night, Pan Gadomski brought a man, whose name he never gave, to dinner. The meal Sophie and Terri prepared was Sophie's best *gołąbki* recipe—meat-stuffed cabbages covered in sauce—though the meat portions were meager compared to prewar standards.

Finishing the meal of forced conversation with a relished and sacrificial glass of wine, Pan Gadomski stayed Sophie's hand when she stood to clear the dishes. "Please, sit down, Sophia. Dishes can wait. Our guest has brought his camera. I wish for him to take your photograph."

"My photograph?" Sophie could not imagine why.

"Yours and Tereza's. I want you both issued new identity cards. I ask that you both remove any trace of makeup, perhaps add some shadows beneath your eyes. Do whatever you can to make your hair less attractive, to diminish your appearance in ways you can maintain."

"You want us to suddenly grow ugly? Why?" Terri demanded.

The two men glanced at one another before Pan Gadomski said, "The Germans are combing public records, listing names and addresses of professionals in academic and medical fields. And they're looking for families of Polish officers and fighter pilots."

Sophie felt her heart constrict. The Germans were quick, efficient, cruel, and they'd done the same among the Jews and intelligentsia in Germany. But she hadn't thought it would come so quickly in Poland. Wasn't occupation enough?

"We can only surmise their intentions. Leverage. Manipulation. Imprisonment. They're clearing the way for their 'living space,' and they want no opposition—no leaders in a nation they dominate. They intend to reduce Poland to a slave state; of that I have no doubt. That does not portend well for academics, and being English will not help you, Sophia. You both need new identity cards, changes of name, new addresses, new occupations."

"I'll no longer work in the library?" Sophie could not imagine doing anything else.

"Isn't this premature?" Terri challenged. "And I am not the wife of a pilot, or a professional academic, or connected with the military."

"Premature?" Pan Gadomski momentarily closed his eyes. "I pray we are not too late, my daughter. Your education alone singles you out. As soon as we have the photographs, I will edit existing library files. Our guest has access to public health and birth records. Father Nowak will alter baptismal records. You'll assume the names of two women killed in the bombing—deaths that the good father did not report. He's done the same for others.

"I've found apartments for the two of you—the same floor of a building near the Jewish Quarter. At least you can be together. Two are better than one alone."

"But what about you, Papa? You will move with us, surely!" Terri's voice rose.

Sophie's heart went out to her friend. Terri loved her dear father, would not want to be separated from him. But she anticipated his answer.

"I am too well known, my daughter. And you know there are other reasons."

"You mean that Mother was Jewish. You're sending me away because I'm half Jewish?"

Sophie winced at the sudden thrust of pain Terri's words caused her father, the anguish palpable in his eyes. She had not before imagined what being Jewish could mean for her new friend.

"You know better," he said.

Terri turned her face from him. "You don't want me to stay."

Their guest stared at his empty plate but did not move, did not shift uncomfortably in his seat as Sophie wanted to.

Pan Gadomski reached for his daughter's hand but she pulled it away. "When they comb the records, they will find that your mother was Jewish, yes. That she died in childbirth will not matter. They will know that you are half Jewish. What they will do about that frightens me more than anything. Frightens me for you, Daughter—a Jewess and the daughter of an academic, a beautiful and intelligent woman with a stellar education of your own. You are a light so bright I cannot hide you in this house. If we convince them that you have been missing since the bombing, and if Father Nowak issues a death certificate for you, then you can have a new life as a Pole with Aryan lineage. It is the only way I know to protect you."

Sophie pitied them both but nursed her own worries. The thought of not working in the library, of leaving the home of Pan Gadomski, her last safety net, panicked her nearly as much as changing her name. But she voiced her greatest fear. "How will Janek find me if I do these things?"

The two men exchanged another glance. This time, the guest spoke. "You've heard that our military was ordered to pull back after the capitulation. They didn't surrender. As many as could made their way to Romania to regroup, intending to launch another attack."

"But Romania has claimed neutrality—yes?"

Pan Gadomski sighed. "Yes. And for that reason the Romanians now refuse to help—terrified of German retaliation, of occupation.

Our soldiers, our pilots, are being held mostly in warehouses with no hope of military assistance."

"Held? As prisoners?" Sophie's breath caught.

"We're doing all we can to send them food and clothing, but the borders are closed. Every entryway is patrolled by Germans. Getting information—much less food, money, or supplies—is very difficult."

"How do you know this?"

Both men hesitated. Finally, the guest—the photographer—spoke.

"We have contacts in Romania. Depending on where they are located, many are subsisting on prison rations. If things don't change quickly, we—they—must make their way to a country that will help, a country allied in the fight against Germany." He said more quietly, "I don't believe your Janek will be back for quite some time."

The brick in Sophie's throat lodged itself more firmly. She imagined Janek—her smiling, loving, brave Janek—imprisoned in a warehouse, cold, hungry. But at least, if he was living . . . "Do you know anything of Janek? Is he—anything at all?"

Now Pan Gadomski looked her fully in the eyes. "The moment I know anything of your husband, I will tell you."

"Even if—"

"No matter what. I promise."

Sophie both needed that promise and was terrified by its potential fulfillment.

"Whenever he returns, we must make certain our brave pilot has his beautiful English wife to come home to, safe and sound, even if that means spending this war as a more homely Pole."

Sophie could not return Pan Gadomski's smile. Janek might come home—and she desperately wanted that, prayed for that very thing. But he'd not return to the radiant wife he left; he would return to a barren one.

CHAPTER FOUR

ITZHAK HURRIED HOME FROM WORK, praying he'd make curfew, praying for a little quiet time with his wife, praying he would not waken his mother-in-law from her evening nap.

He'd lost count of the times over the past weeks that Marya had asked the hour, asked when her husband would come home, asked what was for supper, asked who the woman in the kitchen was, asked his name, then begun the ritual again.

He ached for his Rosa, who stayed by her side, urging her out of bed, down the stairs, into the kitchen, and out to the garden each day. It saddened him to see weary lines frame the mouth of his normally cheerful wife as she nursed her mother through self-pitying cries in the night and accusing tantrums in the day. Her shrill insistence that she should have been left alone to die, that she had nothing left to live for, and what did Rosa know of hardship, anyway?—that was the worst to bear.

It was a good thing she could not remember all that Pani Dobonowicz reported. According to Marya's longtime neighbor,

Rosa's father, who'd owned two apartment buildings, had been forced to turn them over to the Nazis right away, even before the late-September general decree that deprived Jewish landlords of their properties. He'd gone to protest, to plead that the apartment buildings were his sole source of income and that he would be willing to share the income with the German officer in charge.

"And what did the officer say?" Rosa had asked, her shoulders squared.

Pani Dobonowicz had looked away. "They gave him no answer but sent him home. Late that night, after midnight, a Gestapo car pulled up in front of the house. They dragged him from his bed and shot him at the curb, like a dog in the street, in front of your screaming mother. She has not recovered, poor woman." And Pani Dobonowicz, Catholic in a mixed Jewish and Gentile neighborhood, had crossed herself.

It was a mercy Itzhak needed to find work each day, and a mercy that the Germans needed his electrician's skills to repair the devastation and mayhem they'd wreaked upon the wiring of the city through their incessant bombing—though he hated working for them as much as they did not want to acknowledge or use skilled Jewish labor. The hours away gave him peace from his mother-in-law, as well as purpose and livelihood to support them with enough to buy food—something few Jewish men could claim. At least he was not forced to dig ditches or latrines or unearth bodies or collect the stones and rubble of buildings for who knew what purpose. There were old men aplenty for that—even rabbis.

Most of the young men who'd not been captured and sent to labor camps were off to war. If the rumor was true, if the Polish army and air force had regrouped in Romania and were busy preparing to go on the offensive, to drive the Huns from Poland, they could not come soon enough. But for whatever reason, they did not come. Nor did the French or the British, no matter that they'd declared war on Germany and promised to rally to Poland's defense the moment Germany attacked. Where was the world? Why the delay?

Without electricity—and none had yet been restored to Jewish or mixed Jewish and Gentile neighborhoods—Marya's wireless would not work, and now all units were confiscated. Without the wireless to reach lands outside of occupied territory, they were forced to read the German propaganda touted in print and broadcast through loudspeakers in the streets. The only news of substance that they'd heard of Vilna was that the Russians, who had been on the doorstep of Itzhak's hometown when they'd left, had wreaked havoc while there and then turned the city back over to the Lithuanians.

Now the Lithuanians were persecuting Jews—robbing, beating, shooting, humiliating them in the streets. *Everyone getting in their shots, taking their turn to dehumanize the "inhuman Jew."* Itzhak prayed that his parents, his sisters, and their families were alive, were well, were spared. Mail delivery had fallen off. Jews were forced to present themselves at the post office to receive mail. What mail could be worth drawing such attention? What could be worth exposing your relations to German scrutiny and censorship? Neither Itzhak nor Rosa had written or received a letter since they'd reached Warsaw.

Itzhak brushed the street dust from his shoes and stepped through the back door, shrugging out of his coat, just before curfew. The fragrance of simmering root vegetables and what he knew could not be real chicken broth filled his nostrils. In better days his mother-in-law had taught her daughter to cook and cook well, with anything in the larder. "Stone Soup" was a folktale told in truth in her house. Now, no matter that Marya could not cook or remember having cooked, Itzhak was thankful Rosa had enjoyed those early lessons and that she seemed to enjoy having her own kitchen—a peace he'd not seen since the day they'd moved into his parents' home.

Even with the world turned upside down, during moments such as this, when he could slip in the door unnoticed, Itzhak often found his wife singing as she stirred the pot or kneaded bread. Her voice came as music to his weary soul.

◆

Rosa pushed and pulled the black bread dough. It was nearly elastic. *Another few minutes and it will be ready to cover and rise.* She loved the next part of making bread. *So like tucking a little one into its cradle to sleep.*

She smiled as she heard the soft click of the latch, her back to the door. *He thinks I do not hear him. He tiptoes in his stocking feet and holds his breath as he sinks into the chair by the oven. He must be chilled through. Relax there, my love, and I will sing a lullaby for you as I prepare your meal.*

> *"Ah-ah-ah, ah-ah-ah,*
> *There were once two little kittens.*
> *Ah-ah-ah, two little kittens,*
> *They were both grayish-brown.*
>
> *"Oh, sleep, my darling.*
> *If you'd like a star from the sky, I'll give you one.*
> *All children, even the bad ones,*
> *Are already asleep,*
> *Only you are not.*
>
> *"Ah-ah-ah, ah-ah-ah,*
> *There were once two little kittens.*
> *Ah-ah-ah, two little kittens,*
> *They were both grayish-brown.*
>
> *"Oh, sleep because*
> *The moon is yawning and he will soon fall asleep.*

And when the morning comes
He will be really ashamed
That he fell asleep and you did not."

Rosa could feel Itzhak's smile as she turned the bread into the greased bowl and covered it with a tea towel, leaving it to rise on the back of the still-warm oven. She knew he sat in the chair by the stove, weary eyes watching her, growing sentimental and content. Still, she pretended not to see him as she ladled his bowl and cut a slice of bread.

"No butter today, my love," she whispered. "So very sorry." Though in truth there had been little butter since they'd left Vilna. Little butter, no milk except for children, poor excuses for flour, the rare egg—except when she bartered with their neighbor for eggs from the chicken she was certain had been stolen from her tata's empty coop.

She would not tell her husband that she had taken needed bread from the Germans the day Hitler paraded through Warsaw—bread distributed to Poles for propaganda purposes and the benefit of the plane that flew back and forth, a cameraman leaning out of the cockpit to film the "benevolent Germans and grateful Poles." She would not tell him of the ways she improvised in her cooking, what he was actually eating. Not yet. He did his best to bring money home for her to buy food. She did her best to make each zloty stretch, to purchase what she could in the long queues before nearly barren shelves. *When the French come, when the British come, things will get better quickly.* She told herself this over and over until it had become a prayer. *Please send the French, send the British, send somebody—anybody—to save us. Why do they not come? Can they not hear our pleas?*

For now she would sing to her husband each night, grateful he had work the Germans valued, grateful that he walked through the kitchen door before the violence imposed after curfew, grateful her father had acted in foresight to dig a small well and rig a hand pump in the back garden. *We may not have electricity, but we have water. Far more than most. Thank you, Tata. Thank you, Itzhak. Adonai, help us for all the rest. Adonai, have mercy.*

Itzhak reached for her skirt on her last trip to the stove and pulled her onto his lap. Rosa smiled and sighed, kissing his hair, his temple, his cheek. He lifted his mouth to hers and she forgot about deprivation or worry or her mother or soup.

CHAPTER FIVE

In November, Sophie signed her new name on the apartment lease: *Zofia Marek*. At least Father Nowak had settled on the Polish version of her own given name and altered the baptismal records accordingly—easier to remember and respond to than a completely foreign name. He'd done the same for Terri—now Tereza Lis—though both young women had formed a pact. In private they would always be Sophie and Terri, a silent clinging to their true identities.

The census Pan Gadomski feared had been taken in late October. By the beginning of December, every Jewish shop was ordered to display a large star of David at its entrance, and white armbands—four inches—with blue stars of David began to appear on the arms of Jewish men, women, and children over ten years of age. Failure to obtain and wear the armbands meant imprisonment.

"Are you not afraid they'll find out?" Sophie asked her friend over coffee, late one evening.

"What? That I'm Jewish?" Terri shrugged. "I was not raised in my mother's faith. I have no Jewish mannerisms. I speak no Yiddish. How would they know?"

"You're right. They won't know. Of course they won't. We don't even know any Jewish people—hardly any."

Terri drew a deep breath but did not answer.

"We don't," Sophie repeated, insisting.

Slowly, deliberately, Terri placed her cup in its saucer. "That's not true."

"I only mean that we don't know them now—don't see them now. The Bukowskis were my closest friends before the war, but I don't even know what's become of them."

"If you did, what would you do?"

"What do you mean?"

"Would you help them? Would you acknowledge them? Food rationing's started. Did you know that Jews are rationed only a fraction of what Poles are? Not enough to live on."

"That's impossible."

"That's what the Germans hope, what they intend. The only way for Jews to survive—to not starve—is if they buy on the black market at five to ten times prewar prices, or if someone gives them food."

"Helping is illegal." The horror of the situation sank in, but Sophie held her breath.

"Yes," Terri said, not looking at her. "That's true."

Sophie waited, but she knew what was coming—knew without any doubt. "That won't stop you, will it?"

"No," her friend responded quietly.

"Why are you telling me? Are you asking me to help? Do you know how dangerous this is?"

"No, I don't want or need your help." Terri met Sophie's gaze. "I'm telling you because it is dangerous, and the risk I take is my own. Maybe you should distance yourself from me . . . at least for a time."

Sophie couldn't stop the prick behind her eyes. She couldn't lose another friend—her only friend. "Please, please think about this,

Terri. Think what it would mean to your father if something happened to you."

A sad smile crossed Terri's lips. "My father, of all people, would understand. He might try to protect me—has tried—but he'd expect nothing less. He gives nothing less himself. Look what he's already done for us. We're not the only ones."

That realization swept through Sophie's mind in a moment. Of course. He'd hidden her in the basement of the library, had taken her into his home when she had nowhere to go, had given new identities to her and to his daughter, had arranged with his priest to alter baptismal records and death records. He himself had altered personnel records in the library and given her a new job with her new name. And he knew details of the pilots and other military in Romania—things she'd not heard on the streets or seen in print. All those things—those connections—didn't materialize in a moment. He must be involved in networks she'd never imagined. If he'd helped her, who else might he be helping?

She looked at her friend with new eyes. *What are you thinking? What are you already doing?*

◆

Pan Gadomski had arranged for Sophie to work as an archivist and ancient manuscript specialist in the dry underground floors of the library, away from the prying eyes of German officials and the sharp ears of the few Aryan Poles hired to replace Jewish maintenance workers. One of the quickest means of detection for Jews—or for aliens whose first language was not Polish—was the tripping up of accents, the mispronunciation of or stumble over words. Both Sophie and Pan Gadomski knew her Polish was tinged with English inflection, try as she might to eradicate that from her tongue.

It was impossible to know whom to trust. Allies came in the

strangest places, and former neighbors could be turned traitor by a piece of sausage or a wad of zloty slipped into the pocket.

For the moment, there was plenty of work for Sophie. The Reich had determined that all rare and first editions, hand-drawn and embellished maps—some centuries old—illuminated manuscripts from ages past, and countless irreplaceable archives be carefully boxed and shipped to Berlin. Pan Gadomski had actually wept, saying that all the best libraries, from universities to public institutions to private collections, were being torn from their homeland, even as academics in every field were ousted from their posts—some disappearing into the night and never seen again. He deemed it "the dehumanization and intellectual rape of Poland."

Sophie knew Pan Gadomski preferred someone he trusted to carefully pack the treasures, hoping against hope that they would one day be returned to their home library in a free Poland. Her heart warmed to the trust he'd given her, and her stomach thanked him for the paycheck that allowed her to buy meager rations. She'd had to agree to showing no sign of familiarity with her employer. She was a new person now, with a new name. None of the former staff remained since the Germans had closed the libraries. By working in the darkest regions of the library, Sophie rarely saw another person. She knew Pan Gadomski believed her safer that way; she hoped he was right.

Carefully, she lined each crate and placed each wrapped manuscript within its own box as tenderly as if she cradled a baby. Sophie sighed when the current crate had accepted all it could hold and marked the outside with its contents. *What will the archivists and librarians in Berlin do with all these crates? Will they store them in warehouses?* She could not imagine they would display Polish-language literature in their capital. She feared they would destroy these treasures. *But if that is their purpose, why transport them at all? Why not destroy them here and now?*

For weeks, smoke and sparks from bonfires of Polish books and texts, everything from medical journals to Bibles, had lit the streets outside libraries, bookshops, schools, and the homes of private collectors. The Germans seemed determined to rob Poland of literature and learning. Hope for a free and restored Poland seemed very far away, very far removed—as rare and unobtainable as the last illuminated manuscript she'd packed.

Sophie checked her watch. The next collection of crates should begin within the half hour. There was enough time for her to slip upstairs and out the door, to go home for an hour while the loading of crates was supervised by Pan Gadomski. He wanted her nowhere near the German officers and their lackeys. But rain had started just as she'd entered the library that morning. She'd not brought an umbrella and had no desire to catch her death, cold as December had already proved. She'd brought her lunch with her. If she could only wait out of sight until the men had finished.

Sophie had been working in the cellar of the library two weeks before she came across the opening to the sealed room where Pan Gadomski had hidden her during the bombing. If she hadn't known it was there, hadn't actually been looking for it, she didn't think she would have ever found it.

In the moment she'd walked through the opening, she'd regretted it, half expecting to find the bloodstained pallet she'd left when Pan Gadomski had taken her home. Instead, the room had been emptied and scrubbed clean. That was a mercy. But why had he bothered? Or had someone else? Who else, since former staff was gone, would know about the room now?

How had Pan Gadomski known about the room? She'd never heard it mentioned in all the time she'd worked in the library, even before the occupation.

Still, it made the perfect place to eat her lunch on days too frigid or rainy to leave the library.

Sophie pushed through the opening and lit her torch. She didn't turn on the electric light, uncertain as she was whether any light might shine through the cracks and give her hiding place away.

She slipped off her shoes and tucked her legs beneath her skirt, spreading her coat over her toes, glad to give them a rest. She poured weak tea from her thermos and pulled a wrapped crust of buttered bread from her pocket. It was a wonder she still had butter. She'd rationed it as stintingly as the unreformed Ebenezer Scrooge might. Even so, it couldn't last much longer. While it did, she leaned her head back against the wall, flicked off her torch, and closed her eyes, savoring each bite and dreaming of her Janek.

The first Sophie knew of the movers' arrival was a crash on the other side of the wall. She jerked awake, astonished she'd been able to fall asleep in the chilled room.

"Raus! Raus!" The German voice came through the wall, as if through a thick cloud. "This is the last."

"The last? The last you want today?" It was Pan Gadomski's voice.

"The last we want at all. The rest is to be burned."

"Burned?" The horror in her friend's voice stole through Sophie's chest. "These are valuable, irreplaceable manuscripts. To destroy them would be—would be criminal!"

"You question the orders of the *Reichsführer*?"

"No, of course not. But surely, if they cannot remain in Poland, Berlin will want these."

"Soon, Herr Gadomski, there will be no 'Poland.' No Polish language. Then, who will care? Who will read your books? What are they good for besides fire kindling?" The half laugh chilled Sophie's arms, made her heart spasm.

"You have orders to move all the most valuable pieces; you said so yourself. Please, I beg of you, don't—"

"This is taking too long."

"I'll bring in more packers. We can finish quickly."

"We are finished. In consequence, the Reich no longer requires your services, Herr Gadomski."

Sophie swallowed the nugget rising in her throat.

"And the woman—where is the woman?"

"The woman?" Sophie knew that Pan Gadomski feigned ignorance, that he was buying time.

"The woman who works here—the archivist we have paid. Where is she? Her services will obviously no longer be required either. I do not leave loose ends in my work."

"She must have finished, gone home for the day. Perhaps you have work for her, and for me, in other libraries—here in Warsaw, or elsewhere?"

"Simpleminded for one so 'well educated.' Poles are like children, naive."

The sudden gunshot, muffled through the thick wall, reverberated through Sophie's body. She shuddered, bit her lip to keep from crying out, and cringed against the wall.

"One less Pole. One pseudointellectual the world did not need."

Grunts of agreement followed. Sophie could hear the hefting and dragging of crates, the stomping of boots upon the stairs, and finally silence. Then came the acrid smell of burning.

She pulled on her shoes, straining to hear any sound on the opposite side of the wall, afraid to move, yet afraid that if she didn't, she'd be caught in the building inferno of books and boxes and papers. She was afraid for Pan Gadomski, afraid she'd find him dead, afraid to wait and do nothing to help him if he lived and bled, afraid the Germans stood outside the room or up the stairs or in the street to shoot her.

Please, God! Help me. Help me help him. She pushed open the door an inch. Smoke swept in. She pushed it wider. Flames burst from stacks of boxes across the room. The wooden packing crates she'd not yet filled were kindling, the books and manuscripts not yet packed already curling in the heat and spreading flames. Smoke swelled, filling the room.

"Pan Gadomski? Pan Gadomski!" she cried, crawling across the floor, holding her coat hem to her nose and mouth, doing her best to see through the rising smoke. She'd nearly given up, knowing that if she didn't get up the stairs and into the air now, she wouldn't be able to. Then she saw a shoe, a man's shoe and pant leg protruding from behind a stack of crates. "Pan Gadomski! I'm coming. I'm coming!" She pushed to her feet and sprang across the room, falling across his body, reaching for his face. "We must get out—now! Get up, oh, please, get up! Do you hear me?" she cried, pulling his sleeve, his arm. She shook his shoulders and face, but there was no response. The bullet had been clean and sure. Still, she tried to pull his body to the stairs. He was too heavy, too long, too solid.

Terri! Terri needs you! I need you! Don't leave us. Disjointed thoughts, flashes of memory of her own parents gone in a moment, raced through her mind. But she knew, even as those scenes sprinted through space, that there was nothing she could do for her friend. She saw his wedding ring, the ring she'd seen Terri twist round his finger whenever she'd tried to wheedle her will from her father. Sophie gasped, barely able to breathe, and pulled the ring from his finger. She tripped, stumbled, tripped again, and fell against the stairs.

One, two, three stairs . . . She struggled to the top and pushed open the door, coughing. She slammed the door behind her, containing the fire as best she could.

The magnificent, stately library was silent, dim, the Germans gone. Cold December sunlight filtered through seams of boarded, shattered windows. It had stopped raining.

Though the building was largely stone and its exterior might survive the fire, Sophie knew Pan Gadomski's body would be unidentifiable. *The crime will be listed as one more casualty of a bombed building, blamed on an exploding boiler or gas line or some nonsense—assuming the Germans bother to invent an excuse.* Even as Sophie leaned her head against the yet-cold floor, she knew the futility of seeking help. She knew the fear of all the days ahead.

Janek, gone. Pan Bukowski, gone. Pan Gadomski, gone.

How will I tell Terri that the father she loves, who gave her up only to protect her, hoping against hope to reunite after the madness of Germany passes, has been murdered? That his worst fears have been been realized?

Sophie pushed Pan Gadomski's wedding ring onto her thumb and pulled her coat more tightly about her. She straightened her hair, wiped the tears from her face, and slipped through a side door and into the street, while the library burned behind her.

CHAPTER SIX

GRAY DAWN FILTERED through the garden workshop window. Itzhak wiped sawdust from his father-in-law's lathe and returned it to the rack above the workbench. He pushed the Star of David armband—known among his fellows as the Jew's badge of shame—over his sleeve.

It was nearly time to leave for work. While sweeping shavings from the floor, he smiled. He missed Jacob, Rosa's father, nearly as much as he missed his own parents. Jacob had not been eager about Rosa's marriage to anyone outside of Warsaw, but Itzhak knew he'd recognized the love-light in his daughter's eyes. Itzhak liked to think his father-in-law had come to trust him in the months prior to their marriage, had understood how much he loved and would do anything for his Rosa. It was an honor, a privilege to use his tools now. He only wished that he and Jacob might use them together. The man's murder had left an indescribable hole in his family, and in the mind of his wife, Marya, most of all.

Images Itzhak conjured of the rotund little man were ones of perpetual motion, inexhaustible energy. If he hadn't been collecting rent or repairing pipes or painting things that barely needed a touch-up in the apartment buildings he'd owned, he'd been building something in his back garden workshop or hoeing around vegetables that could rival those grown by a botanist or breeding fatter, meatier chickens or crossbreeding roses—all in an already crowded neighborhood.

Itzhak, though never lazy, hadn't been able to keep up with the older man—a fact in which Jacob had taken great delight and more than a little amusement.

He'd been a strong spiritual leader, too. That was something Itzhak wished he aspired to. He wasn't sure he'd ever feel impassioned enough to step out in such faith, either at home or in the synagogue. And now, prayer in synagogues was forbidden. Right away, rabbis had visited homes. Plans, he knew, were being made for secret services. Itzhak was reluctant to participate, or allow Rosa to do so. The risk was unimaginable.

Meanwhile, despite streets still riddled with rubble from the bombings, despite meager stores of supplies or gifts in the shops, and despite the hated German occupation, Poles and Germans alike prepared for their Christmas celebrations.

It shouldn't annoy Itzhak. Christmas had never annoyed him before. It wasn't like Easter with the Passion Plays that inevitably raised Christian ire over the "evil Jews" blamed for crucifying their Jesus. Christmas didn't bring on persecution or pogroms, as the Easter season did.

But it rankled Itzhak that fellow Poles and occupying Germans celebrated a common day—for them, a holy day commemorating the birth of one who came into this world as a peasant. A prophet who, even Itzhak knew, taught love and compassion and mercy and kindness to the poor—who was himself a Jew. Yet even in this season of goodwill and abundance, this year they persecuted Jews with renewed vigor. It seemed as if the cold weather made them not warmer or kinder as it had in Christmas seasons past, but colder, harder. . . .

He needed to do something more for Rosa, something to lift her heart, to help her remember better days and hope in life to come. *Hope.* He sighed. *An elusive thing.* He ran his fingers over the neatly turned spindles of the menorah he'd been fashioning for her— a Hanukkah surprise. *So little for a need so great. Still, perhaps it will give her some semblance of her old life, good memories, perhaps hope for a miracle.* Itzhak still believed in miracles. A woman he'd met as he stood in a short queue in a dark alley for candles had shrugged and reasoned, "It is the season of miracles. They come, you know, at the most unlikely times."

Itzhak had squandered too much of his pay to buy candles on the black market. Rosa would chide him if she knew. But with limited electricity across the city, especially in the Jewish Quarter, candles were scarce indeed, no matter that nearly everyone used carbide lamps. He'd found not one candle for sale in the shops he'd dared to frequent.

Before extinguishing his own carbide lamp, he glanced up at the mahogany wood he'd found carefully stored and labeled *For Rosa, when she bears my grandchild.* Itzhak was not the craftsman his father-in-law had been, but he knew the already cut and sanded wood was a thing of beauty and had probably cost Jacob a week's earnings—or more. Where he'd found it or how long he'd stored it, Itzhak had no idea. Rosa would love this gift from her father, when the time came.

Itzhak had hoped the cradle would be his privilege to finish as a Hanukkah gift. He had but to secure the pieces—like a puzzle— sand again, and decide if a simple varnish would do or if he should do something more to enhance the beauty of the wood. But Rosa had endured another disappointment a couple of weeks ago, when the clawing cramps came, and then her menses. She'd cried into his chest for an hour that night. In the morning, she'd dried her tears and pasted on a brave smile. But Itzhak saw that the squaring of her shoulders was gone, as was the spring in her step. He wasn't sure how much more his wife could endure.

◆ ◆ ◆

Rosa set her darning egg down and rubbed her eyes. The late afternoon light waned, but she refused to turn on the carbide lamp so soon. It gave off the most putrid smell, and the fuel must be rationed, else they would run out before the end of the week.

Her mother, who sat in her rocker by the window staring out at nothing, as she did each long day, whispered, "When will he come home?"

Rosa swallowed. She hated the daily ritual of her mother's questions, over and over, and her answers, every day the same. "Tata won't be coming home anymore, Matka. Remember?"

Her mother said nothing, but continued to stare. Five minutes more and Rosa stood and stretched, grateful her mother had not rattled on this day like a scratched Victrola recording. It was nearly time to prepare the evening meal. *If you can call it a meal. Perhaps I can—*

"I didn't mean your tata. I meant Itzhak."

Rosa nearly dropped her darning egg and socks. Her mother had not spoken Itzhak's name once in the two months since they'd come to Warsaw. She hadn't thought her mother knew it anymore. Mustering as much steadiness as she could, sounding as natural as she could, Rosa replied, "Itzhak will come when his work is finished. Sometimes they keep him long."

When her mother didn't say anything more, Rosa stepped toward the kitchen, fearful of breaking the spell. She had just tied her apron over her skirt when her mother called her.

Rosa thrilled to hear her name—the first time in over a week. "Yes, Matka?"

"Where are the booties you were knitting?"

Rosa's heart sank. Three weeks ago she'd started her baby's layette.

She'd had no idea that her mother had noticed. She'd never spoken of anything Rosa did. "I put them away, Matka. I won't be needing them now."

Her mother looked up, into Rosa's eyes. Rosa's skin tingled, the hairs on her arms standing to attention. "You will need them. In the new year, my daughter, you will need them. They must be ready."

Is that a premonition? A prophecy? A lucid moment, or one of her meshugge *moments?* Rosa turned toward the kitchen, unable to escape quickly enough as the tears coursed over her cheeks. What did her mother know of her fears? Who was she to speak words of hope—a woman who had given up, who spread more despair than indifference?

Rosa filled the kettle, her teeth gritted, sobs pushing down her throat and into her chest, where they writhed and spit. *Why? Why can't I carry a baby? Am I not like other women? Am I not strong or good? Why? And what does she know? What does my mother know of such things—ever, let alone now?*

She heard the rare creak of her mother's chair in the next room. Rosa closed her eyes, knowing she should check on her. Matka was likely unable to go to the necessary by herself, or wherever it was she intended. Usually Rosa had to initiate the trip. But she didn't want her mother to see her tears. As exasperated as Rosa sometimes felt with her mother, she loved her and did not want to frighten her. She must see only peace and strength in her daughter, only confidence. Anything less, the doctor had warned, might set her off—"like a frightened child who throws a temper tantrum because she doesn't know what else to do with herself."

She found her mother standing by the window, unsupported—another miracle of its own.

"Matka? Are you all right?" Rosa swiped at the last of her tears with her apron and crossed the room to lay a hand on her mother's shoulder.

"He's not coming home ever again, is he? Your tata?" Her mother's voice sounded frail but lucid.

"No, Matka. No, he isn't. I'm so very sorry." Rosa wrapped her arms around her mother, drawing her close, too aware of how very thin she had become.

Her mother simply nodded, as if she understood.

Rosa had no way of knowing if her mother would remember tomorrow, but she was grateful for today, for this moment, dark as it was.

CHAPTER SEVEN

HOURS AFTER SHE'D CROSSED the threshold to Terri's apartment, Sophie still sat on the floor beside her friend, alternately holding her hand or drying the tears that rained freely. Dusk crept through the window. Sophie watched as Terri fingered her father's wedding ring.

"I saw this each and every day of my life. It is the one thing remaining from the life my parents shared before my birth stole Matka from him. I felt horrible for that, but never because he made me. He never blamed me—not once." Terri turned the ring to the light and read the inscription engraved within the circle. "Micah 6:8."

Sophie recognized the Scripture Terri recited from memory. "'He hath shewed thee, O man, what is good; and what doth the Lord require of thee, but to do justly, and to love mercy, and to walk humbly with thy God?' He did that every day of his life, you know. Matka would have been proud of him." She sniffed, wiped her nose, and kissed the ring.

"I could not stop them." Sophie's voice broke at last as she confessed the thing she knew she must. "I did not try. I hid. He didn't even know I was there."

Terri shook her head. "You could not have stopped them. They would have shot you, too." She choked back anguish, but tears forced their way through her eyelids, and the sob she tried to swallow came out. She reached for Sophie's hand. "It's good you hid."

Sophie's arms encircled her friend again, her hand caressing her hair and the back of her neck as she would comfort a child, vulnerable and in need. Sophie felt the same need, only she felt she'd grown old in the last hours, too old to be comforted.

Both women cried until their tears were spent and the dark of evening filled the room. At last Terri pushed away, dried her eyes, and accepted the damp handkerchief Sophie offered her. At least it wasn't sopping, as was Terri's own.

"If you hadn't been there, I would never have known what became of him. I would not have this ring." Another sob escaped. "Thank you for that."

"What can I do for you, my friend?"

"Nothing. There is nothing more to do. I cannot claim his body. They'd discover who I am. They'd know someone was there, maybe search for you—perhaps they will still. You must be careful. Stay away from the library. Tata's provision—though I didn't want it—has protected us, given us life. He knew what was coming, so much more than he told me. If they didn't believe I was dead, they would come for me, too. I saw the death notice for two of his colleagues. They're killing them off—teachers, lawyers, clerics, professors. Warsaw's best and brightest. Or they're sending them away, only God knows where."

"Let me fix you some tea."

Terri glanced at the window. The night crept in. She pushed herself up from the floor and closed the drapery. "You should go now."

"I don't want to leave you alone, Terri. I can stay the night." Sophie didn't want to be alone either. If left alone in her apartment, all she'd been through, all she'd witnessed that day would loom even more menacing.

Terri didn't answer at first. She simply walked back and forth, across the small room. She stopped and checked her watch.

"It's not good for either of us to be alone. Remember what your father said: 'Two are better than one.'"

"It isn't safe, Sophie. I'm sorry, but you must go." Terri didn't look at her. "I must ask you to go now."

The statement came out as a command. It felt like a punch to Sophie's stomach. "At least let me make you tea. You must eat something, drink something."

"I'll take care of myself later. I know you mean well, but truly, you must go. Please."

Sophie waited a moment more. Surely Terri would reconsider. She'd said she didn't blame Sophie for her father's death, even for hiding, shameful though Sophie felt that was. Why was she ordering her away? Why now?

"I know we haven't been seeing each other as before. I'd like that to change, Terri—especially now. We're friends. We need each other. You know your father would have wanted us to do that. I can help you—"

"You must go now. I'll see you in a few days. But for now, it's best you stay away."

Sophie swallowed the objections in her throat. Confused and hurt, she pulled herself up from a sitting position that had left her feet nearly numb for the last hour. Terri did not turn to look at her, not even when Sophie walked toward the door and grasped the doorknob.

Sophie slipped through the door and closed it gently behind her. Bewildered, lonelier than before, and frightened to face the long night ahead, she walked to her apartment door at the end of the hallway and inserted the key. Just as she stepped through and was pulling the door shut, she saw two dark forms—one taller and slender, one surely a child—slip into Terri's apartment.

December brought bitter and record cold to Poland. Though electricity had been restored in most of the city, there was a shortage of coal. Sophie slept in her winter coat.

By January she'd gone through most of her meager savings. The Gestapo had not come knocking on her door, though they could have discovered where she lived from the library's personnel records. Since they had not come for her, perhaps they would not. It was past time to find a new position. Her savings and ration card could only get her through another month.

Sophie had just surrendered her week's ration coupons for bread and tinned meat and a few paltry potatoes. She'd rounded the corner on Leszno Street when she saw a man being mercilessly beaten with the end of a truncheon.

"Faster! You lazy fool! Faster!" The Jewish policeman struck the man over his back.

Sophie kept her eyes down and hugged the shop side of the walkway, walking faster, hoping to distance herself from the cruel scene. Jewish police—known as SPs—were often as brutal as Gestapo to their own people.

But as she passed the man, beaten to the curb, he glanced up at her. Sophie felt cold then heat wash over her. *Aaron Bukowski! Can that be you?* The man was thinner, by far, than she remembered, his hair streaked in grime and his clothes unwashed, unlike her old neighbor's. But something in the face—no, the eyes—rang familiar. He didn't seem to recognize her, and she couldn't be sure. She dared not stop.

No matter that she'd twice searched her old neighborhood for the son and wife of her old friend, Sophie had not been able to locate them. She'd supposed they'd left the city and hoped they had found a place in the countryside or somehow struck a bargain to gain a visa to Palestine. That had been Pan Bukowski's hope for his entire family . . . *Next year in Jerusalem!* He would die another death to see his beloved son beaten in the gutters of Warsaw.

Sophie hurried home. With trembling fingers she inserted her key into the lock. Once inside, she slammed and locked the door behind her, her heart racing. She dropped her packages to the floor—packages she'd thought meager less than a half hour ago. But after seeing her former neighbor's son, she knew she'd been living in luxury. Clean clothes, enough to eat. No telling where he was living. *What about his wife and child? Where are they?*

Despite the cold, Sophie felt rivulets of sweat form beneath her hair and in the pits of her arms. She unbuttoned her coat and threw it over the kitchen chair, leaning on the table for support. Quickly, she stored the tinned meat and bread in her cupboard, placed the potatoes on a shelf near the window, as if putting everything in order would also heal the trauma of her former neighbor's son. As if it could make her forget, relax, go on with life.

But it couldn't. Nothing could purge the image of his beating, his suffering, from her brain. Sophie closed her eyes, trying to still her mind and gather her wits. There was no question. She must help him . . . but how?

It was nearly curfew by the time she'd decided. Clearly, Aaron was part of a forced labor detail. Wherever he'd come from, he'd be returning there soon. He might not labor in this part of the city again. She might not have another opportunity.

She buttoned her coat, pulled the tin of meat from the cupboard, and stuffed half the loaf of bread wrapped in a cloth bag inside her coat. The potatoes she pushed into her other pocket. She couldn't be seen giving him the food, and he couldn't be seen carrying it. *Please, God, help me help him. For his sake, for the sake of his wife and child, for the sake of my friend.*

Sophie hurried back to Leszno Street. She'd have to act quickly, surely, and return to her own courtyard before curfew. Violators were shot on sight. No one asked if you were Jewish or Polish or German or Russian. There were no exceptions, and she did not want to add either of them to the growing list of executions.

Her best approach was to circle the block, then pretend she was coming from the grocer's and stumble near the spot Aaron labored. If she dropped enough and asked him to help her, she could at least pass him something—whatever he could carry. She moved the potatoes from her pocket to the bag, thankful she'd not been robbed by one of the perpetual street urchins—mostly Jewish orphans living on the streets. It was never safe to carry more than you could truly hold on to.

Her steps slowed as she approached the labor site. Men were collecting bricks from piles of rubble—buildings demolished in the bombing. The SPs must have spent their cruel energy earlier in the day. They seemed less engaged in punishment or even guard duty and more concerned with stamping their well-booted feet, keeping warm against the cold and talking to one another. She scanned the gloaming for Aaron but didn't see him. It cut her heart to realize how alike the men looked—all bent and thin, all in ragged clothing, none of it warm enough. If she gave everything she carried and every morsel in her cupboards, it could not fatten these men, could never feed their families. *How have I not seen? But I have seen—and turned away, more concerned with the battle of staying alive.*

She was about to give up on finding him and drop her parcel beside anyone when she glimpsed Aaron. Sure it was him, she placed her gloved hand to her mouth and hissed, "Aaron! Aaron Bukowski!" She coughed, drawing attention to herself, and turned toward a shop window, pretending to examine the goods there.

The two SPs, intent on sharing something funny, glanced her way, then turned back to their conversation. She saw, in the reflection of the shop's window, that Aaron had stopped and looked her way. He hesitated, then continued to work, gradually making his way toward her. She stepped back, as if to better observe the contents of the window. When she was within five feet of his labors, she turned, preparing to walk away, but stumbled, spilling the contents of her package into the gutter.

"Take what you can!" she whispered, not looking at his face but doing her best to provide a shield between him and the SPs.

"Sophia? Sophia Kumiega?"

"Not anymore. Hide—hide anything you can. Quickly!" She stood, aware that the crunch of boots neared her.

"Oh! Clumsy me!" She spoke loudly. "I never should have worn these shoes in the snow."

"Are you all right, Pani?" The SP's feigned concern did not impress or frighten Sophie. But she was terrified for Aaron.

"Yes, yes, thank you. Clumsy from the cold. I'm anxious to get home before curfew—that's all." It took less than a moment for her to retrieve the loaf of bread, surely too big for Aaron to hide, and the two potatoes, and stuff them in her bag. "Have a good evening, gentlemen."

They tipped their caps to her, clearly pleased that a Polish woman would refer to them as gentlemen.

CHAPTER EIGHT

TYPHUS CAME TO WARSAW'S Jewish district in January 1940.
The Germans, responsible for the overcrowding and loss of sanitation, enforced a new decree—a "public health measure" to contain the spread of the "Jewish epidemic." All synagogues, yeshivas,
study houses, and ritual baths were closed. Even public prayer was
forbidden—any gathering of Jews.

New decrees were issued almost daily. Itzhak had no question the
decrees were designed to make the historic cold that came to Poland
more keenly felt, especially among Jews.

"The misery they conjure is inventive; I will say that," Itzhak
muttered as he pulled off his work boots at the close of a long day.
"Isolation, dehumanization. It gets worse every day. Four families in
most every two-room apartment—and no running water." He peeled
off his damp socks and handed them to his waiting wife, who spread
them across the back of the stove. They ran the stove only once a day
now. Rosa waited to light it until he came home, just so he could enjoy
its warmth and dry his socks, and so they might share one hot meal.

Coal was scarce and expensive. Their only hope was to buy on the black market—a practice Rosa no longer spoke against or questioned. Families grouped together for lack of housing. Sleeping as many as could fit in a bed became necessary not only for numbers but to keep from freezing. It was only for the mad ravings of his mother-in-law that they did not have half a dozen or more people living with them now.

"News today."

"What now?" Rosa shook her head. "What more can they invent?"

"All Jewish welfare in Poland is to be consolidated under one organization—something called 'Jewish Social Self-Help.' We Jews are responsible for ourselves. No more Polish public assistance. The noose tightens, day by day."

Rosa bit her lip. "Matka depends on the welfare for her medicine."

Itzhak reached for his wife's arm. He wouldn't say that he was certain there would soon be no more welfare of any kind for Jews, no matter that he believed it. "Try to get some extra—to store in case the winter prevents you from the trip to the pharmacy."

Rosa looked at him, managing a half smile. He hadn't fooled her. "She knitted today. The first she's done any handwork since we came."

Itzhak's brows rose. Why did his wife look so sad? "A good sign, yes?"

"Baby booties." Rosa turned away to stir the simmering pot of cabbage soup. "She's convinced we will need them this year. Every day now she says we must make ready."

"Perhaps she is right. Perhaps she knows some—"

"Don't. Don't, Itzhak." She thumped the wooden spoon against the stove.

Itzhak saw his wife's chest heave and knew she stifled a sob. He was behind her, rubbing her arms and shoulders, in a moment. "I'm sorry, my love. I wasn't making light. Our time will come when Adonai deigns."

"Why can't He deign now? Why, when all we have is gone, why won't He give us this?" She could hold her sob no longer.

He turned her into his arms, pulling her to his chest, rubbing her back, beseeching the ceiling, for he wasn't sure any longer that he believed Adonai would help them, would answer their prayer, no matter what he said to Rosa.

"Faith. You need faith. You'll see."

Itzhak and Rosa started. Neither had seen or heard her mother step to the kitchen doorway.

"You both think I am an old woman who knows nothing, who sees nothing, but I tell you, you need faith."

"Matka, we—"

"Nothing will happen if you do not believe, if you do not hope."

Her chiding angered Itzhak so that he stepped between his wife and her mother. *Who is she to reprimand Rosa after all the self-pitying tantrums, the shutting down, the—*

"You think you help your wife by understanding, by pitying her. You must help her by doing, by being strong."

"Matka, Itzhak works hard. He provides the food we eat."

"He is the head of your house. He must set the example. Why does he work on Shabbat? Why do you not light the candles? If you don't keep—"

"The Germans force me to work on Shabbat. If I tell them, 'No, so sorry, I cannot work today—it is Shabbat,' they will shoot me. Is that what you want? Is it?"

"Itzhak!" Rosa whispered.

"Then you must work. I see that. But there is more to even this changed life than work."

"What candles would you have us light, Matka?" Rosa spoke softly.

Itzhak knew Rosa was glad her mother reasoned after a fashion, carried on a conversation, even if she didn't understand the implications of all she said or comprehend their circumstances. He wasn't sure he preferred Marya's interference.

"Candles. You don't keep Shabbat because you have no candles." Marya shook her head in disbelief, withered them with pitying eyes, and shuffled from the room.

◆

That night, as they huddled close in bed, Rosa stroked her husband's cheek. "Never mind her, my love. Matka is not right in her mind. She thinks things are as before the war, before the Germans."

Itzhak pulled one arm away and crooked it behind his head. "Each day she speaks more. Perhaps she returns to her old self."

"I don't know if I would recognize her."

He grunted. "She's right about one thing. We've lost hope. We've lost purpose."

"How can we not? It takes every fragment of fortitude to get out of bed, to trudge through each day." She sighed, fighting bitterness, then reached up again to trace the long indentation in his cheek, the one so ready to smile, even now. He smiled into the dark; she could feel the pleasing change in his facial muscles.

"I am thinner. Each week I tighten my belt." He tickled her beneath her arm.

"Stop that!"

"You, too, are thinner. But you are beautiful, as always, and we are together." He stroked her hair. "We're not living with my parents anymore?" He ended the sentence like a question. "Don't tell me you don't think that an improvement."

She couldn't help but smile.

Though she knew he was concerned for his parents and sisters, he still knew how to make a joke only the two of them shared. He understood her so well. That was music, her music. She pulled him closer yet. How could she not be thankful for this man? For this time in life together, come what may? "I love you, Itzhak Dunovich. I love you madly."

She felt his fingers probe her neck, reach for the delicate chain that held her medallion. It had been a long while since he'd traced the filigreed Tree of Life. Minutes passed. She would have thought he'd fallen asleep if he did not still hold the medallion.

"Day after tomorrow."

"Yes?" Rosa looked up at him in the dark, unable to see his face.

"Shabbat. I will find the candles left from Hanukkah, and we can use them—two of them. Not for long. We'll light them and hold a shortened service. If we're careful—conservative—we can make them last for months."

"Is this because Matka bullied you?"

"No . . . yes . . . partly." He shrugged. "But more because it is right. She is right. The Germans do their best to make us forget who we are, Whose we are. Not just today, but for all time. We must work that much harder so that we don't forget. How can we hope that the world will not forget us if we forget ourselves?"

Rosa breathed deeply. It seemed that the world had forgotten, or that it wasn't listening. Still, Itzhak, she knew, was right. What he said was true, was wise. There were so many reasons to love this man. This was one more.

CHAPTER NINE

SOPHIE READ EACH OF the new decrees as they were posted. Forced labor was now mandatory for all Jewish men between twelve and sixty years of age. Those who did not register with the *Judenrat*—the collaborative Jewish administration organized by the Germans—could not labor, and those who didn't work, didn't eat.

For weeks, upon her return from her new job of keeping books for a Polish grocer, Sophie walked the path that would take her past the work site where Jewish men collected bricks and cleared rubble. Sometimes she glimpsed Aaron and sometimes she did not. Each time she could not find him she worried something had happened, that she would not see him again, and expanded her route, searching for him.

Always she carried with her whatever she could—some small food item, wrapped in a rag, or once a pair of men's gloves, once a pair for women, so if she dropped the item near him, it would not be noticed . . . not if she was careful. Scarcely a line was spoken between them, but she always heard Aaron whisper beneath his breath, "Adonai bless you and keep you."

By the time spring came to Warsaw, the men who'd been collecting bricks were building a wall, snaking it through and around the Jewish Quarter. By following the wall, watching it inch higher and higher, she eventually found Aaron laying brick.

Pretending to examine her shoe, as if the heel had come loose, Sophie paused and set her shopping against the wall near the place he labored. He laid a row of bricks, slowing as he neared her but continuing to work.

"Why the wall?" she whispered.

"To cut us off, to separate us from the Aryan side of the city."

"A ghetto," Sophie gasped. She'd read of ghettos being formed in other parts of Poland—never good for those confined, no matter what the Germans touted in their propaganda.

"I'm afraid for my son. He's getting weaker."

"Typhus?"

"No, not yet. But . . ."

The hopelessness she saw in the young father's face tore at Sophie's heart. "Can't you move before—"

"Where would we go?" Frustration glistened in the pools of Aaron's eyes. "We are marked in every way, and soon they will cut us off." He straightened, pocketing the small package of meat she'd pushed toward him on the low wall, then bent for another brick as an SP walked their way. "Adonai bless you," he whispered and turned away.

Sophie shook an imaginary pebble from her shoe, picked up her shopping bag, and walked on.

Through the long night she tossed and turned. She owed the Bukowskis. She cared about the Bukowskis. She could do nothing to stop the atrocities and barbarities of the Wehrmacht or the Gestapo or even the Jewish Police. She couldn't prevent the suffering of hundreds, of thousands, but she must do something to help Aaron and his family. He'd mentioned his son. Why hadn't he said anything about his wife? What was her name? Ilyana. Such a pretty name, and as Sophie remembered, a delicate woman, a woman who loved beauty and flowers and soft laughter over candlelit dinners and made the most delicious brisket and savory kugel Sophie had ever eaten. How could such a woman survive in a ghetto with no running water, inadequate food, a weakening child?

Please, God. There must be a way to help them, to get them out. But where can they go? You're the God of making a way where there is no way—Pan Bukowski said so. He taught me that. He lived it. Please, help his son and his family as he helped me. Help me help them.

◆

Sophie had not been back to the library since the burning, since the day she'd left Pan Gadomski's body to the flames. But this late spring morning, as soon as curfew allowed, she pocketed her smallest torch, donned her kerchief and spring coat purchased at a secondhand store, and walked directly there. The streets in the Aryan districts, largely functional once again, were just beginning to hum with early morning trams and droshkies delivering milk. Laborers hurried to their jobs as housewives pulled back heavy draperies and blackout curtains.

Sophie kept her eyes focused forward, her head down, and her pace clipped and purposeful, hoping to avoid the attention of Wehrmacht soldiers on patrol. Her heart hammered a rapid beat as the library came into view.

Clearly fire-damaged, the front door, as well as previously smashed windows, had been boarded up. There was no sign of occupancy and no clear point of entry. She crossed the main street and walked down the avenue beside the library. The side door, too, was boarded over. There were no patrols and few pedestrians on this side street, no one to recognize her.

She kept walking and turned again onto the street behind the library. With a quick glance behind her, she slipped through the alley that sloped down to the garbage bins. To the left of the bins, shielded by a hedge, was a narrow doorway used only to wheel barrels of trash from the library. At least it hadn't been boarded up. The Germans must not have thought it necessary. But the door was locked. Thankfully, Sophie possessed a key given to her by Pan Gadomski. Though protected by the hedge, she scanned the street and houses beyond before pulling the key from her pocket and inserting it in the lock. It stuck, wouldn't turn. She tried to twist it, pulled on it.

Setting her jaw, she remembered Pan Bukowski—the time she'd locked herself out of her apartment and he'd had to borrow a skeleton key from the landlord. Even then, she'd not been able to open the door. He'd laughed and said, "You're not holding your mouth right, Pani Kumiega! Let me show you." He'd pursed his lips, then twisted them into a silly grin and slid the key in, turned it just so until the old tumblers complied, and opened her door with a flourish.

If only you were here now, Pan Bukowski!

She drew a deep breath, pulled the key out in what felt a miracle in itself, and tried again, this time imitating Pan Bukowski's silly grin. The lock clicked, and the knob turned in her hand. *God bless you, my friend!*

Silently, quickly, Sophie slipped inside and closed the door behind her. She was in a basement room, furnished only by a carboy—a large bin on wheels at the bottom of a giant trash chute. Thankfully, the door to the basement's hallway remained unlocked. She flicked on her torch and crept through the darkness. She didn't suppose the electricity was still connected, but feared to test it lest it alert someone, somewhere, somehow. The basement was dry but smelled of old burning and ashes, though not as strongly as she'd imagined.

She made her way the length of the building to the storage room where she'd worked. Empty, it had been swept clean. She'd been terrified of what she might find, but there was nothing. All trace of

Pan Gadomski's body and the remaining crates of burned books and manuscripts had disappeared, as if none of it had ever been.

She found the hidden room and lifted the latch built into the wall. Inside was dark, but as clean and spare as the last time she'd been here. In her mind she heard again the footsteps on the stairs, the urgency of Pan Gadomski's pleading for her and for himself, then the sudden gunshot. She pushed the panic of those memories from her mind

Could the Bukowskis hide here? Could they live here if she supplied them with food? Would they be safe? It was an unreasonable risk unless Sophie could get them access to food and water. And what about sanitation? Without running water, without a means to rid themselves of human waste But that would mean going upstairs to use the facilities.

Sophie closed the paneled door behind her and flicked off her torch. No daylight crept in from any quarter. There were no windows in this portion of the basement. She flicked on her torch again and stole up the stairs on tiptoe. As she opened the door at the top, a rush of pigeon wings erupted from a burned rafter and ascended through the broken glass of the library's dome. The room opened up to full view and broad daylight, but at least the walls were intact. She couldn't be seen from the street.

Sophie made her way across the library, avoiding glass and shattered plaster busts as best she could. Bookcases had been emptied or turned over, thousands of books torched. It seemed strange that the basement had been cleared but this room left as it was trashed.

The cleanliness of prewar Poland, the orderliness of the library in days gone by, was hard to recall. But Sophie could well imagine the gasp and tears of the librarian who'd ordered her to remain and run stacks of books in the early days of the bombing, everyone doing their best to guess the direction of the next explosion . . . the day Pan Bukowski had been killed, the day she'd begun to lose Janek's baby. Sophie pushed back on her memories. She couldn't, mustn't, think about that now. She needed to check on the facilities, to see if they were operational.

Silently, navigating the debris, she crossed the library floor to the darkened hallway of the nearest washroom. Not a soul. She opened the door to the ladies' room . . . Nothing. She opened the door to the men's room. A bright light surprised her, and even more—a small, naked child, hair dripping with water, turned from the washroom sink. His face framed enormous brown eyes that grew bigger still upon seeing Sophie.

"Who are you?" he whispered.

"Sophie," she said without thinking. "I mean, Zofia." She gulped to catch her breath. "Who are you?"

"Jakob." As if that answered everything. Clearly, the child was Jewish, but why was he here? Were there others?

"Where are your parents?"

"Dead."

Sophie felt the room tilt. "You're here alone?"

Now the child looked wary. "You should go now."

"Yes," Sophie agreed and quickly closed the door, ready to make her way back outside and into the daylight as quickly as possible. But when she turned, she faced the broad chest and shoulders of a man two heads higher than her own. She might have fainted or screamed, but fear clutched her heart so she could do neither.

"What do you want?"

"N-nothing," she stammered. "I was just leaving." She tried to step past him but he blocked her way. "Please, let me pass." She knew her voice quavered.

"You are here alone." It was not a question, but a statement of fact. The voice came low, not menacing.

He must have seen that she was alone, had perhaps witnessed her entry from some high window. "I came in alone, but someone is waiting for me outside."

"Who?" the voice demanded. She could not see his features in the dim hallway.

"Let me pass, or my friend will bring the Wehrmacht." She mustered confidence and authority as best she could.

"Please. I didn't mean to frighten you. We are only here a moment, to wash. We will be on our way. Please." The voice changed, nearly pleading now, and the man stepped back into the broader opening of the doorway, releasing any veil of threat. What she'd taken for a muscular chest was a heavy blanket wrapped over his shoulders and banded across his chest with a rope.

Jews. Hiding out, just as she'd hoped the Bukowskis might.

"You're living here." Now she felt on surer ground. They wouldn't want her to report them.

"We only stopped to wash. We'll be on our way. Let my son come to me."

As if she had any authority. "I don't wish you harm. I just stopped in to see . . . to see the library. I used to work here, before . . . before the fire, and everything."

He nodded. "Step into the light."

She wanted nothing more.

"Sophia Kumiega. I remember you. Archives."

Sophie gasped. "How do you know—?" She stopped. The voice was familiar, but a long, unkempt beard covered the man's face. She couldn't have identified him if he'd been her neighbor.

He smiled. "The beard . . . a good disguise, yes?"

And then she knew. "Pan Garbinski."

He bowed slightly. "Research historian, at your service."

Sophie clasped her hands to her chest and choked out a laugh until tears of relief took their place.

"I'm sorry I frightened you."

"You're living here." Now she spoke as a statement of fact. He hesitated, but she rushed on. "It's all right. I mean, I'm glad. I'm glad if the library's a safe place for you. I truly mean no harm."

"You were always kind to me, to everyone at the library."

"It's good of you to say that. I was here by the grace of Pan Gadomski. He was godfather to my husband, and as like a father to me as I've known."

"He is dead."

"Yes." Sophie swallowed the lump that popped into her throat each time she thought of that good man. "But how do you know?"

"I found the body. We were already living . . . nearby. Pan Gadomski supplied us with food and information. When the fire started, I knew something had gone awry. I feared they'd taken you. I knew you were working in the cellar, packing the crates."

"Did you?" Sophie hadn't imagined that anyone other than Pan Gadomski knew who she was.

He nodded, then hesitated. He seemed to reconsider and confided, "We escaped after the Gestapo had gone, afraid that the entire building would burn, but were able to get back inside before they boarded the doors."

"How have you managed these months? Where did you get food?"

He looked away. "Perhaps the less you know, Pani Kumiega, the better." And then he looked as if he'd just thought of something. "Why have you come?"

If Sophie hoped to hide the Bukowskis, she must be assured of an ally in Pan Garbinski. She lifted her chin, determined to take the plunge. "I have friends. Jewish friends. They need a place to stay."

"You want to hide them here?" Pan Garbinski frowned.

"In the library. I came to see if there was running water, facilities of any kind. I can hardly believe you have electricity."

"We can hardly believe it either. I think it must only be because electricity on this street has been restored, and they've not thought to turn it off in the library. We expect to lose it any day now. No one has been to the building since the Wehrmacht boarded it up. How many? How many do you want to hide?"

"Three, I think. A family—a man, his wife, their child . . . a little boy. Perhaps your son's age."

Pan Garbinski seemed to pull into himself. "Children are always a risk. Two together . . ." He shook his head.

"They would be company for one another, would they not? They could play . . . quietly."

"They could play," he agreed. "Have you ever known two boys to play quietly? It would be a great risk."

"The library is so big. There must be many places to hide." She hoped he would tell her where they were living. She didn't want to give away the room in the cellar.

He turned away. "You can get them food, medicine?"

Sophie wasn't sure, at least she wasn't certain how she could supply them with enough to cover what she'd been sharing as well as the rations Aaron could no longer claim if he was not laboring. But she'd figure it out. She had to. "Yes."

He nodded, accepting her vow without question. "How can I refuse? It is not my library."

"I don't want to endanger anyone. I just want to help. They might not even want to come . . . but the man, the son of a dear friend who was killed, is working so hard, getting weaker each day. He's worried about his son . . . and typhus, in the Jewish Quarter."

"Your friend is part of the forced labor program."

"All men are."

"All Jewish men."

"Yes," Sophie agreed, "all Jewish men."

"Bring your friends. We will do our best."

"I'll explain the situation to him. I won't give you away. I promise."

He nodded. "Thank you for that, Pani Kumiega."

"That's not my name . . . not anymore. Pan Gadomski provided me with a new identity. Now, I'm Zofia—"

Pan Garbinski smiled. "That is good. It is better if I don't know your new name. But, Sophia, never forget who you are. That will help you when all else is taken away, when your home is gone and your heart is broken."

"No." Sophie tried to smile in return and reached for his hand. She already knew about broken hearts and lost homes. She knew too well. "No, I won't forget."

CHAPTER TEN

ROSA LAY IN BED, the windows opened wide to the late spring, almost summer morning. She'd been so tired lately, more exhausted than even their reduced rations should account for. Itzhak had been so very sweet that morning, not minding that she did not get up to prepare his breakfast or even his lunch pail, saying that he would take care of it.

She hated the worry she'd seen, and caused, in his eyes. She must pull herself together. Why did she need so much sleep? No matter how early she went to bed, she woke up feeling as if she'd plowed a field.

Her stomach roiled. She didn't know if it was because of something questionable she'd eaten, like the meat Itzhak brought home from the black market—horse meat, no doubt. Or was she ill? They could not afford for her to be ill. Jews were only allowed to see Jewish doctors, and there were so few left in the district.

As it was, in order to fulfill Matka's need for medicine, they'd had to go to Father Stimecki, a Catholic priest in the Wawer suburb. Rosa had learned through gossip whispered in the bread line that he was known to hold back names of Poles who'd died, to forge *Kennkarta*—identity cards—in their names. His kindness, given freely despite immeasurable risk, provided Rosa's mother with full welfare benefits and an Aryan ration card, brought to her beneath the knitting needles and skein of yarn in the bag of a young social worker. Now Matka was Liliana Wójcik—Polish, not Jewish. That meant that the Polish social worker, Irena Sendler, could make house calls, bring medicine, and smuggle in food, once even leaving a winter coat that she wore on top of her own so when it was left behind, no one noticed. "Blessed angel!" That's what Rosa's mother had called the young woman whose head came only to Itzhak's shoulder. But that was for Matka. There would be no medicine for Rosa. She could not be ill. She must not.

Perhaps it was time for her monthly. She counted the weeks, then realized it was months. She tried to remember the last time she'd needed the clean rags and cotton wool. Could two months really have passed? She swallowed the bile that threatened each morning, her heart fluttering at the thought. . . . Could it be? Was it possible? She remembered the last months. Had she and Itzhak been intimate . . . enough? She smiled. That had never been the problem.

Rosa shook her head, trying to take in the possibility, what it would mean, whether she could carry long enough for a live birth, and again . . . was it possible? Her hand reached for her breasts—swollen, though the rest of her had grown thinner. She ran her hand over her abdomen. No difference there. Too soon to tell. But somehow she knew. She just knew.

Rosa wanted to laugh aloud, to cry, to look into her mother's eyes and beg, *"How did you know?"*

She placed her feet on the floor, her stomach still doing backward flips. She could stand being sick. She could stand anything, as long as this was real.

Hours later, washed and dressed, she stood at the sink to wash the luncheon dishes, humming the lullaby her mother had long ago sung to her, one every Polish mother knew and sang.

"There were once two little kittens.
Ah-ah-ah, two little kittens,
They were both grayish-brown.

"Oh, sleep, my darling.
If you'd like a star from the sky, I'll give—"

She'd just reached her favorite part when she heard her mother clucking as she shuffled—*slip, slip*—into the room. "Didn't I tell you? Didn't I say?" She smiled, wagging her finger with one hand while her other struggled to maintain balance on her cane.

"Matka! How did you know? How do you know now?"

"I'm your matka, remember? That's how I know. One day, when it's your daughter, you will know too. Now, tell me, how many months? One? Two?"

"Two, at least. Maybe two and a half." Rosa's heart beat quickly.

"Two months gone." Her mother counted on her fingers. "March or April, May, June, July, August, September, October, November, December! A baby to celebrate—a Hanukkah miracle!"

"Shortly after Hanukkah, surely. I counted already. If I can carry full term."

Her mother smiled, nodding. "You will carry. You will deliver a strong and healthy baby for your Itzhak and for you, for me. A new life."

"A new life." Rosa could hardly believe this joy, tentative and uncertain though it was. *Please, Adonai, for Matka's sake. I've not seen her so happy since Tata's death, not since we came. This is a new beginning for all of us. Please, make it so.*

Her mother turned and began to shuffle back the way she'd come. "I will eat my soup early, and then to bed."

Rosa dried her hands on her apron, a pinch of worry in her heart. "You're unwell, Matka? What's wrong?"

Her mother chuckled. "Nothing. Nothing, my dear. I think you must be alone when you tell your husband. I remember just such a day, long ago. I am aged and broken by life and this infernal war, my Rosa, but not senile."

Rosa heard her chuckling happily all the way back to the parlor.

◆ ◆ ◆

Itzhak had worried all day about his wife, and now he worried on his way home from work. How pale she had looked that morning, how listless she had grown these past weeks. At first he'd put it down to her latest disappointment, but she'd seemed to rally from that loss, at least for a short time.

She's not eating enough. She gives the larger portion to me each day, and probably to her mother when I'm not there to see. Does she even eat any meat? He pounded one fist into his other palm. *She thinks because I am out in the cold, I need more. She worries about me, dotes on me, but what about her?* Itzhak stopped in his tracks. If it was food his wife needed, then food he would get. He fingered the coins in his pocket and his heart sank. Enough for nothing.

And then he thought of the cradle pieces stuffed into the beams of his father-in-law's workshop. The wood was beautiful, the carving on the headboard so intricate that a family of means would cherish it for a much-wanted little one. Through his work he'd met several families with the means to afford such a cradle . . . mostly Germans who'd been lucky enough to have their wives and families brought into Poland to live with them. Pregnancy had reached a fever pitch among the Wehrmacht officers' wives. *As if the world needs more little Germans.*

Thankful he'd never told Rosa of the cradle, thankful she'd never know he would sell her father's last gift, he knew he must do it quickly, before he lost his resolve or reasoned it through. It wasn't his to sell, he acknowledged, but surely Jacob would prefer the health and welfare of his only child to the far-off hope of a grandchild. And Rosa had had so many disappointments. What if they never bore a child together?

He shook his head, as if to slap away the thought. *There will be no hope of a child or a future life or anything if Rosa does not recover. Her life is worth more than ten children.* He knew he was mustering conviction, dancing manipulated truth over a guilty conscience, but believed himself right just the same.

If he slipped into the work shed early in the morning—before Rosa woke—and if he slipped in again before entering the house after work each night, he could finish the cradle in a matter of three or four days, as long as the varnish sufficiently dried. He must make certain no light shone through the window, but he could manage that. The days were longer now. He could work without a lamp.

I'll begin tonight. The conviction lightened Itzhak's step and he made double time in the long trek home. Opening then closing the garden gate with care, he quietly, quickly followed the cobbled path to the back garden. Through the kitchen window, he could see Rosa, stirring the soup pot. She pushed a stray curl beneath her kerchief as she leaned forward to lift the wooden spoon to her lips. He watched her grimace, then unaccountably smile, and wondered if that meant tonight's soup was tasty or perhaps not.

He waited until she'd turned her back to the window, then sprinted across the garden, into the shadow of the workshop shed, and reached for the lock, high on the door. Inside, he stood a moment, waiting for his eyes to adjust to the dimmer light.

Stretching high, he felt along the beam for the cut ends, the sides, the rockers and spindles. He ran his hand over the wood carving. It was every bit as intricate as he remembered, the wood already sanded just as fine as it needed to be. Itzhak closed his eyes. How could he sell this? And then he thought of his Rosa, so pale and drawn. How could he not?

Pushing indecision away, he pulled all the pieces to the table. The light waned, but he could see enough to begin. Mornings would be better, lighter. He dared take thirty minutes, perhaps forty. He would tell Rosa that he'd had to work late. *This is true, yes? Yes, this is true.* He reasoned with himself under his breath, then aloud, making a convincing case, a story he would tell his wife.

"She'll understand. Many times I have to work late. The Wehrmacht makes a hard taskmaster. But now the Gestapo has me working in their headquarters. They're worse by far. She will believe me. She trusts me." He shivered though it was not cold.

"I do trust you, Itzhak. Why would I not?"

Itzhak jumped—nearly out of his skin—and knocked the stack of spindles to the floor.

"What are you doing out here in the near dark? Your soup is ready." Rosa stood in the open door.

Itzhak's heart hammered in his chest. He turned, to stand between Rosa and her view of the cradle. "I'll be in shortly. Just let me finish here."

"Finish what? What can be so important to be out here in the chill tonight? It's almost curfew. You're late."

"Yes, they kept me late. It will be that way for a little while. Just a little while. Go back inside, Rosa. It's too cold for you here. I'll come. I promise." *Please, Adonai, don't let her see the cradle. She'll think I meant it for her, and now there is no baby. Protect her heart!*

But Rosa came closer. "It's not cold. It's spring—just a little chill." She wormed her way between Itzhak and the workbench, reaching first for one of the spindles that had fallen to the floor. He had no heart or strength to stop her. It was her father's gift, after all.

"What is it? What are you making?" Wonder filled Rosa's voice. He heard the hope, the dawn of understanding in her last words as she placed the spindle on the bench and reached for the carved headboard.

He sighed. He would have to tell her. "I didn't make it."

"A cradle. A baby's cradle," she whispered, her words sacrosanct.

He could hear her swallow and knew she held back a sob. *Idiot! I'm an idiot! Look what I've done!*

"It's beautiful. Itzhak, it's beautiful! But how did you know?" She turned and faced him, clasped his cheeks with two hands. "I didn't even know until today. How did you know?" She shook her head, not in anger, but as if she disbelieved. "How long have you been working on this?"

The temptation of half-truths and blatant lies swarmed in his head. *Which question to answer first? How did I know? How did I know . . . what? I can't lie to her. By all that is right, I can't lie to her!* "I know you are sick, Rosa. I know I have failed you. But I swear, I will make it up to you. I know someone who will buy this, who will give me good money for it. If I'm lucky, I might be able to get the officer to buy food for us instead of giving me money. He'll be able to get far more and better food than we can buy—or find."

She swayed, just slightly, but enough that he reached for her. "You would give our baby's cradle away? The first cradle you've made with your own hands—you would sell?"

"I didn't make it. Your father made it for you, for your first child, for all your children—our children. He cut the pieces and carved the wood. I was only going to put it together."

"Tata made it? For me? For our baby?" Rosa ran her fingers over the headboard. She pulled the carbide lamp from the bench closer and lit it, then pressed her fingers into the intricate grooves of the wood.

"Please, Rosa. We have to sell this. I would never ask you, but—"

"But you were going to sell it without asking me."

"I would never consider it, but—" He shrugged, helpless. "I don't know what else to do. You are worth ten children to me—a hundred. I can't fail you, not now."

Rosa's exasperation came out in a half laugh. "You have not failed me, Itzhak Dunovich, and I am not in need of food. Right now—today—I will only eat because I must."

He shook his head. "You have not been eating enough. You're weak. I have nothing else to sell. I can't let you—"

She grabbed him by the shoulders and shook him. "Listen to me! I am not sick or weak because I have no food. I'm sick and weak because I am with child! Our child! Our child, who will need this cradle in a few short months."

"What?" The mist that had begun to dissipate in Itzhak's brain rolled in, a full-blown fog. "Our child? You are . . . pregnant?" He was afraid to say the word.

She nodded, her mouth a line that held back laughter.

"Are you certain? How do you know?"

Rosa laughed out loud. She turned down the carbide lamp, picked up the torch, and led him through the garden and into the kitchen. Once inside, she sat him down, pulled off his boots and socks, leaving both by the stove.

Before she could stand, he pulled her onto his lap, holding her gently, reverently, as if she might break. He ran his hands over her sides, her abdomen, her neck.

Her laughter bubbled, music to his ears. She pushed his hands away, drew the curtains, pulled the pot from the stove, handed him a thick slice of buttered bread, and led him upstairs.

CHAPTER ELEVEN

THE NOTE SOPHIE WROTE TO Aaron late that afternoon was brief, written on a small scrap of paper:

I know a place. It is dark and quiet, and silence must be maintained at all costs. Nod if yes. Turn away if no.

On her way home from work that evening she dropped the note near his bricklaying and kept walking, uncertain if he saw her. She turned into a shop, pretending to check the price of butter against her ration coupons. She shook her head apologetically at the grocer, then turned back into the street, glancing Aaron's way.

He spread a layer of cement and then another row of bricks. She couldn't be certain, but she thought he spied her from beneath the bill of his cap. He looked up, removed his hat as if to stretch his back, nodded once in her direction, and bent to his work.

Sophie hurried home. There was much to plan, much to do. For the first time since Pan Gadomski's murder she felt alive, purposeful.

Adrenaline rushed through her veins in a way that it had not even from dropping packages of food for the Bukowski family.

They would need pallets or cots for sleeping, bedding, torches, a chamber pot for hours they dared not go to the washroom, soap, food, whatever clothing they could not wear to their destination. *Getting soap and small packages of food there is one thing—even clothing. But how will I transport bedding—or pallets or cots—into the library?* Sophie sat down at her kitchen table, her legs wobbly and suddenly weighted. *And if I could, how would I afford it? Is there some way they can bring their own possessions? No, of course not. They're going into hiding! It's not as if the Bukowskis can carry luggage through the streets without notice. They must go in whatever they wear, whatever they can conceal beneath their coats.*

Sophie closed her eyes and buried her face in her hands. Why hadn't she thought through everything more carefully?

"Adonai makes a way when there appears no way. It is His specialty. Remember the Red Sea." The words of her old friend came back to her, just as they did so often when Sophie felt at her wits' end.

What would Pan Bukowski or Pan Gadomski do in this situation? Both men had seemed capable of pulling rabbits from hats—hats with no tops.

She'd simply have to work out the details as she went along. The first thing to do was to get the Bukowskis out of their quarters and into the library. Everything else could happen after.

Faith. I need faith. There will be a way. Pan Bukowski used to say that God didn't open the Red Sea until Pharaoh was at the Israelites' backs and a miracle was the only option. Sophie pulled the paper wrapper from a chunk of cheese and wrote:

> *Tomorrow, I will go to the park after work—where we used to picnic. Follow at a distance.*

She was asking the Bukowskis to trust her, to have faith. She dared not fail them.

• ◆ •

The next day at work was the longest and most tedious Sophie could remember. If she made three mistakes in tallying purchases, she made twelve. As soon as the grocer switched the sign on his door to Closed and lowered the shade, she pulled on her coat.

"In a hurry today, Pani Marek." The grocer was always too interested in Sophie's life, the company she kept or didn't keep. His curiosity might unnerve her, but he was that way with everyone. Sophie imagined him selling information to the Gestapo for zloty or sausage.

"It is the naming day of a friend. I promised to celebrate with her." It was the lie that came first to mind. "I want to find some flowers before the vendor closes."

"Flowers . . . ah, better a lump of coal and a package of coffee for . . . who did you say?"

"My friend." Sophie avoided the trap of giving her name. The only friend whose naming day she knew was Terri, and that was October 3, not spring of the year. "Yes, you're right. Perhaps I should reconsider my gift. Good night, Pan Mencher. I will see you in the morning."

"Good night, Pani Marek." He locked the door behind her.

Sophie walked quickly toward Twarda Street, where the wall continued to climb higher day by day. Soon she would not be able to see over it and the workers would be hidden from view. Guard stations were being formed at breaks in the wall. If the Germans limited traffic entering and leaving the walled-off area, moving the Bukowskis could be much more difficult, perhaps impossible.

By the time she'd purchased enough food to get the Bukowskis through the next few days and reached the park, light had faded into gloaming. The park was nearly empty. Polish families would be gathering around their tables soon, locking their doors against Germans and curfew.

There was no time for her to sit on the bench and pretend to watch the birds, as she'd planned, then meander down a garden path, trusting the Bukowskis to follow at a distance. None of them could risk being caught outside after curfew. As quickly as she'd walked to the park, she forced herself to slow along the garden path.

She stopped to caress a bright spring blossom, brave to show its face despite the occupation. As she stood, she scanned the park. A movement near one of the hedges caught her eye. She dared not look closely, dared not linger. She lifted her umbrella against the sudden slight drizzle and walked on through the gardens and out the gate at the far end of the park, never looking back.

Sophie held her breath, praying they followed, praying they wouldn't be stopped, praying . . . praying . . . praying.

She kept going, walking purposefully for a time, then slowed, remembering that the Bukowski child might have a hard time keeping up. She hoped he wasn't becoming soaked in the increasing rain. The basement of the library would be colder yet, and she feared what that might mean for him. A thousand worries plagued her. A thousand worries drove her on.

At last the library came in sight. Fewer pedestrians showed themselves on the street, and those that came rushed by quickly, as intent on reaching their lodgings as she. Despite the downpour, by the time she reached the side street of the darkened library she lowered her umbrella, hoping the trees and the gathering dusk would make her less conspicuous and that as women closed their draperies against the night, they would not see her or the little family that followed.

At the last possible moment, Sophie slipped through the hedge, unlocked the library door, and waited just inside. A tentative tap came a minute later. She opened the door and two forms—one tall and gaunt and one small—rushed past her. She pulled the door shut but hesitated in the darkness. "Aaron?"

"I am here, and my son."

"Your wife. Is she coming?"

"Mami," the child whispered.

"My wife gave way in January. We are only two."

Sophie tried to think what that meant—"gave way." Did she refuse to come? Had she mentally, emotionally broken? Was she dead? All she could say was, "I'm sorry." She locked the door and flicked on her torch. "This way."

She never even heard their footsteps behind her. By the time they reached the hidden room, she was exhausted from the worry, the sleeplessness, the relief of getting them into the library. And yet she knew the work had just begun. She felt for the panel in the wall, all but invisible if you didn't know what you were looking for, and pushed open the door, holding the light for Aaron and his son to make their way, then swept the room with her torch.

Sophie gasped. The room was no longer empty. Three simple beds—two long and narrow and pushed together, and one shorter—had been knocked together, clearly from damaged bookcases. There were no mattresses or pillows, but each held a worn comforter. There was a small table and two rough chairs, also made from shelving, and a carbide lamp sat on the table.

"How did he know?" Sophie had no doubt that the guardian angel was Pan Garbinski. She remembered from her years at the library that he'd been handy at repairing things, often not waiting for the elderly caretaker to mend chairs and windowsills, to repair bookcases and little things that needed tending. *But how did he know about the room? And then she realized. Of course, Pan Gadomski hid them all this time. He probably hid them in some other part of the library so I would not know, would not be at risk or risk giving them away. But he must have shown them the secret room. Perhaps it's even a secondary hiding place for the Garbinskis.*

"Come in, come in." She motioned to Aaron and his son as if they were her guests.

"Someone else is staying here?" Aaron sounded uncertain. "Are you sure—"

A knock came beside the door before he could finish, and a head with a long, dark beard ducked to enter the small doorway. Sophie sensed Aaron's fear as he pulled his son behind him.

"Pan Bukowski, allow me to introduce Pan Garbinski. If I am not mistaken, he has already welcomed you to the library."

Pan Garbinski extended his hand to Aaron. "You are welcome. The furniture is rough, of course, but the best I could do with what we have here."

"You made this—all this—for us?"

"The room was bare when I left it last." Sophie shrugged, smiling, barely able to comprehend such generosity, especially when she knew Pan Garbinski feared bringing more people into their sanctuary.

"We—my wife and son and I—live behind panels in the attic, above the third floor study rooms. We are quiet by day and show no light—ever. Just before dawn we use the washrooms. I'll show you where. There are electric lights there, for now. No windows, so it is safe. But we must be quiet at all times. Perhaps we could come some evenings—after curfew, or better yet, after midnight—and visit. Our boys could play together, quietly."

"We would like that." Aaron smiled for the first time, then looked at his son, who cowered behind his leg. "Wouldn't we, Judah?"

"Sleeping in the day passes the time and helps us remain quiet . . . although my wife and I take turns staying awake to keep watch, to listen for intruders. Sometimes—" he winced—"I'm afraid I snore . . . my wife says, 'like a freight train.'"

"Pape doesn't snore." Judah spoke for the first time.

Mr. Garbinski grew serious. "That is good. Then you can both sleep at once."

Sophie felt as if the weight of the world had been lifted from her shoulders. She pulled the package of sausage and two roasted potatoes from her pockets, and a jar of drinking water from her purse, and set them on the table. "I'm sorry it's pork. It's all I could get."

"Please don't be sorry." Aaron looked near tears. "This is more than we've had in months."

"I'll bring more tomorrow." Sophie smiled, relieved.

"No, Pani Kumiega." Mr. Garbinski was firm. "We will share what we have with the Bukowskis tomorrow. When you come again, bring enough for the week. If you come too often, people will notice. Residents may even recognize you—remember you from before and wonder where you live, where you go when you walk toward the hedge in back. The library is believed to be empty and boarded up. You are supposed to be dead. The less often you come, the less you are seen at all, the better for all of us."

"Of course. You're right." Sophie didn't know why that realization felt like a punch in the gut.

"Perhaps you should go now," Aaron said, "before the curfew begins. It must be nearly time."

Sophie hesitated. This was not what she'd planned. She'd thought to stay the night when she believed Pani Bukowski would be there.

"We'll be all right."

"I will look after your friends," Pan Garbinski assured her. "Go now. Go, quickly."

Sophie nodded. She wanted to reach out, to reassure Aaron that she would be back, that she wouldn't forget them, but it didn't seem appropriate somehow . . . now that there was no Pani Bukowski. So she nodded again, gave the second torch she'd brought for Aaron into his hand, and using her own, made her way back down the dark hallway.

Though she walked as quickly as she could, the route back to her apartment felt longer than it ever had, and far more lonely. It was as if all the adrenaline of the past two days had rushed through her body and was now seeping out through the soles of her shoes into the gutter.

Lights went out along the streets. Running out of time, she picked up her pace, her calves protesting and her heart pumping madly, punishing her each step of the way. She checked her watch with a quick flick of her torch. Sweat broke out across her forehead. Curfew had passed by ten minutes and there were still three blocks to go through a bombed portion of the city. Patrols walked both ends of her street. How would she get past?

She stepped into the darkened doorway of a fabric shop, pressing her back into the crevice between the door and the shop window, and waited as two guards walked by—laughing, talking, or they would have seen her.

She waited until they turned the corner, then picked up a broken brick in the street and hurried along, slipping beneath stairwells and making her way from building to building as quickly as she dared.

The crunch of boots turned the corner and came up the sidewalk. Every few yards they stopped, checking doors. She knew the Wehrmacht looted Polish shops in the night, helping themselves to anything they wanted. What did they care? Poles had no recourse.

The rattle of doorknobs came closer. She would be discovered in the stairwell and there was nothing she could do.

She waited for the next rattle, slipped to the street and threw the broken brick with all her might, then dove back into the stairwell. Gunfire poured into the street as soldiers came running from before and behind, all headed toward the imaginary sniper. Sophie bit her lip and ran down the nearest alley. She was good at climbing fences—something she'd learned as a child in England when pinching apples from Sir Lawrence's tenant farmer. She made it to the back of her building's courtyard, circled the perimeter, and waited at the corner for the patrols to pass.

By the time she made it upstairs to her apartment, she was out of breath, her coat torn and the heel of her shoe cracked. Her hands shook as she inserted the key into her door.

Just before the knob turned, Terri opened her door and took in the scene.

"Sophie!" she whispered down the hallway.

But Sophie, with all the urgency she could muster, shook her head and closed the door behind her.

CHAPTER TWELVE

THOSE EARLY SUMMER NIGHTS, Rosa lay in her husband's arms, content and happy beyond her wildest dreams. Morning brought sickness, but even that was evidence and affirmation that another life grew inside her.

Rosa returned home late one afternoon with their ration of bread, weary but determined to create a new recipe she'd learned from a woman in the bread queue to stretch their meager rations with a jar of her mother's canned plums.

Rosa pushed open the kitchen door to find her mother perched on tiptoe on a chair, rummaging through the top shelf of a cupboard.

"Matka! Whatever are you doing? Get down from there! You'll fall!"

"Pishposh," Marya retorted. "I was standing on chairs before you were born."

"That was a quarter century ago! Not now.'"

"Here, take this." Marya handed Rosa a jar full of coins.

"Where did all this come from?"

Her mother grunted, leaning heavily on Rosa's shoulder, as she climbed down. "You know your tata . . . always saving, always pinching away a groszy here, ten there, bless him. I didn't appreciate it then as I do now." She reached the floor and heaved a sigh of relief.

"Please don't climb like that when no one is here, Matka. What if you'd fallen?" Rosa didn't want to lose sight of the real concern.

"That's all. Everything else up there can stay. We won't have room for everything."

"Room?"

"When we move, and we must move soon."

Rosa's heart constricted. *Is she regressing? Is her mind going?*

Marya looked annoyed, as if she could read her daughter's thoughts. "It's better we go before we're forced, while we can choose our housing. Already the district is filling. We'll be lucky to find something with two bedrooms."

Rosa shook her head as if to clear cobwebs, while refusing the truth that assailed her. "What are you talking about? This house is perfect. You and Tata lived here all your married lives. Why would we move?"

Her mother sighed, the heaviness that Rosa had rejected settling squarely on her shoulders. "You know why. We'll be forced to move soon. You've seen the wall. It grows taller each day—and we're outside its perimeter."

Rosa had heard the rumors while standing in queues for bread—fearful knowledge that the rising bricks collected by forced laborers would wall the Jewish Quarter, or a portion of it, to form a ghetto. Ghettos had already been formed in other cities, physically cutting Jews off from the rest of the world. Within the ghettos came new decrees, new restrictions, a slow starvation of health and dignity, of food, of life. But she had pushed such fears from her mind.

"You haven't even been outside," Rosa accused. "How would you know?"

"Our good neighbor was quick to tell me." Marya harrumphed. "I think she waited until she saw you leave, until she knew I was alone."

"Pani Dobonowicz?"

Her mother nodded. "Protecting me, she said. Not wanting me to hear it elsewhere or be unprepared, she said. Mostly, she wants this house. She's always wanted it. I could see her eyes measuring my windows, wondering if her curtains will stretch the width."

Rosa pulled a kitchen chair from the table and sat down heavily.

Marya rubbed her daughter's shoulder in sympathy. "I'm sorry your little one won't know the home his *zeyde* built with his own hands."

Rosa gasped. It was unlike her mother to revert to Yiddish; only in such a sentimental moment might she do so. From infancy, Rosa had been drilled to speak Polish.

"I'm sorry you won't be here for his first walking in the grass of the garden." She shook her head at the futility of it all, then pulled a determined face. "But it's better if we don't wait for another decree, if we find a place now . . . sell what we can and move what we must . . . the food from the cellar, most of all. We can't let them know how much food we have; it would be gone in a moment."

Rosa couldn't draw a deep breath. Her mother would say it was the baby pushing up, but she knew it was sorrow weighing down. She hadn't wanted to face more than the bread lines, the rubble in the streets outside. She hadn't wanted fear to touch her, or Itzhak, or their baby. And now her own mother had opened the door and invited the mercenary in. Her throat caught. She must be very careful, or the sorrow might consume her.

◆

Itzhak returned home that night, weary from work and worries of his parents, his sisters, in Vilna. Most days he was able to focus on his tasks and commit his family to Adonai's care. But today he'd heard rumors that the situation in and surrounding Vilna had grown worse, more violent. There was nothing he could do to help them, and that helplessness rankled. He dared not think of leaving or urging Rosa to go back to his family, as much as he wished them all under one roof.

My wife is strong; our baby grows stronger and healthier each day. Rosa, my love, my joy! You are my family now, and at least you and our little one are safe—for now.

By the time he reached the walkway to the back kitchen door, his heart sang, in hope and anticipated joy of the days ahead.

Stepping inside, he found his mother-in-law stuffing a tin box into a hole carved in the wall behind the stove. As he closed the door she slapped a layer of plaster onto the wall and slathered it over.

"What is that?"

"Memories," Marya said. "Photographs."

"You hide photographs in the wall?"

Marya, recently energetic and full of vitality at the prospect of becoming a grandmother, looked away, suddenly old. "They'll take our house, you know. They'll take our belongings and all our money. They did that in the last war." Moments passed before she finished her task. She looked up and spoke, almost fiercely. "But wars end, and when this war is over, we shall prove this is our house by these photographs in the wall. And we will need money to begin again. This brooch, these rings are not much, but it will be a start . . . if the house stands."

Itzhak felt as if he'd been run over, as if the joy discovered on his walk home had been sucked from his lungs. In one day, the two women of his household had sorted and packed cases for each of them to carry and had mentally allotted crates of dishes and jars of food wrapped in linens and bedding to a wheelbarrow that he would push. But moving Rosa now might be the undoing of all their care. He wasn't sure what she knew—how far she'd walked to find bread each day, how much she'd seen in the streets—but he'd imagined that not talking about the horrors was best for her and their baby. "Don't you think we should wait? It might not come to this. Britain and France—"

"Are doing nothing!" Marya all but spat. Itzhak blinked at his mother-in-law's fervor. "Jacob and I, we barely survived the Great War, and only because he made preparations, because he knew to go before it was too late, knew how to barter and hide from the pogroms. He's not here now, and you, Itzhak, must be the one to lead. But you've not lived through a war—not been responsible for a family through war. So listen to me. Find us a decent place before we're forced to go, before there is nothing. Do not wait until they come for us in the night, until they push us out at gunpoint. Your child won't be born here, no matter how much you wish it."

Itzhak looked to Rosa, certain she would refuse, certain she would claim that her mother was overreacting. But resignation was written in his wife's eyes. He clasped her hand, then the hand of his mother-in-law. "What you say is hard, Matka, but wise. Tomorrow. Tomorrow, I will find a place."

That night, as he held Rosa in his arms, as he listened to her breathing and her trembling sigh beneath the comforter, he cradled her head beneath his chin. "Your mother is a brave woman. I never imagined she could bring herself to leave here, or that she would be the one to insist." He pulled her closer. "I wish it were different. I wish you could deliver our child in this room. I wish your mother could live here all her days and die an old woman in her bed. I wish that our child could see all the clever things his grandfather built in this house. I wish . . . I wish I could give you the world."

Rosa leaned into him and her tears washed his chest. He pulled her tighter yet, so close that he could just hear her muffled words. "You are my world, Itzhak. As long as we're together, my world is intact."

CHAPTER THIRTEEN

THAT SUNDAY, Sophie piled every zloty she'd hidden and hoarded onto her kitchen table. She placed the gold signet ring Aaron Bukowski had given her to sell on top. Even with the pay she would receive that week from work and by using every ration coupon she possessed, it would not be enough to feed herself and the Bukowskis . . . at least not enough to keep them going for more than two weeks.

The task of supplying her friends with enough food for a week or more at a time had become daunting. There was no way for them to cook in the library's hidden basement room. The Garbinskis managed a tiny coal grill in the attic, despite the fire hazard . . . but it was a ter-rible risk, a risk they only dared on Sunday mornings, when residents of the Polish Catholic neighborhood were most likely to attend mass and not be there to notice cooking smells as they walked by.

Sophie needed to purchase food that required no cooking or that she could cook before dropping it off. How to inconspicuously carry such a quantity and only once a week—preferably less often—posed a greater problem. Her temples throbbed. The library had seemed such a good hiding place. But she'd not counted the cost, not planned as she should. Poor planning was not like her. She'd wanted to help, wanted to be generous. How had Pan Gadomski managed to help the Garbinskis so long? Even when he was killed, they had not been discovered, and still they were supplied. How? Dared she ask them? Could she work with their supplier to help the Bukowskis?

Early that evening, Sophie timidly knocked on Terri's door. She'd not visited with her friend since the day of Pan Gadomski's murder. That Terri had sent her away while accepting others into her home still rankled, still hurt. But she needed help.

"What is it?"

"May I come in?" Sophie's throat thickened with each word. Friendship was what she craved, but she feared to risk rejection . . . again. Terri closed the door behind her and Sophie forced out the words, "I need your help."

Terri pulled Sophie into her arms. "I know. I know, my friend."

Sophie lifted her chin and sniffed back tears that insisted on welling in her eyes.

Terri led her to the sitting area and pulled Sophie to the sofa. "I know you're helping the Bukowskis."

Sophie felt her eyes grow wide.

"I saw the Garbinskis this morning."

"You've been helping them?"

"Since . . . since Papa cannot. I knew he'd been working with them. So after a few days I found a way into the library."

"The trash chute door?"

Terri smiled. "There are more ways than one to skin a cat, as Papa once told me."

Sophie didn't know whether to feel relieved or rebuffed.

"We can help each other help them—all of them, if you're willing. Remember how Papa said, 'Two are better than one alone?'"

Terri's clear gaze unnerved Sophie. It was a good idea, and such a relief. She needed help and Terri obviously knew her way about this business.

"Why did you leave me out before? Why did you push me away?" Sophie needed to know that.

Now Terri looked away, studied the cuticles of her nails, took longer to answer than Sophie wanted. "I needed to begin alone. I needed to be connected to Papa and to the work he was doing." She looked up at Sophie, her eyes pleading for understanding. "Papa thought the world of you and Janck. Janek was like a son to him . . . the son he never had. He'd hoped to be a sort of grandfather to your children." Terri turned away when Sophie winced at the mention of children. "I couldn't give him that, couldn't be that ongoing family for him—not with the war and Piotr going off to fight. We were stupid. . . . We waited too long and missed our chance to marry. Piotr wanted to establish his school, wanted Papa to be proud of him.

"Can you understand? I wanted to do this work with Papa—this something special between us—especially after he sent the two of us away from home. You had Janck—at least you will have him again. I needed Papa. Even though he's gone, I need—needed that connection, that intimacy with my father." She stood and crossed the room, lit the stove in the kitchen, and placed the teakettle to boil, keeping her back to Sophie. "Sometimes I pretend he's alive, that I will see him when I take food to the Garbinskis, when I sneak into the library. I pretend we're still working together."

Sophie didn't speak. She tried to put herself in Terri's shoes. Sophie had grown up without parents. Her father and mother had been killed in a car accident shortly after her tenth birthday. She'd spent five months in an orphanage in London—a miserable existence—while lawyers sorted out the reality that she had no family. No aunts or uncles or cousins or grandparents—no one to take her in and raise her. That's when Sir Lawrence Chamberlin, after having been out of the country for a year, learned of the death of his old comrade in arms from the Great War. Immediately, he'd set about looking for his friend's orphaned child, taken Sophie in as a companion to his own daughter, Caroline—Carrie—and raised her. Always Sophie had known she was "second child, second best" and had sensed Carrie's desire to keep her in that role.

They'd never discussed it, never identified it as Terri just did. Academically, Sophie understood Carrie's desire for a closer relationship with her own father. Academically, she now tried to understand Terri's desire for the same—even with her father gone. Sophie sighed, just a little. She had no father, could barely remember his face, let alone his voice, or her mother's. She had no claim to the close and special relationship her friends had with theirs.

"Tea is in the canister in the cupboard," Terri whispered, her back still to Sophie. "I'll get the pot."

Sophie pushed Terri's plea for understanding away. There was nothing more to be said. Pan Gadomski was gone. Terri had claimed her brief moment in time with her father. Sophie still hoped that Janek was alive and would return, whether or not she was able to bear their child. She hoped the same was true for Piotr, that he and Terri would marry, would have children, would be a family. For now, they needed to help the families they'd promised, and they needed one another to safely fulfill those promises and to bolster courage.

They sipped their tea in silence, the ghosts of loved ones between them.

At last Sophie changed the subject and asked the thing she needed to know. "How do you get enough food for the Garbinskis? How do you get it to them without anyone seeing you?"

"I buy on the black market. I'll introduce you to my sources, or I'll buy for you, too—if you have money."

"A little . . . not enough, not for long."

Terri nodded. "There are others who will help. A network."

Sophie felt her pulse quicken. "Isn't that risky? The more who know . . ."

"Papa helped me form connections. But yes, always, the less any one person knows, the better."

"The German at the library spoke as if he was following orders to get rid of intellectuals. But do you think the work your father was doing—that network—was the real reason he was killed?"

Terri sighed, a heart-wrenching, deep sigh. "I think there may have been many reasons. They are killing off academics. Papa knew that, expected it. That's part of why he sent us away. He wanted to do all he could to help while he could. He was involved in the underground and in the resistance. He had connections to the Polish government in exile. He was helping to get Jews out of Poland—into Palestine, for pity's sake. He was hiding the Garbinskis in the library and who knows how many others I don't know about. But in the end, I believe it was an informant . . . Someone earned their thirty pieces of silver—or a packet of sausage—that day. Killing him as an academic was as good an excuse as any—as if they needed one."

Sophie marveled that her friend's voice held only sadness, but no bitterness.

"We have to be careful. If we can separate ourselves from the library, so much the better."

"I don't want to separate myself. I want to help the Bukowskis. Pan Bukowski was killed while saving things for me and for neighbors. He's the reason I have my photograph of Janek. Do you have any idea how that makes me feel? An old man, deprived of his life, because he cared about me . . . a son deprived of his father, and his son deprived of a grandfather." Sophie shook her head. "I'll go every week if—"

"If you want to get them killed. Don't you see how dangerous that is? How quickly you'll be observed and reported and—whoosh!—the library searched? Is that what you want?"

"No! Of course not . . . but I promised them. I want to help. I need to help someone. I can't just sit here doing nothing! I've no idea whom to trust. Every day I see people coming into the grocer's with their coupons and their zloty—hungry, poor. And then one day, though we have one or two fewer customers, they come with more money to spend and more ration coupons than they should have. Do you know what that means? It means they've ratted out someone— a neighbor, a friend, their aunt or uncle or grandparents!"

"Trusting can be dangerous," Terri agreed.

"Trusting can be deadly!" Sophie nearly shouted.

"Do you trust me?" Terri's hand covered Sophie's arm.

"Yes," Sophie admitted, though she pushed away layers of hurt to do it.

"Then listen to me. It's safer if we each go to the library only once every other week or so. I know someone else we can trust—implicitly— who could spell us for the third week, break it up even more."

"No . . . no one else. It's too risky."

"All right, then . . . you and me."

"You and me," Sophie agreed. "I don't want to just drop off food. I want to visit with them, bring them books, maybe a radio."

"You're getting too involved. You can't do that. You end up making emotional decisions, not smart ones. In this work, sometimes you need to make tough decisions."

What Terri said rang true. It was the kind of thing Pan Gadomski would have said. Still, it hadn't kept him from getting killed. If Sophie was going to run that risk, she would run it her way.

CHAPTER FOURTEEN

THE THREE STOLE AS quietly as possible into the newly walled section of the Jewish district—the ghetto—just after sundown. Just as Shabbat ended, and shortly before the curfew. Itzhak had bartered for an apartment on the second floor—less concern of rain from a leaking roof above the third floor, and not so much foot traffic as on the first floor. He hoped that meant more privacy. He hadn't told the women how much of his current and future pay he'd given and pledged in order to move in. There were takers lined up for each and every place. With more refugees pouring into the city each day, it was a miracle they'd found a place for the three of them.

Though his muscles groaned, Itzhak hefted the wheelbarrow and set the pace, slowing every once in a while when Marya or Rosa fell behind, needing to catch her breath or tend a stitch in her side.

Itzhak whispered to his wife, avoiding the glare of the Wehrmacht soldier stationed on the corner, who scrutinized their little party and its possessions as they passed. "Pace yourself, my love, but know that the curfew will come soon. We still have several blocks to go. We must be at least inside the—"

"Yes, I know. We know, Itzhak; stop fretting. We do our best."

It wasn't like Rosa to snap at him, but nothing was as it should be. Marya had surprised him the most. The way she'd strolled from room to room of the house she'd lived in and loved for more than thirty years, caressing her tiled stove, running her fingers over her work-worn bread table, lingering beside and finally touching the mantel that had long held her siddur, her elaborately tooled prayer book—it had all moved him to pity. But in the end, she'd squared her shoulders, lifted her chin to tie her babushka beneath, then walked into the street carrying the case she'd packed.

One small case, to carry a lifetime of memories. He'd no idea what she'd packed, only that Rosa had slipped in more of her mother's dresses and shoes, tucking them around jars and books and pots and pans in the wheelbarrow.

"She's packed pictures and the candlesticks her mother gave her, but not enough clothing—no matter that she told us to. She'll rue that come winter," Rosa had whispered as she'd collected more than the wheelbarrow could possibly hold.

Itzhak packed a few hand tools from his father-in-law's workshop. It hurt to leave so much behind, but the decree was explicit—they were allowed to move only what they could carry. The cradle pieces he'd tied to the bottom of the wheelbarrow, roping the load securely over the top of their piled-high heap. He scrunched and shoved and vowed to carry all he could with his arms and on his back. If they had to leave something behind in the street or if the Wehrmacht helped themselves to goods as they passed, there was nothing to be said, nothing to be done. The women were giving up so much as it was.

It had been all he could do not to mockingly bow to Pani Dobonowicz, who'd peeked beneath her curtain, watching them go. *Vultures. Lions. Licking their chops. She'll be rummaging through Marya's house before we reach the end of the street.* There'd been nothing to do about that, either.

• ◆ •

"Come, Matka." Rosa tugged her mother's sleeve. "Itzhak said it's not far now . . . one block more." She all but panted beneath her layers of clothing and winter coat and the July heat. "We must get inside before it's truly dark, before the curfew." She knew her mother knew this, but Rosa could not keep herself from repeating the fearful threat. They'd known too many Jews who'd suffered the fate of being found out after curfew. If only her mother could walk faster. If only she would.

But her mother's whole bearing was one of walking to the gallows. She'd left the house so purposefully, so bravely. But as they'd walked through each familiar street, as longtime neighbors and shopkeepers who'd known them all their lives turned away or shook their heads in pity or disgust, Rosa had felt her mother diminish, had seen her shoulders round and her feet reduce from walking to trudging.

Rosa had wanted to shout at the woman who'd sneered, loud enough to be heard across the street, "Oh, how the mighty have fallen!" It wasn't aimed directly at them, but at the several Jewish families making their way toward the ghetto.

Matka was right. If this many go now, how will there be room for all once a decree is issued? Rosa sighed. She hadn't wanted to believe it.

Despite her vow to find her home wherever her husband might be, before they'd loaded the wheelbarrow that morning, she'd argued with Itzhak, begging him to wait and see. "Maybe things will change; maybe we won't need to move," she'd pleaded.

"Oi! Nit heint, nit morgen!" Her mother had intervened, reverting again to her forbidden Yiddish. "We must be as prepared as we can. Pretending the inevitable won't happen is like trying to hold back the sea with your hands."

Now, to see her mother so wilted frightened Rosa. *I need you to be strong, Matka. I need you for the days ahead. Please.*

The block passed as Rosa walked and worried. Children sat on street corners, thin, dirt smeared on bare arms and legs, their eyes listless. The difference between the city streets and the newly walled ghetto was stark—something Rosa did not remember from years gone by. *Such poverty—so much worse since the occupation.*

And then the apartment building stood before them, bare and dirty, in need of paint and so much more.

"There is no grass, no trees," Rosa whispered.

"No," Itzhak agreed. "It is the city."

"The city." Rosa had never lived where there was absolutely no grass, no trees, no window boxes of geraniums spilling out into the sunshine. She hadn't even noticed that change as they'd marched through the city, intent on their destination. This area was not only different—all blocks of apartments with tiny common courtyards—but the buildings were rows upon rows of the same, leaving no room for sunshine or imagination, no room for a vegetable or flower garden, no workshop as her tata had built, no swing hanging from a garden tree for her child to grow and dream upon.

Rosa felt Itzhak's eyes upon her, gauging her reaction. She drew in her breath, holding it until she could force a smile. *I cannot change the present. I can only hope for the future, and I cannot fail my husband now.* "Let's get Matka inside; then we can make trips for the things inside the wheelbarrow."

"You go up with your matka. I'll bring the wheelbarrow into the courtyard, then carry all I can, a load at a time."

But Rosa saw the hungry eyes and thin faces watching them. "One of us must wait with our belongings." She leaned close. "Make certain the food is wrapped in clothing."

He nodded, the sadness in his eyes showing he understood. Rosa stood back. How had it come to this? That she and her husband would not share openly with their neighbors, with those children begging on the street? Would they hoard—if they could, if they had enough to hoard? Yes, she knew they would, for the sake of their unborn child, and for the fear growing inside them day by day, just as real as the life cradled beneath her breast.

Rosa walked her mother up first, following the directions Itzhak gave her—second floor, turn right, and second apartment in the corner. *Good. A corner apartment. There will be windows on two sides. At least there will be sunlight.* Rosa craved sunlight as she craved food.

But the apartment reeked of sewage and urine. The windows were dim with age, scratches, and city soot. Trash—boxes and wrappers and crumpled papers—accumulated in the corners, covered by clumps of dust and what might be animal hair. The kitchen stove and tiles were crusted in grime. Her mother gasped. Rosa swallowed and squeezed her arm. "We'll clean it, Matka. We'll make it shine." But the prospect was daunting. How had anyone lived in such filth? Had anyone lived here in ages?

Rosa found a dusty chair, its caning broken through, and gingerly seated her mother near a window. "I'll be back, Matka. We won't be long."

Rosa's head swam as she descended the stairs. Weakness, weariness, and a dread that deepened every day pressed down on her. But she knew Itzhak would be watching for her reaction.

"How is it?"

"You haven't seen it, have you?" The realization struck and relieved her at the same time.

He shook his head. "I was lucky to get it. Ten men bartered and the auction crept higher and higher. Most families expect to share space with two or three others. By getting a smaller space, we could be—"

"It's all right, my love. We'll manage. As long as we're together, we'll manage."

The relief in Itzhak's eyes was palpable.

"Let's get our things inside. If we can sleep tonight, we can begin cleaning and sorting tomorrow."

"I'll bring a bucket of water before I go to work—two, if we can find something to carry the water."

Rosa stared at him, not understanding.

"There's still no running water here, not since the bombing."

"What?" Rosa heard his words, but could not comprehend. "We've had water for months—at least the pump in the garden."

Itzhak sighed. "In the Aryan district, they have water. Now, we're in a ghetto—made for Jews only. Repairs here are slower, if at all."

"How will we clean the apartment? It's filthy. How will we clean ourselves?"

Itzhak looked away. At that moment Rosa saw the dirty children on the corner in a new light—as children with no running water in their homes, rather than as dirty beggars. Her heart pierced and it was all she could do not to cry out. She swallowed the dry and dusty heat of July. "We'll build our home here, our baby's first home." Rosa voiced her plans bravely, but the empty well inside felt bottomless.

◆ ◆ ◆

Summer waned, and at last the heat of Warsaw gave way to cooler nights and brisk mornings. In October, the German decree was issued by Ludwig Fischer, governor of Warsaw, broadcast through powerful loudspeakers attached to trucks that roamed the teeming streets. All Jews were to move into the sealed section of the "Jewish district," taking only what they could carry or move by handcart, by the end of the month.

"Why does it still surprise me that the Germans declared their hateful decree on Yom Kippur—our holiest of days?" Rosa's mother sat by the kitchen window, staring out at the river of mournful people pouring into the ghetto, laden with all they could carry, everything they now possessed.

Despite severe rationing and deprivation of fats and vitamins, the children looked stout. Rosa knew it was only because they were layered in all the clothing and overcoats their mothers or grandmothers could strap onto their frail bodies. The sight of children weighed down by pillowslips stuffed with bedding, clothing, sometimes a favorite toy made Rosa feel sick. She wished she'd bought—that she could have bought—a toy for their baby before they'd moved. *A book. A child's book. What I wouldn't give for that now. Wherever can I find such a thing?*

Rosa sighed but did not answer her mother. She determined to count herself blessed to be settled, as settled as they could be. Day after day, Itzhak had carried water up the stairs before leaving for work. Day after day, Rosa and her mother had rationed that water for scrubbing, for cooking and drinking, and for what could barely be called bathing. At least their apartment was now clean, if threadbare.

She stepped behind her mother and laid a hand on her shoulder. Together, they watched as families streamed by, moving deeper and deeper into the already crowded district.

"*Ghetto*. The Germans will never use that word." Marya turned away from the window. "But a ghetto is what it is, what it will remain. We'll live here until we die—sooner, if Hitler be pleased, than later."

"Matka, don't say such things. Please." Rosa felt the baby kick at her protestations. *How much do babies understand? What do they know? What do they think or fear?* "At least Itzhak has a job—better than most. We have food. That's something."

"Not enough food, not for long," Marya lamented. "It was like this in the last war, you know. You were only a baby for the worst of it, though the years just after weren't so much better. I vowed I would never face such hunger again. And here we stand, ready to starve."

"No, we're not. We still have a dozen jars of food you canned. We have ration books, and Itzhak said the agent he works under believes he can get him some extra canned goods once in a while. We're not starving."

"Not yet." Her mother closed her eyes. "Don't be fooled, my Rosa."

CHAPTER FIFTEEN

SOPHIE DIDN'T NEED TO read the papers or the kiosk postings on the street to know that mid-November brought the last day of the extended deadline for Jews to enter the ghetto, or that the ghetto was then sealed. Forced Jewish laborers were allowed out of the ghetto at checkpoints. The only Aryans allowed in were those who held special permits, approved by the Wehrmacht.

She knew, instinctively and through the mounting decrees, that hiding outside the ghetto took on ever more threatening consequences. Any Jew hiding outside the ghetto would be shot. Any Aryan caught helping or hiding a Jew outside the ghetto would be shot.

Two days after Christmas, Sophie locked the basement library door behind her and flicked on her torch in the dark hallway. It had been three weeks since she'd visited the Bukowskis. Terri had convinced her to go longer between visits once she'd secured new connections with the black-market community—a windfall of rations to tide their friends over. With the Wehrmacht skulking through the streets in search of Jews violating the ghetto mandate, it seemed a good idea for everyone to avoid the library.

This time, Sophie brought books for the children and a set of watercolor paints. Jewish schools had been closed since last December. The boys, living in the basement and the attic, must be starved for stories, for pictures, for life outside these walls. This library had never specialized in children's books, and those it had shelved had been removed in the early days of occupation, even before it was officially closed.

The Germans did not believe Polish children, destined to become laborers, needed an education. If they did not need an education, they did not need books. The Germans understood nothing of the Poles' love for literature. Thankfully, they had no idea of the growing number of used books circulating within the city.

Sophie gave the gentle, coded tap on the Bukowskis' door panel. Young Judah flung the door wide. "Pani Zofia! You've come at last! Did you bring the books? Pani Tereza promised you would. You did, didn't you?"

Sophie laughed, despite the straight face and tensed shoulders she'd maintained all the way there. "Yes, yes, I did. And I brought the very one you begged her for—the one by Dr. Korczak."

"*King Matt the First*! I love that book! Jakob has not read it, so he will love it, too."

"Jakob?"

"Garbinski—my friend!" Judah smiled from ear to ear, showing two missing teeth.

"Ah, you'll enjoy it together."

"The best way, yes?"

"Yes," Sophie agreed.

"Come in, come in. You are most kind, Pani Kumiega." Aaron pulled his son back from the doorway, allowing Sophie to step inside.

Sophie pulled her packets of food from the pockets sewn inside her coat and held them out to Aaron. "Food for the body." She removed her coat and then the books and paints from two flat pockets sewn inside its back, smiling and handing them to Judah with a flourish. "Food for the mind, young sir."

"Paints! Look, Pape! Can I take them to show Jakob? Can I go now?" Judah danced a ring around his father.

"Tonight. You know the rule. Tonight, when it is safe, he will come here."

Judah's face fell, but only for a moment. "Yes, Pape."

"But—" Sophie knelt before him, grinning—"how would you like me to help you get started? We could paint a picture together."

"And read a story?"

"And read a story."

"Don't let him deter you, Pani Kumiega, not if—"

"No, it's all right, Pan Bukowski. I have the time—no work today, and it is better if I wait a couple of hours before leaving."

Aaron smiled and pulled out one of his two chairs from the make-shift table. "Then, by all means, please join us. Can we offer you something to eat? One of the apples you brought?"

"No, no, thank you." Sophie felt warmed by his generosity— generosity that meant true sacrifice. She tapped the tabletop, smiling at Judah, inviting him to join her. "I'm eager only for a painting partner."

The light in Judah's eyes was more than reward. Two hours passed quickly as Sophie taught Judah to mix the colors carefully and to wash the brush in between. She showed him how to conserve paper and said that there was no reason why he could not paint on the walls, as long as his father agreed.

"Ah, we will have art on our walls again!" Aaron enthused. "Masterpieces! Original works from my budding artist!"

Sophie laughed, happy for the good and comfortable relationship between father and son. It was what she'd imagined Janek might be like as a father . . . if their child had lived . . . *if Janek lives*. She pushed the thought away, knowing she must not grow morose. Her visit was a bright spot in Judah's life, and possibly Aaron's.

She realized, too late, that frequently changing the paint water posed a problem. The Bukowskis made their trips to the washroom only once a day, just before curfew ended. Water stored in their secret room was for drinking.

"Perhaps I can get us some more water, Pape?" Judah all but pleaded. "I will be quiet—like the mouse!"

Sophie saw the uncertainty behind Aaron's eyes . . . the desire to continue to please his son, whose childhood knew so little pleasure, and the concern over bending a rule meant to save their lives.

"Perhaps I can go," Sophie offered. It wasn't wise, but it probably wasn't harmful, either. "I'll be just a moment."

"No! No . . . I will go," Aaron insisted. "I cannot let you take that risk, Pani Kumiega."

"But it's my idea, my—"

He laughed, attempting levity. "What would my pape say? 'That's no way to treat a lady! For shame, Aaron Bukowski!'" He shrugged. "How can I live with his voice chastising me from the grave? I would go mad in these four walls!"

Sophie watched him go, and even as he did, she knew it was a bad idea. Like so many other times, she'd pushed her inclinations aside, chiding herself for useless, groundless worry.

But when Aaron did not reappear, she feared her worry was not groundless. When she bade Judah be very, very quiet and heard the stripping of boards from windows, the shuffle of boots across the floor, the *clop-clop* of what could only be horses—all above her— she knew they'd made a terrible mistake.

◆

Six hours passed as Sophie and Judah remained in the sealed room. Sophie held the little boy, whispered stories to him, did her best to reassure him that his father was clever and knew a hundred places to hide within the library. But she knew that the Germans were clever and could search a hundred places, too.

Sophie had heard of destroyed libraries converted by the Germans for a multitude of purposes—none of those for which they'd been meticulously, artistically designed. One stabled horses; one was a repair shop for motorcycles; one stored valuable prizes—artwork, gems, collections of every kind—looted from Jewish homes and institutions, awaiting transport to Germany. If she could guess from the clops and snorts and click of jackboots above her, this library would never house another book, another treasure.

But what did that matter now? Where was Aaron? Each time she heard boots march purposefully across the room, she tensed her jaw until it ached. *Have they discovered him? Surely, if they're planning to use the building, they will search each floor, each room. What about the Garbinskis?* The attic was a huge and open room, even though they'd boxed off a smaller area in an attempt to preserve body heat and make it seem more cozy.

Sophie closed her eyes. *Cozy.* How could an attic seem cozy for a young family? Pani Garbinski was expecting a baby any day now . . . if she'd not already given birth. When Terri saw her last, she'd expected to labor within the week. *How can the woman deliver an infant in silence? How can she keep one quiet?*

"You won't leave me, will you, Pani Zofia?" Judah's voice came as no more than a whisper, the fearful sob behind it choked back.

"Never. Never will I leave you until your pape is here, safe and sound, beside you."

"What if they never leave?"

Sophie drew a deep breath. "They have to leave sometime. If they decide to live here, well then, so will I." She tried to smile, but it took all the courage she could muster.

Another hour passed, and another. She checked her watch. Ten minutes until curfew. The door at the top of the stairs opened, and at least two sets of boots rumbled down. Even though Sophie was certain that no light shone through the paneled door, she turned off the carbide lamp.

"Stinks down here." Sophie knew enough German from her school days to understand that.

"Friederich said there was a fire—perhaps a year or so ago. It smells like that."

"Maybe." The boots shuffled slowly around the room. Sophie could imagine the men stomping through the empty room, assessing its usefulness. *Judah and his father must leave their hiding place.* She pulled Judah closer and he quickly burrowed into her side. His face turned up, as if to speak, but she pressed her finger to his lips.

Moments later the boots echoed down the basement hallway. They were gone only a few minutes before they hurried back and up the stairs. The last she heard was good-natured bantering.

"That door should have been boarded over."

"No matter. It will come in useful. We can shovel dung down the chute—easier than hauling it out the back."

"Ha! And then we'll be sent down the chute ourselves to clean it! *Danke, nein.* I'd rather do the work the first time."

Finally, she heard the door at the top of the stairs close, a shuffling of boot soles and clicking of heels, then the forceful closing of the front door.

Judah sighed in her arms. She hadn't realized they'd both been holding their breath. Still, they waited in silence. No more feet crossed the flooring above them.

"Where is Pape?"

"I don't know, my dear boy, but I'm sure he will come when it's safe. We must wait."

"Adonai will make a way, yes?"

"Yes," Sophie affirmed, hoping it was true.

"Zeyde always said that Adonai will make a way, when there appears no way at all."

Sophie smiled into the dark, unable to keep tears from trickling down her cheeks. "Yes, he did. He said the same to me . . . many times."

"Then we must have faith." Judah spoke as if the matter had been decided.

Sophie closed her eyes and prayed.

⋄ ◆ ⋄

Another hour passed before Aaron gave the coded tap and Judah flung the door open, falling into his father's arms.

Sophie stood from her sitting position on Judah's pallet, realizing for the first time how stiff and sore she'd become. "Tell us."

Aaron sat down on the chair, running one hand through his hair, securely embracing his son with the other arm. "Wehrmacht. They're building a stable in the library."

Sophie nodded. That much she had guessed.

"I got to the Garbinskis in time . . . nothing more. We moved their belongings behind a panel in the eaves Pan Garbinski had built, just in case they needed a hideaway. If not for his forethought . . . Thank Adonai, he is a clever man."

"Pani Garbinski—and her baby?"

Aaron stroked his son's hair. "The baby was . . . The baby did not live past its birth. A little girl. Two days ago."

Sophie sat down again. She'd feared to see the baby, feared comparing her own loss to its birth, but she didn't want this. Not this. "Poor Pani Garbinski." It was all she knew to say. It was not enough.

"She still has the body." Aaron spoke softly. "Pan Garbinski has begged her to let him take the child away, but . . ."

"But of course she won't." Sophie understood. If only she'd been able to hold her own babies in her arms. She would not have let go.

"It will have to be done. Especially now."

"Yes," Sophie answered. "Especially now." But she could not think, refused to think, what he meant for her to do.

CHAPTER SIXTEEN

HANUKKAH CAME TO THE GHETTO without so much as a light in the window. Rosa guarded their meager supplies as a lioness protects her cubs.

"Every candle must be saved for when the baby comes—for the delivery, and afterward. Who knows what light we will need and when?"

Itzhak agreed and worried as each day Rosa's face, her arms and legs grew thinner, the baby bump beneath her chest the largest part of her.

"Babies have a way of getting what they need from the mother," Marya reassured her son-in-law.

"I'm more worried about Rosa," Itzhak objected. "Will she be strong enough for the delivery?"

"Adonai knows, my son. Adonai knows." Marya sounded tired beyond words. Itzhak worried for her, too . . . but not as he worried for his precious wife.

He took to working longer hours, limping into the ghetto just before curfew and out again as soon as allowed. Each day he hoped for favor from an appreciative Nazi, an extra coin or two tossed into the air or thrown on the ground as a tip for work Itzhak would have charged mightily for in days gone by. But that was then—when he was a professional electrician. *Now,* he silently lamented with grim determination as he stooped to pick up the coins, *I've become a professional beggar.*

· ◆ ·

Rosa pushed back the sheet they'd hung over the window and scraped against the late December frost. She lifted her hand in farewell to Itzhak, hoping he would turn before he reached the corner and see her, smile, return her salute. It would be another long day without him. The waiting, the wondering, the hoping all would be well with their child . . . and the fear of childbirth. It couldn't be much longer.

As if in response, Baby gave a good-morning kick—or possibly a head butt in Rosa's side. Rosa smiled, almost laughed, in spite of the discomfort. *You're getting stronger each day, my little one. I can hardly wait to hold you in my arms—to see you kicking on the outside, to cradle your head against my breast. Oh, my darling! When will you push your way into the light?*

Her mother had assured her that babies come in their own time, that Adonai numbered each person's days and that the One who knit a baby in a mother's womb knew when it would come forth. "There's little you can do or not do now that will make any difference as to the outcome. It's all in Adonai's hands."

But Rosa had seen women go into labor in the street—in the bread queue of all places, unwilling to lose their hard-won place in line. And she'd seen Wehrmacht soldiers roughly push a laboring woman off the street and into an alley. What became of the woman and her baby, Rosa hadn't wanted to know . . . but that didn't keep her imagination from running wild.

It had become plain that the occupiers wanted no more Jewish babies. There were rumors that an edict would soon be issued prohibiting Jewish pregnancies . . . as if the nature Adonai had created could be undone. Itzhak insisted that she no longer go to buy bread, that he would find a way to get what they needed. How he might, she didn't know, but her relief was great.

Rosa let go of the sheet, shutting out the street. Itzhak had not turned to see her. *He's preoccupied . . . as I am, as we all are.*

A clang of spoon against pot made Rosa smile. Her mother was up, and if Rosa had her guess, she'd broken out the rationed porridge watered down to be sure, perhaps sweetened with a dollop from the last sacred jar of plums.

Rosa closed her eyes, remembering the bounty from the tree in her parents' garden each summer, the jewel-tone jars of purple red plums that lined the kitchen shelves each fall, and the pockets of plums her mother had wrapped in sweetened dough and baked until golden. Would her child—son or daughter—ever know the sweetness of plums? Would she walk on grass, picking flowers at whim as Rosa had done? Would he climb that plum tree—or any other? Would this hateful war ever end? Were they doomed to live in squalor forever— no running water, no heat, no electricity?

Her mouth formed a straight line. She knew she should be grateful. . . . They were together, the three of them, and soon a fourth.

"Rosa, come. Eat." Her mother pulled her from the window and her reverie. "It does no good to worry for days to come, to lament the past."

"How did you know?"

Marya shrugged. "What else do we do? We wonder. We wait."

"Can't we hope?" Rosa nearly begged.

Her mother's sad eyes did not give the answer Rosa needed.

◆ ◆ ◆

Itzhak dreamed that he and Rosa walked along the seaside, that the tide washed over their feet, that the sky reigned blue and the sun warm on their faces and arms.

"Itzhak! Itzhak!" Rosa hissed in his ear.

He didn't want to leave the dream. His wife was as young and beautiful as she'd been the day he'd asked for her hand in marriage, as strong and smiling and slim as she'd ever been. The sea breeze blew her hair, tendrils curling around her eyes—eyes sparkling with freedom and hope and happiness.

"Itzhak! Wake up! My water has broken."

Itzhak pulled himself from the dream, away from the sea and the sun to find his wife trembling in cold, wet bedclothes.

"T-tell me what to do."

"Get Matka."

"Should I go for the midwife—for Pani Cohen?"

"No—Matka. She can do this. She said she knows how. She's seen it done."

"Rosa, I think—"

"Don't argue with me now, Itzhak. Edna Cohen is not a Jewish midwife of Egypt. She's not going to hide our baby from Nazis. She'd just as soon sell us out for a bag of flour."

Itzhak drew a deep breath. He cared for his mother-in-law—he did. But could she safely deliver their child? Could she save Rosa's life if anything went wrong? Why hadn't he insisted on a doctor?

"Itzhak! Get Matka!"

Itzhak lit the candle by the bedside and pulled on his pants. Before he reached their doorway, his mother-in-law stood on the threshold.

"It's time . . . time for you to leave, Itzhak, time for your baby to come."

"You're sure—you're sure you can do this?" Itzhak needed a promise, a declaration of faith.

"I do what I'm given to do."

That wasn't the answer he wanted.

"You'll have to get your own breakfast this morning and pack your lunch for today," his mother-in-law declared.

"I'm not leaving Rosa." Of that he was certain. He'd not step a foot outside the house until his wife was safe, until their child nursed at her breast.

"You must go to work, Itzhak. This may take hours. You can't lose your position—not now of all times." Rosa's deep breath told him her panic was subsiding.

She was right, of course. The Nazis would not take a Jewish baby coming into the world as an excuse to delay their plans or their agenda for anything—certainly not progress on the building he was helping to rewire. To lose his job now would be their ruin and starvation.

"We will be fine. Your Rosa will be fine."

The soothing in his mother-in-law's voice did not reassure him. "What if something goes wrong?"

"I will get the doctor. I won't risk my daughter. . . . You can trust that."

It was the only thing that reassured him. Itzhak knew Marya loved and lived for her daughter and the coming grandchild.

"Go . . . go, now," Rosa insisted, just as a contraction stole her breath, drawing her face pale, ghostly, in the dancing candlelight.

Itzhak closed his eyes against the nightmare. What choice did he have?

Less than an hour later he trudged through a fine layer of snow, hating each step that took him from his Rosa, not able to imagine how he would get through this day—how she would. With every step he prayed for her protection, her safe delivery of their child, his mind reduced to three words he trusted Adonai would understand. *Adonai . . . Rosa . . . Baby . . . Adonai . . . Rosa . . . Baby.*

CHAPTER SEVENTEEN

SOPHIE WOULD DO WHAT needed to be done. She'd carry the baby, cold as stone, all the way to the address Pan Garbinski had given her—an address useful before the war, but now . . . who knew? Pani Garbinski had insisted the baby be taken to the Jewish cemetery and given a proper burial. It was terribly dangerous. Sophie could be shot, believed to be Jewish and outside the ghetto without the proper papers, or she could be shot for who she was—an Englishwoman posing as a Pole with false identity papers, illegally helping Jews.

She might have laughed at the incongruity of it all had she not been so utterly terrified that she could barely breathe.

Pan Garbinski had first told her she should carry the wrapped baby to the curb nearest the ghetto gate where the wagon regularly retrieved dead bodies. It was too risky for her to take the baby to the cemetery herself, too risky to trust someone—anyone—to take the sapphire ring Pani Garbinski had saved of her mother's jewelry and actually believe they would supply a coffin, a grave site, and a marker. But Pani Garbinski had refused to let her daughter go unless she knew that when the war was over, there would be a grave to visit, a place to leave a stone of remembrance.

Sophie understood this. *If only my babies had lived and breathed a day, this is what I, too, would want: a place to go, to leave flowers or candles or stones. A place to sit and weep and pray and remember her dimpled fingers, her soft cheek.* But even her last baby had not grown sufficiently within her womb to know if it was a boy or a girl. So she'd named the baby Alex, suitable for a girl, if Alexandra, and suitable for a boy, if Alexander—a strong and beautiful name, and her own private way to remember her, or him.

Sophie forced those thoughts from her brain, determined to remain focused. The baby's body, though slight, had grown heavier as she walked, but she'd dared not take a tram and be discovered with a dead baby in her arms.

At the gate of the cemetery she walked in, looking for an office of some kind, as if going to arrange for a funeral . . . for someone else, certainly not for the "sleeping" baby she carried. By the time she'd found a man she presumed to be an undertaker, Sophie felt ready to faint. The reality of what she'd done and all she'd lost overwhelmed her.

"The baby of a friend." She placed the small body, wrapped in a soft cashmere blanket, on the counter. "She wants a coffin for her daughter, a grave site, a marker with the name in Hebrew . . . a proper burial." Sophie got the words out in a rush. "Can you do it? Will you?"

The man looked Sophie up and down, his eyes boring into hers for a moment, then looked away. "You're not from the ghetto."

"Can you do it?" Sophie pulled a tiny bit of bravado from someplace she could not imagine.

"It will cost."

"How much?"

"You're not Jewish."

"The baby is Jewish."

"Then I'm risking my life to do this for you. How much is a life worth?"

Sophie had no answer for that, but she withdrew the sapphire ring from her pocket and placed it on the counter. "This is enough, surely." Her last word came out weak, almost a plea. She hadn't intended that but was at her wits' end. What could she do if he refused? She couldn't bring herself to leave the baby in a pile of corpses for mass burial or whatever they did with the hundreds of bodies collected each month from the ghetto.

The muscles in the man's face did not move, but his eyes momentarily lit at the sight of the ring. He looked away, placed his palm over the ring, discreetly sweeping it from the counter and into his trouser pocket. "What name, what date on the headstone?"

Sophie wrote the words Pani Garbinski had dictated and handed the paper to the man. "Thank you." It was all she knew to say. "It will mean so much to have a place to come."

She was almost out the door when the man spoke softly. "Tell the mother I will care for her little one. Tell her the grave will be near the wall at the back of the cemetery. Look for the marker in a month, in the new year."

"Thank you." Sophie could not turn, could not look him in the eye again, but walked out, relieved of the burden in her arms, weighed down by the one in her heart.

CHAPTER EIGHTEEN

ALL THAT DAY ITZHAK WORKED, nearly in a frenzy, the cords of his neck straining against his skin. The faster he worked, he reasoned, the quicker the day would go. Perhaps they would let him off early; perhaps they would give him an extra coin and he could buy a bigger ration of bread, maybe a fruit on the black market. Would it be possible to barter for meat? Rosa would need red meat to resupply her blood loss.

Adonai! Help her. Deliver her. So many women died in childbirth. So many children perished before drawing their first breath. What would life be without his Rosa?

"Dunovich!" The barking of his name came as a command, and Itzhak jumped, causing him to cut a wire that he should not have cut.

He swallowed, swearing under his breath. He'd have to make that repair without it being noticed. He set down his wire cutter and turned. "Yes, sir?"

The German lifted his chin, appropriately pleased at Itzhak's show of respect. "Work on this building is behind schedule. We need the wiring finished by the end of this week. You cannot expect officers to work in darkness."

Darkness was all Itzhak saw in the German officers, but he could not say that. "Yes, sir. I'm doing my best."

"Your best? Your best is not good enough, Dunovich. Shall I find another Jew to finish the job?"

Itzhak pulled a ragged breath. "No, sir. It will be done."

"See that it is." The officer turned away, but threw over his shoulder, "If you need a permit to stay here—to work through the night—it can be arranged."

Itzhak trembled inside, determined to hold back the retort that sprang to his lips. "It will be done."

The day went faster than Itzhak could have imagined. The work required for the first floor alone should take three electricians at least two days . . . for the building, a fortnight. But a fortnight was not available, nor were the additional men. Itzhak remained an hour and a half past his normal quitting time.

At last he raced home, knowing the dark streets would stumble him and that he might not make curfew. But he couldn't stay away, couldn't bear the thought of not seeing Rosa, of not knowing that she was safe. He could not imagine the first night of his child's life passing without seeing him—or her. All along he'd imagined a son, but now he knew he would love a daughter just as fully . . . *if only she looks like Rosa, and not me.* He smiled into the darkness, sweat pouring from beneath his cap and pooling in his armpits as he ran through the cold.

He'd heard of women, weakened through deprivation, taking days to labor. He prayed that was not so for Rosa. She hadn't the strength.

Curfew came. Two more blocks, then one, then their apartment building. A light flared on the corner. Itzhak ducked between door stoops. A Wehrmacht soldier lit a cigarette, a pinpoint of light in the inky black. Itzhak crouched low and held his breath. The cigarette passed to another figure in the dark—a figure Itzhak hadn't seen before—and he thanked all of heaven that he'd waited, that he'd not been heard. He waited until the two walked on, farther down the street.

As he was about to stand, about to steal into his apartment building, a lusty, quavering infant cry came from the floor above . . . a cry that screamed of life and hope and another branch on the Tree of Life. Itzhak's eyes widened and his heart pounded. He sank to his knees in thanksgiving and wonder. *Thank You, Adonai! Thank You!* For the first time he noticed that the cold December sky was filled with stars, alive with stars, dancing with stars in their heaven. How had he not noticed before?

Tears streaming down his face, Itzhak crept into the building and softly bounded up the stairs, joyfully breathing his wife's name. It was the dead of night, but a new day had dawned for the Dunovich family—a day no one could diminish or take from them.

CHAPTER NINETEEN

THE PLAN SEEMED A GOOD ONE, the only one. Sophie had forced Terri to break her rule of silence and introduce her to her underground contact, Renat. Sophie suspected that wasn't his real name, but of course, that didn't matter.

She'd learned that Renat was a Pole. Before the war he'd attended law school, but his new identity papers identified him as a doctor of veterinary medicine, and he presented himself as an authority in his field.

"Now," Terri had said, "he will pose as an expert in horses, offering his veterinary skills for the Germans' horses stabled in the library. Those skills, he will convince them, may be desperately needed once he reveals the crushing news that there is an outbreak of equine influenza, which he is doing his best to contain before it infects the horses of the entire German cavalry. They must be quarantined and checked—each and every horse—and observed for at least twelve hours. Any horse showing symptoms must be removed and isolated for the duration of the disease, then given a week's rest for each day of fever."

Dusk came early. Curfew was nearly upon them when Sophie peered from behind the window shade of another underground worker, who lived half a block from the library.

Renat stood at the front door of the library, rattling his sheaf of papers and identity card before the guard, as officious as a Pole dared to be before the occupiers. Sophie couldn't hear what he said, but his body language, the urgency with which he leaned forward, all but closing the space between him and the guard, was convincing. The guard disappeared into the library with the papers. It wasn't long before Renat was shown inside.

Sophie closed her eyes and prayed. *Let them believe him. Let them leave him alone long enough to steal away and reach the cellar—and the attic. Please, let Aaron and the Garbinskis get the message.*

If all went according to plan, Renat would persuade the skeleton crew of night guards to remove themselves from the building and not expose themselves any further until he was certain it was safe. Humans may carry, but not contract influenza from horses. Still, the Germans feared germs of any kind. A Pole concerned for their health was a Pole to appreciate.

Renat would offer to stay the night with the horses, urging the men to guard the outside entrances if they chose. Once the streets were empty, deep into the cold night, he would take a break from his work and offer the guards a drink laced with a sedative strong enough to knock them out for hours.

It was during those hours that Aaron and Judah and the three Garbinskis would escape. Sophie would be waiting to guide Aaron and Judah back to her apartment, where they would hide until a new safe house could be found. Along the way, another contact, unnamed, would fall into step with them and guide the Garbinskis to a safe house. Their rescue plan was in the hands of others, and though Sophie wanted desperately to follow them—to know they were truly safe—her first responsibility was to Aaron and Judah. She trusted the daring scheme Renat had created. She just didn't know what she'd do with the Bukowskis later.

Terri had objected to the plan, saying it was too risky, that they needed to know where the Bukowskis could go before moving them—they must wait. But there was no more time. The Bukowskis weakened daily. There was no way to get them food or water, and waiting only increased their chance of discovery—a cough, the smell of poor sanitation. Waiting, Sophie had convinced her friend, could mean as sure a death for the two as any risk they'd take.

Sophie sat by the window, peering beneath the shade every few minutes, trying to focus on the darkened street, to make out the steps of the library and the alley beside it. Hours dragged on, the tension in her neck and shoulders increasing. The knot in her stomach tightened.

Just after ten the library door opened. The two Wehrmacht soldiers standing guard accepted something—a bottle, perhaps, to stave off the cold. It wouldn't be long now.

A half hour passed, the guards still drinking, their talk louder and more raucous. Another few minutes and the talk had stopped. In the pale moonlight she saw that one had fallen asleep on the steps. The other sat down beside him, his head in his hands. They could be shot for such behavior, but if all went well, who would know?

Sophie buttoned her coat, wrapping her black scarf around her head. Reassuring herself of the key in her pocket, she slipped out the back of the apartment building and through the alley. The night cold bit her. She hoped Judah would be layered in everything he possessed.

Minutes passed before two dark figures, then three more stole toward her, silently making their way between one shrubbery and the next, between one building and the next, and finally across the street to the alley where she waited. She clasped Judah's hands, so glad to see them all.

Judah wrapped his arms about her and started to speak, but his father was quick to press his palm against his son's mouth. Sophie hugged the boy in return, a hug she needed as much as he, and motioned for all five to follow.

Street after street felt like minefields. Sophie couldn't be sure of the guards' patrols, where or when they'd turn a corner. Every few feet, every possible shadow they could slip into held only a moment's safety. They listened for footsteps, for the guttural language they knew to fear, for the loosening of safety clasps on pistols or rifles. When all was silent, they ran on cats' feet to the next shadow.

Two blocks into their journey, a man stepped from behind a kiosk, blocking their path. Sophie gasped, but the man whispered, "Three— come with me." That quickly, the Garbinskis were gone, peeled from their group like the layers of an onion. Sophie drew a shallow breath of both loss and relief, then steadied her nerves and kept going.

Before they slipped through the courtyard of her apartment building, Sophie removed her shoes and motioned for Aaron and Judah to do the same. They tiptoed through the courtyard and up the stairs, holding their breath as they crept past the apartment of the superintendent, a man openly paid by the Gestapo to report any clandestine behavior.

Just as Sophie went to slip her key into the lock, her door swung open and Terri beckoned them all inside.

"What are you doing here?" Sophie feared there had been a slipup.

Terri motioned for the group to sit down and not say a word. She whispered into Sophie's ear, "The Gestapo raided the building tonight, just after curfew. They wanted to know where you were. I told them that I heard you had to work late, past the curfew, and would be staying with your employer's sister, though I didn't know who either was. I don't know if they believed me. We can't show a light."

"What about the morning? What—"

"We'll hide them in my apartment until we can move them. Renat can help. He knows someone who may know of another hiding place . . . or can sneak them into the ghetto. He knows a woman with an epidemic control pass, a woman who is able to get in and out of the ghetto. She's already moved children. He's sure she'll help us."

Sophie closed her eyes. *I don't want to get them into the ghetto! That was the point of everything . . . getting them out. Hiding them, saving them.* But she couldn't push any more tonight. "They must be starving. I've got to feed them."

Terri had thought of that, too, and unwrapped two half loaves of black bread and a portion of cheese for father and son. She passed Aaron a flask of water and another of tea.

"You've thought of everything. Thank you." Sophie pressed Terri's hand.

"You must understand. The woman across the hallway, Pani Rusnak, is suspicious. She confided to me that she doesn't trust you. She knows we are friends, but she warned me against you, said she's keeping her eye on you."

Sophie sighed deeply and leaned back against the headrest of her chair. She couldn't keep all the wolves at bay. There were just too many of them. Her employer was already suspicious, had all but voiced his doubts. If the Gestapo checked Terri's story about working late and staying with the grocer's supposed sister, she could be arrested, sent to Pawiak Prison, even if she didn't admit to any wrongdoing. The Germans didn't need reasons. They didn't need law. . . . They were the law. And few people were known to survive the brutal and bloody interrogations at Pawiak. Fewer still returned home.

Sophie whispered to Aaron that they could not speak, could not move lest the tenants below them hear multiple sets of footsteps in the night. He nodded his understanding, wrapped the blanket Sophie offered him around his son, and together they stretched out on the floor.

Sophie tried to stay awake, intent on nudging Aaron if he snored, but he didn't, and it wasn't long until she fell into a deep and dreamless sleep.

CHAPTER TWENTY

ROSA KNEW ITZHAK WAS HAPPY. Despite working long hours for little pay, despite the constant hunger, despite the frost on their coverlet at night and the horrors of dead bodies on the streets awaiting collection each morning, Rosa knew her husband rejoiced in their small family. She was happy, too—happy beyond all bounds she'd ever known.

Each morning, before Itzhak rose, he drew a sleeping Ania from her cradle into their bed—their makeshift mattress on the floor. He made up silly songs that he whispered in their baby's ear and tickled her cheek with his beard. Ania gurgled and cooed—a beautiful way to greet each new day—and reached thin baby arms for her tata's face, sticking her tiny finger up his nose and tugging on his beard. Itzhak laughed with each new antic Ania displayed, declaring there never had been such a baby, such a darling, in all the world before. Daily, before Itzhak forced himself from bed, he placed a hand on Ania's head and whispered a blessing on her and on Rosa. It was all Rosa could do not to cry for the singing she heard in Itzhak's voice, in her own.

Itzhak and her mother made sure she ate enough to keep her milk flowing, to nurse Ania—the beautiful brown-eyed miracle daughter they all loved with every breath in their bodies. Beyond sustenance, beyond survival, they made no plans. They'd agreed on this . . . for now. If Itzhak found a new path, they would reconsider, might even dare to hope. But for now, food for each day was enough.

The winter drove refugees from all over Poland into Warsaw, and thousands more into the ghetto. Housing was not only at a premium, it had become unavailable. By February, there was no way to turn the needy away without sentencing them to death on the street. That realization came home to Rosa anew one afternoon, as Ania slept in her arms, and before Itzhak returned from work. Her mother stood in the doorway of the kitchen, surveying the room where Rosa had just nursed Ania.

"We must move into one room and give the other." Rosa was surprised that it was her mother who stated the obvious. "And the sitting room. We could house two more families."

Rosa swallowed, cradling her daughter even closer. Their tiny-enough sanctuary would now be given to others. She agreed. She understood the need, but it didn't keep the lament from her heart. *We've given up so much, and we've adapted. Why more? Why now?*

But Rosa knew she hadn't given it up; their home had been taken from them as surely as if they'd awaited the German decree. That they were placed as they were—better off than many in the ghetto—she could only credit to her mother's foresight and her husband's ingenuity. They had a roof over their heads and food in their bellies, even if their bellies grumbled from hunger in the night. Ania was fairly healthy—a gift in these desperate and uncertain times.

Her mother was right. She must face the inevitable before their sanctuary was taken from them by force. Perhaps by offering it to someone, they could choose a family that might be more compatible with them.

She explained their decision to Itzhak as they lay in bed that night.

"Your mother is wise. If we don't open our door now, we will be forced to open it soon. And it's right."

"I know it's right. I've just been so grateful for our time together—just us, as a family." She nestled deeper into her husband's arms. For the first time she sensed he was not altogether with her, despite his strong arm encircling her shoulders. She waited, knowing that, given time, he would share whatever burdened him.

At last he spoke, tentatively, softly. "We have more family."

"Matka will share this room with us," she acknowledged, though she knew that wasn't who he meant.

He didn't speak, and the silence weighed on her heart.

"Your parents. Your sisters. I know. I think of them too."

"All of them. I've no idea how they've fared, what will happen when the Germans come. I wish they could be here, with us."

Rosa remembered the tension of life with her mother-in-law and could not answer.

Itzhak shifted to his side, and Rosa knew that he searched for her face, even though he couldn't see in the dark. "Can you imagine my mama with a Gestapo agent on her doorstep—telling her she must move to an 'enclosed district'?"

Rosa could, and she knew her mother-in-law's response would put the entire family at risk. She shuddered, even though she wasn't cold. *Thank You, Adonai, that we are here . . . not there. Thank You that despite our poverty, we're safe . . . for now.*

Itzhak rolled onto his back, the arm that had held her now crooked behind his head, the hand that had stroked her shoulder now riffling through his thinning hair. Rosa longed to hold him, to draw him back to herself, but she sensed the distance of his thoughts between them. She knew her husband loved her, loved their child, but she also knew he worried for news of his home and parents, his sisters and their families. She'd felt just the same before they'd left Vilna to come to her matka in Warsaw—and that was before they'd known just how cruel the Germans could be. Still, she must soothe his mind. "The Germans are not there now—not yet. They're probably better off than we are."

"We don't know that. The Soviets are brutal—the pogroms—"

"There must be a way to get word to them—to find out how they are."

"We're no longer allowed to receive mail."

"I know, I know. But I've heard talk in the bread queue . . . talk of an underground network, men able to get in and out of the ghetto, through the sewers, and travel. We could ask them to find out—maybe not about your parents, but to learn what's going on in Vilna. Maybe they could find someone who knows your family. It can't be so bad as here."

"Through the sewers . . . I hadn't thought of that."

Rosa closed her eyes against the imagery those three words created, and she could have bitten her tongue. *Why did I tell him? What have I done?*

"If I left now, I could be back before spring, perhaps bring them with me."

Rosa tensed. "You'd never get your mother through the sewers, and the Germans won't allow them to come in. They couldn't register for work, and we can barely feed ourselves. If you leave now, we will starve. Your pay is all that keeps us from starving. The ration books are not enough—you know that." She conjured every objection she could, knowing, loving, and fearing the weight her husband carried on his heart.

"But my parents . . . I'm responsible for them, too."

"You have two sisters—and their husbands—right there in the city."

"I am their only son. They're my responsibility, just as you and Ania are."

Rosa rolled to her back, staring at the darkened ceiling. She and Ania were his family—not a responsibility to be borne.

"I didn't mean that as it sounded."

Rosa couldn't respond, couldn't keep the tears from her eyes or the choke from her throat. She knew him, knew in that moment that he would go and do the thing he believed his duty. But how would she manage without him?

"I've been saving. There is enough for you and your mother and Ania for a month—longer, if you're very careful. And I won't be here to eat for that time, so things will stretch."

"You'll lose your position, and then there will be no pay. If you leave, the soldiers will come after you. They may retaliate against me—they may take Ania away. Are we not more important to you than your parents?" It was a desperate ploy to keep him from going, and she was sorry the moment she'd said it.

Itzhak said nothing for long minutes. Rosa wanted to scream, to demand what he was thinking. Had she gone too far? She'd vowed never to become a nagging or manipulative wife. She'd seen that in his mother too often. But her fears were real, and he must know that. He must have seen the brutality of guards on the streets. He must have heard the tales of late-night Gestapo visits—ramming in doors, dragging people from their beds to who knew where, never to be seen again . . . or shot in the streets, on the spot. How could he consider leaving his family at their mercy? The Gestapo showed none.

"The building I'm working on is nearly finished. I'll be transferred in another month. It won't be so noticeable."

"Ania is too young. If you leave now, she won't know you. You can't travel by foot in winter—you'll freeze. You'll starve." Images multiplied and compounded in Rosa's imagination—all of them horrid. All of them ending in Itzhak's death. No, she could not bear it. "I've never begged you for anything, Itzhak. But I beg you now. Please, wait. Please."

Silence. Moments passed. She knew her husband wrestled within, but she would not relent . . . not now.

"Yes," he said at last. "You're right. I love you and Ania first, my Rosa, and most. I'll wait. For now."

CHAPTER TWENTY-ONE

SPRING ARRIVED IN WARSAW and gave way to summer. Seven months had passed since Sophie had been forced to relinquish her care of the Bukowskis. Renat's friend, a woman who went by the code name of Jolanta, had tried to find a safe house willing to take father and son together, but could not. The risk was too great. She'd arranged for a Polish Catholic family to take Judah, to care for and hide him throughout the war, in the hope of reuniting him with his father afterward, and finally found someone willing to hide Aaron nearby, at least temporarily. Sophie didn't know where.

She knew that Terri, Renat, and Jolanta had done all they could for the Bukowskis—had surely saved their lives. But she felt bereft without the responsibility and privilege of helping them.

Worse, she felt useless, purposeless, and in this world gone mad she could not live with that. There were too many who needed help. Yet she didn't know how to reach them or how to obtain and filter ongoing supplies without working through Renat or Terri, and Terri was loath to risk her. Sophie wasn't even sure how to let someone know they could trust her or how to be certain that what she did would not bring the Gestapo down upon them all.

Janek, though she prayed for his safety each day, may or may not return. Sophie had no sixth sense telling her he was dead, or if alive, where he might be. For better or worse she was stuck in Poland for the duration of the war.

Ostensibly Polish, and certainly Polish by marriage, she must help those she could in her current homeland, Jew and Gentile alike. She needed to help. She could live with nothing less, even if it meant she died with them. Tomorrow or the day after was not guaranteed to anyone. The streets were filled with random shootings. You didn't need to break the law to be gunned down at the whim of a patrol.

Sophie knew Terri had promised her father that she would not involve her in the work of the underground, for he had promised Janek. But both men, so concerned with her safety, were gone. Terri had broken that promise once, to help Sophie help the Bukowskis. Perhaps she would again. Sophie had proven she was trustworthy and capable. Surely the underground could use her.

On a warm Saturday afternoon, she whispered her plea over tea in an outdoor café not far from the ghetto. To her surprise, this time Terri didn't try to dissuade her.

"It's true; we need more help. There will never be enough hands or feet, never enough money or food or forged papers or hiding places or couriers to meet the need. It's staggering in a way I'd never imagined . . . never understood, till recently. And the need grows every day." Terri looked older, sadder, had grown thinner than Sophie had ever seen her. The shadows beneath her eyes had darkened.

"Let me shoulder some of this." Sophie reached for her friend's hand. "You know I can, and that I want to. I know—my accent could give me away, give anyone I help away. Let me do something where

I don't have to speak, at least not to anyone Polish. My German is pretty good. Let me interact with them, if you need someone to. They're not likely to notice my Polish accent isn't perfect."

She could tell that Terri listened, was considering. "There's no way you could hide someone in your apartment—too many eyes and ears on our floor. You'd be pitiful in the black market. You don't drive a hard enough bargain."

Sophie straightened. Both things were true, but it didn't mean she was weak. Surely she could do something.

"You were good with Judah. You're excellent with children."

Sophie nodded. *Even though I've not been able to carry my own. Why am I best at something that can't be used?*

"There are children who need schooling. You could teach them."

"But the schools are closed—long now."

"Yes." Terri leaned forward. "But there are underground schools, in private homes, and . . ." She stopped.

"And what? Where?"

"In the ghetto." Terri's eyes locked with Sophie's, as if taking her measure.

Sophie blinked, doing her best to understand what her friend had just said. *Teach . . . in the ghetto.* It was just the thing Sophie felt made for. *But how?* If Terri believed she could do it, she must know a way. "How do I get in?"

Terri whispered, "Is there anyone sitting behind me?"

"No, they've gone."

"How important is your job to you? Your identity?"

Sophie all but snorted. "I hate my job. But I'm grateful for it. It's paying my rent and supplying food. My identity—"

"You remember Jolanta, the woman who helped us before?"

Sophie nodded.

"She has a pass into the ghetto. She goes every day, multiple times a day, carrying in food, medicine, supplies—anything she can." Terri leaned over her teacup and whispered, lower still, "She gets children out, too—with the help of others."

"Out?"

"I'm going to help—on this side of the wall. A temporary stop until they can be moved to a safe location."

"Then let me help you—on this side of the wall." Sophie could imagine nothing more important than saving children from the ghetto. Once Jolanta and her network got them out, she might give them some semblance of life, of normalcy—education, if nothing else.

"But you'd need a different job, a different identity, something where you wouldn't be watched so closely, would be allowed to come and go. And you'd need to get rid of everything that identifies you as who you really are."

"I've already done that."

"What about Janek's photograph? Do you still have it?"

"You can't be serious. It's all I have." Sophie felt her throat go dry.

"You know that would link you to him and, with your new identity, spell *underground* in a moment." Terri looked away. "We can't be seen working together. Meeting like this once in a while, outside our apartments—two friends over tea—is one thing. But if we're seen to work together or spend too much time at the apartment by anyone, especially in caring for children clearly not our own, we'd be investigated. You know that."

Sophie knew that everything Terri said was true—knew it in her head, but her heart brooked strong arguments, especially concerning Janek's photograph. Still, she wanted to help children in any way she could. If that meant sacrificing her last tangible link to Janek, if it meant teaching illegally or taking in children who could not be seen by outsiders, she would do it. She would do whatever it took.

◆ ◆ ◆

True to Terri's word, Sophie found herself with a new job—a clerk, at least in title, in the office next door to the Social Welfare Department where Renat's friend Jolanta worked. Only her real name was Irena Sendler, and it was clear that the people she worked with either didn't know or didn't want to know what she was doing in the ghetto under the guise of her nurse's uniform and her indisputable epidemic control pass.

The woman was so careful, so circumspect and exacting in all her dealings, that Sophie would not have guessed if Terri had not told her. She tried very hard not to stare, not to wonder at Irena's daring and the extensive network of helpers she'd built, but it was all Sophie could do not to inquire and to go about her assigned tasks as if they were the only thing that mattered.

They did matter, she knew. Jewish teachers, professors, lawyers, writers, and artists had been executed or deported to labor camps in droves. Polish intelligentsia had been targeted too. The Germans wanted to make certain that Poles were equipped only to follow orders, mostly for menial labor. They espoused the belief that a thinking Pole was a dangerous Pole. Hence, Polish schools were closed and thousands upon thousands of children did not learn to read or write—unless they were taught in secret. Students from every stratum of society craved the stimulus of learning. That was a craving, a yearning Sophie could understand, a need she could fill.

By November 1941, Sophie taught three English classes per week to the same group of students outside the ghetto—some Polish Jewish children in hiding with Catholic families and some Polish Aryan children within their families. Classes were kept small, moved regularly, and were attended by a variety of ages to avoid the dangerous suspicion of neighbors. The underground did its best to keep students moving at a normal academic pace, but because so many underground schools had to be taught in one room to a variety of ages and academic achievement, some students fell behind. Few accelerated, despite the individual attention. All were hungry, cold as winter crept near, and afraid of the slightest noise outside the door. All weighed on Sophie's heart.

There was little she could do to relieve the physical deprivation, but she did have her old coat cut down to size for Estera, a young Jewish child who had no coat and who had long outgrown her shoes with none to replace them. It gave Sophie great pleasure to see the little girl fold back the brown paper and her eyes grow bright with delight at the buttons—large for a child's coat. She wished she had a hundred coats, a thousand pairs of gloves and new shoes to give to all the children in need.

For all Sophie couldn't do, she found things she could. She saw that there were often younger, preschool-age children in the home—children who longed to be included with their older siblings. It was for them that Sophie started a reading circle, arriving a half hour before the designated class time. She read children's stories in English to all who wanted to listen, giving the children the pleasure of time, attention, and illustration, as well as an introduction to the language. And though she was able to find few books for children in Polish, she read over and over again Judah's favorite, *King Matt the First*, by Dr. Korczak, always leaving them hanging in a particularly perilous adventure of the young king, with a promise to continue next time. It seemed especially fitting because the book had been banned, the doctor being Jewish, and poor King Matt's life in some ways reflected their own—uncertain, challenging, adventurous, dangerous.

Sophie began to feel alive again, adrenaline pumping through her veins despite the danger, or perhaps partly because of it. She was doing something worthwhile, something purposeful. It changed no one's circumstances, but for those few hours three times each week, the classes transported teacher and pupils far from Warsaw and the cruelties, the deprivations of war, to a different time, another place, and the memory that once there'd been another world. Perhaps there would be again.

Sophie's enthusiasm spilled over into her weekly café meetings with Terri.

"I can't tell you how I love reading to the children. It's what I was made for. They love King Matt—he's perfect for them now!" She almost laughed, something she'd rarely done for more than two years . . . not since Janek left, not since the bombs began to fall.

But Terri was not laughing. In fact, she paled and looked as if she might cry.

"What is it? What's the matter?"

Terri looked away, across the street, as if she might find words or answers there. "I've met him."

"King Matt?" Sophie half laughed at the idea of the joke, but Terri's face told her otherwise.

"Dr. Korczak. The author of that book."

"Have you? I heard that he lived and worked in Warsaw. Where did you meet him?"

"In the ghetto."

"The ghetto?" Sophie sobered. "Of course."

Terri sighed. "A good man. A remarkable man. A champion of children." She tucked her napkin into her lap, smoothed it once, twice. Sophie saw that her friend fought back tears. "He's been offered a way out, several times, but he won't leave. He's running an orphanage there . . . Jewish children who'd be on the streets, starving more quickly than they already are, if not for him. It breaks my heart to see him, to see those children, their arms and legs no more than sticks, their faces showing the bones of their skulls, the skin stretched tight across their cheekbones. Some are losing their hair for lack of nutrition. There's so little we can do, so little we can get past the guards."

Sophie had not realized her friend was going into the ghetto. The knowledge of what that could mean if she was caught chilled her heart. The image of so many hollow-eyed, starving children froze it. "I just don't understand. Why do they do this?"

"*Untermenschen*—human beings they consider socially and racially inferior. All along we've thought it was persecution. The Germans claim they want more living space, so they confiscate countries. But they don't only want to confiscate the living space and property of Jews, or confine them to contain the spread of disease, as they claim." Terri snorted. "There was no ghetto, no typhus before they came." She looked into Sophie's eyes now, and Sophie could not look away. "They want to exterminate them, like vermin. Not like humans at all."

Sophie shook her head.

"You know it's true. They're starving them, freezing them out in winter, and creating disease—swarms of lice and cesspools with no sanitation or clean water. Dysentery—"

"Stop. Stop!" Sophie could not listen. "I know what it is. I don't know what to do about it."

"Neither do I," Terri whispered. "Neither do I."

CHAPTER TWENTY-TWO

ITZHAK WAS GLAD TO SHED his winter coat, to leave the winter and old year behind, to feel the warmth of the spring sun on his face as he walked to work. Each day he practiced gratitude as he walked, naming off the gifts in his life—his wife, his daughter, his mother-in-law, a roof over their heads, even though they now shared it with others. It was 1942, and they had food in their bellies, meager as it was. Work that paid him almost nothing—but something. And each day, as he walked, he prayed for his parents, for their safety and well-being. He prayed for his sisters and their husbands, for his nieces and whatever children had been born into the family since he and Rosa had left Vilna for their temporary visit to Warsaw . . . a visit that it now seemed would never end.

He'd waited a year past Rosa's begging him to stay—through news of the German occupation of Lithuania, through tales of the burning of the Great Synagogue and snippets received through the underground of ghettos formed in Vilna. Still no word of his parents or sisters had reached his ears. And still Rosa begged him not to go.

Ania had grown puny through the winter—a cough that would not leave her small and heaving chest. But just that morning, she had crawled out of her cradle and onto the pallet on the floor that Itzhak and Rosa shared. She'd crawled right onto his chest and tugged his beard! Itzhak had pretended to be asleep but in truth had held his breath, relishing each movement of his precious daughter. It was the first time she'd climbed out of her cradle and to the floor on her own—a feat as great in Itzhak's heart as if his daughter had climbed Mt. Everest!

"We knew she'd climb out of there sooner or later," Rosa had chided. "It's not far to the floor." But to Itzhak it was a sign that Ania was gaining strength, tiny and frail though she was.

Ania did not wail; she cried in whispers when she cried at all, as if it cost too much energy to fill her lungs and howl. That worried Itzhak, who'd lived in a family of nieces climbing and running and wailing by Ania's age. So any sign, any reason to hope, was joy.

Rosa did all she could to alleviate the cough—without medicine. Aryan doctors were not allowed to attend Jews, and Jewish doctors had few or no supplies. But it was spring. Surely Ania would revive with warmer weather, with sunshine, even if it was only the sunshine through their tenement window.

When Ania grew stronger, Itzhak would again broach talk of the trip to Vilna. His daughter knew him now, and Rosa could manage life without him for a month or more. If he didn't go soon—go now—he could not guarantee returning before the fall, and his parents would not be fit to travel in cold weather. He could not, would not leave Rosa or Ania in winter, could not leave Rosa's mother, for that matter. Was she not his responsibility too?

Work had slowed for him—not so many urgent or long days. He was able to get home before curfew, sometimes able to bring a little extra bread or cheese, once a slice of pork . . . unclean food they would not have considered eating before the war. Now every morsel waged a battle against starvation. If he were absent for a few weeks, could they not form some excuse?

Itzhak sighed, nearly missing the turn his feet knew better than his head. He would not fool himself. If he didn't show up for work, he would lose his position . . . unless someone else could take his place for a time . . . unless he transferred to a new building project where he would not be known, and that impostor could pretend to be him. Itzhak nearly laughed. What an idea! Who was trained to do the work he did that was not already doing it, making his own way? But it bore thinking upon.

◆

Later that morning, Sturmbannführer Weiss called Itzhak to his office—a call no one working wanted to receive. But he couldn't think of any way in which he'd offended or failed in his work. He also knew that was no insurance against dismissal or punishment.

"You have finished the work on the second floor." It wasn't a question, but Itzhak answered the gruff statement anyway.

"Yes, sir, I have."

The Sturmbannführer smirked. "Don't look so frightened, Abraham. I know not to bite the hand that lights my office."

Itzhak steeled himself against the anger of being called "Abraham." It was the German name for all Jewish males—a sacred name used in derogatory terms. This German was no different from the hundreds that had invaded Warsaw. He must remind himself of that . . . daily . . . hourly. He waited for the Sturmbannführer to continue.

The man scribbled something on paper. "Do you read?"

Itzhak bit the inside of his lip to keep a scathing remark from leaving his mouth. "I read Polish, Lithuanian, Russian, German." It was dangerous to boast, even when it was the truth.

The Sturmbannführer reddened. "Then you'll have no trouble

finding this address. Go to the back door. Do what needs to be done for the doctor. Don't come back until you do."

Itzhak hesitated before reaching for the paper. "This is electrical work?"

"Take your tools. Do what he says, and do not mention it outside this office. I owe the man a favor." The Sturmbannführer leaned back in his chair. "Keep your mouth shut about that. If you don't, imagine the consequences."

"Yes, sir." Itzhak waited until the Sturmbannführer turned away, dismissing him. He coughed.

"What is it?"

"A pass, sir. I will need a pass."

"Yes, yes." The Sturmbannführer turned and scribbled a pass, stamped it with his official insignia, and shoved it across the desk.

Outside the office Itzhak looked at the two papers. The Sturmbannführer had forgotten to date the pass. Itzhak stopped, his hand poised to knock on the office door. But he hesitated, knowing that disturbing the Sturmbannführer again was not a good idea. What might it mean to have an undated pass? A freedom? Or a risk of execution?

The address he'd been given was deep into the Aryan district, nearly the other side of the city. It would take him longer to get home at night. He could only hope that he wouldn't be stopped and his papers searched, that the work wouldn't take many days, that it wasn't something illegal, that he could still find a way to make his trip to Vilna and provide for Rosa and Ania in his absence. He closed his eyes. It was too much to know, to decide. One foot in front of the other. One day at a time. What more could Adonai expect of him?

It was late afternoon when he stood in front of the two-story brick building—an imposing house, now no doubt the home of some Nazi officer. Itzhak sighed. He hoped it was only a lamp or a room that needed rewiring. But if that were true, why the not-so-thinly-veiled threat?

As Itzhak rounded the corner of the house he saw a door with a shingle hanging above it: *Dr. Leja, General Practitioner. Surgery closed pending repairs.*

A doctor. What relationship could he have with the Sturmbannführer?

Before he knocked, the door opened. A petite woman in house-dress and apron beckoned him inside. "Come in, come in, then. The Sturmbannführer phoned that you'd be coming. The doctor's expecting you." She all but pulled Itzhak through the door and into the kitchen set directly off the corridor. She closed the door and placed her hands on her hips. "We're glad you're here. A relief, it is." The woman cocked her head to one side. "By the looks of you, you haven't eaten in a week. Is that right?"

Not waiting for an answer, she pushed Itzhak into a chair beside the worktable and proceeded to cut a fat slice of bread and slab of cheese. "A man can't work on an empty stomach."

Itzhak wondered if he'd been led into a magical land—maybe something like the books Dr. Korczak, the renowned children's doctor, wrote. At the sight of such a feast, the dizziness born of hunger that sometimes came upon him made his head swim.

"None of that. No swooning at my table. It's not done. Eat."

Itzhak ate . . . wolfing the bread and cheese, as if someone might take it from him. Too late he realized the sight he must present. "I'm sorry. I—"

"You're not the one to be sorry, poor man. I'll wager that's the first meal you've eaten in a while."

Itzhak swallowed against such kindness, compassion. "You're very generous. I thank you." Too late he wished he'd pocketed half of the largesse to take home to Rosa and Ania, to Marya. "There is electrical work here for me to do?"

"Yes, the doctor will explain."

"The doctor? Not an officer?"

Her eyebrows crept to her forehead. "A Nazi officer? The doctor? I should say not! It's the Nazi that owes my good husband the life of his son."

Itzhak did his best to follow the woman.

"Saved the boy's leg, my husband did—after that man foolishly allowed his young son to ride a Wehrmacht motorcycle. The boy turned the bike over on himself and it crushed his leg. The German doctor wanted to amputate the leg, but the father couldn't stomach that. Couldn't face his wife after such foolish behavior, if you ask me. To let a child—no more than eight—on one of those heavy machines!"

She cut second slices of bread and cheese, pushing them toward Itzhak. "Blood everywhere and draining fast. But my husband reset the bones and sewed him up. The boy's plagued with a limp, but hardly any scarring. The limp may lessen, given time."

This time Itzhak pulled a dirty handkerchief from his coat pocket and wrapped the precious meal.

"You needn't hoard that. I'll give you more."

"You are kindness, madam. I will save this for my wife."

"You're married?"

Itzhak nodded, amazed that this Aryan woman spoke to him of such normal things. "Rosa, and a little girl, Ania." He couldn't keep the smile from his face, the light from springing to his eyes at the very thought of them.

The woman smiled—a strange combination of compassion and pity. "You live . . . behind the wall?"

Itzhak looked away, the smile falling from his face. "Yes. Behind the wall."

"I hear food is scarce there."

"Everything is scarce." And then Itzhak realized. A doctor—an Aryan doctor would have medicine. "My daughter—my Ania—has coughed all winter. There is no medicine for her." He knew it was a shameful plea, but for the sake of his daughter he musn't mind shame.

"How old is she—your little girl?"

"Fifteen months."

"Walking and into everything, is she?" The woman smiled again.

"No." How could he explain that there was nothing for her to get into, that she was too weak to walk on her own? "Not yet."

The woman nodded, as though she understood without Itzhak's explanation. A silence came between them, one Itzhak felt too weary to fill.

"Well, come along now. Let me show you what needs doing. I'm sure the doctor will see you when he has a moment, but I can get you started."

For the next two hours Itzhak tore plaster from the wall in the doctor's small operating room until he found the break in the wires. It was a simple matter to repair. Replacing the plaster would be easy, too. If the doctor wanted that done, Itzhak could return on the morrow. Today, there was still time for him to walk home, time to be off the streets before curfew.

"You can't be finished already," the small woman, the doctor's wife, accused.

"Come, I'll show you." Itzhak was always pleased with the flood of light a simple repair could produce. The difference between total darkness and a way to see, to walk, to move about and perform one's duties—all because of electric light. It was a wonder that never ceased to move him.

The doctor's wife walked to the wall switch and turned it, on and off, alternately spilling light into every corner and then taking it away. She shook her head. "This will never do."

"This is not what you wanted?"

She sighed. "Well, yes, and no—not so quickly."

"I do not understand."

"No, you wouldn't, would you?"

He understood less all the time.

"Are you trustworthy? What is your name?"

"Itzhak Dunovich. I am trustworthy." Itzhak's shoulders pulled back.

"Then tell no one what you've accomplished here and come back tomorrow. My husband had to go out for an emergency." She looked away. "I want him to meet you for himself."

Itzhak hesitated, trying to remember the Sturbannführer's exact instructions.

"I know what you're thinking. But the Nazi won't be expecting you. We told him it was an old house—a very complicated wiring system and likely to take days . . . even weeks. My husband assured him that we would pay your expenses, and he said we can keep you until you're done with the work. Is that satisfactory to you?"

Itzhak thought of the bread and cheese in his pocket. Would the woman continue to send him home with food? Even if they did not pay in cash, if only they would send food home . . . or medicine. "The Sturmbannführer told me not to return until the work for you is done."

"Good. That's good. Come back tomorrow."

"Yes." Itzhak tipped his cap and picked up his tools, heading for the door.

"Wait. You said your little girl has a cough."

"All the winter. Less now, but still, especially in the night."

"Wait here."

Itzhak waited until the woman returned and handed him a package wrapped in strips of cloth.

"Put this in your pocket. Don't let it be known where it came from, but give your daughter a teaspoon in the morning and a teaspoon before bedtime. Do this for a week, and let me know how she is."

"Will I be coming here for a week?"

"At least." She smiled. "Now, go, before curfew catches you."

Itzhak had barely crossed the threshold of his apartment when the latest *Aktion* by the SS began—the Night of Blood. By morning, sixty well-known Jews had been dragged from their homes and executed in the street. All were connected in some way with the press—printers, writers, financiers, distributors of the over fifty underground newspapers published in Poland.

The next morning German posters appeared all over Warsaw: *As long as the secret press continues to appear, there will be executions. The Jews must put a stop to this treason.*

Itzhak kept his head down on his way to work. He would not jeopardize his family by reading so much as a poster in the street or on a kiosk. But that also meant he navigated with less information. Less information could prove as deadly as too much.

CHAPTER TWENTY-THREE

IT WASN'T UNTIL SPRING THAT Sophie learned Aaron Bukowski had left his hiding place with Jan and Antonina Żabiński at the Warsaw zoo that winter, just as the terrible cold set in.

Renat, whom she'd not seen since he'd helped the two families flee the library, sat on a bench in the park, reading a newspaper, the first pleasant day of April. With benches back to back, Sophie faced the opposite direction, picking through her purse.

"He went to find his son," Renat whispered into the air, just loud enough for Sophie to hear. "Antonina begged him not to go, insisted he wait until Jan could try to get the boy out after Christmas, but he was desperate beyond reason."

"Out? Out of where?"

"Young Judah was ratted out by a 'friend' of the Catholic family he was hiding with. He made the mistake of running when the Gestapo tried to interrogate him. A Polish policeman discovered him on the street—without papers, and with 'physical evidence.' He was sent to the ghetto—an act of mercy, I suppose, compared to being shot by the SS or incarcerated in Pawiak. Still, Aaron could not bear to leave his son there with no money, no papers, no food, not even for two weeks." Renat paused as a man, apparently an office worker, walked by. "He'd obtained papers and meant to join him."

"Aaron? Sneak into the ghetto—to live?"

"It's been done before—successfully. But not this time."

Sophie held her breath.

"Aaron left the zoo late in the day, thinking he could slip in unnoticed. It was a terrible risk. He stood out. His beard had been shaved. He was not as thin as the workers he walked beside—the workers returning to the ghetto from their daily forced labor outside the walls. Perhaps he would have made it inside, perhaps even his better clothes would not have been too closely observed. But when he was less than half a block from the gate, Judah saw him and screamed—such delight in his voice. Aaron . . . I saw his face—he had no control over his son's jubilant cry or the child's run toward his arms outside the gate."

Renat paused only a moment, then rushed on in a whisper, as if seeing it all again and needing to get the telling out. "It happened so fast—seconds, only. The guard shouted, 'Halt!' But Judah did not seem to hear."

Renat stopped speaking. Sophie froze, then thought she'd be sick in anticipation of what must come.

Renat's voice came again through Sophie's fog. "Gunshots tore through the labor force. Laborers hit the street, their faces pressed against the cobblestones, hands over the backs of their heads. Bystanders scattered, terrified for their lives."

Sophie could see every detail in her mind. Judah racing, head thrown back in joy and victory, through the gate, bounding toward the father he loved, the one he'd not seen in so long, who had always saved and protected him from harm. And the chaos, the terror, that followed.

"I don't know how many died in the gunfire. When I looked up from the horror and the bloodbath, Aaron and his son lay in the dirtied snow, ribbons of scarlet trickling from them both, less than a meter from the outstretched arms of one another. . . . The loaf of bread Aaron had hidden beneath his coat lay like . . . like a black pearl in the snow. In a moment it was snatched up and carried away. Odd, how you remember such things."

No! No! Sophie wanted to scream, to cry, to make Renat take back the words. But she dared bring no attention to herself or to Renat, who was risking his neck to inform her. *No, God! No! Poor Aaron! Poor, dear Judah!*

"He was just a frightened boy who saw his father coming to save him." Renat choked and coughed to cover it, as if the weight of that last act of love might prove too much, even for him.

They sat, back to back, for long minutes. At last Sophie heard him rise from the bench behind her, tucking the paper beneath his arm. "Be careful, my friend; be very careful." Slowly, Renat walked away.

◆

It took Sophie weeks to recover enough to teach without losing her train of thought, without her voice breaking. It took longer to bring herself to walk near the ghetto gates again.

But from the day she awoke from her stupor of grief, Sophie took to throwing vegetables over the ghetto wall, one at a time, or small packets of cheese, or half a loaf of bread, whenever she could do so unobserved. Someone would find those things. Someone would eat them. She didn't know what else to do, and she was grateful to find early one morning that she was not the only one.

A Polish woman, older than she, was in the process of throwing three potatoes over the wall when Sophie turned the corner. The last one bounced against the brick wall and fell back. As the woman bent to retrieve it and try again, she saw Sophie. Fear swept her eyes as she backed away from the precious vegetable, prepared to run. But Sophie lifted her hand and threw her own packet of cheese and half loaf of bread over, just clearing the rows of barbed wire atop the wall. The woman stared. She bent to pick up the potato, threw it again, then turned and smiled at Sophie. Sophie felt the ice of her heart thaw and smiled in return, for the first time since that awful day she'd learned of Aaron and Judah's fate.

CHAPTER TWENTY-FOUR

FOR WEEKS ITZHAK RETURNED daily to the Aryan home of Dr. Leja. No matter that his wife, Elżbieta, repeatedly declared that the doctor wanted to meet Itzhak in person, he was always out, visiting patients, working at the hospital . . . something. Except for the white coat hanging in the hallway and the occasional taint of ether in the air, Itzhak might have thought the woman invented—or imagined— her husband.

But there was nothing imaginary about the work Itzhak did. The third day he came, Elżbieta led him to a passageway off the basement—a hand-dug tunnel. The first day he saw the tunnel, it stretched twenty feet, connecting to the basement in the next house, and then the next week, another length, connecting to the basement in the house beside that. In time, the tunnel turned sharply and finally began a steep slant that ended in a chiseled entry into the sewers beneath Warsaw.

Not once did Itzhak ask the purpose of the tunnel. From the face of the clearly Jewish man he'd met coming through the tunnel, ripe with the fragrance of the sewers, he didn't need to ask. His job was to string electrical wire, to install a buzzer and a small flashing light near each entrance to the tunnel, of which there were few, and another inconspicuous buzzer leading to the basement of each connecting house.

The remainder of the day he spent on small projects for Elżbieta. For his faithful completion of each one he was given another simple task—and meals better than he'd eaten since before the war. Each night she gave him a small package of food to take home to his wife and child.

Itzhak worried that one day the Sturmbannführer would come looking for him, that they would be caught, the tunnel exposed. What would happen to Elżbieta then? To her husband? To him? If imprisoned, he could not bring home food or money. What would become of Rosa, of Ania and Marya? Itzhak's worries multiplied, but he also felt that at last he was doing purposeful work—work that clearly helped Jews escape Warsaw.

The question in his mind was, where did they go? Was there a place where Jews could be better off, less vulnerable?

He knew where he would go. Whether his family was better or worse off in Vilna, he didn't know, but he needed to know.

Word had drifted in through the underground by way of a letter, crumpled into a boot. Itzhak remembered the words by heart: *They are killing us. Be careful. Take refuge, because they are killing us.*

There was no way to know where the letter came from. He dared not think it was Vilna. Vilna, the Jerusalem of Eastern Europe—that's what they'd called it. How could you kill half the population? No, it couldn't be Vilna.

Yet if things *were* worse there, perhaps he could get his parents and sisters and their families out and into Warsaw. If they were better off, perhaps he could get Rosa and Ania out through this tunnel. Perhaps even Marya, if she would go.

It was late on a Saturday afternoon when Elżbieta ladled a full bowl of lentil stew and called Itzhak from the stamping of underground brochures that he'd been assigned.

"Eat up, my friend. Sunday is long."

"You've been very kind to me, and more than generous, Pani Leja. I don't know how to thank you."

"You can thank me by remembering my name is Elżbieta, and by eating up and keeping your strength. If I could send this stew home to your family, I would, but I doubt you would get it past the guard at the gate."

He shook his head. "I would not, and we'd all be found out."

Elżbieta sat down with a sigh. "And that would never do. But I have a small slab of cheese here. Can you slip it in your boot?"

Itzhak smiled. *Cheese. Ania's favorite. Rosa will love it.* "Thank you. Yes." He hesitated, frowned, studying the last of the lentils in his bowl. All week he'd been trying to think how to form the words to ask what he wanted.

"You don't like your stew?"

"It's wonderful."

"But? There is something you wish to say?"

Itzhak drew a deep breath. "The tunnel. It leads to the sewers."

"Yes." She sat back in her chair.

"I've long finished my electrical work, and still you have me come."

"Yes," she sighed.

"Why?"

For the first time, Elżbieta hesitated. "Already you hold our lives in your hands."

"You hold mine in yours."

She looked at him steadily. "I told you that my husband saved the Sturmbannführer's son—his leg, but also his life. He believes himself indebted to us. My husband convinced him that the best way to repay us was to provide us with the best electrician he had. My husband knew of you—of your work—because the Sturmbannführer had boasted of his J—" She stopped, her face reddening.

"Of his Jew?"

"Of his 'Jew slave.'"

Now Itzhak felt the heat rise up his face. She'd said the words with remorse and pity. The Sturmbannführer would have said them with pride and contempt.

"My husband told him that our house's electrical wiring had been badly damaged through the bombing, that in order to continue providing emergency care, particularly surgeries, to German families posted here, we need powerful and steady lights. It just so happened that during his son's surgery, the electricity went out."

"It just so happened?"

She smiled. "Yes, miraculous what one can do with a fuse box, isn't it?"

He smiled in return. The woman was wiser than he'd realized.

"So, there really is a Dr. Leja?"

"Of course." She straightened, offended, then shook her head. "You've never met him. I keep forgetting."

"Where is he?"

"Making house visits . . . to the ghetto, to those hiding in the sewers, to partisans outside of Warsaw."

Itzhak felt his eyes widen.

"As long as you're 'working on our electric wiring,' the surgery remains closed, freeing him to do this work. As soon as your work is done and you return to the Sturmbannführer, the surgery must reopen and my husband will be missed. Once he returns, the partisans and all those so in need of his help will be without a doctor."

"How long has he been gone?"

"Since the first day you came. I'm to get word to him when you leave."

"I could have rewired the entire house in this time."

"Can you spread that out over three more weeks?"

Itzhak wanted to ask why three weeks. What would happen in three weeks? But he'd pushed for and been given enough, more than he deserved, more than any other Aryan had given him. "Why does he do it? Why do you?" *Why do you both risk your safety, your lives for others?*

"Why wouldn't we? It's right." She stood, taking his empty bowl to the sink, then turned. "That's not all. I hesitate to say this to you, because you . . . because you are a Jew."

Weeks I have eaten at your table and now you insult me?

"I see you misunderstand. I hesitate to tell you for fear of your own prejudice, but I must. If I don't, I will regret it all the days of my life."

Itzhak shook his head, not comprehending.

"I do it—my husband risks his life each day to save others— because that is what Jesus did, and what He wants us to do. He healed, even when it risked His life, and then He died to save others—all of us. Jesus was a Jew, and as Gentiles, we are privileged, through belief in Him as Messiah and Savior, to be grafted into faith with you. We follow in His steps. . . . We do our best, for Him and for His people—our people. We, too, count ourselves children of Abraham, by the grace and mercy of our Lord Jesus Christ. How could we do less for our family?"

Itzhak's immediate resistance to the name of Jesus and the idea that a Gentile would count herself a child of Abraham gave him pause. The Germans wore belt buckles emblazoned with *Gott mit uns*—"God with us." But he no more believed Adonai fought on the side of the Germans, winning this war though they may be, than he believed he'd sprout wings to fly from the ghetto. He didn't understand how Christians looked at the providences of their Jesus, how two differ- ent peoples—Germans and Poles like Pani Leja, both claiming to be Christians—could hold and practice such different views. The Germans believed themselves superior, a master race, and practiced cruelty to others they deemed "less than"—and that certainly meant Jews. Yet he'd heard and experienced Elżbieta's practice, at great risk to herself, of mercy and loving-kindness. She practiced mercy not only to Aryans but to Jews—Jews she was now claiming brotherhood with.

All the way home Itzhak wrestled with the thought of it. What did he know of Jesus, anyway? Only what the rabbis had said, what they'd warned against. He knew about pogroms and crusades and wars waged in the name of this Jesus. He knew of the reputation of Christians who proselytized Jews, but what did he know of the man himself? Nothing in his experience made him think of Christians as merciful. And yet, here was a woman who claimed her kindness, her goodness at risk to her life and limb, was the result of following in the steps of a Jew.

◆

Rosa divided the cheese gift four ways, but Itzhak pushed his portion back to her. "You need this more than I. Pani Leja feeds me well when I'm there."

"You're not there today," Rosa objected, but she took the cheese. Nursing had depleted her. She dared not stop eating lest her milk dry up and she have nothing to give Ania. Despite her thankfulness for the extra food Pani Leja sent, Rosa envied the attention the woman she knew only by name gave her husband. She would have liked to cook stew and bake apple cake for her Itzhak. It was hard not to resent that another woman was able to do this, and it was *meshugge*, too, when she knew Pani Leja kept them all from starving.

"I've been saving my pay. The extra food helps."

Rosa bit the cheese—a small bite to make it last, to savor the flavors she'd almost forgotten. But it stuck in her throat as Itzhak's eyes met hers. "You're going, then." It wasn't a question. She knew the answer—had known it for weeks.

"I'll ask tomorrow. She wants me there for three more weeks—or at least needs to be able to say I'm needed there for three weeks."

"Why three weeks?"

"I don't know, but I don't think it really matters if I'm there . . . not if she can find someone else to come and go, as if I'm still doing the work. In three weeks I can walk, if need be, to Vilna and back. I can see if my parents can come here, or if things are better and we can go there."

"Matka could not make that trip—not on foot. How would you get us all through the sewers? How would you get us out of the ghetto to the Lejas' house?" Rosa thought hard and furiously of all the possible objections she might raise.

Itzhak pulled her small hand into his. "I need to go. I'll come back; I promise. We won't decide anything until we decide together."

"We're not deciding this together."

He straightened. "No. But I need to know you understand, Rosa. I need to know you are with me." He gave a half smile. "Even if it means bringing my mother into our home."

Now Rosa smiled. Of course she would welcome his mother, as he had been willing to stay with hers. It wouldn't be easy—three women in a tiny kitchen, plus the family that shared the other bedroom. At least the sitting room had remained a common room—a room that should be offered to another family soon if Itzhak's parents did not come. "Your parents will have to share the sitting room with Matka. I'm not having your mother in our bedroom."

He chuckled. "I promise. And I promise I will write you every day while I'm gone—letters in my head, letters I will share with you when I return. You must write the same to me."

"Promise me you'll come back—alive and well. That's the promise I need."

Itzhak nodded. "I swear." He hoped, he prayed, it was a vow he could keep.

CHAPTER TWENTY-FIVE

THROUGHOUT THE SUMMER, Sophie kept teaching. Neither the children nor their parents wanted to give up the classes. Lessons provided a few hours of respite from the deprivation, the suffering, the fear that worked its way through their bodies each day as they waited for news of the block where the children's parents lived inside the ghetto. Were they still there, or had they been ordered to the *Umschlagplatz* to await the deportation trains that had begun leaving in July? Books, literature, and simply meeting together—to see and be seen—helped maintain their sanity.

Rumors from underground newspapers continued: death camps, Jews being shot in the forest and left unburied, Jews being shot in open fields and buried in mass graves. Words that swam together in nightmare proportions . . . words Sophie couldn't bear to believe.

Word through the streets and through the underground was that the cattle cars leaving from the *Umschlagplatz* were going to a place called Treblinka, believed by the Judenrat to be a transfer station to labor camps in the east, or perhaps a labor camp itself. But if that were so, why were there no barracks? Why only smokestacks? Why were the elderly and children among the first to go? What labor were they fit for? And then whole blocks of ghetto residents, indiscriminate of their working abilities, were taken.

One hot, early August morning, Sophie left for class before her usual time. She'd promised Estera, the child she'd given her coat to the winter before, that she would bring embroidery floss and a small hoop. Estera, though in hiding, was certain she could find the fabric. Sophie would teach the little girl to embroider, and together, they would create a handkerchief Estera could give her mother for her naming day.

The route to Estera's home required that Sophie pass near one of the ghetto gates. When she did, she saw, through the gate, a boy with a green flag leading an assembly—a parade of children, some surely ten or twelve years of age, but many not much more than three or four. They marched four abreast, heads held high, small water flasks and a single toy or book in hand, and singing. An old and feeble man accompanied them, walking up and down the ranks, apparently encouraging the children—something significant and rare in the world Sophie had come to know.

Sophie stopped and craned her neck to get a better view, as did others near the gate and everyone inside the gates as far as she could see.

"What is it?" The question was whispered again and again through the gathering crowd.

Sophie had not heard Renat come up behind her. When she realized it was he, she dared not acknowledge him, but heard him say, as if to someone else standing near, "The orphans, and that is the famous pediatrician, Dr. Korczak, and their teachers."

Dr. Korczak! Sophie had heard so much good about the man. His books and radio broadcasts before the war had revolutionized theories for parenting and for understanding and encouraging children. His

novel *King Matt the First* was beloved by Polish children everywhere—
a story in the vein of England's *Peter Pan*, and the one she read over
and over to the children she taught, the one she'd read to Judah.

The green flag from his book. Sophie pressed her hand to her heart.
The flag of hope for a better land—of freedom for children!

"What's that they're singing?" a woman asked.

Sophie felt the crowd strain to catch the words.

"Though the storm howls around us, let us keep our heads high."

"Where are they going?" another asked.

"To the *Umschlagplatz*—the train platform."

"They'll travel? All those children? Where will they go? Are they
being sent away?"

"To Treblinka." Renat spoke softly, his voice broken. "To die."

CHAPTER TWENTY-SIX

SUMMER WANED AND the first crisp days of autumn bit the air, but still Itzhak had not returned. Each night Rosa laid her head on her husband's pillow and composed mental letters—the ones he'd urged and promised in return, letters she meant to fill with hope and love. But in the end, she wept, tears of fear and frustration, of anger and longing.

She'd risked going to the house of the man arranged to pose in Itzhak's stead, to beg for news. But there was none. Pani Leja sent slim packages of food that the man brought back to Rosa through the ghetto gate, tied to his leg beneath his trousers, but nothing had been heard or seen of Itzhak since he'd left.

By the end of September, Rosa was frantic. The money Itzhak had saved was gone, despite her careful rationing of every penny. Her ration book was allowed only because of the hand sewing she took in—the repair of German uniforms. Matka's hands were too feeble to wield needles through the coarse fabric, so they shared the proceeds of two ration books—the one Rosa received, and the one Matka had

161

received from Jolanta—when someone was able to sneak food inside the ghetto. At least the delivery of those uniforms allowed Rosa outside the ghetto for an hour each week—an hour to raid waste cans and beg for bread behind the bakery she'd visited each day as a child. But the Aryans took no pity on her . . . why would they? She knew she was one of hundreds who came to shopkeepers' doors each day.

Late one afternoon, Rosa pulled the latest cheese packet from beneath her coat and unfolded its edges. The note, written inside the paper, came as a death sentence.

S. looking for I.

That was all, but Rosa knew what it meant. The Sturmbannführer had come looking or sent someone looking for Itzhak. It was a wonder it hadn't happened before now. What it meant for her, for Matka, for Ania, didn't bear imagining. A pounding could come at their door any moment. There was no way to know. What she knew for certain was that there would be no more cheese, no half loaves of bread or rare slices of tongue or pork. *We will starve. We will surely starve.*

Matka's shadow crossed the table. She still had the strength to carry Ania in her arms—Ania, who weighed almost nothing. "What is it?"

"They've gone to the Lejas, looking for Itzhak."

"What will they do?"

"What do you think? They will come here next. One day."

"We will be beaten, or shot."

Rosa wanted to tear out her hair. She couldn't think that, couldn't imagine Ania being torn from her arms, her head smashed in the street. "Give me my daughter." She pulled the little girl from her mother's arms and cradled her, roughly, beneath her chin. Ania whimpered.

"You're holding her too tight."

"She's my daughter." Rosa bit her lip until she tasted blood, but refused to cry.

"That woman, Jolanta, who gave me the ration book, came again today."

"Did she bring medicine? Ania's cough is better, but with winter coming—"

"She's taking children out of the ghetto. She wants to take Ania."

Rosa closed her eyes. She'd heard that the nurse—the Polish social worker—smuggled children from the ghetto and found them homes, safe houses, on the Aryan side. She'd met her when she brought medicine for Matka, and once or twice when she brought food. That seemed a lifetime ago.

"I told her not to show her face at our door again, that you will never allow it. We are not so desperate as to give up our own."

I would never have considered it before . . . but now, what if they come for me? What will happen to Ania, to Matka? Rosa swallowed, doing her best to keep her voice steady. "This is the last food Pani Leja will send. Even now she may be in Pawiak, or dead, because she helped Jews . . . because she helped Itzhak go to his parents, because she's shielded and helped us."

"We will manage. We have always managed."

"We won't manage if the Gestapo comes, if the Sturmbannführer comes. They will take me away at the very least. You and Ania would be left alone—with nothing. I can't let that happen to my daughter."

"We can only wait and see. Perhaps they won't come. If they do, we'll make them understand—say that Itzhak deserted us. We don't know where he is."

"And we never reported that—never pleaded for help before."

"The Germans help us? They would never. Even they will see the truth in that."

"We are playing Russian roulette, Matka! They will come for us. They took an entire orphanage of children—of *children*! Do you still think they will not take us? In their eyes we are useless mouths, feeders off of their society."

"Rosa, Rosa." Her mother sat heavily at the table beside her. "What can I say to you? What can I do?"

"Nothing. That is it, there is nothing you can do . . . but I beg you, do not try to stop me from doing what I must."

Her mother grimaced but turned away, saying nothing. Rosa didn't have the strength to try to convince her. She would need every ounce to give up her child.

◆ ◆ ◆

Rosa held Ania through the night. She breathed in the scent of her daughter's hair, nuzzled the soft curve between her neck and shoulder, pulled her close enough to share their heartbeats. Every nuance she committed to memory, engraved on her heart.

"It will only be for a while, my love . . . just until this cruel war is over," Rosa whispered into her sleeping daughter's ear. "You must be safe. I don't know how else that can be. I would do anything to make it otherwise, but I don't know how. I promise I will come for you. I swear, I will come."

In the morning, Rosa clipped a small lock of Ania's hair and folded it in a slip of paper. She tucked it in her pocket. Then she clipped a lock of her own hair, folded it in paper, and slipped it in Ania's tiny pocket.

She slipped the medallion Itzhak had given her on their wedding day from her neck. Using a chisel and hammer left in Itzhak's toolbox, she carefully cut the medallion in half. Filing the cut filigreed edges smooth, she wound a short length of gold chain from her mother's necklace through the split branches of the Tree of Life. The medallion and gold chains were the only things of value the women had not sold—gifts meant for the generations to come. Rosa crimped the chain closed and placed the half medallion over Ania's head, around her small neck. *Let this remind you you are not alone, my love. This Tree of Life is your connection to Adonai, and to me.*

One day these two halves will be rejoined. One day, we will be together again, mother and daughter, whole.

◆

Despite Marya's declaration, Jolanta appeared once more at Rosa's door. This time, Rosa was there and ready. She'd scrubbed Ania from head to toe. Her dress, washed and smoothed as best Rosa could manage, hid the half medallion tucked beneath the smocked bodice. But Rosa no longer cared about her daughter's dress. She crushed the child to her heart.

"Mamusia!" Ania giggled. "You snug me tight!"

Rosa could barely breathe but forced herself to smile for Ania's sake. "I'm giving you a good-bye snuggle, my love. It must hold you until I come for you."

At that, a shadow crossed Ania's eyes. "Come now."

"Soon, my love. You must go with this nice lady. She'll get you food—" Rosa bit back her tears.

"I keep a list," Jolanta began, "of all the children's Jewish names and the Aryan names they're given. I keep a list of all the addresses, so after the war we will be able to reunite families."

Jolanta was speaking, saying words that Rosa would only dissect later. She knew the young woman meant well, that she and her friends risked their lives to save the children of the ghetto, but Rosa had no idea if the woman believed her own speech. *Reunited after the war.* As much as she wanted to believe that, Rosa could not. Still, to save her daughter's life was all that mattered now . . . all that could matter. Rosa closed her eyes, memorizing the warmth of Ania's body.

"Please . . . she's hungry at night, in the day. She hasn't grown as she should. . . . Someone who loves her . . . someone who will sing to her at night. 'Oh, sleep, my darling. If you'd like a star from the sky, I'll give you—'" Rosa could not continue. "She's afraid at night, and the singing helps. Do you know the song?"

"Yes, I know it." Jolanta spoke crisply, efficiently, but Rosa saw the pain in her eyes. "There will be food. She'll be with you after the war."

How wicked—no, how hard it must be to pull children from the arms of their mothers each day. How cruel and kind to lie, to tell us that there will be an end to this war, that we will live to see our babies again.

Jolanta unrolled a blanket on the kitchen table. "Let's tuck her in here. I can give her something to help her sleep—just until we get past the guards. Luminal." She tipped a small amount into the child's mouth and massaged her neck glands, urging her to swallow.

Uncertain of the stranger's hands, Ania shook her head and reached pleading fingers for her mother. Rosa took her up, pushed the foreign blanket aside and wrapped Ania in her own small blanket— the one Marya had crocheted for her granddaughter at birth.

Rosa heard her mother gasp in the kitchen doorway. They'd agreed that Marya would not watch, would not come into the room or attempt to stop Rosa from doing what she believed she must. Evidently her mother had needed one last glimpse of her grand-daughter. Rosa could not blame her. How could either of them let this child go?

Rosa forced herself back to the moment. Singing softly, she held Ania until she fell asleep, then placed her on the blanket Jolanta had provided and tucked her in. *She'll be warm enough now, with two blankets.*

"You go out through the courthouse." Rosa repeated the rumors she'd heard, doing her best to stay focused.

"We used to; perhaps we will again. But there are other ways. Everything depends on silence and secrecy." Jolanta lifted the blanket enfolding Ania and tucked her into a gunnysack stabbed with breathing holes and labeled *Infection Control.*

"Can you promise me? Promise me my daughter will be safe."

"I promise you that if we don't get her out of the ghetto, she will die."

Russian roulette. Rosa could not breathe.

"When we leave, do not look out the window. If we are caught—"

"Yes—yes." Rosa couldn't think about that now. "The Leszno gate. I heard that's a good way out."

Jolanta looked at her sharply. "Since the Night of Blood there's a new guard there. He shoots people for no reason—because he feels like it. Stay away from there."

"They call him Frankenstein." Rosa had heard those rumors, too.

"That's what they call him."

"Then how? How will you get—?"

"It's better you don't know, Pani Dunovich. You must trust me."

"I will never see her again, will I?"

Jolanta looked away.

"Your silence speaks truly," Rosa whispered. "Thank you for not lying to me."

◆

That night, Rosa wept in her bed. Her mother slipped in beside her and held her sobbing daughter. "You did what you could . . . all you could. I'm sorry I discouraged you so long. You love your child more than your life, my Rosa. No mother could love more."

Rosa could not answer, could not trust herself to speak. In truth, she could not have given Ania up a moment sooner. And if Jolanta had delayed another minute, Rosa would have snatched her daughter back into her arms, no matter that it meant both their deaths.

"Now you must decide where you will go."

What? What was Matka saying?

"There is no longer a reason for you to stay. You're free to go, to find Itzhak. Waiting here makes no sense."

"We're here together, Matka. I won't leave you. We're all we have now."

"It's as you said. We're sitting here, waiting for the knock on the door, waiting for them to come and take us away."

"Perhaps they won't. Perhaps—"

"Don't pretend, Rosa. You were never good at pretending, not like some children. Let that stand you in good stead now."

"Where would we go?"

"You go. Find your Itzhak. If you make it through the war—and you must—find your Ania. Build a life, an even bigger family."

Rosa nestled into her mother's chest. *A fairy tale. A lovely fairy tale. But that is all.* Still, it was possible to sleep, dreaming of fairy tales.

Rosa dreamed of Ania, of Itzhak, of picnics they might one day take. Only the gunfire in the street, just before dawn, woke her. The realization that she was alone in bed chilled her heart, made her throw the covers back and run to the window in time to see the German boot kick over her dead mother in the street.

CHAPTER TWENTY-SEVEN

AS ROUNDUPS INSIDE THE GHETTO continued, Sophie felt the pressure increase for anyone helping Jews or hiding Jews outside the wall. Penalties for doing so or for not reporting what one saw or knew became still more swift, more harsh. Rewards to informants doubled, then tripled.

One of the Polish underground schools outside the ghetto was discovered, the teacher dragged into the street and shot—as a warning to others. The children and their parents were taken straight to the *Umschlagplatz*. No one needed to ask where they were being sent, Jewish or not.

Two Catholic families withdrew their children—their own as well as the Jewish children they'd taken in—from Sophie's classes. She couldn't blame them; the penalty, if caught, was unthinkable. She wondered if the education she'd so passionately shared would do the children any lasting good. Would they even grow up to use it, to spread their wings?

• ◆ •

By October, word from the ghetto was that the deportations had slowed, then seemed to stop. Despite warnings from the underground, tentative hope trickled through the attics and alcoves of the ghetto and into members of underground networks. *"Perhaps they'll leave us alone. Perhaps they just wanted to decrease the size of the ghetto. We have more room now—not more food, but more room. Maybe the information we had was wrong—maybe they really did relocate them to a labor camp, a better place. After all, how could it be worse?"*

But Sophie knew that people oppressed clung to any thread, no matter how slender. She also knew it was only a matter of time before the calm erupted into another storm.

During the last few months of the year, Sophie learned through underground newspapers and flyers illegally posted, as well as through angry German responses, that a group of mostly young Polish Jews, the Żydowska Organizacja Bojowa—ŻOB—was retaliating against German cruelty and open murders by assassinating collaborators, Jewish police, and blackmailers who'd made fortunes from Jewish betrayal, misfortune, and execution. With each success, the ŻOB grew bolder. But Sophie knew such vengeful daring, such frightening, reckless success, could not last.

CHAPTER TWENTY-EIGHT

FOR TWO DAYS AFTER her mother's sacrifice, Rosa remained in a fetal ball on her pallet. She did not see when the death cart rattled its way over cobblestones, stopped before their building, and men picked up the nearly weightless body of her mother. But she heard the cart resume its rattle down the street, and though she squeezed her eyes closed, she'd seen the ritual so many times that her imagination flared, vividly painting every detail—the steel gray of her mother's wispy hair, the bone-thin, limp hand that surely fell away from her body.

Rosa heard the couple in the apartment whispering, arguing, just loud enough for her to hear, over who should have the room now—now that there was only Rosa.

"Surely she can sleep beneath the kitchen table and give us the privacy and the pallet. There are four of us!" It was Helga Rosenfeldt. Bitter though the woman sounded, Rosa couldn't disagree. She would have fought for space for her family . . . if she still had a family. Rosa curled tighter into a ball and, shutting out her world and all it held, slept.

"We're sitting here, waiting for the knock on the door, waiting for

them to come and take us away. Don't pretend, Rosa. You were never good at pretending, not like some children. Let that stand you in good stead now." In the near dreaming between waking and sleeping, Matka's words played through her mind.

"Where would we go?" Rosa asked again, sleep lingering at the edges of each word.

"You go. Find your Itzhak. If you make it through the war—and you must—find your Ania. Build a life, an even bigger family."

Oh, Matka, you were the pretender. Ania is gone. Itzhak is gone. They're liquidating the ghetto. Our street, our building will be called any day now.

"Then you'd better get moving." The words, so like something Matka would say, came clearly into Rosa's mind, as if her mother had spoken them aloud.

"Matka?" Rosa's heartbeat quickened. Her eyes flicked open, focusing on the empty room. She waited in the silence. Nothing—no one. But gradually, the idea, the dream crept from the edges of her mind . . . feeble at first, then stronger. *What if I could make it to Vilna? Find Itzhak? What if we hid until after the war—no matter how long? It can't last forever—surely, Adonai, it can't last always! Did Pani Sendler mean it? Are there lists? Could we find our Ania? Could we build—?*

Rosa stopped. Wishing, hoping, even praying had not changed all that had happened. If there was any possibility of finding Itzhak, of making it through the war—through this week or this day, or of ever finding Ania again and becoming a family—she must get up, must take a first step, must begin. *That's what you would tell me, Matka. Get up. Get moving. Oh, Matka, what you gave. Freedom for me to go. I wish you hadn't. I need you—need your strength. How I love you!*

Rosa sat up, pushing sleep from her eyes. She drew a deep but ragged breath, beyond the grief harrowing her chest, and whispered, "Your sacrifice is not in vain, Matka. I promise. I vow."

CATHY GOHLKE

Her vow enabled Rosa to slip from the apartment that night in between the rounds of German soldiers. Her vow gave her courage to remove the bricks from a weak spot in the ghetto wall and steal through into the dark—just as she knew child smugglers had. She was not much bigger than a child herself now, thin and wasted.

She hid in a cellar near the ghetto wall, waiting for another darkness, then made her way to the Lejas'.

Pani Leja—Elżbieta—could not keep the tears from falling when Rosa told her story of her still-missing Itzhak, of her relinquished Ania, of the terrible sacrifice her matka had made, of the liquidating of the ghetto.

Elżbieta pleaded with Rosa to hide in their home, to let Elżbieta feed her, clothe her. But Rosa would not risk their lives further, and she'd made a vow. She would delay only for a much-needed bath, a meal, a night's sleep before begging—demanding—that Dr. Leja send her through the sewers to find her Itzhak.

◆

It was November—just before the freezing time—when Rosa reached the outskirts of Vilna.

The Lejas had done all they could to prepare her, to obtain a guide through the sewers, but they couldn't guarantee anything—least of all the cratered, guarded miles to Vilna—or provide protection against the Poles willing to turn Jews over to the Germans or the Germans too eager to shoot a Jew or rape a woman with no risk of reprisal. The food and funds the Lejas had given her, the cigarettes to barter, the new clothes and coat to keep her warm had long been sold or ruined. But she was within sight of her Itzhak's destination, and surely that counted for everything. She wished she could be clean again, her hair washed and curled, her face not so pale and drawn, but she knew Itzhak would love her, would be relieved to see her.

Please, Adonai, help him understand that I did the best I knew how for our Ania. She is safer wherever she is than she would be in the ghetto . . . if there is still a ghetto.

Mile after mile, Rosa had rehearsed her explanation for Itzhak. She believed he would understand, that they would plan together how to find safety, how to find Ania after the war, how and where to rebuild their lives. Whether her husband's parents would understand her decisions, Rosa dared not guess. She only knew that Itzhak must be on the other side of Vilna's ghetto wall, and she would find him.

She'd hidden in a culvert until dusk, when factory workers dragged through the streets, returning from their mandatory employment. Filthy and thin, but no more so than they, she slipped into their ranks. Keeping her head down, she followed them through the gates and onto Kwaszelna Street, where the workers were counted at the end of the workday, and marveled at how much easier it was for a Jew to slip into a ghetto than to steal out of one. The Germans cared only if their number was short. One more was nothing.

She didn't know the hour of Vilna's curfew, but couldn't imagine it far away. She needed to find the Dunovich family quickly, and little time did not afford niceties. She knocked on the first door of the second street she came to. The occupant pulled the remnants of a newspaper aside at the window but did not open the door.

"Dunovich?"

The face returned a blank stare.

"Dunovich!" Rosa closed the space between her mouth and the window. "Do you know where the Dunovich family lives?" she all but shouted.

The face shook its head and dropped the paper covering over the window.

Rosa clamped her mouth, returned to the street, and kept her eyes fixed on the cobblestones, not wanting to draw attention, fearful of German guards finding her out alone. She tried six houses down, and six across—this time no shouting. She tried the next street, and two over from that. The streets emptied, doors closed, windows covered by newspaper, worn curtains, or blankets. Curfew had surely fallen. The temperature plummeted with the sun.

It was one thing to find a sleeping place in a barn, even a ditch, covered by grasses and the threadbare coat she still wore. But empty streets—and nothing to shield her from the eyes of roaming patrols—were something else . . . something to fear. And what of the morning? First light would expose her fully.

She walked on until she could walk no more. Why had she thought she could simply stroll into the ghetto, ask, and be ushered into the arms of her husband? Now, in the cold and emptied streets, she saw her folly. Not everyone would know everyone else—no more here than in Warsaw. Refugees had flocked to the city in the early days of the war. Now the ghetto was filled with people from every town and even dialects that differed as night from day. Rosa had hardly known her neighbors.

She knocked softly on the next door she came to, praying they would have pity and take her in for the night—to sleep in a corner, just until morning when she would continue her search. There would be no food, but perhaps a little water. *Just a small drink of water.*

◆ ◆ ◆

It was only later that Rosa remembered strong arms lifting her, carrying her through a darkened doorway. Somewhere at the edge of memory she knew someone had smoothed the hair from her forehead, pressed a cool cloth there, and slipped a spoon of warm broth into her mouth.

Matka. She remembered thinking her mother there, yet knew that was not right, could not be true. She didn't remember why that could not be true. Consciousness faded in and out, oblivion a warm blanket.

That had been late November. Over the next few days, word had spread through the ghetto until it reached the ears of Pani Dunovich, Itzhak's mother, and her grown daughters. By the time her sister-in-law led her to the Dunovich ghetto apartment, Rosa could walk again.

CHAPTER TWENTY-NINE

IN JANUARY 1943, Sophie and the few students remaining in her class were warned to disperse and, avoiding streets near the ghetto, go quickly home whenever word came of the next roundup.

The word came one cold morning later in the month, just as Sophie reached the climax of *King Matt the First*.

"Can't you finish before we go? How will we wait another week to learn what happens?" Ivan, the youngest, objected.

Sophie knew they dared not wait. She was tempted to give the book to Ivan's mother and have her return it next week. But based on information Renat had shared, she felt uncertain there would be classes next week, and possessing a book by a Jewish author was a danger too real to allow Ivan or his parents.

"We'll just have to hold on to the suspense," she teased. "I promise I won't lose the book. We'll finish the story next time, even if I read for an hour!"

She waited until the last parent came for their children, then took the long route back to her apartment, avoiding her usual trek by the ghetto wall. Tanks and an unusual number of troops poured through the streets toward the ghetto gates.

Sophie heard later that afternoon that in response to the ŻOB's executions, the SS had swarmed into the ghetto, shooting and rounding up the wild ones—children who lived in the streets, in cellars, in attics, smuggling in and out of the ghetto to survive—most of them orphans. By noon the death march of captives walked four abreast up Zamenhofa Street, toward the *Umschlagplatz*, where they would await transport to Treblinka.

Following the cessation of gunfire in the ghetto, local Poles reappeared on the streets. Some gathered to peer through the gates.

Terri, Sophie knew, had received the same warning to stay home. Sophie crept by Pani Rusnak's door and turned the knob of her friend's apartment.

Terri pulled the door open in a heartbeat. "I'm so glad you've come. I didn't want to be alone."

Pacing and hand-wringing had become the order of the day. Terri switched on the burner beneath the teakettle while Sophie retrieved the pot from the cupboard and tea leaves from the shelf beside the stove. But she dropped the metal canister to the floor, her nerves stretched taut. "Sorry. I'm all thumbs." Sophie pushed damp hair from her forehead, not realizing until then that she'd been sweating. "The ŻOB—what do you think they're planning?"

Terri shook her head. "Renat didn't say. That frightens me more than knowing. He looked so . . . so final."

"Don't imagine things. The reality will be hard enough." Sophie had meant it as a good-natured chide, but she could see the tears her friend fought to hide. *She's scared to death. She loves him. She knows Piotr is never coming back, and she loves Renat. How is it I never noticed? Why would they do that—fall in love—in the midst of war, when life looms more uncertain each new day? Then, why wouldn't they? Wouldn't love for a little while be better than never loving?*

She thought of Janek. He'd been gone so long . . . What she wouldn't give for an hour, a day with him. At least that's what she'd told herself for months on end. Now, she could barely remember the sound of his voice. Sometimes it was difficult to remember his eyes, the shape of his mouth, now that she no longer possessed so much as a photograph of her beloved.

When the kettle whistled, Terri, hands shaking, swished hot water in the bottom of the teapot to warm it. Sophie took the kettle from her. She spooned in tea leaves, covered them with boiling water, and gave the pot a stir. She wrapped a tea towel around the pot to keep it warm and pulled Terri to the table.

"Renat is smart—so quick and clever. He's careful."

"That's no guarantee. Nothing is guaranteed," Terri insisted.

Sophie could not contradict her. She could only cover her friend's hand with her own, and wait.

It wasn't long before the first pistol shots and grenade blasts broke out in the street—a cacophony of panicked screams and explosions, the irregular pounding of boots hitting cobblestones, punctuated by the staccato return of rifle fire.

Sophie held firm while her friend vise-gripped her hand and tears coursed down her cheeks. The tea grew cold.

◆

The next four days unfolded as a living, breathing nightmare for Warsaw, inside and outside the ghetto. Sophie and Terri, as well as many other residents, remained at home, behind locked doors, as the fighting inside the ghetto increased.

Renat stopped by Terri's apartment one night while Sophie was there. How he got in the building and past the superintendent, Sophie could not imagine.

"How—how can you hold out against the Germans, with all their guns and grenades?"

"We use the weapons we've captured and others we've made and collected—knives, steel pipes, petrol bombs, homemade grenades, clubs, our bare hands—to kill as many Germans as possible. This is our chance, our time to stand against them. This is our moment to say we will not be led as sheep to slaughter." Sophie saw the determination, the grit and pride in the pulling back of his shoulders. "We saved some of the children they'd rounded up. Those Jews, at the very least, never made it to the *Umschlagplatz*. They didn't go to Treblinka."

Not yet, Sophie thought, but wouldn't say it aloud. The cost in lives to save lives had been dear, but hailed as worth every sacrifice. Sophie understood the desire to fight, to stand, to not roll over and die . . . but she could only believe there would be one ending to the tale.

Still, as the days went by and the ghetto remained off-limits to Aryans, she heard sporadic cheers erupt from inside, spilling over the wall to a stunned and somewhat respectful Polish populace. Though outmanned and outgunned by the Germans, the ŻOB had accomplished something most Jews and even Poles had not dreamed possible. For the first time, Germans feared chasing Jews into the ghetto's attics or basements, and the Germans, for all the anti-Semitism in Warsaw, were a common enemy.

"That," Terri confided, "is the first bit of solidarity the city has shown for the Jews. It's about time. They're calling it the January Uprising. Renat said the Jews are fortifying bunkers, preparing for a long siege. And since they've started fighting, the smuggling of weapons into the ghetto has increased."

"But the gates are closed—no one in, no one out, but Germans. How do they get in?"

Terri shrugged. "The sewers."

◆

February passed. The winds of March swept the streets of Warsaw as cold as the deepest part of winter.

From the time of the January Uprising, Sophie and Terri had used every resource they knew to smuggle food into the starving ghetto. Children had long become the principal carriers of smuggled food. Families depended on their ability to sneak in and out of the ghetto. Those children who had no families became streetwise, canny. Many such children had been rounded up by patrols, but there were still wild ones surviving any way they could.

Under cover of darkness, undernourished children squirmed or slipped sideways through holes chiseled into the wall—holes they covered and camouflaged or filled with loose bricks during the day. On the Aryan side of the city they retrieved small food caches left by sympathetic Poles or stole from shops or grocers or houses that left their doors unlocked. They raided the dumpsters of restaurants and hotels—if starving Poles had not reached them first.

But the Germans caught on and bricked every hole in the wall. Now, homeless children were driven to the sewers to live and traverse the city. Beneath the streets, in the convoluted labyrinth of stinking tunnels deep with sewage, there stood no ghetto wall.

One bitter cold March night, when Sophie could not sleep, she drew back her curtain. Outside her apartment, a movement in the middle of the street caught her eye. She squinted to better see by light of the half-moon. A manhole cover shifted. Small bodies, eight or possibly ten, scrambled out and disappeared into the darkness. The last one replaced the manhole cover before melting into the night.

The next day, Sophie met Terri for their weekly coffee visit at one of the few operating cafés. Sophie waited until the two women behind them had paid their bill and left before sharing what she'd seen the night before. "They can't come out in droves like that. They'll be caught. Is there any way to get word to them to spread out more? There's not enough legal food on our street, let alone black-market, for that many children to steal in one night."

Terri set her cup down and stared into its bottom. "They're not stealing food. They're getting out through the sewers—running away. We're finding as many urgent care homes as we can. But there simply are not enough, and not enough convents or orphanages or homes able to take them." She closed her eyes, rubbing them wearily. "There's no more time. They're going to finish liquidating the ghetto soon. Most are ready to die trying to escape rather than wait for the Germans to come and get them."

"We? You said 'we.'" Sophie could not help but feel annoyed. Terri had never told her the full extent of her work. Sophie knew she was involved with the underground in more ways than she'd shared. Apparently that had more to do with the rescue of children, but what exactly did it mean?

Now the clandestine work Sophie had done seemed minimal. She'd helped, yes, but whom had she saved? The Bukowskis were dead. The classes she'd taught were no more. The most she was doing was helping to collect milk and get it to a house near the wall where the owner had rigged a pipe that flowed inside the ghetto. Milk for the children—though more died each day, their corpses piled high with others carried on the wagon that daily trekked through the ghetto to retrieve dead bodies.

She'd believed that she and Terri were soul sisters of the heart, yet Terri had not shared this most vital information. Sophie had not pushed her, fearing that her friend was already involved over her head and that talking would convict her to risk further dangerous exploits. Now, she knew there was no point. "Let me take some. You know I'll take care of them."

"I know Pani Rusnak would report you—both of us—in a heartbeat. She's *Volksdeutsche*, you know. I'm sure she collaborated with the Germans to denounce the Cibalskis downstairs. You remember the day our building was raided? They were arrested, suspected of hiding or helping Jews, then shipped off to a labor camp . . . at least that's what they said. And now, with rewards for denunciation increased . . ." Terri shook her head. "I saw her wearing a new coat. How do you think she got it?"

Sophie closed her eyes. Terri was right. She'd lived on her own too long to suddenly manufacture a son or daughter, or a niece or nephew, or a cousin's child from the country. The risk would not only be to her, but to the child.

Not if I move to a section of Warsaw where I'm not known . . . if I obtain a new identity . . . a new job . . . a new life. "The underground can find me a new place. They did before. Tell Renat that I need new papers. I'll take as many children as they bring me."

"You're barely passing for Catholic or Polish now. I don't think you'd make the best urgent care facility."

"Then make me a long-term care facility. Hide me away in some dark place. You know I'd be perfect. There must be some way to supply me with enough money to stay home with the children. Others are doing it, right?"

Terri nodded. "Żegota."

"What's that?"

Terri leaned further forward, as if studying a spot on the table linen. "An organization Jolanta works through—made up of Jews and non-Jews who supply funds to help support Jews in hiding and those who will save them. You wouldn't lack for essential funds, but you don't know what you're saying, Sophie. The risk—I promised Papa. He promised Janek—"

"They're not here, and I am! Stop trying to protect me."

"The underground knows you, knows where you are now."

Sophie snorted. "That doesn't make me—or you—safer, does it? Anyone dragged off to be tortured could give us all up in a moment."

"Yes, but it does mean that they know where you are if word comes from Janek. If you move now, no one—"

Sophie threw up her hands in frustration. "Janek may be dead, Terri. You know that as well as I do. He's not going to suddenly appear in Warsaw, even if he's alive. But I am alive, and I want my life to count for something!" It was all she could do to keep her voice down.

She'd prayed and wept night after night, month after month, longing for Janek. But when the year turned over on itself again—more than three years since she'd heard from him—something inside her had broken. She still had no information, no sense that he was either alive or gone. In fact, she felt almost nothing, as if that part of her life—life with her husband before the war—was some other woman's story.

All she knew was that she needed to move on, to continue living, or she would die inside the shell of her body. "The underground will know my new identity, my new address. If they ever need to reach me, they'll find me. I'd be a good mother to the children. . . . You know that, don't you?"

Terri sat across from her in silence. Sophie could see the struggle in her friend's shoulders. Her help was needed. Surely that must count as much as Terri's promise to her father.

At long last Terri lifted her chin, her eyes resting in worried resignation on Sophie's. "I'll miss you, my friend, being just down the hallway."

CHAPTER THIRTY

THE LAST SNOW MELTED, and Vilna's ghetto drowned in a sea of March mud. Now that the freezing was past, young men ran into the forests to join the partisans, to save themselves from the all-too-common whippings by police.

Rumors of purges in Białystok and Grodno raced through the streets, increasing fear and trepidation. Still the ghetto swelled with women and children from other regions brought by force and by choice, as if Vilna were safe, as if it might provide sanctuary.

But the women in the Dunovich apartment knew better.

"They're taking caravans and trains of people out," Talia, Itzhak's sister, whispered into Rosa's ear.

Rosa shrugged her away. She didn't want to hear. She knew that the trains from Warsaw disappeared, that the reports of liquidation rumored death. She could not think about that now, not again.

Rosa's strength had returned only enough to plow through each day, to relieve her mother-in-law and sisters-in-law of just enough burden to make them willing to share their rations with her. It was no small thing to feed one more mouth, and Rosa made certain they knew she was grateful. Staying strong, alive, was the only hope she had of finding Itzhak . . . sometime, somewhere.

Whatever fears Rosa had harbored of the opinions of her once-proud, officious mother-in-law dissipated on the first day. A tiny, broken woman had replaced the disapproving officer of the home. She knew her daughters and grandchildren, and sometimes she knew Rosa, but she rarely spoke, seemed not to have the energy to speak.

According to her daughters, Itzhak's mother had begun losing her will to live the day her husband was taken, along with their husbands.

For months the younger women had tried to discover where their husbands and father had gone, what the Germans had done with them, but to no avail. It was only through the mercies of a secret courier that they'd eventually learned the whereabouts of their men—Stutthof concentration camp. But that didn't help Rosa.

"I told you," Talia had insisted, "if Itzhak made it anywhere near Vilna, it's likely the Germans picked him up. He may even be in Stutthof with our men for all we know."

"There must be a way to find out. Can't you ask the courier who discovered your Avner?" Rosa had asked.

Talia closed her eyes and turned away.

Rosa clamped her lips, determined not to cry. There was nothing Talia could do—Rosa knew this. But she begged, cajoled day after day. It had become as much a litany as anything, a way to pass the interminable hours. Rosa knew the answer. The courier had been found out and shot in the street as an example to others. But in her weakness, in her desperation, sometimes she forgot that and asked again and again.

It was easy to forget things when you were hungry, when the veil between sleep and daylight fogged. In those half-asleep moments, day and night, Rosa dreamed of Ania, imagined that she cradled her precious daughter in her arms. Sometimes Talia pinched her arm to wake her, for she'd sing Ania's favorite lullaby in her sleep.

If only I could stay asleep. If only I could sleep and never wake up. Yet even in those moments Rosa knew she dared not give up. Giving up meant giving up on Itzhak and Ania. Giving up meant Matka had sacrificed in vain.

Late March brought more Jews—mostly old women and hordes of children—from surrounding ghettos in the process of liquidation. Jews from Oszmiana brought food—potatoes, meat, flour, even honey, which no one in Vilna had seen for ages. Before the precious food could be begged or bartered, Germans confiscated most and the best—all of the flour. What was left was quickly stolen by desperate men, hungry men. And then more people came, with nothing—Jews from Michaliszki and Święciany. Starvation set in in earnest.

The trains began pulling out again in April. Eighty-three train cars crammed with nearly four thousand people who'd been promised a future, a better life upon resettlement in Kovno, went first. Willingly, eagerly, they said good-bye to Vilna. But the cars returned too quickly, empty, and few in the ghetto held any illusions.

Murer, the German in charge, acted as if nothing had happened, nothing was amiss.

A few days later, nine who had escaped the massacre resurfaced in Vilna, among them six children. And then twenty-five Jewish policemen were sent to help bury the dead.

All of this Rosa pushed from her heart, from her consciousness, telling herself she could change nothing, could do nothing . . . until the next morning as she neared the gate, picking up scraps of paper to burn for a little heat, a little light. A Lithuanian peasant stood at the gate, pushing a child into the ghetto—a child no bigger than Ania.

Rosa stepped closer, inclining her ear to the guard.

"He's not mine," the peasant asserted. "Found him sitting by those dead bodies in the Ponary Forest, crying his eyes out. Those bodies are your doing, so I suspect you'll know what to do with him. I don't. I can't feed my own children. His family must be here."

The man, gruff and grim of mouth, but with eyes betraying tears, looked away. Rosa was certain the guard knew as well as she that the child had no family—not anymore.

When the guard fingered his revolver, Rosa rushed forward.

"He's mine." She pushed between the two men and scooped the little one into her arms. "I don't know how he got mixed in with those leaving. He must have followed them onto the train."

"Your papers," the German demanded, clearly annoyed by the interruption.

Please, Adonai. Mercy. I beg You for mercy. "I didn't bring them. I'm in the ghetto—why do I need to carry my papers?" It was a foolish and brazen question, but the only way she knew to stall for time. "You took my husband. What more do you want?" She turned and walked away, squeezing the child to her chest so hard that he cried out. Any moment, she was sure to hear the report of the guard's gun, certain she'd slip into nothingness. If she did, she would take this child with her. At least they would die together and he would not be left crying on a heap of corpses.

Rosa's legs trembled, barely supporting her, all the way back to her street. No gunshot sounded; no one followed her. At last she reached their building and set the child on the steps, helping him climb the stairs to their third-floor apartment. When they reached the top stair she sat down, pulled the pencil-thin child onto her lap, and cried.

Finally, Rosa dried her eyes with the hem of her skirt and did her best to wash tearstains from the little boy's cheeks. But he, like she, was dirty, and there was little she could do to conceal the rivulets his tears had made down sunken cheeks. At least he was healthy enough to cry. So many children in the ghetto could no longer do that. His mother must have fed him with her own life's rations. As must Rosa.

Rosa drew a deep and ragged breath, stood, and clasped the small child by the hand. She knew a battle lay before her, but what was one more battle compared to a life?

Help me, Adonai. Help me feed this child as some woman feeds Ania. The prayer stabbed her heart. She clutched the toddler's hand more firmly and pushed open the door.

Her mother-in-law's eyes grazed the child and rose to meet Rosa's. It was a good day for her, Rosa could tell. There was "someone there."

"Ania?"

Rosa's breath caught. "No." She couldn't bring herself to call this woman "Mama," so simply avoided appellations. "I don't know his name. He was discovered—" She stopped. *What good will it do to frighten her, to tell her—to tell any of them—what I know? Where the others went? Where we will all likely go in the days ahead?* "He was separated from his mother when the last train pulled out. He's all alone."

Talia stood at the window but did not even turn to face her. "Why did you bring him here? You know we can't keep him. There is not enough food now."

"You saw him at the gate?"

"I saw you foolishly intervene in whatever took place there. That guard nearly shot you."

Rosa lifted her chin. "I saved his life."

"And who will save yours?"

"I will share my ration with him, just as you share yours with Regina."

"Regina is my daughter. What is this child to you? Nothing. No one."

Rosa felt her heart slam the thin wall of her chest. "He is someone, a life, a child."

Itzhak's mother interrupted quietly, "He is not your Ania. You cannot replace your child with another."

Rosa would not listen to more. If only she could scoop the little boy into her arms and run to another room, another apartment.

But there was nowhere to go. Already fifteen people crowded the two-room living arrangement. So she pulled him into her arms and cradled his head, walked to the corner of the room, and sat with her back against the wall. *At least he's alive . . . and my arms are no longer empty.*

The women in the room turned away from her. Fighting was useless, a waste of limited energy, and for that—for once—Rosa was grateful.

CHAPTER THIRTY-ONE

APRIL SWEPT IN WITH THE promise of spring, but Sophie barely noticed. Raids, day and night, had become the norm and sapped all the strength and focus she could muster.

Before Sophie turned off the light in her new apartment each night, she made certain her small case, beneath her bed, was packed with toiletries and a change of clothing—ready to go, just in case the pounding came at her door, just in case they sent her to a labor camp or prison. Though that, she knew, was wishful thinking.

Word on the streets whispered the real and dreaded procedure. Sophie first heard it from a woman in her office.

"They wait until they believe all the family is at home—usually the middle of the night—then break down the door, drag them into the street, and line them up. First they shoot the father, then the Jewish children they've been hiding . . . then, one by one, the children of the family, leaving the mother until last . . . forcing her to watch each member of her family murdered." The woman hesitated, trying to get control of herself, then whispered, "They leave their bodies in the street, as a warning to others . . . until the morgue wagon comes for them, next day."

Sophie did not doubt the woman's word, did not think she'd exaggerated; she'd witnessed enough SS brutality to overflow her nightmares. The woman was warning her to be careful, without divulging that she suspected her secrets.

Sophie nodded, but could not respond. She prayed desperately that no one else in the office knew, that no one would report her as she fled into the washroom and, shaking, retched into the toilet.

Still, it didn't change the fact that children needed rescue. Families throughout the ghetto who'd long refused to be separated now begged Jolanta to take their children, to save them any way she could. Not only were they starving, but illusions about "relocation" were a thing of the past. There were too many reports of the fast train to death to deny.

Despite Terri's earlier misgivings, Sophie's new apartment immediately became a short-term rescue site by night—a place to scrub sewer grime from small waifs whose arms and legs were little more than sticks. A place to launder their clothes or replace the rags they wore with something—anything—that might get them through the streets to a better location unnoticed. She did her best to teach them the Lord's Prayer, the Magnificat, the rules of Confession and Communion, in case they were stopped and interrogated. Always, they received new names, and both the old and new names were recorded for Jolanta's lists in the hope that children would be reunited with family somewhere after the war, or at least know that they were Jewish.

Sophie might have the children overnight or for three or four days before they were taken to a longer-term care facility—a convent or home where they could be hidden or incorporated more openly into a Polish family.

Each starving, frightened child who came tore at Sophie's heart. Each child who left the temporary shelter of her home broke it a little more.

♦ ◆ ♦

The third week of April, an urgent *rat-a-tat-tat* came to Sophie's door. It wasn't the normal courier coded knock. It surely wasn't the angry pounding of the Gestapo.

Heart in her throat, Sophie stepped close to the door. "Yes? Who's there?"

"It's me," came the whisper. "Please, let me in."

Sophie opened the door immediately and Terri nearly tumbled in, her arms loaded with bags and a bundle.

"Close the door."

Sophie didn't need to be asked twice. She and Terri had absolutely agreed they would not go to each other's apartment now that Sophie possessed a new identity and new address. The risk of being followed, if suspected, was too great. Only some peril could have brought her, and Terri was either dizzy with weakness or shaking in fear. "What's wrong? What are you doing here?"

"Help me unload."

Sophie removed the string bags and heavy, overstuffed purse from Terri's shoulders, but Terri kept the hefty bundle in her arms.

"I'm in trouble. Can you peek out the window and see if anyone is there? I don't think I was followed, but I can't be sure. I'm so, so sorry."

Sophie stepped quickly to the side of the front window and peeked behind the drapery. She scanned the sidewalk, the corners, the shops across the street, the alley—as much as she could see. Then she casually walked to the other side of the window and did the same, scanning the other direction. "No one. At least, no one looks like they're watching the building or standing around. What's going on?"

Terri sighed heavily, relieved or exhausted—Sophie couldn't tell which.

"Sit down and tell me."

But Terri ignored the offer of a seat on the sofa and sat on the floor, placing her bundle between her legs. It was a large cloth sack, like something in which you might carry potatoes or grain. She untied the top and folded it down, revealing a head of dark-brown curls, tucked into its small chest and fast asleep.

"A child!" Sophie reached for the tousled head and stroked damp curls from the little one's forehead. "She's beautiful!"

Terri's chest still heaved as she tried to catch her breath.

"Let me get you some water . . . some tea?"

"Water . . . I can't stay. I'm so sorry to ask this, but I don't know what else to do."

"Anything. I'll do anything. You know that."

Tears pooled in Terri's eyes. "It's Pani Rusnak."

"That nosy old woman!" Sophie handed Terri the water and returned to the floor beside the sleeping child.

"I think she's reported me."

Sophie felt the world spin. "How do you know? What happened?"

"The woman who took over your apartment . . . she's been taking in children. Someone reported her—accused her of hiding Jewish children in her home. Someone tipped her off that the Gestapo was coming. She got them all away before the Gestapo came, except this one." Terri closed her eyes as if reliving the nightmare. "They stormed the building. Just before they reached our floor, she pounded on my door and pushed the baby into my arms, begging me to take her. She said to get her to Jolanta, and she ran back to her apartment."

"That doesn't mean they'll suspect you!"

Terri swallowed and breathed deeply. "Just as she ran back to her apartment, I saw Pani Rusnak's door close. It must have been open just a tiny bit. I can't be sure, but I think she heard. I think she heard everything. If she did . . . she may have been the one to report that poor woman."

"You can stay here . . . absolutely." Sophie began to tick through her mind how best to accommodate Terri and the child. They could have her bed. She would sleep on the sofa.

"No—you don't understand. I have to return to my apartment, or else I'll look guilty. I have to go about a normal life—no risks for a time—until things calm down."

"You can't go back there! You know what they'll do if—"

But Terri was vehement. "I need you to take this little girl, to keep her until Jolanta contacts you and finds her a safer place. If my neighbor—I don't even know her name—is released, I can come get her and return her . . . but it might be best if we wait a few days. I don't think she will be released." Sophie saw the worry in Terri's eyes. "I don't want to give anyone else your address, but Jolanta knows where you live. As soon as I can, I'll tell her you have the child. Can you manage her? You'll have to pretend she's yours, or make up some story why you have her if anyone besides me or Jolanta or someone from the network comes."

"Of course—anything. I'm no longer working in the office. Jolanta's providing me with enough to stay home and help the children smuggled out. Żegota's being supplied with tons of money to provide for the children—just not enough safe homes to take them."

Terri nodded. "Right. I know. Good. That's good you're here."

"I don't like this. . . . I mean, I'm glad to take the little girl, but I don't think you should go back. I'm frightened for you."

"I'm frightened too." Terri's hands shook. "But the sooner I get back and appear normal, without a child in my apartment, the more convincing I can be, if arrested." She stroked the head of the little girl. "Her name is Ania. That's all I know. I don't even know if that's her Jewish name or the Aryan name they gave her. My neighbor said she gave her a sip of Luminal to make her fall asleep. I think she'd hoped to hide her, then thought better of it. It should wear off soon." Terri's eyes softened as she stroked the little girl's arm. "She'll be frightened when she wakes up."

"I'll do my best." Sophie could not help that her heart yearned toward the little girl.

Terri smiled through her sadness and worry. "You're a great mother. I know."

Sophie swallowed the lump in her throat as her friend stood to go.

"Oh!" Terri slapped her head. "I can't believe I didn't give you this right away." She pulled a creased and somewhat worse for wear sepia-toned photograph from her pocket. "Renat brought it to me last night. He was looking for you."

Sophie had to hold it beneath the lamp to see the faces: four men in RAF pilot uniforms—uniforms with Polish insignia—smiling, as if congratulating one another. Sophie studied each face in the picture a moment before they came into focus. Her breath caught before one face in particular registered in her brain. *Could it be?* "Janek! It's Janek!"

Terri's eyes filled as she laughed with her friend.

"What does this mean?"

"Renat said it means he's alive—they're all alive and flying with the RAF in England. It came in with a courier bringing money for Żegota. It's their way of letting us know. They're trying to locate family members of each of the pilots to show them, to let them know the men are alive. So far, you're the only one they've found."

"Janek? In England?" Her head spun with the joy that he was alive and the irony that he was at her home—in England—and she was here, living in his Poland. She felt the need to sit down, to shout, to sing, to ask if it was real.

"I'm sorry . . . but I have to take the photograph back. They want it to show the families of the other pilots."

"No!" Sophie could not let it go. Not to have it, not to touch it and see it, would seem that it was unreal—a dream she couldn't hold, a thing that had never happened. But of course the other wives, the mothers and fathers, would want to know, to see that their men were alive. "I'm sorry. I don't know what I'm saying. Let me look—just one more minute." *Let me memorize his face, his smile, the way his hair falls across his forehead. He looks well—anxious, but well. Thank You, God! He's alive! Janek is alive!*

Gently, Terri tugged the photograph from her fingers. "I'm sorry. I have to go."

"Yes, yes, I know. Thank you. I don't know how to thank you, Terri—for everything. Be careful, my friend. Be so very careful."

Terri nodded. She reached for the doorknob, hesitated, then turned. "Don't worry. I will never give you away. Be safe. Find Janek, when this awful war is over. Be happy, dear friend."

Sophie smiled, nodding through her own tears, accepting the blessing and love of her friend. But everything in her resisted the horrible resignation in Terri's eyes.

◆

While the room darkened, Sophie's heart pounded as she thought of Janek. From the photograph he hadn't changed—perhaps a little thinner, a little more muscular, a little tired or worried around the eyes. But his smile was just the same. *And he's alive! Alive! Oh, Janek, to find you again. To be with you, to feel your arms around me.*

Memories flooded her mind—memories she hadn't allowed herself to relive in months, in years. But now she reenvisioned their last walk by the Vistula, two days before he'd left for what seemed forever. They'd picnicked late in the day in the shade of a grove of linden trees.

They'd packed a quilted coverlet that Sophie had brought with them from England, a wedding gift from her friend Carrie. It had seemed frivolous to spread it on the ground, to risk grass stains on the keepsake, but Sophie had wanted everything to be perfect, a beautiful day to remember in every sense. They'd watched the sun go down and couples, walking arm in arm, leave the path, headed for home.

As the stars came out, Janek flicked a match and lit the lantern they'd brought. Sophie poured tea for them both from a flask and arranged small sandwiches—bread and cheese and ham, or had it been beef tongue? She'd cut apple slices and pulled apart the segments of an orange, arranging everything on small plates . . . just so.

Janek smiled, and she knew he enjoyed watching her. With one hand she'd smoothed her hair, swept up into a chignon, and spread her dress prettily around her, covering her toes. The fingers of her other hand were still sticky from the orange. She looked for a napkin, but Janek lifted her hand, kissed her fingers, and slowly, lovingly, licked each one, and then her palm.

She remembered how her heart had raced, the sensation flooding her body. Janek turned down the wick of the lantern and led her to the far side of the coverlet, away from the midnight tea, readied and spread so daintily across one corner. They'd been married three years, but when he gently pulled her to him, beneath the stars that came out one by one, it seemed like the first time. They'd slept in each other's arms, wrapped in the coverlet, until morning. And then they'd laughed to drink cold tea and eat dried-bread sandwiches for breakfast.

Sophie heaved a great sigh, a longing for the reality of that memory. For so long she'd thought all her life, all her love with Janek was a thing of the past, hidden as surely as she'd first hidden his photograph in uniform, before being forced to leave it behind. She remembered how she'd folded it away like a cherished linen, tucked in a drawer—saved, but not used and seldom remembered. Even that was given up when she enlisted in the underground. Now, as improbable as it seemed, to learn that he was alive . . . it was almost too much. She'd savor the knowledge a bit at a time, and she'd dare to hope—just a little—for their future.

But now she must think of the child before her. As Terri had said, she would surely be frightened when she woke.

Sophie turned on a lamp to help chase away the darkness, and so she could get a better look at the sleeping child. The little girl appeared to be somewhere around two years of age—a few months younger than the child she and Janek might have had. She searched the little one's head for lice and her limbs for signs of bruising. There were none, and she was clean, which meant she had probably been well treated, though she was pitifully thin. But then, every child coming out of the ghetto was malnourished.

Sophie wondered how long it had been since the child had actually been with her mother, what she would remember, what she might know, what she might have endured.

There was something around the little girl's neck . . . a delicate gold chain holding an unusual pendant or medallion—or part of a medallion, as if someone had cut one in half and filed the edges. It looked like half a tree, too big for such a tiny child. Something from her family? Sophie didn't know, but tucked it back inside the little girl's neckline.

Ania squirmed. She pushed the blanket Sophie had placed over her off with her feet and stretched in her sleep, arms overhead, small hands clenched into fists. She rolled from side to side, then lay very still, her hands tucked beneath her cheek. At last she opened her eyes. It took a moment before she seemed to register her surroundings.

Sophie waited.

The child sat up, took one look at Sophie, and screamed. She pulled back against the sofa, huddled into a crouched kitten position, and wailed over and over for her mamusia, even fighting when Sophie reached for her, trying to hold and calm her.

Sophie had had no experience with screaming children. The children she'd worked with so far—Judah Bukowski, the underground classes, the children smuggled through the sewers—had all been older, and all seemed glad to see her and grateful for her help. Sometimes they were afraid, mistrustful, reticent, but they'd never screamed as if she were beating them. She couldn't afford to bring nosy neighbors to her door.

"You must be hungry." Sophie tried to speak calmly, but still the child cried. "Would you like something to eat?"

Ania's screams decreased to whimpers.

Thankfully, Sophie still had an apple, left over from her week's shopping. She sat the little girl on a blanket on the kitchen floor and let her watch as she cut up slices of juicy red apple. Ania's eyes widened. Sophie drizzled the slices with honey and set the plate on the blanket before her. "This is for you, Ania. Eat. Enjoy." Sophie sat on a chair at the table, giving the child space, hoping she would feel free to reach for the treat.

Ania's sniffles subsided. She looked up with enormous brown orbs framed in dark lashes, eyes too big for her tiny face.

"Yes, it's for you." Sophie smiled.

Ania looked longingly at the fruit, then up at Sophie again, clearly trying to discern if she was truly allowed or if this was some kind of trick.

The fear in her eyes smote Sophie's heart. "It's yours, sweetheart. It's all for you."

Still, Ania didn't reach out. Sophie knelt on the floor beside the blanket. Ania scooted away. "I don't mean to frighten you. See, watch me." She took a bite of the apple and smiled. "Mmmmm. So good!" She held out the plate. "Want some? We can share."

Ania blinked. Still wary, but with little pink tongue moistening her lips, she drew closer. At last she reached for an apple slice, her worried eyes glancing up at Sophie. But Sophie nodded in approval.

When at last Ania lifted the fruit to her lips and licked the honey, it was all Sophie could do not to laugh out loud in pleasure at the little girl's reaction. Perhaps it was the first time she'd tasted anything truly sweet. Her pale cheeks took on a pink hue, and she looked up at Sophie in surprise.

Sophie smiled again and said, "Mmmm. Good! Linden flower honey."

Ania took a bite of the apple, clearly another new sensation to her teeth, on her tongue. Sophie didn't have to offer the plate again. Ania reached for slice after slice. Near the end, both tiny fists grasped slices, honey dribbling sticky from her palms, cheeks puffed out to a more natural, childlike shape. When she'd licked every last taste from her hands, Ania looked up, her eyes daring to hope.

"I don't have any more, but in a little while I'll make our tea. You'll like that, too. Best to give your tummy a little while to get used to things."

Ania blinked, this time in understanding, and Sophie's heart melted.

CHAPTER THIRTY-TWO

THE NEXT *AKTION* CAME TO Vilna in mid-April—a week before Passover. The Kovno powers that be refused, at the last minute, to take the influx of Jews from Vilna. A few hid within the ghetto. More young people, the strong ones, escaped into the forest to join the partisans. But most, having no more will to fight and no more food to live, were led to the train. This time the Gestapo made no pretense of resettlement for those loaded into railroad cars. A rail worker revealed that the train had been given only enough oil to go as far as the Ponary Forest.

Men and women barely met the eyes of those beside them.

Rosa's mother-in-law struggled to her feet and allowed her daughters to help her down the apartment steps. Arm in arm, they walked to the train, a trembling wall of support for one another. Rosa wanted to urge her nieces to run to the forest, to follow the older teens, but the girls were too young and their mothers huddled them close.

Perhaps it is best. At least we will all die together. Who knows what awaits young girls in the forest? It didn't bear thinking about.

Rosa pulled the little boy she'd rescued to her chest. He lacked the strength to walk and she needed to feel his heart next to her own. He'd not spoken a word since she'd pulled him from the guard's arms a few weeks ago. She didn't know his name—his given name or his family's name. What did it matter now?

There'd been moments over the last weeks when she'd called him Ania. It was not that she meant to replace her daughter, and not that she meant to recast the very real child before her. It was simply a slip into memory, a hope, a prayer that her daughter was loved and held as she loved and held this small child. *Survive this horror, my daughter. Grow strong and well. Know who you are and that you were loved more than my life, more than your papa's life. Please, Adonai, care for her. Give her family—a mother and father. Somehow, someday, let her know I loved her. Let her know she is a child of Israel—but only when it's safe . . . if it is ever safe.*

Rosa pulled herself and the child onto the train and pushed toward the wall, hoping to steady herself and the boy before the crush of people knocked her off balance. She'd heard of the Ponary Forest but never been there. Itzhak had spoken of his years, as a child and teen, of camping and hiking amid the towering evergreens, of the beauty of the place. He'd said he knew the trails like the palm of his hand, that it was the place in all the world where he'd felt most clean, most sure of himself and his future.

We never expected our future to end there, my love. I'm glad it's a beautiful place. When I close my eyes for the last time, I will see your face.

Rosa fingered the half medallion beneath her dress. It hung lower now that she'd lost weight. She remembered the day Itzhak had placed it around her neck. She remembered every word of their vows.

In her mind, Itzhak held her face in his hands. *"I am my beloved's, and my beloved is mine. Rise up, my love, my fair one, and come away. For, lo, the winter is past, the rain is over and gone. . . ."* And then he turned her, so gently, and she felt his fingers fasten the chain around her neck. *"I give you this ring, my wife, with no adornment, its symbol eternal. And I give you this medallion, for you and for our children's children—"*

The train lurched to a stop even as Rosa's heart lurched in memory—the great hope of children fulfilled in Ania; the medallion she'd cut in half, carefully filing the edges so it would not cut their daughter's chest, and how she'd placed it around her slim and fragile neck.

The Tree of Life, Itzhak! Eternal hope—eternal connection to Adonai—to you and all that was meant to come! I vowed, my husband, to wear it always. And now "always" has come. I'm sorry, my love. I'm sorry I could not save our Ania. I could not save my matka. I cannot save myself.

Wooden doors slid open on steel bars and guards shouted in German, *"Raus! Schnell! Schnell!"* Pulling people from the car, shoving them along, as if going to their deaths would be more final for their hurry.

In the pushing and shoving, Rosa lost sight of Itzhak's mother, of his sisters and their daughters. She clung to the child in her arms, even as the guard at the door tried to jerk him away.

Shoot me here! You will not have this child! She could not understand why no words poured from her mouth. They screamed inside her head. But the guard shoved her on. She stumbled, fell, cradled the little one against her neck. This time he didn't cry. His eyes were open. *Do you remember, my darling, that you were here before? If I could hide you, make you live . . .*

And then the words around her blurred her own. Words, prayers whispered or spoken aloud, a jumble of dialects, but they all began with the Shema: "Hear, O Israel, the Lord is our God, the Lord is One. Blessed be the name of the glory of His kingdom forever and ever. You shall love the Lord your God with all your heart, with all your soul, and with all your might. And these words which I command you today shall be upon your heart. You shall teach them thoroughly to your children, and you shall speak of them when you sit in your house and when you walk on the road. . . ."

Rosa swallowed and began, whispering into the ear of the waif in her arms. "Hear, O Israel, the Lord is our God, the Lord is One. Blessed be the name—"

"Schnell! Schnell!" With his riding crop, the guard struck the backs of women walking too slowly.

Rosa hurried, stumbled, picked herself up, followed as quickly as she could the running Jews in front of her. *Don't beat this child. Don't beat this child!*

Before she realized the change in terrain they were there, herded into a single line around the edge of a huge crater in the earth—a crater full of dead bodies, skewed limbs. The rising stink made her gag. How had she not noticed it before? Her heart slammed the walls of her chest, pulsed in her brain. The little boy whimpered, burying his head into her neck. She clung to him, tears running down her cheeks.

And then the rhythm of those surrounding her took hold. Haltingly, she joined the chant. "The Lord is my shepherd; I shall not want—I shall not want. He maketh me to lie down in green pastures: He leadeth me beside the still waters. He restoreth my soul: He leadeth me in the paths of righteousness for His name's sake. Yea, though I walk through the valley of the shadow of death, I will fear no evil—"

Gunfire exploded on the far end of the line. Few screams rent the air, the thud of bodies falling into the crater behind the only response.

"For Thou art with—"

CHAPTER THIRTY-THREE

THE DAYS PASSED, and Terri did not come. April became May. The days of May melted into one another. Sophie kept Ania indoors for the most part but opened her window wide each day so they could sit on the floor beneath it and take in the sunshine.

During those long mornings, Sophie read storybooks to Ania, the very ones she'd read to the young children in her classes. She taught Ania to count, to color, and the names of those colors . . . though the little girl already knew the names of most. She pointed out a rainbow one day, much to Ania's delight. Gradually, the fear in Ania's eyes faded. The day wariness was replaced by light in the brown orbs came unexpectedly, over nothing in particular. But it was in that moment, when Ania looked up at her with gladness and pleasure, with a twinkle in her eyes, that Sophie knew she could not give the child up . . . at least she could not give her up without ripping apart her heart.

To be on the safe side, Sophie deemed it best to give Ania a new name.

"Karolina," Sophie tutored the little girl. "Your name is Karolina, and you are my daughter. I am your mother." She hated drilling the child in falsehood, in an assumed identity that would likely be torn away at any moment, but saving her life—both their lives—must take priority. "You are three years old." Sophie knew that was a stretch, but these were difficult times, and though Ania was small, she was particularly articulate; she could pass for the age Sophie's own child would have been, had he or she lived. Whether she'd learned so much vocabulary from her birth mother or from the Polish woman who'd cared for her, Sophie didn't know, but Ania—Karolina—was certainly bright and quick to learn. With the scarcity and cost of food, children everywhere—Jewish and Gentile—tended to look younger than they were, undernourished or underdeveloped for their age. Their wizened faces and eyes told a different story.

"Pretty name," Ania whispered.

Sophie's heart swelled. "Yes, yes, it is." It was the name she and Janek had picked to name their baby, if the baby had been a girl. "Charlotte was my mother's name. It means 'feminine' and 'free.'" She smiled. "Karolina is the Polish form of Charlotte."

Ania blinked up at her, as if waiting to hear more.

"That simply means, should anyone ask, that you were named for my mother, your grandmother." Sophie felt the stab of wishing for her own child, the pain of revealing something so deeply personal— a wish, a hope, a dream, a part of herself that only Janek knew, and Janek was not there. She feared she would regret giving Ania her chosen name—not that she couldn't still use the name if she one day had a child of her own, but it was giving away something sacred.

And yet, what if she didn't have a child? Wasn't this the perfect opportunity to honor her mother's memory, to pass on her cherished name? Her mother had not lived to become a grandmother; this way her name continued . . . at least for now.

"I like Charlotte best. My name is Charlotte."

Sophie squeezed the little girl's hand. "Charlotte it is. But here in Poland, it must be Karolina. Okay? The day we are truly free, I will call you Charlotte . . . I promise."

The child smiled.

Sophie hoped it was a promise she could keep.

As the days ticked by, the fighting in the ghetto continued—it could be heard all over Warsaw. No more children were brought for short-term care, or for any care. No word came from Jolanta, and no courier gave the coded tap on Sophie's door. It was as if the underground world that had so long supported her had disappeared, dried up. What that might mean for her ability to buy food or pay rent frightened Sophie. What it meant for the safety of her friends and the unknown workers terrified her.

Where was Terri, and did anyone else know Ania was in hiding at Sophie's? There was no one she dared contact, no one she dared telephone or track down and question. Going to Terri's apartment was out of the question. If Pani Rusnak had reported Terri, seeing Sophie suddenly reappear, with or without a child, could be disastrous for them both. Sophie didn't know, but she assumed Jolanta and the network had concocted a story that Sophie had been killed in some way or other when she'd disappeared. Her identity had been changed, so she dared not show up in her old neighborhood or at the office where she used to work.

Finally, Sophie had no choice but to take Ania with her when she went to stand for two hours in the breadline. She'd been careful to keep to herself since moving to her new apartment, but she knew that neighbors realized she had a child. Sometimes Ania had nightmares and woke up screaming. In those times Sophie would lift the little girl from her pallet on the floor into her own bed. Sophie stroked her brow, singing softly to her, until Ania fell asleep. Certainly, the neighbors knew of her presence.

Once, when coming out of her apartment, an older woman had

asked if her baby was well, said she'd heard it crying in the night. Sophie smiled and gave the speech she'd prepared. "She's so much better, thank you, but still has some pain that wakes her in the night. She was a sickly baby and spent ever so long in hospital. But she's really coming along now, and I'm so thankful to have her back home. You're kind to ask."

She thought the woman bought her story, was flattered at Sophie's smiling thanks. She knew word of the sickly but recovering child would circulate through the building.

Sophie was new enough in the district that as long as she shopped late in the day, she was not apt to bump into women who stayed at home with their children, women who might notice that suddenly she'd appeared with a child who was never there before. It also meant that the best rations were gone, but she'd have to deal with that for now.

The breadline was a good place to hear the latest street news of the city, and even gossip concerning the ghetto, but she must be careful.

The line inched forward; all the while Sophie prayed that there would still be bread by the time they made it to the front, and cabbage at the greengrocer's. If not, she wasn't sure what she could feed Karolina.

She'd just retrieved her ration of bread and cheese when a woman with a package, her head and most of her face covered in a babushka, stepped close, bumping into her, making them both drop their parcels. Sophie instinctively reached for Karolina's hand and then grabbed her bread. While they were stooped on the ground, the woman shoved a small packet of cash into Sophie's hand and whispered, "Your friend was arrested. Keep the child for now. Jolanta will contact later. Be ready to move."

Stunned, Sophie found herself still groping for her packages after the woman had risen and gone. *Terri! Arrested! Does that mean Pawiak Prison . . . or a labor camp?* She knew it meant interrogation, brutal interrogation. So many people who went into Pawiak never came out. The blood pounded in Sophie's ears.

"Mamusia. Mamusia!" Sophie became aware that Karolina tugged at her coat sleeve. She was still at the child's eye level. "What is this? Is this snow?"

From the sky came wisps . . . white-and-gray wisps floating on the air of the spring day. But it was not cold, not even chilly. The smell of woodsmoke filled the air.

"Ash," she heard a man passing by say to another. "They're burning the ghetto."

Sophie stood, looking up, Karolina's hand still tight in her own. The sky was filled with ash. It floated—like snow—on the breeze and covered everything . . . the tops of awnings, the women standing in the breadline, the few flowers that still grew in the square. She looked down at Karolina, who held her free hand up to the sky, trying to catch the ashes as they fell.

"Snow!" she cried happily. "Like in the storybook!"

It isn't snow, and it's no storybook. It is people, their homes, your family! Sophie wanted to scream. Instead, she swept Karolina into her arms, burying the child's face in her neck, blindly grabbed her parcels, and stumbled, as best she could, back to the apartment.

◆ ◆ ◆

Five weeks after the burning of the Warsaw Ghetto, Sophie ventured toward the wall. In her purse she held the new identity papers delivered by an unknown courier for herself and Karolina, their new names and address carefully intact. In her other hand she held Karolina's small fingers. They both wore summer dresses—almost identical mother and daughter outfits, both a little drab, a little worn. Clothing donated through the underground.

They blended easily into all the other women with children who walked the city streets. Around the perimeter of the wall was a long hike for Karolina, but for Sophie it was a pilgrimage, the closest thing she knew to visiting a cemetery. Residents of the ghetto had long gone—either in cattle trains to Treblinka or through the sewers beneath the ground, or they'd been murdered in the ghetto uprising or the burning of the ghetto.

Sophie did not explain to Karolina, who now seemed content to be with her and easily called her Mamusia. There were moments when the girl grew quiet, and Sophie wondered what she remembered, or if she did. The nightmares came less often now, but still they came. In those moments, Sophie would cradle the child, stroke her long, dark hair, and sing to her until she finally fell asleep again.

Sophie relished the hours that Karolina slept spooned against her chest. She loved the still-baby smell of her after a bath, and she loved combing out the tangled curls of her hair. She'd thought of cutting Karolina's hair into a bob—many little girls wore their hair that way now. But there was something very relaxing and even bonding in sitting Karolina before the mirror and running the brush through her unruly locks. Together they would count aloud, *one, two, three* . . . No, she would not cut it, not yet.

Sophie breathed deeply and closed her eyes for just a moment as they walked. Silence, except for the morning sounds of any other city. No more bombing. No pistol shots, no machine-gun fire, no screams.

All these weeks later, there was still the smell of woodsmoke in the air. The last night of the uprising, an explosion had burst the sky, so loud that Sophie was certain it had been heard over all of Warsaw. The next day, word was that the Great Synagogue of Warsaw had been set aflame. Even now she saw the synagogue's shattered dome, the walls broken, the rubble piled high. Heartache, devastation, emptiness everywhere. Still, she walked on.

They'd nearly circled the ghetto, as close as they could reasonably come to it, when Karolina looked up. "I don't like it here, Mamusia. Can we go home?"

In that moment Sophie made a decision. She would stop pretending. There would be no home to return Karolina to at war's end, no parents or siblings for her to find. From today Sophie would stop guarding her heart and give it completely to this child, this precious little girl. Karolina would be her daughter, and she, Karolina's mother. Whatever the future held, and that future loomed uncertain, they would face it together. Nothing but death would separate them.

"Mamusia—please. Can we go home now?" Sophie felt the child's tug on her skirt.

"Yes, my darling. We're going home."

CHAPTER THIRTY-FOUR

Stutthof Concentration Camp

My beloved Rosa,

How many hundreds of letters have I written from my heart to yours? I know the month only because of these words I mentally pen to you each day. Do you hear them? Do you understand that I dream of you each night and pray for you by day, that I miss you with every breath I draw, that I am sick with sorrow that I left you and Ania alone? I should have stayed, should have continued my work and protection of you both, just as you said. My coming did nothing to help my family in Vilna.

But enough of that. Tell me, my love, are you well? And Matka? Do you have food? Is Ania talking more? Is she running now? I love to imagine that she is strong and smiling, that she laughs and that her belly is full, that her cheeks are pink and round. I know this is a dream, a fantasy, but it carries me—

"*Raus! Raus! Schnell! Schnell!*"

Itzhak shook his father awake on the hard bunk beside him. The guard would not wait for an old man to limber his stiff bones. He'd barrel through the camp barracks within the next three minutes with a riding crop and fury in place of coffee and breakfast. *Breakfast! A joke. Barely a cup of lukewarm water.*

Roll call in the hard-baked camp yard, the prelude to that cup of tasteless water, was misery. For months his father and brothers-in-law had endured this in camp, even before Itzhak was arrested and joined them. Hours of standing ramrod straight became a battle between mindless boredom and physical pain, depending on the weather, until they were released at the whim of the fiend in charge. Hard labor inside the camp for the hours of daylight remained the only relief from boredom, and lately there had been less of that.

In that reprieve, Itzhak found hope. If the Germans seemed less determined to drive them to their deaths or re-create the camp, then perhaps it meant the tide of the war truly was turning. Perhaps, this time, rumors might be true that the Russians were just beyond the gate.

"I cannot keep this up, Itzhak. What's the point? Another day, more or less. I'm an old man. Let me be. Let him shoot me."

"Papa, get up. Get up, now," Itzhak urged as the riding crop made its way through the barracks. "What would Mama say?" he hissed. "She'd tan my hide if she knew I let you slumber off."

That made the old man smile. "Your mama, she was a slave driver."

"She is still a slave driver. Count on it. She'll want a good report when we get back to Vilna."

Chaim Dunovich groaned but sat up. He smiled with his mouth, but Itzhak saw that the quirk did not reach his father's eyes. Perhaps it was a story, a child's fairy tale that they would live to see their loved ones again. But it was the only story Itzhak allowed himself to believe, allowed his brain or mouth to repeat. Anything less was unacceptable—a ruse spawned by the Germans to break their spirit. *There's more to me than that. More to Rosa and Ania. We will survive. We'll tell the world what happened here. We'll live to do it.*

For the first time in months, roll call did not last for hours, and they were given a bowl of soup—thin, watery, but with a skimming of cabbage.

"What's this?" Avner, the husband of Itzhak's sister Talia, studied the bowl before lifting it to his lips. "They're feeding us? Why?"

"Perhaps it's our last meal," Uri, Regalia's husband, surmised with his usual gloom.

"They wouldn't waste the food on us if that were so," Chaim reprimanded. Itzhak knew his father was right.

"We'll know soon enough. Eat up, Papa. It's probably the best we'll get today."

No sooner had the last ladle of soup been poured than the commander's whistle pierced the air. Two transport trucks pulled into the courtyard.

"This does not look good," Uri whispered.

"Stand up, Papa. Rub your cheeks. Look healthy as you can." Itzhak felt the pulse in his brain. He couldn't lose his father. They'd take the old and sick first, if they were clearing the camp.

But the lines ahead of them, all the men from their barrack, disappeared into the trucks. No one was left behind. "Stay together," Itzhak ordered his father and brothers-in-law. "Don't let them separate us."

"Where are they taking us?" Uri, the youngest, sounded as if he'd swallowed pebbles rather than soup.

"Steady. We will learn soon enough, my son."

Itzhak was relieved that his father donned his shepherding voice. He was the head of their family, after all—a position Itzhak wanted him to cling to for the sake of the others, for his own sake—a reason to stay alive.

Their line snaked toward the trucks. Itzhak jumped in first, then reached for his father's hand, pulling him up into the truck bed. *They wouldn't have fed us if they were going to take us out and shoot us.* Itzhak repeated the thought over and over, convincing himself that it was so.

◆ ◆ ◆

My beloved Rosa,

I am Jewish but walking through the hell painted by Dante's Inferno. It is good that you will never read the epistles I write in my brain, for you would not believe them, and I would not want you to know. But I cannot bear this alone, and everything I think, everything I am, is open to you. So listen, if only for tonight.

They took us to the Ponary Forest this morning. The forest I told you about—the forest I ran through as a child, the place we held festivals and spent holidays. Everyone in Vilna did. The birch trees have grown taller yet, and the firs, beautiful as they were in the days of picnics and overnight camping trips, now tower far above. I remember the smell of the forest then, the damp earth ripe with mushrooms, and the towering evergreens. I remember lying on the ground, arms folded behind my head, and staring up into the treetops—green canopies scraping the sky—and dreaming of days and years to come, of all the things I would do, of the man I would become.

But the fragrance of the forest and the beauty of trees, even the blue of sky, are gone. Were they ever there? Perhaps that forest was nothing but a myth from long ago conjured by a boy in his dreams.

I was certain they were going to shoot us. The stench of death—of rotting human flesh and feces—was so strong, even before they ordered us out of the trucks, that many gagged, losing the watery soup we'd been given before leaving camp.

Guarded by machine guns, we were led to pits—so wide and so deep—a block long, probably more. Filled with corpses in every stage of decay. Spread over with a slight covering of chlorine that did nothing. Layer upon layer of corpses. And the shoes and clothing piled nearby. Why? I wanted to vomit.

All around me, men began reciting the Shema and then "The Lord is my shepherd; I shall not want . . ." We waited for the gunfire. If only they would do it and get it over with!

But they didn't kill us. Not today. They diverted us to the forest to cut trees, make planking.

We're to build bunkers in one of the pits—an empty one—and a latrine. Why, I don't know. Do they mean for us to live there? In that hole in the ground? For what purpose? For what purpose do the Germans do anything? To debase us . . . dehumanize us.

Oh, my Rosa. I will do my best to remain sane. I will do my best to come back to you.

Your Itzhak

◆

My Rosa,

The bunkers are finished, so we no longer report back to the camp, and we are no longer able to walk about as men. They shackled our ankles, so we can only step so, and so.

The Gestapo moved us tonight—permanently. Building bunkers in a pit—an open grave—is not the worst. What they demand is unthinkable.

Beginning tomorrow, we are to dig up the martyrs and burn them. They want us to dig up each and every body, carry it to a pyre we have yet to build, and burn it. Then we're to mix the ashes with sand and bury them. We are forbidden to call them human, or the dead, or victims, and never martyrs. We are ordered to call them Figuren*—manikins—or a foul word I cannot say to you.*

My heart is sick. I can tell no more tonight.

I pray for you, my love, and for our Ania, that you will never see such a place, never know it exists.

Shalom, my wife. Somewhere there is shalom, but not here.

Your Itzhak

◆

"Raus! Raus! Schnell!"

The barking of German orders rang in Itzhak's ears, pulling him from fitful, tormented sleep. Opening his eyes to the walls of the pit that surrounded him made him realize that his nightmares were not the stuff of dreams.

Itzhak caught his father's trembling hand in midair.

"I cannot do this, Itzhak. I cannot do what they say."

"If we don't, Papa, they will shoot us."

"Let them shoot me. Please, HaShem, let them shoot me."

Itzhak closed his eyes. He could not blame his father. "Think of Mama. Think of her, Papa."

The older man sighed, shaking his head.

Itzhak knew his father's marriage was not the joyful, motivating force that Itzhak experienced with his beautiful Rosa. But he didn't know what else to say, how else to infuse determination to live in the old man. Itzhak could not imagine letting his father go. He felt responsible to keep him alive, to keep him willing to breathe, get up, walk, work, pray.

"Schnell!" the order came again.

Somehow they managed to pull one another from the cold pit and climb the ladder let down for them, despite the clank, the discomfort, the limitations created by their shackles. Itzhak climbed behind his father, giving the older man a firm push, a helping hand up the rungs.

"Dunovich! Itzhak Dunovich!" an officer with a clipboard screeched.

Itzhak felt his heartbeat quicken. To be singled out was not good.

"Here . . . I am here." Itzhak swallowed.

The guard jerked his head, indicating Itzhak should follow to the Obersturmbannführer's car.

He waited, several feet away, while the Obersturmbannführer talked over plans spread across the hood of his car with a man of lower rank.

The Obersturmbannführer glanced at Itzhak and questioned the younger officer, the Sturmbannführer, more closely. At last the

Obersturmbannführer seemed satisfied, rolled the plan back into a tight scroll, and thumped it against his subordinate's chest. "See to it."

Without another glance or word, the officer entered the rear seat of the car, his door closed by the attending driver, and the black car roared away.

"Bring that man here!" the remaining officer barked.

Itzhak was jerked forward by an overzealous underling and brought to his knees before the Sturmbannführer.

The man circled him, scrutinized him. Itzhak didn't know whether to look up into the man's face or keep his eyes downcast.

"You registered as an electrician. Yes?"

It was not the question Itzhak had expected.

"Speak up! Answer the Sturmbannführer!" The underling punched the side of Itzhak's head, sending stars through his vision.

"Yes—yes," Itzhak croaked. "Electrician. I worked as an electrician before the—" He stopped, fearing anything he said would be used as a trap.

"Come." The Sturmbannführer moved forward in long strides, heading for the forest's edge.

Itzhak pulled himself from the ground, prodded by the boot of the guard behind him, and shuffled along as best he could.

The Sturmbannführer never turned to see if Itzhak followed, but spoke to the air. "I demand lights circling the perimeter of the site—to keep an eye on the prisoners, and enough for prisoners to work at night. Lights in the guardhouses—strong beams—and lights at stations here, here, and here." He pointed to distances beyond the eight craters of bodies.

Itzhak nodded to show he understood, but didn't know if he dared speak.

"You can do this?" the Sturmbannführer barked.

Itzhak nodded again. "Yes. With the right equipment, the right tools."

For the first time the Sturmbannführer looked him in the eye. Then he addressed the guard with the nervous punch. "See this man gets what he needs. If he fails, shoot him."

CHAPTER THIRTY-FIVE

ONE CHILLY AUTUMN DAY, Irena Sendler appeared in her nurse's uniform outside Sophie's door. As Sophie let her in, she saw the neighbor across the hallway peer out of her door. Sophie closed the door softly, relieved and startled at once to finally see her old coworker again.

"What news of Terri?" It was the first thing Sophie asked, the thing that had grated her heart each day for weeks.

Irena shook her head, handing Sophie an envelope filled with zloty. "No news. Usually Żegota can bribe a guard—someone—for word, but as far as we can tell, she's not at the prison."

"There's been no death notice posted," Sophie declared. "I check every day."

Irena nodded, sympathy apparent in her eyes. "It could mean a camp, but where, I don't know. The minute I hear anything, I'll get you word."

Sophie swallowed. There was nothing more to do. "Come, see Karolina. See how she's growing." She forced herself to focus on the child before her, the child she loved and who poured love into her heart each day.

Irena smiled. "She's thriving! It's so good to see a child thriving now."

Karolina tilted her head and looked up at Irena. "I remember you. Your name is Jolanta."

"Yes." Irena knelt before her. "You have a very good memory. What else do you remember?"

The child seemed to study Irena's face. "I remember you took me away and gave me to another lady, but then I woke up here." She reached for Sophie's hand. "Please, don't take me away again."

"No, I'm not here to take you away. You're happy here, yes?"

Karolina didn't answer but snuggled into Sophie's knee. Sophie picked her up and kissed her cheek. "We're a team, Karolina and I. Inseparable." She smiled, intending to convey her determination.

Irena stood, observing them both. She looked relieved, but Sophie saw a cloud pass through her eyes for just a moment. "I don't know if Terri was able to explain, but long-term caregivers must all agree to return the children after . . . after the war."

"If there is ever an end to this war."

"It can't last forever." Irena stood firm.

Sophie set the little girl on her feet. "Karolina, can you go in the kitchen and find an apple and plate? We should make a treat for our guest."

"Apple and honey?" Karolina beamed.

"A very good idea!"

Sophie smiled as the child ran toward the kitchen, calling behind her, "Yes, Mamusia!"

Irena's eyebrows rose.

"Is there word of her parents?" The words almost choked Sophie's throat.

"None. The father left months ago to find his family in Vilna. He never returned. I heard that the mother went after him—or wanted to. I don't know if she ever made it out of the ghetto. And now there's no way to find out."

"It is most likely, then, that they are both dead."

"That is most probable, yes. But there may be other family—somewhere. After the war—"

"After the war, come and talk to me, if either of us is still alive." Sophie felt an edge of bitterness. "In the meantime, Karolina is my daughter, and I will do everything I can to protect her, to hide her if I must. If no family comes forward later, I want to raise her as my own."

Irena looked as if she warred in her heart. "We must do what's best for the children. Ania—Karolina—is a Jewish child. She needs to be with her own people. I promised her mother that we would do our best to reunite them after the war. Ania is not only Polish, she's Lithuanian by her father—and she's not Catholic."

"Did her mother believe she would be alive to take her? Isn't that why she sent her now?"

Irena turned away.

"Do you really believe, after we've bonded as mother and child, that it would be best to send her to people she doesn't even know? Just because they are related to her parents?" Sophie saw the hackles in Irena rise and softened. "I'm not Polish and I'm not Catholic, either, but we are both pretending in order to stay alive."

Irena whispered, insisting, "I promised her mother."

Still, Sophie would not give any assurance, would not promise to relinquish the child she loved and who loved her. *What recourse does Irena have anyway? She needs me as she needs the many nuns in convents to hide children. We're all doing our best, and my best is to give Karolina—my daughter now—a home.*

Irena left before Karolina returned with the apple and honey. At first the little girl seemed disappointed but, seeing Sophie's tears, crawled into her lap, wiping them away with gentle fingers. Sophie cradled the child to her heart. *Please, God, show me the way. I don't want to steal this precious child from her mother. But if her mother is no longer alive . . . I don't want someone else to take her from me. Make our way clear. Give me a heart to do what's right. And please, God, protect and help Terri, wherever she is.*

◆

Barely a month later, a coded rap came to Sophie's door, just before curfew. Sophie opened it, expecting to find Irena—Jolanta— standing there. But Renat slipped through, quickly closing the door behind him.

"Renat! Is it really you? I never expected—"

"I can't stay, Sophie. Just brought your packet. It may be the last one for a while. Make it last."

"I don't understand. What's happened?"

"Irena's been arrested."

"No!"

"They came for her last night. She's in Pawiak Prison." He pushed his cap from his head and sank into the nearest chair, no matter his declaration to be quickly gone. He pushed his fingers through too-long, thick hair. "She knows everything. If they break her . . ."

"She'll not break. She's strong. She won't."

"Strong people break too." He shook his head. "I don't know if she took a capsule with her or not."

"Cyanide?"

"Yes. She told me just two days ago that she has more requests from couriers for capsules now than ever before. The Gestapo is on an all-out witch hunt, ferreting out everyone they can."

Sophie sat down beside him and closed her eyes. She couldn't imagine this world, this network, without Jolanta leading it. "Who reported her?"

"I don't know." Renat spoke quietly. "I would like to know. I would kill him . . . or her."

"Do you think the network's been infiltrated? Is it possible they could gain records—details—anything that would lead to all of us?"

"Anything's possible." His eyes bored into hers. "Be careful. Be very careful."

CHAPTER THIRTY-SIX

FOR THREE WEEKS ITZHAK'S SHACKLES were removed as he collected cables for the wiring. He and Sol Goldberg, a man assigned to
assist him, were guarded, but driven to neighboring villas where they
were to cut apart and retrieve existing wiring and all that they needed
to install an electrical system in the forest.

Near the end of the third week the two men were left alone for a
length of time at the far end of a villa, near the forest's edge.

"Itzhak, he's gone—the guard, he's gone."

"He's been gone for the last half hour. You only notice now?"

"Where has he gone?"

"How do I know? To visit the woman at the villa would be my
guess. Perhaps he convinces her why she no longer needs her electric
lights."

"The forest. We could go now. Come—before he returns. We
can run. He has no dogs, no reinforcements. He'll never find us. It's
nearly dusk."

Itzhak looked up. Goldberg was right. *The forest, so near. The guard, not in sight. How easy it would be to walk away—to escape.* "It's too cold. We'd never survive."

"You think we'll survive the winter in that hovel? You think they'll let us live when we've done their work? They'll want no survivors—no witnesses. We're as good as dead men if we stay. There are others in the forests. Surely we can join with them."

Itzhak swallowed. *What if we did? Can I find Rosa? Perhaps, if I—*

"We'll join the partisans. They have ways to survive. We can fight with them come spring. We can tell them what we know."

Itzhak began descending the pylon, weighing the pros and cons. He pictured seeing Rosa, telling her he'd left his father in the camp, that he didn't know what had become of him. And in the end, he knew what his answer must be. "My father. I cannot leave my father there alone."

"Your father would tell you to go, to live. You know he would."

Itzhak reached the ground, pulling up the cable that he'd dropped. "Yes, he would say that. But if I run, they will beat him to death."

"We have a chance to live; won't you take it?" Goldberg pleaded.

Itzhak shook his head. He might dream, but he didn't need to weigh the options. "Go, if you want. I won't stop you. But I can't leave my father."

"They'll beat you if I go, if they think you let me go."

"They'll beat me anyway. It's what they do. Go, Sol, with blessing." Itzhak meant it.

But Goldberg stayed. It was their last trip outside the camp. There was enough cable to appease the Obersturmbannführer.

◆ ◆ ◆

For weeks Itzhak had been excused from the burning brigade to run lighting, but his father and brothers-in-law had not. Seventeen pyres were built of gathered wood, and a routine of jobs and men had been established. Men to dig up the bodies—a minimum of three hundred each day. A man to extract gold teeth from the corpses. Men to stack the bodies. Men to add a layer of wood, and then bodies again, and pour on the gasoline. Men to light the pyres and keep them burning. Men to pound, to crush the bones to a fine powder. Men to scoop the ashes, mix them with sand, and spread them into the ground.

At night, the electric lights surrounded the camp and illuminated the gruesome pits. It took eight days to burn an entire pyre. Even in the dark, lurid flames flared into the night sky.

It was grueling work that stole the souls of the eighty men forced into labor. The stench of decaying bodies, combined with the smoke of the pyres that burned day and night, filled their nostrils. Soon the men could not be separated from the smell around them. They reeked of death. Even the guard dogs ignored them, unable to distinguish them as living.

By night those eighty broken men barely had the strength to stumble down the ladder into their own pit and crawl into the shabbily built bunker housed against one wall. No one spoke. No one joked. There was no end to the nightmare . . . waking or sleeping. They all walked and slept as if dead men.

"By hand," Uri whispered the night before Itzhak was turned into the pit to dig. "They make us dig them up by hand—no shovels, no gloves, nothing. The flesh falls apart."

Itzhak closed his eyes against the vision. It wasn't news to him. He'd watched the horrors from every vantage point as he installed lighting.

"Don't cry—don't break when you work in the pits. They beat you if you do. The first day, we all fell to our knees, sobbing like children. They beat us with riding crops and whips. And in the end our cries made no difference. It only spurred them on. Save your tears for the darkness. And, Itzhak, be prepared. There are no faces—no faces left the further down we go." Uri turned away then, and Itzhak knew to expect no more.

Itzhak wouldn't have blamed a man for lying down on the heap and begging to be shot—only to end the horror. But no one did. Silently, methodically, the men dug from the heaps with their bare hands. What they could be thinking, what they could pray to keep going, Itzhak could not guess. But his time had come; he would no longer have to wonder.

◆ ◆ ◆

One day in the putrid pits was all it took for Itzhak to know he couldn't keep going. He'd taken Uri's warning and had not cried, though he'd wanted to scream—to scream and never stop.

That night he lay on his back, listening to the other men's whiffling snores—men too exhausted to talk or eat. Sleep was the only sedative for the work they were forced to do.

My beloved Rosa . . .

Itzhak drew a ragged, shallow breath. Twin tears oozed from his eyes. He swiped them away with the back of his hand and bit the filthy sleeve on his arm. *I can't do this, my darling. I tried. But I can't do this. I'm sorry. . . . Tomorrow I will walk into the barbed wire at the edge of the camp, and they will shoot me. I am sorry, my love.*

He turned over and closed his eyes, but neither the nightmare nor the resolve left him.

CHAPTER THIRTY-SEVEN

TWO WEEKS PASSED. Sophie checked the posters listing the death toll and their names daily. Neither *Irena Sendler* nor *Jolanta* nor the different aliases for Terri were ever on the list. Each time, Sophie breathed a prayer of thanksgiving, and one for help for Irena and for Terri.

She prayed each day for Janek, and prayed that she and Karolina would one day join him in England, if God willed. She'd been so shocked at Renat's visit, at hearing of Irena's arrest, that she hadn't asked him if there was any more news of Janek through the underground. Sometimes it seemed that Terri's bringing Janek's photograph had been a dream.

In November, Sophie observed, from her apartment window, a man standing across the street. He stood for quite some time in the same spot, ostensibly reading a newspaper, but never turning the page. After a while, he walked away. A day later she saw another man, this time taking in the shop window across the street. He stood so long that Sophie realized he must not be looking at anything inside the window, but at the building behind him, reflected in the window glass. Her building.

Sophie stepped back from the window. As far as she knew, there was no one else in her building hiding Jews, no one involved with the underground in any way. Not that she would necessarily know. The less any one person knew, the less they could tell if arrested, if interrogated . . . as Irena surely had been.

Two hours later the man had gone. If the Gestapo suspected her, why were they waiting for the arrest? Why send different men? She knew they specialized in terrorizing during the night, but she was just one woman with a child.

My child. What will happen to Karolina if he is——? She'd kept the little girl safe thus far; she couldn't let anything happen to her now. But the thought of giving her up to someone else pierced Sophie's heart.

It's just the crossroads that her mother faced . . . only hers was certain death. Mine is fear . . . but real fear, fear based on experience. Dear God, what should I do?

"Mamusia? What's wrong?"

Sophie hadn't realized she'd been wringing her hands. "Nothing, my darling. Mamusia's just thinking."

"Will you read me a story? Will you read me the one about the animals in the circus?"

Sophie smiled between her worries. Dear Karolina had never seen a circus—perhaps she never would—but she loved the picture book Sophie had found about two children going, with their parents, to see a circus for the first time. Each time she read it to her, Karolina would exclaim, "It will be just so when we go to the circus, won't it, Mamusia?"

Poor Karolina. She'd never even seen animals other than the weary horses that drew droshkies through the streets, or the strong ones that the Germans rode when on patrol.

And then she remembered—animals—Jan and Antonina, keepers of the Warsaw Zoo. Aaron Bukowski had hidden there. She couldn't imagine how they'd managed it or exactly where they'd hidden him. Did they hide others? Were they still hiding people?

Sophie pulled back the edge of the drapery and peered out the window. It was nearly four o'clock. The man had gone. If she hurried, they could just make it to the zoo before dark, and she could make her way back again if they wouldn't take her—if they would only take Karolina.

Sophie bit her lip to keep from crying. Hiding her there was not giving her up.

"Mamusia? The story?" Karolina pushed the book into Sophie's hands.

"I have an even better idea. Would you like to see real animals?"

"The circus! You mean we go to the circus!"

"No, my love. But I know a place where animals live . . . at least where they used to live. Let's go and see if there are any there now."

She didn't need to ask twice. Karolina grabbed her coat and hat, ready to go.

Sophie tried to think. What would they need, going into hiding? To Karolina she said, "Let's dress more warmly. It's very cold outside."

Sophie tugged layer upon layer on the little girl . . . every warm thing she owned, until Karolina looked more like a pudgy child than the tiny waif she was.

"This is ridiculous, Mamusia! Why so many clothes?"

Sophie did her best to smile. "Yes, it is ridiculous. What a wonderful, big word you know. Humor me, dearest. We might be gone for a while, and we need our warmest things."

Sophie layered her own clothing as well, and tucked her Bible into her purse. She carried only a shopping bag, cramming into it every bit of fruit and bread and cheese left in the apartment. They'd just closed the door when Sophie remembered the medallion.

I can't believe I'm doing this. Let us not be too late, Father!

With shaking hands she fumbled the key into the lock and ran to her dresser drawer. She'd taped the medallion into a tiny square of paper in the top of the bottom drawer, just in case anyone searched the apartment. Sophie yanked the paper out and, with trembling fingers, fastened the medallion around Karolina's neck. "There," she said, when the little girl fingered it, pulling it from her dress to look at it. "Very pretty. Now, let's tuck your necklace back inside, and we're ready to go."

Walk steadily; don't run . . . Walk steadily; don't run. Sophie repeated the mantra over and over in her brain as she and Karolina traversed the city. She didn't dare take the tram. From a distance, they looked like two well-fed citizens of Warsaw—strange enough in this day and time. Up close, on a tram, they'd be revealed as wearing several layers of clothing, a sure sign of running away.

They'd just crossed the bridge over the Vistula River. Sophie breathed a prayer of thanksgiving, knowing the zoo was not far away. She prayed there were no Germans there now. *Please take both of us, but if not both, please, please take Karolina.* She rehearsed her speech, her desperate plea as she walked, gaining more speed than she should.

"Mamusia, I can't see!" Karolina complained, stumbling.

Sophie looked down at her daughter and stopped, kneeling before her. "That's because your hat is slipping over your eyes. We just push it back, like this."

"My nose is cold and my toes are pinched. When will we see the animals?"

"I know, my darling. That's because you have three pairs of socks on. We'll be there and soon we'll get toasty warm again. We must hurry."

"Promise?"

"Yes, I—"

"Mrs. Kumiega? Sophia Kumiega?" A man towered over the two

of them, his coat collar turned up and his fedora pulled low over his brow, but Sophie was certain it was one of the men she'd seen across the street from her apartment.

Sophie's heart stopped. She swallowed, wishing she could close her eyes and make everything go away. Instead, she stood, clasping Karolina's hand, and replied in her best Polish. "That's not my name. You've mistaken me for someone else. Excuse me." She tried to brush past him, but he clasped her elbow.

"I'm a friend," he said in English.

Sophie knew it was a trap. She continued speaking in Polish. "I'm sorry, sir. I don't know you. I don't understand what you're saying. Please let go of my arm."

"Perhaps you know this man." He pulled a photograph from his pocket. It was a picture of two good-looking young people, the man dimpled, smiling from ear to ear, his arm wrapped around a radiant young woman in bridal dress, her hair thick and flowing beneath a thin veil. *Janek and Sophia Kumiega* was written on the back . . . the photograph Janek had carried away to war with him, the one he said he always kept in his breast pocket, nearest his heart, and would never let go.

Sophie's heart sank. If a stranger held this photo, it meant that Janek was . . . *No!*

She swooned, reaching out to steady herself.

The stranger caught her, firmly grasping her arm, and steadied her on her feet. "Your husband is very much alive. An amazing pilot—one of the best—doing a bang-up job for the RAF. That's not why I'm here. Sir Lawrence Chamberlin sent me into the fray to find you. It's been like looking for a needle in a haystack."

Janek's alive . . . alive! That was all Sophie could hear as she walked, one hand looped through the man's arm to remain steady, the other clasping Karolina. Finally, she gathered her wits and breath, pulling away from the stranger. "Who are you? How did you find me?"

Sophie wanted to believe his tale, but it was so outlandish, and his accent was strange. *American?* Yet, were it not true, how would he know about her British guardian—the guardian who'd strongly disapproved of her marriage to Janek?

"Call me Alan. I've been looking for a week. Finally, the underground confirmed who I am and helped me. Finding someone who knew you was tricky. Trickier yet, finding someone who knew where and who you're supposed to be now. They're very careful, as they should be."

"What do you want with me?"

"Sir Lawrence sent me to get you out of Poland and home to England. Guess he figured you've probably had enough of Nazi occupation by now."

Sophie almost snorted. "And how do you propose to accomplish such a thing?"

"I know a way. It's risky. You'll have to trust me."

It was just the kind of ruse so many Jews, even so many Poles had been lured onto trains with . . . Yet this was something more than a promise of relocation and work. *Why would anyone go to the trouble to learn so much detail about my past? Does the Gestapo believe I know something important to them?* Of all the people involved in the underground, Sophie believed herself to be the most ignorant of clandestine activities.

"I don't know you, and you ask me to trust you. How did you get this picture?"

"Your husband gave it to Sir Lawrence. I guess he believed a British title would have luck getting you out . . . or getting someone in to get you."

Janek—you're looking for me. Thank You, God—thank You! But Sophie must keep her head about her. "You're not British."

"American."

"Why are you doing this?"

"Cash on the barrelhead. A third up front, two-thirds when I deliver you into Sir Lawrence's hands . . . or your husband's. Whichever comes first." He lit a cigarette and blew smoke into the air. "Plus, I'm a bit of a romantic. Your husband's a hero back in England—ace of the skies. You coming home would make him happy, keep him focused."

The man was surely American. She'd never met a German able to imitate that American laissez-faire attitude or perfect slang.

"There's not much time. We need to leave today—tonight at the latest. I have two train tickets. You in?"

"Train tickets? Just like that? You think the Germans will let the three of us ride away to—to where?" Sophie shook her head and walked on. The man was a lunatic.

He kept in stride. "Not you, nor me, but a Sturmbannführer and his wife. No one said anything about a kid. I've got no plans to get a kid out."

Sophie felt the landscape spin. "I go nowhere without my daughter."

The man looked from Sophie to Karolina, then studied Sophie's eyes. "Janek doesn't know he has a kid?"

Sophie wanted to cry. She was so near the zoo and hopes of hiding, but she dared not take this man there. What if he wasn't who he said he was? What if it was all a trap she was too simpleminded to see? She didn't know what to think, what to believe, but she couldn't risk the good Antonina and Jan were doing, the lives they were saving.

She clasped Karolina's hand all the tighter. She'd simply have to wait until this man gave up, then come back. "Janek knew I was pregnant when the war started. There's been no way to write him since. Look, I don't know what to believe. Let me think. Let me think about it. I'll let you know tomorrow." She tucked the photograph in her coat pocket.

"Tomorrow might be too late."

"Then you will have discharged your duty, won't you? You'll be able to collect your reward."

"If you're not coming, you have to sign the back of the picture. That way he knows I found you."

"You'll be paid, yes?"

"Believe it or not, sister, that's not all this is about. Give me back the picture."

"I'll return it tomorrow." She turned and walked back the way she came. *If he really means to save us, he'll have to find a way to take both of us. If he's connected with the Gestapo, I've just sealed our fate. Please, God, help us!*

"Where are we going? You said the animals were the other way!" Karolina cried, stumbling after Sophie, who walked as quickly as she dared.

"I'm sorry, darling, we can't go there today. We were too late. We'll try again tomorrow." Sophie did not look back to see if the man followed. *If he is Gestapo, he could pull me off the street at any time. He knows who I am. He knows I'm English. He said Janek is an RAF ace. Why does he not simply arrest me if they want to interrogate me?* Sophie swallowed, remembering the wedding photograph in her pocket, thankful it was still there. She was eager to look at it again, to touch it with ungloved fingers.

"Who was that man, Mamusia? He talked funny. I couldn't understand him."

Thank heaven that you couldn't. "He thought I was someone he knew. He was mistaken." They hurried along in silence, Karolina too breathless from Sophie's fast pace to ask more.

They'd almost reached their street when Sophie realized people were ducking into shops and behind stairwells. She turned the corner and froze. A black car screeched to a stop outside her building. Three men in Gestapo uniform spilled from the car and marched inside. Even from this distance, Sophie could hear the shouts, the screams, the firing of a pistol one, two, three times. One of the Gestapo returned to the car, dragged a man in plain clothes from its interior, and pointed to the building.

The man wore a dark coat and a drooped fedora—the same man who'd watched her building the day before. He pointed upward, toward an apartment above the first floor. Sophie followed his finger . . . to her apartment. The other two Gestapo burst from the building, holstering their pistols, anger and frustration written on their faces. The three piled back into the car but pushed the informant out.

Sophie ducked behind the corner of the building, her heart beating fast against her rib cage.

"Ready now, Mrs. Kumiega?" The familiar accent came from behind her.

Sophie closed her eyes, bit her lip, and breathed. *What choice do I have?*

◆

The escape plan was so outlandish Sophie could only believe it was invented by an American. Either that, or Britain's special forces had lost their minds.

The man calling himself Alan had taken Sophie and Karolina directly to a house he'd vowed was safe, an apartment more luxurious than anywhere Sophie had been since the war began.

"You'll have to get rid of those rags," he ordered.

"These 'rags' are all we have. We can't—" But before Sophie could finish, the man left the room, closing the door behind him.

Sophie pulled Karolina to her lap. She didn't know who else lived in the house, if it was truly safe, or why Alan had left so abruptly.

She heard voices in the hallway, low at first, then a little more urgent.

Less than five minutes passed before the door opened again. A petite woman slipped through the door so laden with clothes that Sophie could not see her face. Karolina gaped in wonder and Sophie knew she'd never seen so many clothes in one woman's arms.

The woman piled the clothing—silks and wool, jewel tones and paisleys—on a table beneath a blacked-out window. "Here." The woman turned and gave a tight-lipped smile. "There should be a few things in here you can wear or that I can alter to fit you well." Her smiled relaxed when she saw Karolina. "We were not expecting a little one, but we will find a way to make do."

"You're French."

"*Oui*, I am French. I was told that you are fluent. Perhaps now we can speak in French. I would like to hear your accent. The child, I presume, does not speak French?"

"*Non.*"

"*C'est bon.*" The woman began separating outfits, holding up one after another for Sophie to view, all the while smiling and speaking in French. "I do not wish to frighten the child, and the less she knows, perhaps the better. Little ones have a way of speaking when spoken to and telling tales out of school."

"*Je comprends.*" Sophie was relieved not to involve or worry Karolina more than was necessary. "We have our own clothing."

"Not for the journey you will be making. These are French couture pieces—satin, silk, the very finest by excellent designers . . . at least they were so before the war. You are traveling as the very wealthy and fashionable wife of an important man . . . wife and daughter."

"To England? I don't understand how that's possible."

"By walking into the lion's mouth and out again, my dear. Your first stop is Berlin." She handed Sophie a dress to try on.

"Berlin! That's the last place I want to go." *The last place I want to take Karolina!*

"How old is your daughter?" the woman asked innocently, ignoring Sophie's panic while pinning her hem.

Such questions always made Sophie bristle, but now, still uncertain what to believe, mental fog added to her trouble. To keep to her story, she knew she must claim that Karolina—Charlotte—was older than she clearly was. Not everyone would realize the age discrepancy, but a woman, a mother, might. "Three."

"Three?" The woman's brows rose. "Ah, yes. The paper manufactured from the hospital says she was born in May 1940." She looked directly at Sophie. "Three and a half. She is petite, *n'est-ce pas*?"

Sophie lifted her chin. "These are difficult times. Perhaps, in other circumstances . . ."

"*Oui*, of course." The woman tickled Charlotte's rib cage to make her lift her arms and pulled off her simple woolen dress. She lifted the delicate chain from the little girl's neck and studied the medallion. Sophie held her breath. She didn't know what the medallion meant, if it signified something in particular, but the woman rubbed the half between her fingers and sighed softly.

She stood and looked directly at Sophie. "You must be very careful, madame. You are playing with fire."

CHAPTER THIRTY-EIGHT

JUST BEFORE DAWN, A RAIN of pebbles came down on the bunker, waking those near the opening. Itzhak opened his eyes, relieved that morning had almost come and they would send the ladder down into the pit. He wouldn't have to wait long. He didn't need to deliberate longer. He wanted only to end it.

The pebbles came again. The men began to stir. One stuck his head out to see where the pebbles came from. He turned back to the others. "It's one of the guards—he's asking for Dunovich."

Itzhak heard his name. His father's frail hand reached for him. "He means you. They don't know any of our names but yours."

"What does he want?"

"Go on. He wants a new lightbulb, can't change it himself," Uri scoffed. "I don't know; why don't you ask him? At least you are a name."

Itzhak did not want a distraction. He didn't want to think about anything but what he had purposed to do.

"Dunovich! Get out there. Something's up." The prisoner by the opening spoke with something foreign in his voice—a trace of hope. That small flicker carried through the ramshackle sleeping quarters. "Go on! See what he wants. He's whispering."

Itzhak crawled through the mass of rousing bodies to the door and out into the pit, his hands and knees raw from the work of the day before.

"Dunovich? Is that you?" The whisper came from the top of the pit.

"Yes. I am Dunovich. What do you want?"

"I heard them talking."

"Who?"

"The Obersturmbannführer."

"Why do you tell me?"

"He's scared. They're all scared. The Russians are near. It won't be long. That's why you're burning bodies. High Command wants them to all disappear before they come. They don't want anyone to know what they've done here."

"Everyone will know. We all know."

"When you're done with this work, they'll shoot you—all of you. You're going to die, just like them. I'm telling you, escape if you can. But don't do it on my watch. They'll kill me."

"Who are you? Why do you tell me this?" It was knowledge and responsibility Itzhak did not want.

But there was no answer. The man was gone, just before the gray light of dawn seeped into the forest and over the pits.

"What is it? What did he say?" Men crept out into the open. The guards would be bringing the ladder soon anyway.

"He said the Russians are coming."

"When? Will they save us?"

"Who knows? Why do you ask me?" Itzhak didn't want to think about it, didn't want to hope. But hope stole through the eighty men as a flame rips through a forest. Even his father stood a little straighter.

"What else? What else did he say?"

Itzhak squeezed his eyes shut. He couldn't hold on to his determination to reach the barbed wire at the fence and think about this at the same time. *Escape . . . escape . . . escape . . .* The word seeped through his brain, quickening his heart rate until he blurted out, "He said we should escape—before they shoot us all. They want no witnesses to these murders, no one left to speak. When we've finished the work, they'll shoot us—like they did them."

A hush fell over the group. The hope that had crept into the pit dissipated before the morning fog.

"Escape? How does he expect us to do that?" Anger flared in the company.

"Did he say?" asked Uri.

"No, he did not say." Itzhak would have ridiculed his brother-in-law for simplemindedness, but he didn't have the heart or the energy.

"He did not say because he knew you would devise a way," his father said softly. "Itzhak will make a way." He whispered louder now, to the men near him. "Itzhak is a clever man, an electrician. That is why the guard spoke only to him."

"Papa! That's not true."

"You are an electrician, are you not?"

"Yes, but—"

"He spoke only to you, did he not?"

"Yes, but I don't know why. I have no plan of escape."

"Then you will think of one. We count on you, Itzhak Dunovich."

◆

All day, in between carrying mounds of human flesh to the pyres, Itzhak eyed the barbed wire surrounding the pit site—where he'd planned to be shot while making the guard think he attempted escape. And now the men from his barracks believed, thanks to his father, that he could devise some real means of escape that would end in freedom, in life.

He could imagine no such plan. *Eighty men walk free from the pits of hell, while guards with machine guns trained on them, stationed every few meters, let them go? Ludicrous. I am not Moses and this is not the Red Sea!* Anger at his father's misplaced confidence, at his ridiculous, feeble hope and belief in the impossible rankled Itzhak, giving him renewed energy for the afternoon.

By night he'd determined to tell his father to forget it, to find someone else to fulfill his *meshugge*, broken dream, this fairy tale. He had other plans—plans for his own form of escape. Itzhak swiped the sweat, even in the cold, from his blackened brow and finally straightened his back when the siren blew to stop work.

Men filed out of the pit, walking across layers of bodies to reach the edge and haul themselves up. No more did Itzhak think of the bodies as human beings. He couldn't. No one could. They'd all go mad. *We're mad already.*

They'd almost reached their sleeping pit when a guard called, "Dunovich!"

It wasn't the same voice as the man at the top of their pit that morning. All day, Itzhak had searched the faces of guards when they weren't looking, trying to connect the voice he'd heard with the faces looming over the pits.

"Dunovich!" Itzhak stopped and turned. It was the Sturm-bannführer's nervous underling. "Follow me." He punched Itzhak in the side with the butt of his rifle, pushing him forward.

Itzhak didn't ask why.

"See that light in the far tower? One of those flickers."

"A short in the wiring might do that . . . or a loose connection."

"Fix it."

"I need tools."

He nodded and jerked his head toward the supply building. Itzhak followed without a word. It would be good to hold tools in his hands one last time, even if it meant repairing a German's prison light.

◆ ◆ ◆

The job took longer than Itzhak had expected. An infestation of rats had eaten through the wiring, leaving half a dozen dead and a trail to their hideaway in the guard tower. New wiring had to be strung and cut, then connected.

"Look! I'm getting cold down here," the guard shouted. "How much longer?"

As if Itzhak weren't cold. "Thirty minutes maybe."

"Here, now. My replacement comes. Let him stand out here. When you're done, give him those tools. He'll escort you back to your pit."

Itzhak was tempted to take his time at the top of the tower just to make the guard stand longer in the cold, but he was no warmer in the high tower. His hands shook so that it was hard to to cut, connect, and twist the wires.

Finally he was finished and replaced the tools in the belt. He looked over the edge of the tower.

The guard below looked up, shifting from one frozen foot to the other. "Done?" He was young—new, perhaps.

He's barely out of knee breeches. What does he know of electrical tools? Itzhak looked into the distance, his eyes narrowed, barely able to make out the barbed wire tangled through the fence surrounding the camp. He readjusted his tool belt, slipped a pair of pliers and a screwdriver beneath his armpit, and hoisted his leg over the wall to climb down. "Finished!" he called.

◆ ◆ ◆

Itzhak lowered himself through the opening of the bunker, intent on keeping his arm against his side, though the pinch of the pliers bit his skin. But he sensed the tension in the group before he'd taken two steps—tension focused on him. He glanced from man to man. Even his father seemed to hold his breath.

"What? What is it?"

"We're going to do it."

"Do what?" But Itzhak knew already. The men had whispered throughout the day, speculating, imagining, trying the sound of ideas in their mouths beneath the eyes of oblivious guards. Itzhak shook his head. "It's foolish to try. You'll be shot before you reach the fence, and there are mines—between the rows of barbed wire, there are mines."

"They won't shoot us if they don't see us." Sol spoke, as if for the group.

"Madness." Itzhak looked away, keeping his eyes to himself. He'd find a way to reach the fence. If he could cut through the wires and get free, good—a miracle. If he stepped on a mine, he'd never know. If he was caught cutting the barbed wire at the far fence, he'd be shot, and it would be over. Anything was better than another day of this.

But if these madmen attempted to rush the fence, they'd all be shot—or caught. He wouldn't take that on his conscience.

"You did not hear me. . . . They will not see us."

"What—you have an invisible cloak now? You are ghosts? They will see you before you get out of this pit. And you forget your shackles. They'll hear you before you walk two steps." Itzhak claimed his place on the floor and lay down, as if to sleep, careful to keep the pliers and screwdriver between his back and the floor.

"Beneath the ground. We'll dig a tunnel through the back of this wall and into the forest."

Truly, they have gone mad.

"Listen to the men, Itzhak," his father ordered. "It's a plan—a good plan."

"And just what will you dig with? Your hands? It's one thing that they make us dig soft and rotting flesh with our hands. How do you think you will dig a wall of earth?"

"The earth here is sandy. Not so hard. We'll dig with our hands." Sol sounded sure, as if hands were enough.

Itzhak closed his eyes.

"And with these." Avner's voice quivered with excitement.

Itzhak heard a clank behind him. Finally, he turned. Sprawled across the ground lay five metal spoons. "Spoons. You'll dig a tunnel with spoons," he scoffed. But he saw they were serious. "Where did you get them?"

"From the pockets of the dead. We'll search for more tomorrow, and the next day, and the next." Uri all but challenged Itzhak to disagree.

"An army of spoons."

"Yes. We begin tonight. But we need you. You know the forest. Your father said you know it—" Sol again.

"Like the palm of his hand!"

"Papa! Don't listen to this madness. How can it be done?"

"One spoonful at a time," Avner insisted, his voice firm now.

Itzhak closed his eyes. "It would take months."

"You have something better to do with your time?" his father asked quietly. "Help us, Itzhak. Promise that you will be the first out of the tunnel, that you will lead us through the forest."

Itzhak weighed his desire to escape—or die—alone against the first real hope he'd seen in his father's face since joining him at Stutthof. That same hope flickered through the eyes and determined lines in each of the ten faces around him. *A tunnel dug with spoons. One spoonful at a time.* "Where will you put the dirt? A tunnel leaves a lot of dirt."

Doubt blinked in the eyes before him. But his own father would not be discouraged. "We'll carry it out in our pockets."

"Our pockets?"

"Ten of us know now. Eighty are here. Every morning we each carry out all we can. We dump it in the latrine pit. They'll never notice. Never see."

"There is one problem." The voice came from the back of the group.

"Only one?" another voice jested.

"We won't know when we've dug past the fence. What if we miss? What if we come up short? Even if we clear the mines, what if we come up before we clear the last of the barbed wire?"

"We'd be no better off than we are now. We couldn't get beyond the wire." Defeat crept into the speaker's voice, a voice Itzhak didn't recognize.

Itzhak saw his father's eyes shift in uncertainty, his breath catch, his shoulders slump, just a little. Itzhak swallowed, and he shouldered the pain of his father's last hope.

He moistened his lips, drew a breath he prayed he would not regret, and pulled the pliers from beneath him. "Unless we cut the wire with these."

CHAPTER THIRTY-NINE

KAROLINA, SOUND ASLEEP IN HER ARMS, was a deadweight, and Sophie was no longer used to walking in dress heels. Striding through the train station and along the platform as though she were the self-assured wife of a German Sturmbannführer and mother to his child, and keeping up with Alan, proved more of a challenge than she'd anticipated. But their papers were in order, the forged seal on their photographs perfect. Her instructions were to speak as little German as possible—to feign a toothache or sick headache if necessary. Alan was fluent in German, his accent impeccable. He would do the talking and lead the way.

The petite Frenchwoman had altered enough clothing for Sophie to convince the world that she was who she claimed . . . and given her enough silk stockings to bribe anyone she couldn't convince.

Dressing Karolina—who was told she would now lose her Polish name and be known as Charlotte—was more difficult on short notice. But she'd been respectably outfitted for a small child. They could always claim her trunk had been lost, and children grew so quickly . . . they would procure clothing for their only child in Berlin. Stories needed to be manufactured, agreed upon, and rehearsed in short order.

Just after breakfast, the petite woman had brought out a large bottle that looked like cough syrup. Alan had captured Sophie's attention with last-minute instructions. Before Sophie realized what she was doing, the woman had given Charlotte a spoonful of the liquid.

"Luminal. It is best that she sleeps. Her hair is dark; her eyes are brown. She does not look like you, madame, or the 'Sturmbannführer.' Not many brown-eyed children belong to officers of the Reich. Keep that in mind. Keep the warm bonnet on her head. Keep her sleeping or sleepy as long as you can. Do not allow her to speak Polish." The warning was spoken kindly, but Sophie knew all that was at stake.

"I'm sorry, my love," she whispered into her daughter's hair as she swept as regally as possible toward their rail car. "It's safest this way."

The trip to Berlin was painfully slow—giving Sophie time to think, to worry, to regret, to pray. *Father God, thank You for this hope—this hope for life. Be with us on this journey. Blind the eyes of those who mean to hurt us. Let them not see through our disguises. Bring us safely to England, to Janek. And please, God—oh, please be with Terri, wherever she is, and with Irena. Help them, and somehow let them know that I've not forgotten them. Let them know where we've gone, that Ania is safe, that I'll watch over her. Somehow, someday let me know where they are, even if . . .* But she stopped. Even in her prayers, Sophie could not imagine a world without her courageous friend or the woman who had rescued so many.

Delays and trains switched to side tracks to make way for troop trains were common and frequent. Despite restrictions on which cars Poles could ride in and which cars were reserved for German officers and their guests or families, the train was crowded and smelled of cramped bodies. Thankfully, passengers seemed consumed with their own worries and not eager to engage. Alan sat by the aisle, dealing with ticket requirements, frowning when a train employee addressed his "wife" directly, and shielding Sophie and Charlotte from the conversation of other passengers. When possible, Sophie lay Charlotte on blankets on the seat across from them, discouraging new passengers from taking that seat. She kept one eye slightly open and pinned to Charlotte through her lashes, but feigned sleep, alternately against the window glass or the back of the seat. She doubted she and Alan resembled a married couple, much less a family, but she wasn't certain what a German officer's family might look like. She imagined little public affection between them.

Sophie's stomach constricted when at last the train pulled into Berlin. Her German was good, but her accent clearly not native, so her acting skills had best prove above par. She trailed Alan through the chaotic station, keeping her half veil over her darting eyes, watching as best she could for any sign of too much interest from men in plain clothes or Gestapo uniforms. But the capital was filled with foreigners and the Gestapo had no time to take a second look at a German officer and his family walking purposefully to their next connection.

The train to Brussels left half an hour after their arrival, thanks to the delays they'd already encountered. Sophie wasn't sorry. She would have liked to stretch her legs longer, but the sooner they were out of Berlin, the better. She hadn't realized that the train to Brussels would take thirty-six hours. How she would keep Charlotte asleep that long she could not imagine, not unless she drugged the child beyond recognition.

Once they crossed the German border into Belgium, Sophie breathed easier. Not that it should matter. Belgium was occupied with just as many Germans as Berlin, and they'd likely be more watchful. But it was more familiar. Sophie remembered the summer trips Sir

Lawrence had taken Carrie and herself on, the many operas and art galleries and museums they'd visited in those old days of grand tours. For several years, Sir Lawrence had insisted they visit one country per summer, concentrating on its language, its art, its culture. Sophie's love was fostered through poetry and literature throughout England's long, damp winters. For Carrie, it had been a love affair with art from the beginning.

It was only now, as Sophie neared sleep in the rattling train, that she allowed herself to think of Carrie. For months, for the last few years, she'd pushed aside those memories. The two of them had grown up inseparable from the time Sophie came to live with the Chamberlins.

Carrie had lost her mother to tuberculosis when she was barely five. She'd been raised by an indulgent but strict father and a kindly nanny replaced as she grew older by a strict governess both girls had shared. Sophie joined the household at Haverford when she was ten—a year younger than Carrie.

It was Sir Lawrence's great kindness and loyalty to Sophie's father that had driven him to seek her out of the orphanage to which she'd been relegated after her parents' car crash. The two men had been friends since boyhood, both graduates of Eton and almost graduates of Oxford when the Great War began. Caught in the Battle of the Somme, Sir Lawrence had been wounded and lay unconscious through the cold October night before he was missed, in the unthinkable space between the armies' trenches known as no-man's-land. Near dawn, when the shelling stopped and roll call was taken, Sophie's father, James, realized his friend was missing. It had taken two hours, but slithering beneath camouflaging branches topped by a tangle of barbed wire, he'd made it the twenty feet to his wounded and unconscious friend with a flask of water. Together, they'd waited for nightfall, when James had dragged his friend back toward the trenches. Just as they'd reached the trench, a grenade had exploded not thirty feet away, sending them over the edge, down into the murky trench water, and filling James's leg with shrapnel.

Both men had been sent to Blighty for recovery. Ironically, Sir Lawrence had been returned to duty, but for James the war was over, at least active duty. He spent the rest of the war, much to his chagrin and fury, behind a desk in France. But that was where he'd met Charlotte Brodeur, Sophie's mother. A whirlwind wartime romance resulted in the love of a lifetime and a marriage of which Sir Lawrence disapproved. He'd always hoped and expected that James would marry his younger sister. Cold shoulders and no family in England left the couple in France until they realized Charlotte was pregnant.

Desire for British citizenship for their daughter was strong, so a move across the channel changed everything. Sophie's earliest memories were of the Lake District in England, of month-old lambs dotting brilliant green hillsides, butting their mother's side so she would let down their lunch. Sophie couldn't remember her mother's face, but she remembered her brown eyes—dark as the lake at night. She remembered her voice, and the lullaby she sang even when Sophie was surely too old for lullabies. *Or was I? Are we ever too old for our mother's lullaby?*

She'd never met the Chamberlins until after the accident, until someone from the district who'd been in the men's unit during the war had contacted Sir Lawrence, thinking he'd want to know of the death of his friend.

At first, Carrie had seemed uncertain of this newcomer—at least as uncertain as Sophie felt of her and her father—but the girls had become fast friends. Both motherless, they doted on Carrie's father, and it was easy to see that he loved them, if not equally.

Still, Sophie felt like the outsider she was, that she would always be. And when she'd met Janek on holiday in London and fallen madly in love, when she'd told Sir Lawrence and Carrie that she was going to quit university, marry him, and move to Poland, it was, as Mrs. Hettie in the kitchen used to say, "as if the fat hit the fire, mercy sakes!"

Sophie had been certain that time would heal the rift, that they would come to accept and love Janek as she had, unable to resist his old-world Polish charm. But as the weeks passed and her letters were returned, unopened, her heart fell. When she lost her first baby, she'd written to Carrie again but never heard a thing. Now, to believe that Janek had gone to them for help and that Sir Lawrence had actually orchestrated this bold and unlikely rescue . . . it all seemed too much.

Sophie knew she should be as grateful as she was when he'd come to the orphanage and claimed her, but she was no longer a child. She'd moved on, and she'd supposed Sir Lawrence and Carrie had done so as well. What would they expect of her in return? If they'd disapproved so vehemently of Janek, how would they feel about Charlotte? Wouldn't history repeat itself as it had played out for her parents? For her?

Sophie scooped the sleeping Karolina—Charlotte—into her arms and snuggled her against her heart. She'd have to convince them that Charlotte was her child. The way things were playing out, she knew that meant convincing Janek as well.

◆ ◆ ◆

Paris was more neutral ground for Sophie. She'd visited it several times over the years with Sir Lawrence and Carrie, and it was, after all, the birthplace of her mother. Fluency in the language was one thing she had retained from her mother's teaching, reinforced by the orphanage school and fostered through tutors by Sir Lawrence. She was doubly grateful for that now and eager to see the sights they passed upon leaving the station—the Eiffel Tower, the Champs-Élysées.

But Paris was not what she'd remembered and certainly not the beautiful city she wanted to introduce Charlotte to. Upon seeing the dismal, occupied pallor of the city she'd once found beautiful and intoxicating, she wanted only to move to the next leg of their journey as quickly as possible.

But after Alan's short trip to meet his next contact—a woman behind the counter of a local fashion boutique who worked with the Polish underground in France—their trip into neutral Spain was delayed.

"Why? Why can't we go on?" Sophie felt the tentacles of fear creep through her heart.

"No need to get the jitters. It's a delay, that's all. We've done this route before; we'll get you through." Alan lit a cigarette, puffed twice, then smudged it in the hotel room ashtray, belying his professed confidence.

"What do you mean you've done this before?"

It had clearly been a slip of the tongue.

"Alan?"

"We've brought clients through before . . . recently. I've never lost one. You don't need to worry. It's just—" He hesitated.

"It's just what?"

"Things are tricky now, since the krauts took over Vichy France. Appears they've intercepted some of London's radio transmissions. We're not sure how much they know, so we need to wait. Besides, I'm not sure I can bluff my way through, and I've never moved a child through this route. When you get to the border—"

"When *we* get to the border," she corrected him.

"I'll be leaving you in Lyon. A contact there will take you on to Barcelona."

"You're taking us all the way to England. You said you would deliver me to Janek or Sir Lawrence, whichever came first." Sophie felt panic rising in her chest. She didn't know but a few words in Spanish. She could not be abandoned now.

"I'll make certain you have a guide you can trust, a man who knows the terrain and the people. I'm not the person to take you into

Spain. I can impersonate a German officer or peasant, as long as the interrogation's not too long, but I don't want to end up with a detailed background check. Besides, I'd never make it past the border. This was the plan all along . . . just not the delay."

There was no point in arguing. Sophie could see what he said was true and knew he'd only ever planned to tell her what she needed to know when she needed to know it, but to trust someone else, someone new, to rely on anyone other than herself or the underground workers she knew, felt more than she could muster.

◆

En route to Lyon, Alan exited the train and did not return. At the next station, as planned, Sophie and Charlotte stepped off the train, exchanged their outer coats behind a park bench a block from the station, and returned in simpler style, waiting for the next train, two hours later. All their luxurious clothing had been left behind in Paris and would be used as currency for the Polish underground.

Traveling with new papers, as a French mother and child on their way to visit a sickly grandmother in Lyon, Sophie felt more at home in her own skin. Though few French had spoken to them while she and Charlotte had traveled with Alan, she'd sensed their disapproval beneath veiled smiles, blank stares, and sometimes open hostility toward their presumed oppressors. She empathized but had needed to play her role as the wife of a Nazi officer for all their sakes. Now she could better blend into the faces and atmosphere she knew.

Alan had warned Sophie that she might need to stay in hiding in Lyon for a week or more, but the woman who met her at the station—ostensibly a sister she'd not see in years—hurried the mother and daughter onto a train bound for Perpignan, saying loudly enough for those around to hear that they'd moved Grandmother to Aunt Lucille's to recuperate. "She's doing better, but at eighty-four we don't know how long she has. I'm so glad you've come. She'll do better for seeing you and Charlotte."

At the mention of her new name, Charlotte smiled up at the lady, who took her in her arms and chatted with her all the way to Perpignan, not allowing Charlotte a Polish word in or out.

Sophie was relieved for the unexpected help, the sense of camaraderie, even if it was only make-believe. She leaned her head back and closed her eyes. *Perpignan . . . one step closer to England, to Janek, to Sir Lawrence. What will that mean? It's been so long since we've been together, Janek. . . . Will it be as it was before? How will you have changed? For surely I have. I'm not the same young girl you left.*

She wouldn't say it aloud, but she wasn't even certain she wanted Janek, or any man, to take charge of her life now. For four years she'd made every decision—wise and unwise; she'd lived in danger and done what she could to help others in danger. She'd lived an entire life without her husband. How could she go back now to being the woman he'd left behind?

◆ ◆ ◆

Two weeks passed in Perpignan before a guide could be found to take them across the Pyrenees and into Spain, and all that time Sophie drummed her fingers with worry.

"Smugglers were three to a penny," proclaimed their host over breakfast, "but since the Germans took over Vichy France, no one will make the journey. The border is closed—sealed. Germans have searched until they've found nearly every trail. The price to cross has risen dramatically. It used to be ten thousand, maybe twenty thousand francs. Now . . . even the opportunists have disappeared into the woodwork. And it's winter. No one crosses in winter unless pursued by the devil himself . . ." She sighed. "Which may be the only way."

Sophie still had a few gold coins sewn behind the buttons of her dress, still had a stash of cash sewn into the hem of Charlotte's blanket. But would they be enough to get her to Barcelona, and then Madrid? Was that even the route they would take now? Alan had warned her not to share with any of the hosts what she carried, to let them provide the way lest she end up stranded someplace.

"They're equipped, and they've been paid what they agreed to," he'd said. "Trust them. Let the guides do what they do best."

So Sophie waited, and she prayed, reminding herself of Pan Bukowski's words. *"My people came to the end of their road. Egyptians raged at their backs with nothing but the sea in front. That's when Adonai parted the waters and they walked across—on dry ground. He is the One who makes a way when there is no way. Remember!"*

She swallowed at the memory of her encouraging and faithful friend and her own realization. *If Adonai can part the Red Sea, He can surely move my mountain, can't He?* She whispered, smiling through the darkness, "Sometimes He moves those mountains miraculously, and sometimes by having us carry one small stone at a time, doesn't He, Pan Bukowski?"

◆ ◆ ◆

Word came in the dark of night on Christmas Eve. Their hostess, whose real name Sophie never knew, roused her, shook her arm, urging her awake.

"It's time to go. Dress yourself and the child as quickly as you can—wear everything. You will need it against the cold. Take the boots in the hallway. I'll see you downstairs."

When Sophie and Charlotte reached the kitchen, their hostess was gone. A short, wiry man stood at the stove, sipping coffee laced with cognac. Sophie could smell it across the room. He offered her a cup, but she refused.

"Don't be foolish, woman. You'll need it to keep your blood warm . . . and the child."

Sophie hesitated, remembered Alan's words, and took a sip of the lukewarm brew. She'd never tasted cognac and didn't care for it. She grimaced and wanted only to spit it out.

"Swallow!" he ordered, and she did. "Now the child."

"I don't think—" Before she could protest further the man lifted Charlotte from the floor and forced open her mouth.

"Drink!"

Charlotte was so startled that she swallowed and sputtered.

"I won't have her dying on me in the pass. If either of you do, I'll leave you. Understood?"

Sophie nodded, terrified of what she'd committed to.

The man took one look at the suitcase Sophie had packed and thrust it open, shaking his head. He pulled a knapsack from behind the stove, clearly one their hostess had already packed with rations and a bottle of wine. "This is what you'll carry on your back. Take warm socks and one change of clothing. Everything else you must wear or leave. Five minutes. The entire village is at mass. We have half an hour to clear the city. I'll be waiting by the gate."

Sophie's heart thundered in her chest as he slipped out the door as silently as he'd come. Dared she trust their lives to this man? She looked at Charlotte, wide-eyed and frightened, and oh, so small. That's when Sophie knew she would do whatever she must to get them both to safety, and she would make certain that Charlotte did not believe she was afraid.

◆

An hour later Sophie and Charlotte were hunched into the boot of a car, several layers of blankets over and beneath them, crates of wine stacked between them and the opening, a layer of sausages on top. Their guide had said they were lucky. The first part of their trip was feigned as a Christmas delivery to a German officer. They would drunkenly share their booty if stopped by patrols and pray that the Germans did not search the boot beyond their surprising Christmas gift.

Charlotte fell asleep in Sophie's arms, but Sophie was too frightened to sleep. Each time the auto slowed—the auto stolen from a Sturmbannführer already deep in his Christmas cups—she cringed, holding her breath, doing her best not to grip Charlotte tighter and waken or frighten her child.

They'd been traveling for what seemed like hours when the auto slowed to a stop. She strained her ears to hear. German voices, sharp and officious, barked orders she could not translate, but she understood they would be searched. She tucked the blanket tight around Charlotte and willed her heart to slow, fearful they would hear it slamming against her rib cage.

Footsteps rounded the automobile. Doors opened and closed. She heard the French driver and the man accompanying him get out, pretend to be mildly drunk, jovially offer the guards a bottle. The guards did not respond, but a sharp rap came on the lid of the boot.

The boot was opened and a rush of cold air swept through the blankets cradling Sophie and Charlotte. Sophie prayed for invisibility as she'd never prayed before. Crates were rummaged through, sausages pushed aside. The Frenchman offered a sausage, uncorked a bottle, and passed it to the guard, proclaiming, *"Joyeux Noël!"*

More orders were barked, but less gruffly. Another German voice spoke, this one placated, and the boot slammed closed.

Sophie breathed at last. Charlotte squirmed in her sleep and tried to turn over. Sophie held her close, praying she'd not whimper.

At last the car doors shut and the engine roared to life. Cries of *"Joyeux Noël"* and *"Fröhliche Weihnachten"* were thrown to the stars as their midnight journey continued.

CHAPTER FORTY

NIGHT AFTER NIGHT THE MEN DUG IN the dark earth, taking turns. They created a false wall in the back of the bunker, behind the cooking area—a way to hide their work from easy view—and another area to spoon their sand and dirt.

At first it didn't matter that there was no light, but as the tunnel snaked deeper into the earth, Itzhak rigged a lighting system from parts he'd smuggled in his clothing after making further repairs to the Germans' lights, as well as a simple tunnel alarm in case of emergencies—a surprise roll call or inspection by the officers or guards.

Eighty men shared the bunker, but only ten, and soon the twenty closest to the back wall, knew what was going on. Most men collapsed into sleep as soon as they'd eaten and hit the floor. It was not hard to keep the secret, at first. Only those with enough youth and energy to work in the night—after their grueling day—could participate. Many could not. It was too much. But even those sleeping men who knew provided a buffer between the kitchen's false wall and the other sleeping men.

It was not the digging or the light in the earth or even the whispers that spread the word through the bunker, but hope. Hope energized the workmen, even though they lost sleep. Hope kept them going through each vile and gruesome workday. Hope lightened their step as they headed for their underground bunker.

For two months those who were fit enough toiled in the narrow tunnel, taking turns at night. One man dug away with his spoon, then passed the sandy dirt beneath him to the man behind, and that man to the one behind him until it reached the bunker.

Each morning the men carried new portions of the tunneled earth in their pockets, depositing it in the latrine hole. When the latrine filled, the men complained to the Germans that the earth had collapsed and dug a second hole.

"How long? How long until you reach the end?" Itzhak's father asked each morning.

Each morning Itzhak replied, "Until the day we do. Until the day I tell you. You will be the first to know."

His father smiled and nodded, then endured another day.

CHAPTER FORTY-ONE

FOR EIGHT LONG DAYS, through bitter cold, Sophie followed their guide's snow-crunched footsteps, her thighs and calves burning with each step. Though he carried Charlotte on his back and often slowed to check for patrols, Sophie could barely keep pace. Two- or three-hour stretches were all she could manage before begging for rest. At night they slept in shepherds' huts or caves, which must be reached before nightfall, never daring to build a fire for fear of Nazi patrols.

Sophie couldn't tell when she fell ill, when the building heat in her forehead began to rage through her body, or how many days or nights their unnamed host kept them until she'd recovered sufficiently to go forward. She didn't remember the skis or the sleigh or the route their guide brought them through, but was grateful beyond words when they finally boarded a train bound for Barcelona, so very far from whence they'd come.

Faintly, she remembered their guide shaking Charlotte, ordering her to stop speaking Polish. "If stopped, you must both claim to be

Canadian! If a Canadian is arrested in Spain, the British authorities can get you out . . . not so if Polish!"

Sophie remembered nodding in agreement and weakly pulling Charlotte from his clutch.

She grasped only faint and fleeting images of the Spaniards who ran the safe house in Barcelona or of the English-speaking man who appeared the next day to drive her and Charlotte the eight hours to Madrid, then on to Algeciras, where they hid and slept for three days in the attic of a warehouse.

By the time they were transferred to a hotel in the middle of the night, Sophie began collecting her bearings. Her head still pounded, but the fever had diminished. She would have given anything for a proper bath and a hair wash—for herself and for Charlotte—but the man who stood guard declared there was no time. They would not be staying.

They'd been in the booked room less than an hour when two men slipped through the door, spoke in hushed and hurried English with their guard, and they were all driven, cramped in the back of an automobile, to a hidden cove to board a small fishing boat.

Charlotte's arms glued themselves to Sophie's neck, for which Sophie was most grateful. They trolled the Bay of Gibraltar through the black night, shivering, tossed in the rough current, until at last a patrol boat signaled with its blinking light.

The two men who'd joined them at the hotel helped Sophie and Charlotte into the patrol boat. Time stopped for Sophie as she pressed her daughter against her chest and they both gazed up at a sky more alive with stars than any they'd ever seen. It gave her pause to remember how far they'd come, all they'd left behind. *Terri, my friend . . . where are you—you and Renat? Irena? Are you seeing these stars? Please, God, please . . . help them; keep them in Your care.* She swallowed. It seemed a miracle too much to hope for that they would all still be alive, but on a night like this, with stars exploding in their galaxies and beyond, she could believe in almost anything.

As they neared Gibraltar, the patrol boat flashed its signals at other English boats. *This is happening. It's really happening. I'm going home to England. We're going home.*

◆ ◆ ◆

Sophie had loved the tales Janek spun of flying through the air—the thrill and speed and freedom of streaking through clouds, of pushing high into the sky and plummeting to the earth, coming up just in time. All that pumped his blood. But she'd never stepped into a plane, let alone an American bomber.

From the moment they left the ground, she closed her eyes and wished to close her ears, to shut out the thundering rumble through her feet and belly, the frigid cold of the unpressurized cargo bay. For the first two hours of the flight Charlotte cried or whimpered in terror in Sophie's arms until one of the men who'd boarded with them pulled out his handkerchief and tied it in knots to form a rabbit puppet that crept along her arm. He kept the play up for nearly three hours, urging the other men to donate their pocket handkerchiefs and chatting away in funny animal voices, though they could hardly be heard above the roar of the plane. Charlotte was mesmerized until, exhausted, she fell asleep.

"Thank you," Sophie whispered when they finally taxied down the runway. "That was so very kind."

The man tipped his fedora, looking a bit wistful. "I have a little girl, back home."

"And where is home?" she asked innocently.

The man smiled but turned away.

Ah . . . for a moment I almost forgot we're at war.

◆ ◆ ◆

The familiarity of British red tape returned quickly to Sophie. She and Charlotte were quarantined at a site several miles from the runway while she was interrogated and the contents of their knapsack examined. After three hours she began to despair that she'd at best be declared a war refugee. Her various passports and aliases that had proven their ticket through occupied Europe became red flags for the possibility of being declared an alien of suspect or a Nazi spy on British soil.

She completed form after form, declaring who she was, her marriage date to Janek, his name and birth date, Charlotte's name and birth date, the assurance that he was her father. She could not answer questions about Janek's rank or whereabouts in the RAF. She had no idea, only the fuzzy memory of a picture of him standing with other Polish RAF pilots. It seemed they would never be satisfied.

And then, suddenly, it was over. Sophie was declared a British citizen. Her dilapidated knapsack was returned, the forged documents confiscated. She and Charlotte were ushered through doors and driven to a small guardhouse beside a barred road.

There, on the other side of the bar, in front of a limousine, stood Carrie Chamberlin, gloved hands clasped, smiling in relief.

Sophie gasped. It was as if the clock had been turned back nearly a decade. Her friend of most of her growing years looked just the same—lovely and trim, smartly turned out in what must be Britain's latest wartime pseudomilitary fashion: a gray woolen jacket fitted to show her curves, a straight skirt with matching hat, and elegant pumps. But when she turned, Sophie saw the black mourning band that encircled Carrie's arm.

"Carrie?" Sophie didn't know whether to question or run into her old friend's arms. But she pushed the quandary from her mind, as far as she could. Whomever Carrie mourned Sophie would learn soon enough. Whatever had driven Carrie and her father to cut off their relationship before the war was past. It was at Sir Lawrence's behest and thanks to his influence, and probably his money, that she stood on British soil . . . home . . . England. "Carrie!"

"Sophie!" Carrie opened her arms and Sophie ran into them, both women crying and hugging. Little Charlotte followed, clinging to Sophie's skirt.

Sophie could not stop the rainfall of tears. For weeks and months and years she'd held them back. For Charlotte's sake she had forced strength and resolve into her voice and posture that she never felt deep down. Now, to be with someone who'd known and loved her as a child called forth a release she'd not given way to since she'd lost her last baby.

Two minutes of crying and hugging and holding followed, despite the embarrassed glances of the British military guards.

Carrie pulled away first. "And who's this?" She looked down into Charlotte's worried eyes.

Sophie drew a deep breath. *Do what you must.* "This is my daughter, Charlotte. Charlotte, meet your aunt Carrie."

Carrie flashed a questioning glance at Sophie, her mouth a momentary line, but at last reached her hand to clasp Charlotte's. "I'm very pleased to meet you, Charlotte. Would you like to come home with me?"

Charlotte ducked behind Sophie's skirt.

"Polish is Charlotte's native language. She speaks little English yet, but she understands more." Sophie reached down for Charlotte and lifted her to her hip. "We're going home with Aunt Carrie, you and I," she said in slow English. "It will be all right. She's a very nice lady and lives in a wonderful house with her papa—Sir Lawrence. You'll like it. We'll be safe there. You'll see."

Carrie placed her hand on Sophie's arm. "You don't know, do you?"

"Know?" Sophie's brain whirred and her stomach plummeted to her feet. She tried to pull her eyes from Carrie's mourning band but couldn't. "No. Not Janek!"

"No . . . Papa."

"What?"

Carrie looked as if she'd cry—as if she had cried, buckets. "His heart—nearly a month now."

"Sir Lawrence?" Sophie could not comprehend that. "Carrie, I'm sorry. I'm so, so sorry."

"All that stress of the war. Long hours, and the trips he took to France in the midst of the fighting, and the worrying, and . . . and in the end, it was his heart, in his favorite chair, at home." Carrie lifted her chin, clamped her mouth and looked severe. "Not a bad end, but . . . the end. We'll talk more later. Come, let's go."

"Don't make me go with her, Mamusia. Don't leave me!" Charlotte whimpered.

"No, my darling. Of course not. We'll stay together . . . always." It was a promise Sophie made in Polish, vowed to keep, and prayed she would be able.

◆

After bathing Charlotte, feeding her an early meal, and tucking her into the big bed Sophie begged they share, Carrie insisted Sophie bathe—and take her time. Despite her desire to be with Carrie, to hear all her friend had endured through the war and since the death of her father, Sophie did not argue and spent two luxurious hours soaking in a hot tub scented with rose petals. She scrubbed her matted hair and rinsed three times, thankful to find no lice after her weeks of travel and hiding. She might have fallen asleep in the tub had Carrie not knocked on the bathroom door.

"When you're done, wrap up and come to my room. We'll find you something of mine to wear for tomorrow. I have tea and scones at the ready—your favorite, with raisins and marmalade."

"That sounds heavenly, Carrie! I'll be right there." Sophie couldn't remember when she'd last felt so clean or been treated to a scone. Marmalade ranked as something from the prewar world. Even the memory of her favorite childhood teatime treat belonged to another person, someone who lived a different life. And to imagine that afterward she would sleep in a real bed with starched sheets . . . it truly was as if she'd flown to heaven.

But as Sophie stepped from the tub and wrapped the terry-cloth robe warmed over the steam pipe heater around her, cinching the waist, she felt guilty—as if she were walking on Sir Lawrence's grave. How could she bathe and dine and sleep in his house, enjoy the freedom he had provided for her and for Charlotte, knowing he was not here? Knowing he had disapproved of her marriage and would surely disapprove of her child? Had he really not known? Had no word reached him through the underground before his heart failed?

She towel-dried her hair and, sitting at the vanity in her room, ran the brush Carrie had provided through it, pulling out knots and tangles, and with them the stress and worry over running, hiding, getting her precious Charlotte to safety. For now, for tonight, they were safe at Haverford, the Chamberlins' ancestral home. But what about tomorrow? With Sir Lawrence gone, what advocate did she have? What resources? And what about Janek—where was he?

She glanced in the mirror at her sleeping daughter, nestled into the center of the huge bed behind her, and returned the brush to its tortoiseshell set. *Whatever has happened, whatever comes, I must keep you safe, my darling.*

◆

Sophie marveled at Carrie's determination to carry on, to see to the tasks of pouring tea and serving scones and culling her wardrobe for Sophie before sharing all that had happened in her life since her father's death.

Sophie tried not to gawk at the array of clothing Carrie had pulled from her closet and spread across the bed. Since the first bombing of Warsaw, Sophie had not owned more than two skirts, two blouses, and a dress, except for the short-lived couture wardrobe with which she'd traveled incognito to Paris.

Finding something to fit her proved more difficult. Carrie was shorter, so anything for Sophie must be lengthened, despite the shorter wartime skirts. Sleeves were a greater problem, sliding well above her wrists. Sophie held up a fairly modest full-length evening dress that could be shortened. She turned this way and that before Carrie's mirror but blushed at the boyish leanness of her body. Months of deprivation and the trek across the Pyrenees had left her without feminine curves to fill clothing in the necessary places. She touched the dark circles beneath her eyes, took note of the hollows in her cheeks. *Will Janek find me unappealing?* She hadn't had time to care or even think about her appearance in so long.

"When Janek came to Papa for help to find you, I saw him." Carrie sipped her tea, but Sophie felt her watching carefully.

"You did? Is he well?" Though relieved when Carrie nodded, Sophie still felt on foreign soil. Asking after her husband felt as if she asked about a near stranger.

Carrie gave a half smile. "He's as handsome a devil as ever. I can see why you fell for him."

Sophie smiled, uncomfortably, in return. She stepped behind the dressing screen and returned to her robe, then took a seat across from her friend.

Carrie sobered. "Janek told me that you wrote me."

"I wrote every week—for months. You never wrote back."

"I did write . . . but I thought you didn't. Father kept back my letters. I didn't know it then, but he kept them and never sent them to you."

"All the letters I sent you—and Sir Lawrence—were returned, unopened." Sophie still felt the sting of that.

Carrie nodded. "I'm sorry, Sophie. I didn't know—not until Janek told me."

"Why?"

"I confronted Father—asked him why he'd done it, why he'd kept us apart when he knew it broke my heart."

"And mine."

"He wanted to break your heart, because he said you'd broken his."

"What?" Sophie felt the incredulity, the awareness, and the shame all at once. She'd known she'd hurt Carrie and Sir Lawrence by marrying Janek, by moving to Poland, by turning her back on the life they'd provided, but wasn't it her right to marry? To love?

"He wanted you to stay here. To stay as we were—a family."

"I grew up, Carrie. I wanted more—a life, a family of my own. You and your father were a family. I was the outsider. He provided for me in every way, but all those years . . . he had me call him 'Sir Lawrence.' He was never 'Father' to me."

Tears trickled down Carrie's cheeks. "I know. I understand that now. I didn't then. I'm so sorry."

Sophie knelt by the chair of her friend and took both her hands. "You've nothing to be sorry about. It wasn't your fault."

"He was angry when you left us for Janek—for Poland." Carrie's voice dropped to a whisper. "I was angry. I realized—too late—that Father retaliated because he knew I was hurt."

Sophie sighed. "Then why did he agree to Janek's pleas to help me? To get me out of Poland?"

"Because in his own way he loved you, and I think, in the end, he realized that Janek really loves you—that it wasn't a fly-by-night marriage after all."

"'Fly-by-night marriage'? How could he think that?"

Carrie shook her head sadly. "He thought the same of your parents' marriage. Remember how he talked about them?"

"As if my father had made a rash decision—a very 'un-English' decision in marrying a Frenchwoman."

"He was wrong then; it wasn't up to him. And now—Janek's a good man."

"Yes, he is." Sophie felt proud to confirm her friend's conclusion.

"I think Father came to see that. I think he was truly sorry for what he did, and he went to great lengths to get you out. Thank God—oh, thank God, truly, that he set everything in motion before he died!" With that, Carrie broke down entirely. Now it was Sophie's turn to set the past behind her, to help her friend. She folded her arms around Carrie as she wept.

When it seemed Carrie had at last calmed, Sophie took the serviette from her lap and dried her friend's eyes. She sat back on her heels. "There now, that looks more like my old friend."

"Not so old," Carrie protested through the last of her tears with a small smile.

Sophie smiled in return. "No. Not so old at all. You look wonderful, Carrie—just the same."

Sophie would have imagined that would please Carrie, but Carrie hesitated, and furrows appeared between her brows as she reached to pour more tea for them both.

"What is it? What's wrong? I know I don't look the same, but in time—"

"That's not it. I'm just thinking . . . she doesn't look like you, does she? Or Janek."

"Charlotte? No, she's more dark . . . like my mother, I think." Sophie forced a smile, tried to still the sudden rapid beat of her heart. "I gave her my mother's name. It means 'free' and 'feminine.' I think it suits her."

"'Free'? Interesting. I don't remember your mother," Carrie said.

"Well, you never knew her, did you? Our parents, at least our fathers, knew one another in those days. The truth is, I hardly remember my mother. Just little things . . . the sound of her voice as she sang me to sleep—a lullaby I still sing to Charlotte. A dimple near the corner of her mouth. The same with Papa . . . I remember even less of him."

"You're lucky to have any memory at all, I suppose. It was all so long ago."

"Yes, I'm thankful for that." Sophie trod carefully, knowing Carrie might be thinking that she'd known her own mother an even shorter time and aching for the recent loss of her father. She was almost sorry she'd said what she had. "We don't get to choose our lives, do we?"

"We choose some things," Carrie said evenly, setting down her teacup. "Father never mentioned that you'd be bringing a child, only that Janek had asked him to get you out."

Sophie stiffened. "No, Janek doesn't know. I was expecting when the war started . . . when he left Poland. He's never seen her, never even knew she was born. I can't wait to tell him, to have them meet." But it was a lie. Sophie's heartbeat would have betrayed her could Carrie see it thump-thumping in her chest.

She prayed she'd find the courage and know the freedom to tell Janek the truth, prayed that he would want to claim Charlotte as his own. *But how will he feel about another man's child? Another woman's child? A Jewish child?*

"We'd tried so long for a baby. I'd lost two before Janek left." Sophie took a sip of tea, let it slide down her throat and warm her. "Who would have imagined that I'd carry one to term in the midst of war?"

"Yes," Carrie replied softly. "Who would have imagined?"

CHAPTER FORTY-TWO

IT WAS NOT SPRING IN the Ponary Forest—not yet. Winter winds and even snow and freezing rain complicated the burning of the dead. But progress on the tunnel kept the increasing number of men who knew going.

"We can't be too far away now," Uri said. "Before Passover. It will be our miracle to celebrate Passover outside these forsaken walls."

"Passover?" Itzhak hadn't thought of Passover in longer than he dared remember. How would they even know what day that was? What day today was? He'd lost count of the days and weeks since he'd come to the Ponary Forest. He'd meant to keep writing his mental letters to Rosa, but he'd become preoccupied with the tunnel. All his energies, all his focus had gone there.

Now, with the hope of escape near to becoming a reality, every able man put his back and arms into digging the tunnel. Incentive to dig was added by the overheard snippets of the Obersturmbannführer ranting that the Lithuanians had made such a mess, leaving it for the Germans to clean up quickly. Itzhak bit the insides of his cheeks to keep from arguing with the guards who blamed the Lithuanians. He knew the Lithuanians were only-too-willing henchmen—too eager by far to demean, dehumanize, and oust the Jews—but the Germans were the orchestrators of horror. He knew, and he would one day tell the world.

They were nearing the tunnel's end. Itzhak must mentally prepare to rejoin his Rosa. He would begin with a new epistle tonight. The thought warmed him as the guard separated the group of prisoners and directed his half to a new pit. They'd reached the bottom of the biggest one, and it was time to open new graves.

Itzhak steeled his mind against what awaited. This new grave would begin with the more recent dead. Bodies near the top held more recognizable features. He could not pretend they were not people, no matter what the Nazis ordered them to say, to think.

The sun had risen higher, and despite the cold wind, it warmed his back, the backs of his hands.

It won't be long now, my Rosa. We'll escape. We're making a plan for all of us. Half the men know now, but we will tell the rest when we know we've reached the end. Where I go doesn't matter. I will find you. It may be after the war, but I promise, I will find you. All that matters is that I find you and our Ania, that we are together again.

Itzhak stopped the letter in his head. He stopped digging. The dress on the body before him was one he'd seen a thousand times. He'd seen it as his mother lit the candles on Shabbat, as she served latkes on Hanukkah. Her best dress—navy with the ivory crocheted collar. Worn, dirty, too big on the corpse before him, but it was her dress.

His heart pounded, climbing to his throat. He lifted the hand . . . The fingers were too thin, but there was the scar from the gash she'd received when he was a curious child, the day she'd jerked his hand away from the butcher's knife as it fell too quickly. She should have had it sewn, but she didn't.

He could not bring himself to look at her face, if there was a face. The dress on the body beside belonged to his sister Regalia. There were three young girls next to her; two had their fingers intertwined with hers. Her daughters, surely. What about Talia? He looked across the expanse of pits. He didn't see his father or his brothers-in-law. Would it be better if they knew, if they saw, or if they didn't? How to answer such a question?

"What are you waiting for? Put them on the stretcher!" the man partnered to him spat. "We must keep our quota; you know that."

Itzhak looked up, not sure he saw the man.

"What is it?" He hesitated. "You know them?"

Itzhak couldn't speak. He sat back on his heels. Should he say kaddish? Here? Now? A wail formed in his throat, but as soon as it began, the other man punched him in the mouth.

"Are you *meshugge*? They'll shoot us! Here, let me get them. Dig somewhere else."

But Itzhak pushed him away, pushed him to the ground with a fierceness he didn't know he still possessed. *Do not touch my mama! Do not touch her!*

The man huffed, the wind knocked from him. "See to her yourself, then. Don't blame me whatever happens." And he crawled away to dig elsewhere.

Itzhak lifted his mother onto the stretcher, and his sister beside her. They weighed nothing. He could carry them both at once if the man came back and took the other end. He moved the three young girls to another stretcher, an empty one nearby. Two men picked up the ends and carried them away before he could speak, before he formed the thought to say, *"Wait—they are my family."*

But he would carry his mother, his sister. He looked up, searching the pit for his work partner, but the tears blinded his eyes. He swiped them away with the back of his filthy hand. Dirt in his eye made him blink, made him look down at the ground and away from the sun, and that was when he saw the glint of gold.

They'd been told to watch for gold—gold teeth, gold brooches, gold rings, gold necklaces . . . all to be turned in immediately for the greater good of the Reich.

He didn't recognize the dress. But the filigree, the cutting, looked familiar. Itzhak swallowed. He pushed aside the dirt. The earth shifted. The world came out of alignment. *No. No! It can't be . . . It's only half—half the medallion. It's not her—no!*

He couldn't look at her face, couldn't bring his eyes past the medallion. *There must be a thousand Tree of Life medallions among the Jews of Vilna! It is—not—not—her!*

He closed his eyes, rocking back and forth on his heels, his breath ragged, his chest crushed in a brace. But he knew he couldn't take this image with him. He must know for certain. Itzhak opened his eyes. Gently, he brushed the dirty hair from her face.

Rosa! Rosa! God in heaven, why? Why are you here?

"What's going on?" The guard above the pit moved closer, aiming his gun at Itzhak. "Why have you stopped? *Raus! Schnell!*"

Itzhak wanted to rip the man's heart out. But the man held the gun, and Itzhak couldn't risk the guard making sport of his wife. He raised his hand in acquiescence and turned so his back was to the guard above him, so his hands cradled his Rosa's face. He traced the line of her neck and fingered the medallion, the medallion he'd placed there on their wedding day, the medallion she'd vowed never to remove.

An empty stretcher was dumped beside him, ready for the next corpse. Carefully, reverently, he lifted her body, choking back tears of anger and anguish and futility, and gently placed her on the stretcher. He unclasped the half medallion, fingered the filigree he'd had fashioned just for her, and twined the chain through his fingers.

Ania . . . Ania! He searched the earth beside the place Rosa's body had fallen, pushing aside the body of an older woman he didn't recognize. There, as if torn from his Rosa's arms, the body of a child, perhaps two or three, reached its arms toward her resting place. *Ania?* Itzhak's heart broke, irrevocably, truly. He cradled the faceless child to his chest, pressing it closer than the fragile bones allowed. As he did so, its clothing fell away and he pulled back. *A boy. You're a boy. You can't be my Ania.*

Frantically, Itzhak searched the earth—five bodies in each direction and directly beneath. Ania, wherever she was, was not there.

◆

That night, and every night to follow, Itzhak, his father, Uri, and Avner said kaddish, quietly chanting the prayer of praise and mourning with men around them—men they knew by name, men who'd said kaddish for more loved ones than they dared count aloud. Itzhak knew the words but said them more by rote than with the faith long ingrained in him.

Where are You, God? Why have You not come? Why do You not change the hearts of men to stop this?

But Itzhak still prayed—each night and each morning, he silently railed against the heavens. Without Rosa to talk to, to write letters to in his brain, he desperately needed someone, somewhere.

Days passed. Itzhak no longer worked on the tunnel. He no longer ate. By day he worked slowly, methodically, as if he hoped the guard would shoot him for his dullness. Night after night, he curled into a fetal ball, rubbing the edges of the medallion between his fingers.

"We're nearly there," Uri, who seemed to cope with his terrible loss, urged. "Sol said he reached more earth—dark, less sand—last night. He had to divert the tunnel around a tree root, so we have to be at the forest's edge. We'll be free soon. Gather your wits, Itzhak. Pull yourself together if you have any hope of getting out alive."

Itzhak stared at his brother-in-law. *Does he not understand? Is he so simple?* "I'm not going."

"You're not going because Rosa is dead? You think I don't care that my Regalia is dead? My children? What is wrong with you? You're not the only one who has lost someone. We all have. There is not a man in this bunker who believes his family lives. But we live—we are alive, and we owe—"

"I owe no one! Rosa is my reason—was my reason—for breathing, for getting up and living each day. I have no reason to escape. You go. You go, and take Papa."

"It's not so simple, Dunovich." Avner pushed Uri aside. "We need you. No one here knows the forest as you do. No one here knows where the electric cables run or has seen the layout of the mines from the watchtowers as you have. No one has the experience of cutting through the barbed wire so quickly, silently, that you do. You have to go, and you have to be first out."

"The men will follow you, listen to you," Uri urged. "All our lives are at stake."

But Itzhak's heart steeled against them, against all of them. He didn't know how they could go on without their wives, their children, but he could not, would not. *What is left? Nothing. Nothing.*

He was done talking. He turned, lay down, and closed his eyes.

Perhaps an hour passed, and still Itzhak did not sleep. His father rolled over beside him. As if they'd been in deep conversation, he whispered, "You found half the medallion. Where is the other half?"

"I don't know. How would I know?"

"It was cut in half—cleanly—and filed. You showed me, remember?"

"That is nothing." Itzhak wanted him to stop talking.

"You are wrong. It is something. Why would Rosa cut the most precious thing she owned? Why would she cut it cleanly in half?"

"How can I know?"

"Think, Itzhak. Rosa would give the medallion you gave her to no one—unless she gave it to her daughter, to your Ania. Unless she knew they would be separated and she intended to reunite the pieces."

Itzhak didn't speak, didn't trust himself to think what that meant.

"You don't want to live because you are alone. You are without your Rosa. But what about your Ania? What if she is out there—somewhere—waiting for her papa to come for her? What if she is waiting and you do not come?"

"Please, Papa. There is no way to know—she's probably dead."

"'Probably' means she may be alive."

Itzhak locked his teeth to keep from crying out. "I don't know where to look. I can't believe she lives, or that Rosa could find a way to hide her or give her up—"

"You won't find her here, in this hellhole. You won't find her in this bunker. If Rosa gave her up, it was to save her. Can you do less? You must go, Itzhak—and take us with you. There is not another man who grew up in this forest as you did, not another man with trails marked between trees in his head. Do you not think you were given your trade, the tools of your trade, and the knowledge of the forest for such a time as this? Do not spurn the gift HaShem has given you, or this opportunity to search for your daughter."

Itzhak could fight no more. *What if he's right? What if Ania waits for me? I failed my Rosa, but our Ania . . . If there is a chance, even a very slim chance . . .*

The next night he met with the representatives of the men digging the tunnel.

"We must go out in small groups—five, six at most. I will go first and lead you as long as my father and brothers-in-law come out in the first group with me." Those were Itzhak's terms.

"No." Sol Goldberg held his ground. "Your father is old. He'll slow us down. Not the first group—the third. I agree to the third group."

"Going out first is the most dangerous. When I stick my head above ground, if they see me, they will shoot it off. If I make it to the barbed wire, it will take a moment to cut it. All of that adds up to greater risk. If I am going to take such risks, my father in the first group is my deal."

But Chaim Dunovich intervened. "No, my son. Sol is right. The young men must go first. They're most likely to make it into the forest. They can join with the partisans. They can fight. I have no more fight."

"But, Papa—"

"Yes." Chaim's eyes flashed and his chin lifted. "I am still the papa, and this is what I say."

Itzhak knew his father's word was final. He could not shame his father by insisting, and he could not sway eighty men to his thinking.

"Tomorrow night, then," Sol insisted. "We're there—beyond the mines now. You go first. Break through the topsoil. Then there's only the barbed wire to cut. We dare not dig farther and we can't wait. The roof is in danger of collapsing."

"Tomorrow night," Itzhak agreed.

◆ ◆ ◆

It was the first night of Passover. There was no wine, no lamb, no bitter herb or egg or unleavened bread. And they would not be staying within the doors of their "home" this night.

Itzhak cut the shackles from his legs and his father's legs. As the pliers made their way through the room, the only sound was the muffled dropping of chains caught before falling to the floor, the first whisper of freedom.

Itzhak hugged his father, sat back, and took his hands. "I'll see you in the forest."

His father, eyes full, did not speak, but squeezed his son's hands in reassurance.

Itzhak drew a deep breath and crawled into the tunnel, for what he believed would be the last time.

When he finally reached the end of the tunnel, Itzhak was out of air. He'd told the men to wait until he signaled that he'd broken through the topsoil to enter the tunnel, but they were too quick, too eager, and had evidently pushed forward. Now the tunnel, full of men—twenty, perhaps—became a suffocating tomb.

He'd intended to take more time, to slowly and carefully increase the surface area to be certain it would not cave in and block the tunnel, but now there was no time. Without more oxygen he would soon pass out, as would the men behind him. The tunnel would be filled, blocked by dead men whose last thoughts of freedom had betrayed them.

Gasping, he pushed his iron bar through the dirt, straight up, making a hole, then a second one. Soil and dried grass fell into his face, followed by the overwhelming aroma of sweet, clean, pure air. Air unlike anything he'd smelled for all the months he'd been shackled in the pits. Itzhak drew it into his lungs, then drew another, deeper breath. *Fir, damp earth, and freedom.* The moon and stars above him, the earth before him . . . and a group of Nazi guards but a few meters away, looking directly toward the spot where his head had emerged. Itzhak froze. The guards did not move, did not seem to see him, but talked quietly among themselves.

Light flooded the pits, casting gruesome shadows on the forest beyond.

Itzhak felt the hand of the man behind him on his foot, a plea to move. He broke through the surface, a wider opening, wide enough for a man to slip through. He crept out on all fours, keeping flat to the ground, and crawled toward the dark forest. He'd crawled perhaps a hundred meters and was nearly to the outer rim of barbed wire when the voices of guards in the forest beyond made him stop, the man behind him almost overrunning him.

Itzhak changed course, risking a longer route, but could not alert the men behind, silence being their only cover. By the time he'd nearly reached the barbed wire in the new location, he was able to stand, no longer fearful of being seen.

Several men behind him stood. A branch snapped. Dogs barked. Searchlights swarmed the pits. German orders were barked, and machine guns opened fire. A mine exploded and body parts flew into the air.

Itzhak dove to the ground, cut the barbed wire, and wriggled through. Suddenly he was running, running with ten, eleven, twelve men beside and behind him, and then there were five, and more fleeing in different directions.

Papa! Where is Papa? But this time Itzhak did not stop. He ran and ran, as he'd promised he would, in the direction he'd said he would. They would meet near the road—whoever made it through.

Gunfire and barking dogs continued behind him, closing in. Itzhak knew he could not make the road—not now, not yet. Shafts of moonlight penetrated the forest canopy—here and there a tree—and then the dead husk of a giant tree bathed in starlight.

Itzhak dove in, his breath ragged from running. He scraped handfuls of rotted, decaying leaves over his skin, rubbed them through his hair. He pulled his feet, light and curiously free without their shackles, beneath his buttocks and waited. Snarling, barking dogs came closer, surely following his scent of fear.

The barking stopped. He heard the dogs, noses to the ground, sniffing, tracking scent. And then the dog was there, beside him. Itzhak's hand and foot lay most exposed. He wanted to pull them in, tighter, but there was no more room.

The dog sniffed around the tree, and sniffed again. It stopped, sniffing Itzhak's hand, his foot, but didn't bark. At last the German shepherd hesitated, sniffed the earth once more, and moved on—and with him, the guards.

Itzhak remained still as death for the next hour, until he was certain the guards and their dogs had doubled back to the camp.

In time he lifted his hand to his nose. *The fragrance of death and decay. Even the dog can't tell the difference between me and the rotted leaves. Thank You. Thank You, Adonai. Your ways are beyond knowing.*

While it was still dark, Itzhak slipped from the hollowed tree trunk. He didn't hear the other men, had no way of knowing who had made it out and who hadn't. He couldn't imagine more than the first two groups had made it through the barbed wire, which meant his father would not have. He couldn't think about that now. He must make his way as far as possible before daylight found him. He didn't know where to look, but if he didn't find the partisans quickly, they would find him.

For now, Itzhak pushed on, and pushed away the tears that streamed down his face despite his refusal to feel the weight of more loss. He would say kaddish for his father later, when he found a minyan. He was used to saying kaddish.

CHAPTER FORTY-THREE

IT WAS SPRING BY THE TIME the details Sir Lawrence had set in motion before his death ironed out—leave for Janek and an apartment for Sophie and Charlotte as close as possible to the airfield where Janek was stationed, which wasn't really very close at all. Sophie knew that Carrie would have preferred they be nearer to Bristol, where she could see them regularly, but she was quite certain Sir Lawrence had intended to maintain a distance for the sake of his daughter's reputation—and to keep Carrie tied to him—just as he'd done when he'd confiscated and returned the letters Sophie had written. It was a grace to learn that Carrie had been deceived, that she'd also written letters to Sophie and never known that her father had intercepted them. Carrie had not spurned their friendship, as Sophie had so long believed.

Despite the restoration of their relationship, Sophie was glad, even relieved, for the distance. She wanted—needed—time alone with Janek when he finally came, and time to help Charlotte settle into their new life.

She didn't want to lie to Carrie. Perhaps it was her imagination, but she felt Carrie could read her mind, see clear through her brain to the back of her skull. She'd felt that way growing up when they'd declared themselves kindred spirits. So many years had passed. Everything in their lives had changed, and yet it seemed now that nothing had changed.

Carrie had invited the Kumiegas to join her at Haverford for dinner when they were settled, assuming Janek could get leave. That would be soon enough.

◆ ◆ ◆

Sophie spilled Charlotte's milk at breakfast and sopped it with her new tea towel, lamenting that she could no longer hang it prettily from the hook above the sink. While washing up she dropped one of the secondhand teacups she'd found at Saturday's market, shattering it across the tile floor. She burned the rationed mystery meat she'd so lovingly prepared for the day's luncheon. She did her best to twist her dark hair into victory rolls, popular with other British women, but it was still too thin and brittle from years of malnutrition to roll properly or to shine. She sat down in the middle of her bed and cried.

"Mamusia, don't cry." Charlotte crawled onto the bed beside her, stroking Sophie's arm.

Frustrated and helpless at once, Sophie swiped at the tears. *How was it I maintained fortitude and resilience amid the most harrowing of circumstances and now break down over my hair? If it were only just my hair!*

"Is it because Papa is coming today?"

Out of the mouths of babes. Sophie sighed.

"Don't you want him to come?" Charlotte's question came so innocently.

"Of course I do, darling. Of course I do. It's just that . . . it's been so long since I've seen him. I want everything to be perfect.

I wanted luncheon to be wonderful, and I want to be beautiful for him, and . . ." She didn't know how to finish, how to explain it all to someone barely four years old . . . at least she imagined Charlotte to be four, or nearly. That was another thing. She needed to remember the birth date she'd assigned Charlotte: February 14, 1940, Valentine's Day. How could she forget? She'd counted carefully from the time she believed she had conceived. Of course, she hoped to tell Janek the truth. But telling the truth might depend on how he perceived her . . . if he still wanted her, or them.

Sophie had barely been able to keep her porridge down that morning, what with all her imaginings and fears and the countless conversations she'd rehearsed inside her head. She would explain it all after they put Charlotte to bed that night, when they were alone. It would be time enough.

"You are beautiful, Mamusia. You're my special mummy, my very best friend. You're the most beautiful lady in the whole world." Charlotte's brown eyes grew like saucers in her petite face.

So trusting. So precious. No matter what, my dearest, I cannot give you up.

"Mamusia?"

"Yes, my sweet?"

"Will Papa like me?"

"Of course he will! He'll love you!" Oh, how she prayed it was true.

They were still snuggled in an embrace when the knock came at the door. Sophie jumped.

"It's him! It's Papa!" Charlotte jumped from the bed, excited and jubilant, then suddenly shy. "You go first, Mamusia."

Sophie smiled and stood, trying to still her beating heart. She smoothed her skirt, straightened the collar of her blouse, and pushed a wayward tendril behind her ear. There was nothing more she could do but open the door.

As she placed her hand on the knob, the anxious knock came again, Janek's hand still raised as she pulled the door open. They both froze. Janek's eyes so clearly searched for the young and inexperienced, nearly child bride he'd left behind. Sophie silently pleaded that he'd see and love the woman she'd become, that he'd not be disappointed.

Wisps of concern, of longing and heartache, stole through his eyes. He laughed a syllable, or choked a sob—Sophie couldn't tell which—and whispered, "Sophia. You're real."

"Flowers! He brought flowers, Mamusia!" came Charlotte's breathless voice behind her.

Confusion crossed Janek's eyes, then wonder as he looked from Sophie to Charlotte and back again.

"Will he kiss your hand, Mamusia?" Charlotte whispered, loud enough for both grown-ups to hear.

The reminder seemed to catch Janek short, and he bowed, lifting Sophie's fingers to his lips and closing his eyes. It took a moment longer than she remembered for him to stand, to look into her eyes and take her into his arms. He didn't kiss her on her mouth but held her close—gently at first, then more firmly—a treasure redeemed. "Sophia. Sophia."

The tears in his voice broke something fragile within Sophie. He held her and she clung to him, running her fingers up the back of his neck, holding his face, burying her longings into his shoulder, his neck. She let him pull her lips to his. "Janek! Janek!"

"The flowers, Mamusia! They're getting crushed," came the wail at Sophie's knee.

Sophie laughed. She laughed and cried for joy and relief and the unpredictable comedy of it all. Then she prayed, *Thank You, Father.* She pulled away first, attempting to dry her eyes, to release the coveted flowers from their demise.

But Janek couldn't take his eyes from her. Sophie wasn't sure exactly what he saw, but clearly he was riveted, and she rejoiced.

Persistent tugs on her skirt distracted them both, until Janek seemed to fully comprehend the presence of the child. Charlotte gave a hopeful smile, ducking behind Sophie's knee.

Janek looked again at Sophie. Confusion, then indecision, like a man afraid to hope. He leaned down and cautiously said, "Who's this?"

Surprising them all, the little face peeked out and said, "My name is Charlotte. And you are my papa."

Janek paled, glanced at Sophie, who wanted to say everything, but said nothing. In the end Sophie could only nod, half smiling, half crying. *I'll explain later. Let her have this moment.*

Janek went down on one knee. Flustered, speechless for a moment, he handed Charlotte the crushed flowers. "Then these must be for you, for you and your mamusia."

Charlotte beamed. She glowed like sunshine. So seldom had she seen flowers. Even in England few had yet budded in the gardens at Haverford, much less bloomed. *"Dziękuję!"* She stuck out her hand, dropped a curtsy, and said, "I'm very pleased to meet you, Papa."

Janek closed his eyes and lifted her tiny fingers to his lips. He looked as if his heart might explode.

Charlotte giggled and pulled away, happy with her bouquet of flowers. Janek let her go. It took him a few moments to gather his bearings, but at last he stood and whispered, "Carrie told me you had a surprise—that I would be stunned. Is she—is she truly—?"

It was the moment Sophie had wrestled with for months. The love and unbridled hope in Janek's eyes coupled with her sudden anger that Carrie had dared to speak first of Charlotte caught her off guard. The words came out, bypassing reason. "I was pregnant when you left. Do you remember?"

"Yes. Yes! But with the war . . . I never thought—I never imagined you would—"

"Would have been able to carry a child?" she all but challenged.

It was the insufficiency she felt in that moment—weakness that she could not carry a baby when other women popped them out so regularly, a sign not only of fertility but of womanhood. Carrie's eyes had told her she didn't believe her capable. Now Janek.

"I didn't mean . . . ," he stuttered, then stopped, his eyes following Charlotte across the room. "She's beautiful." He pulled Sophie close then and whispered into her hair, "To find you, my Sophia—after all this time—is more than enough . . . is all that I've wanted, prayed for in this world. But you've brought me a daughter?" Tears of disbelief and overwhelming gratitude filled his eyes.

Sophie closed her eyes and leaned into him. She yearned for his warmth and kisses and responded in every way possible to his love and joy. But a dagger thrust into her soul. *How can I tell him? How can I break his heart?*

PART II

CHAPTER FORTY-FOUR

London, England
June 8, 1946

It was a full year after VE Day before the military victory parade marched through the streets of London. By invitation, the many nations who'd come to Britain's aid and fought with the Allies marched—representatives of corps that fought on land, on sea, and in the air.

Janek had, at first, refused to attend, but in the end, Sophia argued until she'd convinced him, saying he was new, as a civilian, in the country. In order to be accepted by friends and neighbors, he must go—for the sake of Charlotte's future, if not for his own. How could she explain his absence to Carrie after all Sir Lawrence had done for them? Surely she would ask in her letters.

So Sophia had dressed six-year-old Charlotte in navy blue with a white collar and hair bow. She'd given her a small British flag, declaring her intent to set a celebratory tone and wave away the set jaw of her husband.

But her teasing was futile. Janek could no more work his jaw into a smile than he could fly to the moon . . . or anywhere else. He'd never fly again, no matter that his squadron had defended Britain from the first day of the London Blitz, shooting down at least fourteen German aircraft—an RAF record. He was lucky, he knew, to be allowed to stay and work as a Polish interpreter in England—a favor from the government, all thanks to the legacy of Sir Lawrence and the supportive recommendations established before his death. Going home to now-Communist Poland would end in a trip to Siberia, without reprieve; of that he had no doubt.

He'd defended flaming London from the seat of a British Hurricane, but Polish military personnel were barred from participating in the parade, for fear of offending Joseph Stalin, the man behind the Polish "Provisional Government of National Unity," which was anything but a free Poland. All of former British prime minister Churchill's lofty declarations of gratitude and honor, his promises to Poles throughout the long war to "conquer together or die together," had disappeared quicker than London's morning fog. President Truman had proven no better. He and the still-mourned Franklin D. Roosevelt had, in Janek's mind, thrown Poland and now its warriors under the bus, to use a popular American expression.

Janek blinked away the moisture behind his eyes and stilled the too-fresh memories of the daring pilots, good men and close friends, who'd given their lives for Britain in order to gain freedom for Poland. It was a mercy they didn't know.

Janek glimpsed Sophia from the corner of his eye, saw her cheering, encouraging Charlotte to wave her little Union Jack. He drew a deep but ragged breath and let it out slowly. England was Sophia's country, not his.

"See my flag, Papa! See my flag!" Charlotte danced, her arms raised to him. He lifted her up, high on his shoulder, so she could see and be seen. Janek was proud of his daughter, of her dark beauty and sparkling eyes, her ready laugh. She was victory over the war in a teacup—small and delicate, a half-pint of resiliency and joy. He could deny her nothing.

Charlotte's soft brown eyes and olive skin contrasted sharply with Sophia's startling blue eyes and pink skin. His heart crimped even as it swelled, and he stroked the little girl's foot against his chest. The two women he loved most looked nothing alike, and Charlotte looked nothing like him or anyone in his family—a reality he worked hard to ignore in light of his love for the child, and for Sophia.

Sophia smiled up at him, a rare occurrence these days, and looped her free arm through his. Janek knew she was doing her best to buoy his spirits. He even wished he could reciprocate the smile. But England's latest betrayal cut too deep in his heart, a gash too fresh to heal. That Sophia didn't understand, or chose to ignore it, cut deeper still.

At last the parade ended with a deafening overhead roar of airpower. Led by a Hawker Hurricane, Britain's best flew low as the crowd cheered wildly. Bombers, fighters, flying boats, and transports filled the steel-gray skies. A final wild cheer and the crowd began to disperse, giving good-natured claps on the back to one another—as if they'd single-handedly won the war. Some made their way home and some stumbled toward pubs to continue the celebration.

The Kumiegas' walk home was quieter. The distraction of the parade gone, it was as if the tense veil fell over Sophia's face once more.

This time, Janek had no energy to try to lift it.

◆ ◆ ◆

Monday morning came as a relief. Even the jostling of the overcrowded buses felt friendlier than the cold and nervous silence of his wife.

Janek stood back while the new company handyman screwed his nameplate onto his office door. *Janek Kumiega.* At least he'd been able to keep his name intact, despite the postwar pressures to anglicize foreigners' names.

He knew he should be the happiest man alive. He'd survived the war, a feat too few fighter pilots could claim. He'd been honorably decommissioned and established British citizenship in record time. He'd gotten a job through favors but quickly shown himself capable— capable enough to be promoted to a recognized linguist position within the first five months. His wife and the child he'd longed for but never knew existed had escaped war-torn Europe. Their daughter was healthy. Her English was perfect. In September, Charlotte would begin school. Life, in every apparent way, was wonderful. What was it Sophia had early on in their reunion quoted from Robert Louis Stevenson? *"The world is so full of a number of things, I'm sure we should all be as happy as kings."*

Janek hung his hat upon the clothes tree in his office and pulled the chair from his desk. *Every reason to be well satisfied, every reason to be the happiest man of the happiest family in the world. But I am not. We are not, and I don't know why.*

His reunion with Sophia had been so sweet, at first. His delight in their daughter unbounded. But Sophia had quickly distanced herself. The more he reached out, the more she pulled back. From the moment Janek had gained the courage to question her about their daughter's birth, the apparent smallness of her size for her age, she had taken his questions as a personal affront. It was as if she thought she had to defend her honor as a woman, and Charlotte's honor as a war victim. She'd accused him of not being there when she needed him, declaring that she'd done the best she could under horrific circumstances and that he should be grateful they were both alive. She vowed she would never return to Poland, no matter what happened politically or militarily in the years to come.

Her venom, her anger, had come as an unexpected blow. He'd only wanted to understand what had happened to her, how she'd survived.

CATHY GOHLKE

To show his admiration for her strength and courage—childbirth alone, enduring the deprivations of war in a hostile environment, her amazing and courageous journey through Germany and France, over the mountains, by way of the sea . . . He'd wanted to know the details of the life she'd lived without him. He'd wanted to share the details of his life in England, of his missions over the channel and of waiting and praying and never knowing if he would ever see her again.

Why can't she understand how I love her, how I need her, how that need is more than physical? Though there's that, too. She sleeps with her back to me and her heart hardened. And there were the nightmares. Born of the horrors of the war, no doubt. Janek had them too from time to time, so he could understand—at least he could if only she would share them with him. Sometimes Sophia whimpered in her sleep, soaking her pillow in tears and sweat. Other times she sat up, screaming the names of people he didn't know—someone named Terri, most often—even though she was still asleep. Was Terri a man? A woman? Each time he asked—and he'd quickly learned not to ask—about people they both knew and loved before the war—Pan Gadomski and his daughter; the Żablińskis from the zoo; the Bukowskis and neighbors in their apartment building—she simply clamped her lips and shook her head, as if talking or even thinking of those days were impossible.

Janek pushed his hand through his hair, making it stand up on end. The secretary walking past his door looked up, smiled as if his unkempt hair was endearing, then walked on. Janek did his best to comb his hair back down with his fingers. It wouldn't do to be distracted by another woman or to let her think he was. He wanted his wife, and only his wife. He simply didn't know how to reach her.

Janek remembered how his mother had enjoyed the company of other women—her sisters and friends and acquaintances. He'd suggested to Sophia that she contact Carrie Chamberlin, that they make plans to meet for lunch or an outing. They could take Charlotte on a picnic before her schooling began.

295

At first Sophia shrugged at the suggestion, as if it might be something she'd consider, but not now. She insisted she was too busy, that the transportation was still uncertain and that letters were sufficient. But Janek couldn't see what kept her so busy or why it would matter if she were late of an evening, or even if she and Charlotte stayed the night at Haverford. He knew how to prepare his own tea. Janek knew Sir Lawrence had wished—insisted—that they keep their distance from Carrie by having a home in town. But Sir Lawrence was no longer here, and Carrie had made repeated overtures to them both, clearly craving time with Sophia.

The more he offered solutions, the angrier she became.

"You just want to get rid of me. Is there someone else? Someone you want to bring home, and you want us out of the house?"

The accusation had stunned Janek. That wasn't what he wanted . . . at all. He wanted his wife, but he didn't know how to make her understand that. He began to wonder if she no longer wanted him. *Is there someone else for you, Sophia? Was there—during the war?* They were words he'd hinted at, but dared not voice aloud. Still, the fear grew in his heart day by day, chipping away at his confidence.

Janek had thought the knocking came from inside him. It took a moment longer to realize that Iwan Nowak, the custodian, stood at his door, grinning and knocking on the doorpost. "So, you'll let me come in? Or are you far away, still fighting the war in your Hurricane?"

"Iwan, I'm sorry. Come in, come in."

"I heard you have a problem with the lighting."

"Ah, yes, a short in the wiring, I think. But I'm no electrician."

"Neither am I. Let me take a look, see if I can do anything. If not, we'll send for someone. Lousy wiring through this whole building even before the bombing. It's on the list to be repaired."

Janek nodded. He knew they were lucky to have a building. The city was pockmarked, whole blocks still in rubble, and would be for a long time to come. Wars might end with the stroke of a pen or political leaders' handshakes, but the devastation, to people and things, went on for a lifetime.

"Not so bad as home, all the same, so I guess we oughtn't complain, eh?"

Iwan was a Pole, from just outside Warsaw, not ten kilometers from where Janek was born and raised. They'd met first when Janek was still in the RAF. Iwan Nowak could tear apart a plane and put it back together in no time, but he was not, as he'd said, an electrician.

Although Iwan never said, Janek suspected the man had been a strong community leader in their home country. He did his best to strengthen ties among the Poles in London, especially within the clustered Polish community—not overtly, but through friendly means. Janek knew Iwan sought out and recommended Poles for jobs wherever he could. "It's good business—for everyone," he'd said with a wink when Janek teased him about recommending a Pole for England's next prime minister. "We work hard; we build strong families—good for the community, good for the economy, better for the British than they know."

Even when it had seemed the underground would never find Janek's wife, even when it loomed unlikely that they'd be able to get her through Germany and back to England, Iwan had believed in miracles. It was a comfort to see the man, even when the two didn't speak. A fellow Pole with a great heart—not rare in London, but a treasured gift, all the same.

"Have you heard anything?" Janek didn't need to ask more. Iwan would know he meant *anything from Poland—about your family, about your neighborhood.*

Iwan shrugged. "Word that my brother-in-law never made it back from the war. Word that my sister is stuck there, in Warsaw, for now. We can't get her out—not yet. Because she hid Jewish children in her home, she's suspect. She might be sent to Siberia. We don't know. She waits."

"I'm sorry." Janek knew, just as all the world did, that not many survived the winters in Siberia, especially those already sick or weakened from war deprivations. It was hard to know what more to say.

"And what about you? How goes life with the 'ice princess'?"

Janek winced. He'd confided his worries to Iwan in a moment of weakness. At first it had been a relief to engage a confidant, but hearing the vulgarity of his own words parroted back to him, he regretted not better defending the honor of his wife.

Now it was Janek's turn to shrug. But it wasn't enough. He couldn't brush it off, remain silent. Ever since the parade he'd wondered if he could keep going, keep breathing. Things at home and in the city—and inside him—were closing in. "Did you go to the parade?"

"Yes, I celebrate freedom. But not as I will celebrate the freedom of Poland, when it comes."

"If?"

"When. We must believe, my friend."

"Iwan Nowak, you have more faith than I."

"But you have a family, which many of us—most of our Polish fighters—do not."

Janek nodded. The option was to assimilate in England or to return to Poland and be arrested. It was not a hard decision for single men, but for married men, fathers with children still living in Poland, the decision had been agonizing.

"You, my friend—"

"Yes, yes, I know. I have everything and should be grateful." Janek hated the sting of sarcasm in his voice.

"That's not what I was going to say." Iwan tilted his head to one side and repacked his tools, unable to repair the short in the wiring. "But it bears thinking on."

"I don't know if Charlotte is my daughter." Janek blurted it out before running it past the filter in his brain. He'd thought it a million times but had not dared to voice it aloud.

Nowak stood, shouldered his tool bag, and nodded, looking at the mother-and-daughter picture on Janek's desk. "Perhaps not."

Just like that? You say it just like that?

"Do not look at me as if I've uttered the unthinkable . . . you think it, yes? It is not so impossible, my friend." Iwan walked to the door and turned. "And it is not the end of the world. Not the unmaking of your family."

"Not the unmaking of my family!" Janek was not a man given to displays of temper, but even he didn't know what to do with the hammering in his chest. "If she is not mine, whose is she?"

Iwan shrugged, as if it didn't matter. "Look, my friend—" he set down his bag—"you have a beautiful wife, a magnificent child. Do you want to lose them? If you do, if you want your Sophia to get fed up with your dark moods and walk away, taking the little girl with her, then you keep this up. You keep asking her, you badger her, you eat yourself inside out with doubts and worries." Iwan narrowed his eyes. "But if you're smart, if you have between your ears the sense you were born with, the good sense of a Pole, you will move heaven and earth to save your marriage—your family."

Janek sat down at his desk, telling himself to breathe, to listen. Iwan Nowak had given him sound advice before.

"Men by the millions lost their families in that war. What they wouldn't give for a face from home—just one face. Don't be foolish, Janek Kumiega. Don't throw away the wife and family God has miraculously restored to you . . . even if the child is not yours."

"But whose, then? And did she love him?"

"Who is to know? Many terrible, unthinkable things happened during the war. She was a woman alone . . . Perhaps, if Charlotte is not yours, Sophia had no choice. How can you know? If you can't believe in that child being yours, believe in the life God has given you now. Embrace what you have, Kumiega, or you will lose it."

CHAPTER FORTY-FIVE

ITZHAK DUNOVICH STILL BORE the limp he'd received from the bullet of a German Luger. Living in the Rudnicka Forest for months, fighting beside the partisans and two of the ten men who'd escaped through the tunnel with him, had fueled his anger, given it a venue to explode. But when night came, when the cold settled in and battles waned, memories of Rosa as his bride, as the mother of their sweet Ania, and finally as little more than rotted flesh and half a medallion, pierced his soul . . . again and again and again.

Before the war ended, he'd been spirited through networks by way of an underground band to London. It was a destination many desired, but few achieved. It would not have happened for Itzhak had the underground not needed his skills—extinguishing the lights on a train in order to get their contingent aboard unseen, then returning them to normal, and later creating chaos and distraction when lights flickered and the chandelier in a ballroom of suspected Nazi sympathizers suddenly crashed to the floor. Once in England, there was no easy way to return to Poland or Lithuania.

There seemed little point in going back anyway. His family was gone. The deaths of his father and brothers-in-law had been confirmed through the underground. He'd seen what remained of his mother and sisters, his nieces. He'd held the remains of his Rosa.

The only person unaccounted for was his Ania, and he didn't even know if Poland was the place to look.

Electricians were in short supply after the war, and England had been pleased enough to grant him citizenship, as long as he plied his trade for their good and kept his nose clean.

Two weeks after the victory parade through London, Itzhak was sent on a new job—to work through a minor government office facility, replacing damaged cables and wiring as needed.

He had no idea what work they did there, but he doubted the faulty wiring was a direct result of war bombing. The building looked ancient, and Iwan Nowak, the Polish custodian who'd recommended Itzhak for the job, agreed.

"The electrical system was probably installed with the onset of electric lighting, if I had my guess. At least that's true of the plumbing and half a dozen other changes forced into the building's original structure." Iwan shook his head. "The war was bad enough but can't be blamed for everything. Still, bombing didn't help. And if they say their war damage was this bad or that bad, it gives them priority for repairs."

"Better than waiting until all the war-damaged buildings are repaired, then?" Itzhak raised his brows. *Everybody's got an angle, eh?*

"Exactly. No trouble for me. Nice to have you on the job, Pan Dunovich."

"Thank you, Pan Nowak. I believe before I'm done rewiring this building we'll get to know one another quite well."

"That long?"

Itzhak adjusted his glasses—glasses he'd only needed after the war—and pulled a nest of tangled and bent wires from an electrical box. "If what's here in the basement is any indication of what I'll find in the offices above, I should live to meet your grandchildren."

"Ha! And I yours, Pan Dunovich!" Iwan Nowak clapped Itzhak on the back. "You have the run of the building. Let me know if you need anything. I'll be on the third floor for the next few hours."

◆ ◆ ◆

It took Itzhak three weeks before his work reached the second floor. To him, it was a wonder any building standing that high had not been demolished in the bombing. Even so, the constant jarring and rumbling of the city under siege had weakened the structure of many buildings left standing and compromised their electric and plumbing. Adding to that the general age and in some cases inferiority of the original materials, Itzhak knew he'd have no shortage of work for years to come.

But it was not enough to work, to go home exhausted, to sleep, to get up again and repeat this life. He'd tried drinking himself into oblivion, but it did no good. The resulting hangover and unsteadiness on the job were not worth it. And he couldn't lose his job. He knew he was lucky to have it, lucky to live in a country with running water and electricity. He'd been without both for more years than he wanted to remember.

Life before the war, life with Rosa in his arms and all the promise of future years before them, seemed like a dream. That was the thought on his mind when he stepped through the office door marked *Janek Kumiega* to investigate a reported short in lighting and saw the photograph on the man's desk.

Itzhak blinked and blinked again to chase away daydreams, and readjusted his glasses. He didn't recognize the woman—had never seen her. But the little girl, who couldn't be more than four or five, was Rosa looking out at him, smiling, a younger version of herself. *Could two people, unrelated, look so much alike?*

A secretary walked by the open door, hesitated, and looked in. "Can I help you?" She looked as if he were scum on the underside of her shoe that she wanted to be rid of.

"No, but thank you. I'm here to repair the wiring. There's a short in the wiring." He felt as if he talked from a mouth of marble dust.

"Then don't you think you'd best get on with it?"

Itzhak realized he'd been staring at the photograph, but it probably looked as if he were taking inventory of the man's desk. He stepped back, set down his tool chest, and, kneeling to unpack his tools, turned his back on the woman. *Let her think what she will. Who is that child? Who is this Janek Kumiega?*

All morning the questions haunted him. All morning he spent in Janek Kumiega's office, though it didn't take long to repair the short. Where the man was, he didn't know, but for the first time in a long while Itzhak prayed, thanking Adonai for this picture, this smile, those eyes.

When the war ended, Itzhak had written letters to distant relatives and fellow workmen forced to do work for the Reich, to the Lejas, to the Żabińskis who ran the zoo and were known to have hidden Jews and others. His letter to the Lejas was returned, marked "Deceased"—a tragedy Itzhak mourned deeply and all too vividly imagined. The Żabińskis knew nothing. No one had seen Ania.

He'd even written to Pani Dobonowicz —though he hated doing so—asking her to open the wall behind the kitchen stove in the house that had belonged to Rosa's mother, to find the box Rosa's matka had hidden in the wall.

He would never see the house again and was not fool enough to think the woman would send the jewelry. He'd told her to keep it, as a gift, but begged her to have mercy on him and send the photographs. They were all he had or could ever hope to have of Rosa, of Ania—of any of his family. Months passed, and he'd heard nothing.

It wouldn't have surprised him if Ania didn't look like her mother as she grew. But this child looked just like the photographs he remembered of Rosa as a child. Rosa in pigtails. Rosa in braids. Rosa with her hair hanging long and loose and thick. The slightly crooked smile, as if she'd been told to smile for the photographer and wasn't quite sure how to achieve the desired effect.

Above all, it was the eyes. He remembered Rosa's eyes with a clarity he could not claim for anything else in life. That, he remembered, had been the most startling thing about finding her in death, though he hadn't credited it at the time. Her eyes did not open and smile at him from the depth of her soul. The pain of that memory gouged Itzhak's chest. Involuntarily, he doubled over.

Thankfully, no one passed the open door. But it was in that moment that Itzhak knew he must have the photograph. He forced himself to finish checking the wiring around the room, hoped he'd connected everything as it should be connected, and packed up his tools. He left the taking of the photograph until the last moment, in case the secretary walked past the door again or in case this man, Janek Kumiega, returned to his office.

Now he was done. Itzhak drew a breath, stared into the face of the photograph, and reached out his hand.

◆

Janek hated long meetings. The English either spoke at a rapid clip or pompously drew out their speech, as if each word bestowed gold. *Masters at saying little and deciding nothing! Why can't they just get on with it? Take their own advice: "He who hesitates is lost!"*

He added a few choice words under his breath as he hurried down the hallway, eager to finish the translation of paperwork due to his superior before the end of the workday. What he didn't expect was to find a tearful workman ogling the photograph of his wife.

"Who are you?"

The workman looked up, startled, fearful, and then angry, if Janek was any hand at interpreting eye movement, and he knew he was.

"I say, who are you, and what are you doing here?"

"I—I am Itzhak Dunovich." The man's face clouded and he set down the photograph, but appeared loath to do so. "I work here . . . electrician. I'm the electrician working on the building."

"Ah, good. I'll be glad to have my desk lamp stop blinking like a neon sign." Janek considered the man. He looked quite pitiful, but his accent was unmistakable. "You are Polish?"

"Yes." Dunovich looked up. "Well, Lithuanian to start."

Janek nodded. He sympathized with those caught in the constant back-and-forth of border claims. "I was from Warsaw." He reached his hand to shake.

But Dunovich looked horrified. "Warsaw?"

"Before the war. I was a pilot, forced into Romania when the Germans came—it's a long story, but finally, here."

"RAF?"

Janek nodded, his heart divided, but proud of all he'd accomplished. "Polish division."

The man seemed to relax. "So, you left Poland in the beginning. You—" he pointed to the photograph—"and your wife and child."

"Me, anyway. It wasn't so easy for my wife. Our daughter was born after I left. All those years we missed. But we're here now—together. That's all that counts." Janek wished he could believe that.

"Your wife and daughter stayed in Poland?"

Janek wanted to be kind to the man. So many Poles had lost everyone, as Iwan had reminded him. Some wore those losses as badges of honor or victimization. Some closed off their earlier life to the world as if it never existed, except in their broken hearts and memories. But Dunovich seemed hungry—uncomfortably hungry. Hungry for what, Janek wasn't sure. Information? Shared misery? Sometimes it didn't pay to get too close to others' sorrow. Didn't he have enough of his own without raking the coals from another man's fire? "So, are you finished here, or shall I come back later? I don't believe we can both work at my desk." He eyed the man, trying to level the discomfort but at the same time put him in his place.

Dunovich hesitated, then shook his head. "No, I'm finished. The lamp works fine now." He eyed the photograph again, frowning. "I'll stop in a few days to make certain all is well."

"Thank you. There's no need. I'll put in a request if I have a problem."

Dunovich nodded, tipping his cap.

Janek closed the door behind the man, relieved to be alone. Between upper management's pompous condescension, Sophie's cold shoulder and sharp tongue, and now a heart-heavy, nosy electrician, he'd endured all he believed he could for one day.

He plunked down into his hard wooden desk chair, thankful for a short reprieve, a little quiet, and no faces, no talking mouths. Closing his eyes, he gathered the fortitude to finish work and go home again.

CHAPTER FORTY-SIX

ITZHAK TIGHTENED THE STRAP ON his toolbox and paced the lonely walk home. At least the blackout had been lifted. Neon lights from the cinema and pubs shone through the glistening mist, casting garish colors on passing pedestrians.

Try as he might, castigate his thoughts as he did, Itzhak could not get the image of the little girl's eyes out of his head. He counted the years, the days, on his fingers. He knew exactly how old Ania should be at that very moment.

Logically, that girl could not be Ania, could not be Rosa's daughter. But she didn't look anything like the tall, blond Kumiega, or even like his beautiful wife.

Something needled at the edge of Itzhak's brain, but he couldn't put his finger on it. It worried him something fierce through the wee hours of the morning until he finally fell asleep near dawn and dreamed of Rosa, of their wedding day, of the moment he encircled her neck with the delicate gold chain of the medallion.

When the alarm rang he woke, crying, desperately wishing he

could return to his land of dreams. But he pulled himself up, splashed ice-cold water on his face and beneath his arms, and began to lather up to shave.

Staring into the mirror and bringing the straight razor to just beneath his jaw, he stopped. It was as if a lightbulb flashed inside his head. *If Kumiega left Warsaw—left Poland—in 1939 and didn't see his wife until the end of the war, the child must be six years old, at least. But she doesn't look six, and that photograph must have been taken here, in England. He didn't see his child before she was born—he said so. In fact, how could he be the father of the girl in the picture, or certain that he is?*

The pounding in Itzhak's heart turned to a pulsing in his brain. Just last week he'd read advertisements in the Polish newspaper circulating the Polish section of London—fathers and mothers, aunts and uncles, even societies seeking to reunite children with their families. The article told of many Jewish children hidden from the Nazi death wheel in convents and in Polish Catholic families. *Could that be true of Ania?*

Itzhak nicked himself three times as he shaved that morning.

He kept going over how the advertisements were worded, how the advertiser appealed to readers, what made one request to find a child stand out from all the others.

All he'd thought at the time was, *Those lucky people have hope.* He'd had no reason to hope—not until now. *Even if this child is not my Ania, and Adonai in heaven knows she cannot be, then perhaps He sent this as a sign that I should renew my search for her.*

By the time he'd dressed and packed a lunch of brown bread and butter, Itzhak had composed a rough draft of the advertisement in his head.

Searching for young girl, five years old, disappeared in Poland sometime between 1942 and 1944. May have been found wearing half of a medallion—a Tree of Life. Any information, please write PO Box 1247, Euston Station, London, England.

A thousand scenarios ran through his head as he marched to the newspaper office to place the ad. *I must be careful not to sound as if I believe she was kidnapped or forced against her will, or even to let on that I am her papa. If someone adopted her, they might not want to give her up. If they believe someone is seeking half of a gold medallion, they might come forward more willingly, hoping for a reward. On the other hand, a Tree of Life medallion may mark her as Jewish, and what would that mean—here, in London?*

Itzhak swallowed. Anti-Semitism had not disappeared with the stroke of the Allies' pen. It was alive and well in England. That, he knew firsthand. He didn't want to arouse suspicion or even notice.

But the medallion was the only thing that might stand out in a reader's mind, the only way he knew to tell the world whom he was looking for.

Itzhak pulled the half medallion from his pants pocket, the half medallion that he fingered through every odd moment. No, he knew he must take the risk. It was a shot in the dark, a prayer beyond the stars, but he must move heaven and earth, as far as he was able and Adonai willed, to find Ania. Seeing the photograph of the little girl so like Rosa had sealed that in his mind. He dared not hope, but prayed for the manifestation and well-being of his daughter, something he'd failed to do for months.

Half an hour later Itzhak stepped outside the newspaper office. He'd done it. The ad would run for a week, beginning with tomorrow's paper. He clapped his hat on his head, shouldered his toolbox, and stepped into the pedestrian flow more lively than he had since coming to England.

At last, at least, he was doing something. He was searching for his Ania.

◆

Each night, after work, Itzhak returned to the post office to check his box. Day after day, nothing.

When the week ended, he ran the advertisement again. When that week ended with no response, he ran it again.

On the fourth week, the newspaper office clerk cast him a pitying glance. "Who is she? Your daughter?"

Itzhak nearly broke down. Months and years of one foot in front of the other, and a simple question became his undoing. "My daughter. My Ania," he acknowledged gruffly, and all but ran from the building.

On the sidewalk his chest heaved. He closed his eyes, drew a deep breath that ended in a fit of coughing. Doubled over, hands on his knees, he pressed his eyes closed, doing his best to get hold of himself.

At last he could stand, could hold his head up and walk forward.

The newspaper advertisement is not enough. Who reads advertisements unless they're looking for something? Who would look to give away a beautiful child such as Ania must surely be?

Itzhak pondered this all the way to work. He'd finished with the second floor of the building and was repairing additional lighting in storage areas. It wouldn't be long until he had no access to Janek Kumiega's office and no opportunity to search the face in the photograph. Even now, Kumiega had taken to keeping his office door closed most days. Itzhak didn't know if that was normal for the man or if he'd become suspicious of Itzhak, who used every opportunity to glimpse the intriguing photograph.

I'm becoming paranoid. If only I could see the child. Surely I would know my own daughter, even after all these years.

The words *surely I would know* reverberated in Itzhak's head throughout the day. *If only I could see her* became a mantra. By the end of the day, he'd decided.

Itzhak stowed his toolbox beneath a painting tarp in a storage closet. It was risky leaving his tools unattended overnight, but carrying them would make him too noticeable, too memorable. He waited outside, just around the corner, until Kumiega left work, which was later than most of the office staff.

Kumiega seemed intent on getting home, but not as a man eager to meet the lovely wife and bright daughter in the photograph. *What is the matter with him? Does the man not know what awaits him?* What Itzhak would give to come home, just once more, to Rosa and Ania.

Kumiega took the bus from the corner. Itzhak was thankful he had coins in his pocket and a newspaper to pretend to read—a way to keep his head down but watch Kumiega from hooded eyes. When the man stepped off the bus, Itzhak followed, at a discreet distance. When Kumiega stopped and turned around, as if looking for something, Itzhak turned, stooped, pretending to pick up a dropped coin. By the time he turned again, Kumiega was gone. Itzhak hurried in the direction he'd last seen him, down a street with houses that got smaller and smaller the farther he went. Ahead, he saw Kumiega's lanky form pass through a garden gate. Itzhak slowed and sauntered along the street. Kumiega stopped in the front garden to kick stones from the path to the door.

Itzhak dared not stop, dared not look at him openly, but kept going. He'd nearly passed the stone bungalow when Kumiega stepped inside. Through the kitchen window Itzhak saw the woman in the picture. It was all he could do not to knock on the door, introduce himself, and demand to meet their little girl. *Their little girl.* The words made him want to retch.

What could he do now? What was the next step? Was he just a lonely, nearly middle-aged man going *meshugge*?

A brilliant yellow flash at the window caught Itzhak's eye again. A girlish figure threw her hands into the air and jumped into Kumiega's arms. Itzhak's heart lurched to one side. He desired yet feared looking into the child's eyes. But he couldn't see her face. The woman pulled the curtains closed. It was nearly dusk, after all.

Itzhak turned and exhaled the breath that cramped his chest. He took two steps, intending to make his way back to the bus stop but uncertain he could make it home. *What now? Adonai, what now?*

On impulse he pulled the folded newspaper from his pocket, took his electrician's pen from behind his ear, and circled his advertisement in bold, dark strokes. He tore the important sheet from the newspaper, folded it, and stuffed the page through the letterbox in the front door.

Whatever happened next was out of his hands.

CHAPTER FORTY-SEVEN

SOPHIE OPENED THE CURTAINS in her kitchen to greet the morning sun. She lifted her apron from the hook and tied it around her waist, a good and sturdy bow. She liked things sturdy, simple, routine.

She'd just pulled eggs from the pantry when she remembered that today was the day for milk delivery. She'd forgotten to put the empty bottles with money on the front stoop and only hoped it wasn't too late, that she hadn't missed Mr. Kreeley.

She didn't see the newspaper on the mat by the door until she stepped on it, milk bottles in hand. She might have thought the folded paper beneath it unlikely trash, except for the crudely circled text on the page.

The light was poor in the foyer, so she took the newspaper into the kitchen, set it by Janek's place at the table, and placed the folded paper on the crockery cabinet, intending to read it later. Perhaps her neighbor had circled information for a sale. They sometimes did that for one another.

First, she must get the kettle on and the tea made. Janek would need his breakfast before catching the bus for work.

Early mornings were the most pleasant time of day for Sophie. All her family still snuggled in their beds. She knew where each one was and harbored no fear of separation. Even a year after the war's end, that relief came as a new feeling each morning, a gift, albeit tentative.

The moment Janek walked out the door, fear began its slow and ugly creep into her heart. *Will Janek be all right? Will he be able to keep his job? Will the British treat him well? What if things get ugly with Stalin? Will Britain turn against the Poles and deport them? Is his British citizenship enough to keep him here?*

And then she focused on Charlotte. *Will someone come knocking at my door, seeking to reclaim her? If they do, I'll deny knowing what they're talking about. She's mine. She has papers now, legitimate British papers. But will they believe me? And what would I ever tell Janek? How could I possibly explain?*

Sophie didn't understand herself why she'd not told Janek the truth about Charlotte. At first she'd maintained that she didn't want to break his heart, didn't want him to think of Charlotte as less than his . . . especially when Sophie was convinced she could not carry a child to term. They'd been together over a year now, and no pregnancy. Perhaps there never would be.

But as time went on, Sophie knew she feared even more the discovery of her deception. *If he learns that I've lied about this—foundational to our family, our marriage—how will he trust anything I say, anything I do? Will he believe that I love him? Will he think I love her more than him? Will he be hurt that I didn't share my fear with him?*

Although she knew Janek had no choice in going to Romania with his troops, Sophie told herself that he'd abandoned her and the baby she'd carried early in the war. No matter that he—that they all—had believed Poland's military would regroup and return victorious in short order, it hadn't happened. Except for Pan Gadomski and

Terri, she'd been alone for years in war-torn Poland, not even her own England. *How could he expect that I wouldn't look for love, for comfort elsewhere? For all I knew he was dead. I was never unfaithful to him with another man. I had no desire for anyone else—only him. But I needed Charlotte as much as she needed me.*

Still, in her heart she knew that she'd not trusted God, and not trusted Janek. She'd taken matters into her own hands time and again. *But I did it to survive, and to save Charlotte.*

Her arguments were fair and true; they were simply not the entire truth. It was this vicious cycle that wore her down, day after day, that kept her from turning to Janek with an open heart and unclouded eyes. She knew he felt her coldness. *But it isn't coldness, Janek, my love! It's fear. I can't lose you again. I couldn't bear for you to walk away from me . . . from us. All my dreams of a happy family . . . and I'm destroying them, one way or another.*

"What is it? Has something happened?" Janek was behind her, turned her into his arms and gently wiped the tears Sophie didn't realize coursed over her cheeks.

"No, no," she lied.

"You don't cry over nothing."

She shrugged him off and forced a laugh, but it came out brittle. "Sometimes women do that, you know. Especially when it's that time of the month."

He stepped back, dropping his arms, and she perceived the slight slump in his shoulders. *Does he remember I used that excuse last week?*

Janek pulled his chair from beneath the table and sat down. Sophie busied herself at the stove, cracking an egg, then slicing bread for toast. Janek unfolded the newspaper and began to read. Silence reigned in the kitchen until the whistle of the teakettle pierced the air and clawed against Sophie's nerves.

"What's happened to us?" Janek spoke quietly.

Sophie swallowed the sawdust in her throat. She stabbed the bread with a long fork and held it over the burner to toast, pretending she hadn't heard him.

"Won't you answer me?" He didn't turn to look at her, but sat, the newspaper in his hand.

Sophie closed her eyes and felt the heat creep up her hand. She pulled the bread away from the burner. "I don't know what you mean. We're busy, that's all. You work. I take care of the house and Charlotte. We're fine. We're just like any other family in London."

"Do you remember us . . . before the war? The way we made love? The picnics by the river?"

Sophie's heart clenched. She scooped the eggs from the skillet and slid them onto a heated plate, setting it down before Janek. He took her wrist in his hand. She tried to pull away, but he held on and brought it to his lips.

"What's happened to us, Sophia?" he asked again.

She pulled away; this time he didn't stop her. "I don't know. I don't know, Janek." She felt the sky falling, the floor tilting, and knew she must regain control. "We could try a picnic, the three of us, on Saturday," she offered, but lamely. "Take it to St. James, if you want."

Janek stood without eating and reached for his coat.

"Your breakfast. Aren't you going to eat?"

"It's not a picnic that I want, Sophia." He pushed his arms through his mackintosh and grabbed his hat from the tree in the foyer.

She followed him, hands wringing in her apron. "What do you want?" She'd do anything to keep him, but she couldn't give up Charlotte. *Please, God, don't let that be what he wants. Life before Charlotte . . . I can't go back there.* "Are you sorry we have a daughter?"

Janek turned to her, his face confused and clouded, a thunderbolt of disbelief written in his eyes. "No, of course not. You know I love our daughter. I simply want you—I want *us* again. And I don't understand the problem. Am I the problem?"

"No, no." Sophie couldn't keep the tears from her voice.

"Then what is it?" Janek reached for her but she stepped back, shaking her head.

"I don't know. I just don't know."

He sighed the sigh of the defeated, opened the door, and walked out into the morning fog.

◆

It wasn't until after Charlotte had eaten her breakfast and gone into the garden to play that Sophie finished washing the dishes and returned the crockery to its cabinet. That's when she picked up the folded sheet of newspaper and looked closely at the circled advertisement. But it wasn't a food advert or information about rationing normally shared by the women on the street. It was a request for information:

Searching for young girl, five years old, disappeared in Poland sometime between 1942 and 1944. May have been found wearing half of a medallion—a Tree of Life. . . .

Sophie's hand grasped instinctively for her throat, as if to cover the filigreed branches of the Tree of Life. She'd guessed that was what the half medallion was, the medallion now buried beneath the lining of her jewelry box. She'd told herself she would save it, would one day give it to Charlotte and perhaps tell her the truth, at least what she knew of the truth. But she also knew that was a lie she told herself. She would never tell her daughter that another woman had given her birth, another father given her life.

Someone knows . . . someone suspects. The force of that truth hit Sophie like a hammer between the eyes. Stunned, she grasped the back of the nearest chair and sat down. She closed her eyes. Her head swam and her heart beat a pulse into her brain, throbbing, throbbing, throbbing. Panic surged up her throat, but she forced the bile down.

Who? Janek? He wouldn't do this. He's an honorable man. He would ask me straight out . . . like he did this morning. And he's never seen the medallion . . . has he?

But perhaps he had. When they first moved into the little house, when they moved all their possessions from the apartment they'd first shared near the air base. He'd given her a brooch with lilies, and a jewelry box to hold it "and all the other gifts I will give you as we grow old together." He'd spoken with such love.

She'd slipped the half medallion beneath the lining that night. But he'd walked into the room as she was doing it and asked what it was.

"Nothing, nothing," she'd replied. "Something I picked up in Warsaw . . . a memento of the war, that's all." She'd tried to sound offhanded. He hadn't asked more, but her silence, her lack of explanation sealed the first layer of bricks in the wall between them.

Evasion. Deception. I never meant for it to go this far. . . . And now. What now?

Sophie opened her eyes. *Someone suspects . . . someone knows.* The words repeated themselves over and over until she could barely breathe. *What do they want? Is it money? I have no money! But if it is that, wouldn't they come out in the open? Unless they know I've deceived Janek. But who would know? How could they know?*

The last she knew, Jolanta had been arrested, perhaps killed, if the posting of her death had been true. Terri was gone. But Sophie knew she could have tried harder to find someone in the network. She'd written to Jan and Antonina Żabiński, owners of the zoo, searching for Terri and Renat, to no avail, but had not asked about Jolanta, had not shared that she'd taken the child in her care from Poland. One person or another could have led her to someone who might know if Charlotte's parents lived. *But how could they? The ghetto was liquidated and burned! I saw it myself. There was no one, nothing left.*

Sophie read the ad again. No name, no signature. Only a post office box. She folded the paper in half, whispering a prayer of thanksgiving that Janek had not seen it, had not picked it up from the cabinet and read it, asked what it meant. She couldn't wait. She must discover who sent it, and what they hoped to gain.

It took her less than half an hour to tidy the kitchen, to dress to go out, to arrange for their neighbor to watch Charlotte. Hers wasn't an errand for a child.

Sophie hurried along the street, checked the posted schedule, and took two different buses to reach the designated post office.

Questions clicked with her heels up the post office stairs until she stood in the great hall. Lines and walls of post office boxes surrounded her. Even knowing the number would not help. A card bearing a post office box registration had to be presented to the clerk behind the desk before one could obtain mail. If they didn't say the number out loud—and why would they?—she would never know which person used which box.

How futile! How stupid of me! She'd just wanted to see, to know who sent the advertisement without showing herself. *But they do know me, at least they know where I live. They know where Charlotte lives.* The thought struck terror in her heart.

By the time she reached home, Sophie had formed a plan. She would write an anonymous letter, just a couple of lines, and post it to the box number, not giving a return address. She would place the notice in a distinctive envelope—perhaps an odd shape or color—so she could watch who came out of the post office with it. Then she could follow them.

There was a park with benches across the street from the post office. There was a tea shop two doors down. She would go every day and watch and wait until the person with the envelope left the post office. She had just enough coins squirreled away for a rainy day to pay her neighbor to watch Charlotte—at least for the week. Surely, in that time, she would know.

CHAPTER FORTY-EIGHT

JANEK CLOSED HIS OFFICE DOOR and slumped in the chair behind his desk. He ran long fingers through his unruly hair in frustration, then planted his face in his hands, his elbows on the desk. How had things gotten so mixed up, so strained?

If he'd been courting Sophia and she'd treated him like this, he would have walked away, baffled by her inconsistent behavior. One moment she jumped like a kitten pounced on by a wolf and either turned away from him or pushed him away. The next moment she clung to him, as if terrified he would disappear into thin air.

Iwan Nowak's reprimand played through his mind a hundred times a day. If he wanted his marriage to work, he must step forward, woo Sophia, let her know he loved her, not risk losing her and Charlotte. How could he be other than himself? Himself had been enough for her before. Was he so different now? Was she?

The last time he and Iwan had talked, Iwan suggested doing something to surprise her, to capture her attention—something she would like but not expect.

Janek looked at the stack of work on his desk. Nothing urgent, finally. He could afford to take a half day, perhaps surprise Sophia and Charlotte and take them out to an early tea in a restaurant. He checked his watch. If he hurried, he could catch the 11:30 bus and be home just after noon. It was unlikely Sophia would have served Charlotte her luncheon by then. Would she be glad to see him? Glad for the three of them to venture out on a weekday for a treat? Perhaps they could take in a cinema film as well—a matinee—and make it an early evening.

Janek grabbed his coat and hat and was halfway down the block when he spotted the flower seller. Violets—a London tradition. Sophia would like that. He was certain of it.

By the time he reached the front door of their bungalow, it was just past noon. He pulled out his key, determined to keep the surprise, and opened the door. "Sophia! Charlotte! What do you think? Papa's home!"

No small running feet came to greet him. No longer strides from the kitchen or the sitting room.

"Sophia? Charlotte?" He didn't call quite as loudly.

Janek stood in the middle of the downstairs hallway and heard the house echo around him, its odd creak in the pipe, and the tick of the mantel clock. But no human sounds.

Where can they be? Shopping? Not this time of day. A friend's? Who? Janek had urged Sophia to make new friends in the neighborhood, among the other women, but she had steadfastly refused, declaring that she didn't have time now, that she didn't feel the need for others in their lives.

What is she hiding from? What is she hiding?

Janek didn't know where the questions came from . . . perhaps his subconscious. Would he entertain them? He thought he might.

For now, he would return to the office. He thought to leave the violets for Sophia with a note that he was sorry he'd missed her. But she might take that as a reprimand, if indeed she had gone out with friends, or better yet, gone to visit Carrie Chamberlin. He picked up the violets and took them along. Removing his hat and bowing, he handed them to an older lady, just coming off the bus he was ready to hop on. The pleased surprise on her face was worth more than the cost of the flowers, and Janek was glad he hadn't thrown them away.

◆ ◆ ◆

That evening, Sophie burned the only meat ration she had for the week. She made an omelet instead, using her egg ration, and fried potatoes. What they would eat tomorrow, she didn't know and couldn't imagine. She scalded her hand pouring the tea and nearly broke down in a frenzy of tears.

"What is the matter now?" Janek asked softly.

"Nothing. I'm tired, just tired."

"You didn't sleep well last night?"

"No, I never sleep well. You know that."

"You did at first—when we first came together again."

"Not anymore."

"Tell me what has changed. Why are you so unhappy?"

"I'm not unhappy!" She wanted to slam the teapot on the table. "How can you say such a thing? You expect too much." But she knew he expected very little. He expected her to be truthful, to be honest with him. And she would be, once she took care of whoever and whatever was behind the newspaper notice.

Janek spoke more softly yet. "Calm down, Sophia. You're frightening Charlotte."

It was true. Charlotte's wide and fluid eyes aimed at her mother spoke volumes.

"I'm sorry. Just, please, let's eat." Sophie took her place at the table and shook out her napkin, spreading it deliberately across her lap, willing her hands to stop shaking.

Janek prayed, and they ate in silence.

Sophie had just begun to butter her bread when Janek looked up from his omelet.

"Did you have a nice day today?"

"Yes, and you?" Sophie swallowed her anxiety and pasted on a half smile.

"An interesting day."

"Me, too!" Charlotte piped up.

Janek smiled at the little girl. Sophie held her breath. "And what did you do today, my little cupcake?"

Charlotte smiled from ear to ear. "I played outside—for hours!"

"You did?"

Charlotte nodded.

"It was such a lovely day and the garden was not muddy for a change. It seemed a good idea to let her play in the fresh air."

Janek blinked. "She played in our garden? Here?"

"Of course."

"All day?"

"Yes, why?"

"You were here all day?" Janek looked as if he didn't believe her.

"Where else would we be?" She all but laughed.

"But, Mamusia, remember—"

"It's 'Mummy' now, remember? And please don't speak with your mouth full, Charlotte. Now, eat up. I have your favorite dessert if you stop talking and eat."

"Sweet charlotte?" The little girl sat up straighter.

"Yes." Sophie smiled, relieved the distraction had worked. "Mrs. Tucker and I shared sugar and milk rations. We're all having sweet charlotte for dessert."

Sophie knew Janek continued to stare at her throughout the meal. She didn't know why, but it did not help her nerves.

✦ ◆ ✦

Janek was not fooled. His wife had lied, deliberately deceived him. She had shepherded Charlotte into forgetting. *Where were they? Why wouldn't she say?*

Janek spoke little that night or before leaving for work the next morning. Sophia made up for it with nervous chatter. The next evening she alternately cajoled and bantered with Charlotte, more and at a higher pitch than was her custom. The child laughed herself into a frenzy and still Sophia prodded her until bedtime.

At last Charlotte was in bed and all was quiet. Sophia walked into the sitting room. Janek rose from his chair beside the fire. "I'll say prayers with her."

"Not to worry. I did it tonight."

Janek stopped in his tracks.

Sophia's face flamed. "I'm sorry. I know you do it, but she was so wound up. Just this once, to calm her down, I stayed with her. She's nearly asleep now. You'll wake her if you go in."

If he hadn't realized that Sophia was trying to keep Charlotte from sharing her day with him, or that Sophia worked to deceive him, he wouldn't have minded so much, wouldn't have given it a second thought.

As it was, it was all he could think of the entire night.

✦ ◆ ✦

Janek left for work early again the next morning, before Sophia or Charlotte awoke. He couldn't pretend that all was well. Nothing was well, and he didn't know why, but he would get to the bottom of it.

Mornings in the city were warm and he was glad to doff his overcoat and hat before knocking on his superior's door.

"Come in." Rudolph Sheffield's voice rang above the clatter of the tea cart just coming up the hallway.

"Good morning, sir." Janek bowed slightly. He winced, realizing that old habits and customs died hard.

"Good morning, Kumiega. What is your business this morning?"

"I'd like to ask a favor, sir, a privilege."

"Oh? And what might that be?"

"I'm in need of a few hours in the middle of the day. I have—I have an appointment that I cannot make in the evening."

"Hmm. Appointment, eh? I hope it's not something medical."

"No, sir. Not exactly, sir. It's a family matter."

"Family matter. I see."

Janek knew it was an expression. He only wished he himself could see. "I recommend, if it suits you, sir, that on the days I need an extra hour or more, I come in early—as I am today—and work late, after returning to the office."

"Well." Mr. Sheffield considered. "I suppose that will do. For a limited time, mind you."

"Yes, sir. Not a day longer than is absolutely necessary."

"And do you know how long that might be?"

Janek swallowed. "No, sir, I do not, but I hope not long . . . not long at all."

"Very well. See to it."

"Thank you, sir. Thank you." Janek bowed his way back to the door and slipped through, relieved beyond words that it was over and that Mr. Sheffield had not asked more questions.

◆ ◆ ◆

Janek took the 11:30 bus home, and just as before, Sophia and Charlotte were gone. He returned to work, worked an extra hour, and went home.

"You are late" was all that Sophia said as she poured his tea.

"I needed to finish some work at the office. You don't mind, do you?" Janek couldn't bring himself to look at her.

"Not if that's what you need to do, of course not."

"You had a busy day?" He swallowed the lukewarm tea.

"The usual," she replied, not looking at him.

"Home all day?"

"Of course." But she squirmed and he saw her dart him a worried glance. She stood. "Charlotte and I have eaten, so I'll get her ready for bed."

Janek didn't say anything, didn't offer to say prayers with their daughter. He knew he'd be rebuffed or the privilege usurped.

◆

For two more days the pattern repeated. The next Monday, Janek left work soon after the tea trolley made its second round through the offices, arriving in his street about ten thirty. As he turned the corner, he saw Charlotte bound out the front door and Sophia turn to lock the door behind them. Janek pulled back, desperate by this time to see where they would go.

Sophia took Charlotte by the hand—Charlotte, who skipped happily along the broken walkway—and led her across the street and down two doors, to Mrs. Southerly's. She knocked on the door. Mrs. Southerly must have been expecting them, for she opened right away and ushered Charlotte inside, waving Sophia off.

Sophia turned into the lane and hurried up the street toward the bus stop. Janek felt foolish hiding from his wife, but he needed to know what she was about, where she was going and why she was so secretive. He didn't believe that asking her would produce the truth. Janek swallowed his pride and ducked behind an overgrown holly shrub, kept his head down, and untied then retied his shoe.

By the time he stood, Sophia was stepping up into the front of a double-decker city bus. He walked, long strides and double-time, to hop on the back and bound upstairs. He knew she was not likely to move beyond the first floor in her heels and hat.

He paid the fare clear to the end of the line, uncertain where she might get off. It was an easy thing to watch passengers leave from his vantage point. The bus had traveled a good twenty-five minutes, including regular and random stops, when Sophia stepped down into the street. He waited until she'd headed across the street and followed.

"Here, chap!" the bus conductor called after him. "This i'nt your stop!"

Janek held up his hand in recognition and hurried on, keeping a distance from his wife, who seemed to know exactly where she was going and be very eager to get there.

But then she stopped, abruptly, in the middle of the walkway. She looked to her right, up the stairs to a post office, and left, to a park across the street. She checked her watch, then headed for the park.

She's set to meet someone. The realization made Janek's heart sink. He remembered the Polish laborer who'd been so taken with his wife's picture. *Why wouldn't another man go after her? She's beautiful.* But the thought sickened him. Despite the troubles in their marriage, he couldn't have imagined that Sophia would be unfaithful to him. But what did he really know of the woman she'd become, the woman he could no longer understand or predict?

Sophia reached a bench, in full view of the street, and sat down. She looked weary, tired, stressed. She took a book out and began to read.

Janek kept to the shrubbery near the corner, but he could see her face. From time to time she looked up at the post office—each time someone came out. She didn't seem to pay attention when they entered, only when they exited. Even then she didn't seem taken with their faces, didn't seem to recognize anyone in particular, but carefully screened each one.

Once she strained forward, seemingly unable to see what she required, and stepped out into the street, heedless of the traffic. She trailed a woman half a dozen feet, then pulled a notepad from her purse and called after the woman, suggesting she'd dropped it. The woman searched her mail, seemed to thank her, but shook her head and walked on. Sophia stood in the street staring after her, then walked slowly back to her bench and took up her vigil.

Two hours passed and Janek could think of no acceptable reason to continue standing in the street. A local shopkeeper came out his front door, giving him a suspicious eye. Janek tipped his cap and walked on. He circled the park and found a bench some distance behind the bench Sophia still occupied. *What are you doing here, Sophia, my love? What is going on? It's as if you're searching for someone, but you don't even know whom.*

He waited another hour, but she did not move from her seat. When the local church bell bonged six o'clock and the post office closed, she rose from her seat, placed her book in her bag, and walked toward the bus stop.

Janek spread his hands in frustration. *What does this mean?*

He milled in with men, women, and children and waited until he saw Sophia step onto the bus. Knowing he would need to put in several extra hours to make up for the work he'd lost today, he headed for his office, less than five minutes away. *If this is where you go, I don't need to go home to follow you.*

That night he came home late, well after nine. When he joined her in bed, he asked about her day, as he always did. She lied again, saying nothing unusual had occurred, that it was just another day at home with Charlotte.

Janek turned over, sick at heart, and equally confused.

CHAPTER FORTY-NINE

THE NEXT DAY, Janek could not leave the office. Meetings, important to his superior and their clients, were held in tandem. Thursday was the first day he dared leave the office early. He waited until one, his normal lunchtime, and took the bus directly to the park. He got off one street over and spotted Sophia at her same park bench, keeping a surreptitious eye on patrons of the post office.

Three hours passed. Janek had just determined his wife had gone mad when he saw her sit up straight, smooth her jacket and skirt, and stand. She clutched her bag and hurried across the street toward a man. It seemed she headed straight for him, then stopped, turned, and stood aside, pulling her hat low over her eyes. But when he'd passed, she followed him. She didn't approach him more closely, didn't try to speak or distract him, but she was clearly following him, and openly perturbed.

The man stopped as he read a letter, apparently a short letter, then looked up, searching the area, as if he feared someone might be watching him. His eyes paused briefly on Sophia's downturned hat and swept on. No one was watching him—no one, Janek knew, but Sophia.

As the man scanned the crowd once more, Janek paused. Where had he seen that face before? Dressed as a laborer, the man stood apart from the office crowd thronging the walkway this time of day. He shouldered a bag, or a box, as Janek saw more clearly the closer he came. *The electrician. The Polish electrician. The man who couldn't take his eyes—or hands—off Sophia's picture.*

Janek reached into the air, attempting to steady himself. *They knew each other in Warsaw, during the war. They were both there.* The thought made Janek's heart race and sink. The only possible solace was that Sophia did not seem glad to see the man, though she clearly stalked him, and he—what was his name? Dunovich, perhaps?—didn't seem to be aware of her. It was not a clandestine meeting. *What does this mean?*

◆ ◆ ◆

Janek returned to the office but accomplished precious little work. He left, finally, at nine, confident he'd caught up enough to satisfy his employer, should he ask.

All the way home, Janek argued with himself about how to proceed. He regretted opening this Pandora's box, but now it was open, he could not slam the lid and forget it.

It was late when he let himself in the front door. Charlotte would be sleeping. Janek left his hat and coat on the rack, thumbed through the few bills and newspaper that Sophia had left for him on the hall table, and prayed up each and every stair to their bedroom.

His wife wasn't asleep but sat in an armchair in the corner. She looked so small, so pitiful and careworn, but Janek steeled his heart. "How was your day?"

She didn't answer.

"Home again? You and Charlotte—all the day?"

CATHY GOHLKE

She turned her face away, her nails digging into the soft wood of the chair's arms. He pretended he didn't see.

"Did I tell you about the Pole in my office a few weeks ago? Dunovich. Itzhak Dunovich, from Poland. Warsaw, as it turns out." He registered her every move, each facial expression. "Rather taken with your picture, he was. Couldn't seem to tear his eyes from your face."

Sophia looked up, aghast. "The one of me with—with Charlotte?"

"Yes, the very one." He spoke evenly. "Do you know the man, Sophia?"

She began to tremble, to cry. Janek tried to brace himself for whatever might come, but he had to ask, had to know. "Did you have an affair with that man?"

"What?" she gasped. "What did you say?"

"He looked at the picture as if he knew you, as if he'd seen you."

"That's how he knew."

"Knew? What did he know?" Janek's heart thumped in his chest. He didn't want the answers to his questions, but he desperately needed them.

Sophia sat up, her face a picture of unguarded horror. "He came here to the house. He followed you home. That's how he knew where we live."

"He followed me here?"

"How else could he have found us?" Terror and helplessness flitted through her eyes, then fury.

"You know him, then?"

"I never had an affair with that man! I have never loved anyone but you, Janek. I waited for you! Prayed for you! And you ask me this?"

"Then why did you go to meet him?"

"What?"

"I saw you at the post office today. I saw you approach him."

Sophia shook her head, buried her face in her hands, and wept, loud, wrenching sobs. "I've been so afraid, so afraid!"

"Afraid of what? Of Dunovich?"

She nodded, unable to speak.

"What did he do to you?" Janek knelt before her. "In Poland—what did he do to you?"

She turned away, shaking, her arms wound about her middle.

"Did he—did he—" The relief that Sophia did not love this man and the horror of the crime he could all too well imagine Dunovich had perpetrated on his wife built a raging fire in Janek's bones. Despite Sophia's shaking head and attempts to wriggle away, he pulled his wife into his arms, cradling her head against his shoulder and stroking her hair, as he would comfort young Charlotte. "My darling, why didn't you tell me? Why have you carried this burden alone?"

But Sophia cried all the harder. Her words jerked out, barely coherent. "I was . . . so afraid . . . he would take Charlotte."

Walls of protection flew up in Janek's mind. *The man take Charlotte? No wonder you left her with the neighbor. No wonder you moved head-on into the lion's den.* "Brave, brave wife. You can't do this alone. You mustn't. We are one, Sophia Kumiega; we are one. Let me take care of this. I know the man."

"No! Please don't go to him. Stay away from him. We must all stay away from him! Promise me! Promise me, Janek!"

The terror in her eyes undid him. *What hold can this man have over her?* But he knew, at least he feared. *Could this man, this Itzhak Dunovich, be Charlotte's father?*

Janek did not ask his sobbing wife if she'd lost their baby, if Charlotte was not their own. It was enough to hold her, to wrap his arms around her, to protect and comfort her in ways he hadn't been there to do through those long years of war.

Iwan is right. Whatever happened during the war is in the past. Sophia survived. She survived and bore a child and brought this child to me. Whatever it takes to keep our family whole, together, I will do. With God's help, I will do.

CHAPTER FIFTY

THE CRYPTIC LETTER HAD appeared in Itzhak's mailbox with only three words: *Who are you?*

Itzhak didn't know if it was in response to his advertisement or if someone stalked him because he was Lithuanian, assumed to be Polish, or because he was a Jew. There was no shortage of anti-Semitism in England, and Itzhak knew better than to believe otherwise. There was no return address, so the sender must not expect an answer, but must intend to inflict fear.

He couldn't afford fear, not if he was going to find and raise his daughter.

In the evenings he imagined Ania setting the table, so he'd bought another set of cutlery and another bowl and plate. If she was growing up in England, she would drink tea. So, even though Itzhak no longer drank tea, to save the pence, he bought a kettle and a teapot. He would wait until she came to his home to buy the tea and milk, so it would be fresh.

These dreams kept him going, even when the post office box remained empty.

He would file a report with the society that worked to reconnect families. He had little hope they could help, and part of him feared sharing his Jewishness with strangers, but anything was worth a try to find his Ania. This, at least, he could do for Rosa, for Ania, for himself and the last of his family line.

But first, he must see if he could get the picture on Kumiega's desk. His Ania, he would explain to the society, might look like the girl in the picture. Itzhak knew that he would have to steal the picture, that he could not walk up to the man and ask for a photograph of his wife and child and expect to be given it.

Stealing went against Itzhak's grain. Yes, he had stolen food during the war, had stolen tools and himself through the tunnel in the Ponary Forest, but he had never stolen when he could provide for himself or for his family through honest work. But this . . . how else could he show someone what his daughter looked like? What she might look like now? Without it, Ania would be just a name lost in a million other names of missing persons.

Adonai, forgive me. Forgive me for stealing.

Itzhak took money from his pocket and counted the coins. Perhaps if he left enough money, the man could have another picture taken of his wife and child. And Adonai would understand. It was like Abraham insisting to pay for the cave in which he buried his Sarah . . . wasn't it?

Itzhak waited until the lunch hour. Janek Kumiega was likely to leave the building, walk to the tea shop next door but one. That had been his habit when Itzhak worked in the building. He would approach the building just after one, when most of the staff left for lunch.

◆

Sophie had agreed with Janek that she and Charlotte would not stay alone in the house during the day, at least for a time. When Janek

334

was unable to locate Dunovich at work, he had confirmed with Iwan Nowak that the Pole had finished his electrical repairs in the building and had no reason to return. That didn't mean he might not come to the house. Janek wouldn't take the chance that she or Charlotte would be there without him.

Her husband's concern comforted Sophie's heart. At last they were on the same team—for different reasons, perhaps, but on the same side, nevertheless.

Each day, for a week, Sophie had taken Charlotte on another outing in the city, often meeting Janek for luncheon. At first it had been great fun. They'd bought the little girl her uniform, Charlotte's first term in school set to begin in another week. Charlotte had proudly stood and held it against herself for Janek's enthusiastic approval over tea and crumpets.

They frequented all the historic sites and museums Sophie thought might interest Charlotte—all those that had reopened after the war. There were precious few, and it didn't take long for the little girl to tire of the daily excursions.

Sophie realized that beginning next week, she must be home at noon with a meal on the table for Charlotte's tea hour from school. Friday would be the last day she dared go out for luncheon. So she left Charlotte with Mrs. Southerly and took the bus into town to meet Janek—to surprise him.

He'd been so kind and solicitous of late, asking no more questions, but extending his love and compassion in every way possible. She hadn't even dreamed the last two nights—no horrors from the war, no fears of the present. This was the life Sophie wanted, and she wanted to reciprocate, to reassure Janek of her love for him. Despite all that had happened in the past, despite all the tension of the present, romance was still possible for the two of them. It must be possible.

She had checked the newspaper advertisements each day. The quest for the little girl with the half medallion had run its course and not been renewed. *That might mean that some other little girl was found to match the need, mightn't it? That we are no longer under suspicion . . . couldn't it be so?*

If the man, Dunovich or whoever he was, was truly gone from Janek's building and gone from their lives, perhaps it meant they could live in peace. Perhaps there was no more to worry about.

Sophie told herself these things a hundred times each day, reciting them as a benediction, a blessing. If the truth would not surface on its own, why resurrect it? What did it hurt to let Janek think the worst of a stranger he'd never see again if it made him love her more, love and protect her unreservedly? She knew she invented fantasy—that it was wrong to deceive Janek or by her silence cast suspicion on Pan Dunovich. Her conscience protested, but she pushed it away. The still, small voice that had led her through wartime hardships and all of life—her life before Charlotte—must be quieted. But was that a price so high to pay for her daughter, her husband, her family?

Sophie jerked the cuffs of her gloves over her wrists and straightened her hat, stepping off the bus just before one o'clock. As she painted a determined smile on her face and anticipated Janek's glad surprise when she walked through his office door, her step lightened.

Itzhak shouldered the strap of his toolbox and took the stairs to the building two at a time. Walking confidently and purposefully through the door might eliminate suspicion. Thankfully, it looked as if it might rain. People hurried out to lunch and about their business, not bothering with him or one another.

"Itzhak Dunovich!" A voice boomed from just inside the doorway, making Itzhak jump and nearly drop his toolbox. "I didn't expect to see you again so soon. Did you get another call? What is it this time?"

Itzhak blinked, desperate to adjust his eyes to the dimmer indoor lighting. "Pan Nowak." He swallowed. "How are you? Good to see you again."

The friendly custodian nodded, smiling. "I'm just on my way to tea. Won't you join me?"

"I—I'm sorry. I promised to take a look, as a favor, at—at a problem on my lunch break. I must be quick and get back to my regular job."

"Don't be helping them out for free, man," Nowak whispered. "They'll be calling you night and day!"

"I—I'll remember." Itzhak forced a smile, desperately trying to regain his composure.

"I won't keep you. Get on with it, then; the building's pretty well cleared out. Just some of the brass in a closed meeting. None to hold you up."

"Thank you, sir." Itzhak tipped his hat and the older man laughed, apparently glad and surprised at the show of respect.

Itzhak reached the stairwell and closed the door, drawing deep breaths.

* ◆ *

Sophie reached Janek's office only to find it disappointingly dark and empty. She closed his office door, remembering that he'd mentioned something at breakfast about an important meeting with the military. She hoped that didn't mean they would meet over luncheon. She'd dressed especially to impress him, wanting more than anything to rekindle their romance, their hope for the future.

She didn't turn on his desk lamp. There was a little stream of sunlight through the transom high above his desk, casting a pale yellow glow over the area where he worked. She ran her fingers over the wood grain of his desk, the place he'd spent so many extra hours of late, and sat down in his chair.

Smiling, she picked up the photograph, the one of Charlotte and herself, glad her husband kept it nearby, despite all she'd put him through since their reunion. She remembered when it was taken—not so long ago. She'd had to force herself to forget the times pictures were taken to forge false identities and escape incognito with her precious cargo, her Charlotte. But the smile in the photograph, for Janek and for the pleading hope of their future, had been real.

The door opened. A man slipped through, closing the door just as quickly as he'd opened it. She'd thought it would be Janek, but he was dressed as a workman.

Startled, Sophie barely held on to the picture in her hand. She must have gasped because the man turned quickly, surprise and fear written on his face, and then it went blank. It was in this blank moment that she recognized him, and the breath left her body.

"Pani Kumiega," he said.

This is the man from the post office. This must be the man Janek spoke of. She swallowed cardboard, and the panic in her chest raced the wind.

"I recognize you from your photograph." The man's eyes traveled to the frame she held. He looked as if he wanted to say more, as if he struggled in the speaking, but she did not want to hear what he would say, what he might ask, might demand.

Sophie forced herself to stand, ready to fight or flee. She grasped the photograph to her chest, determined he'd not wrench an admission, let alone her daughter, from her.

"I want only to speak with you."

"Stay there," she ordered. "Not one step closer or I'll scream."

His eyebrows rose and he blinked twice, a nervous tic. He set down his workman's box and slowly straightened. "I want only to ask about your little girl."

Sophie's breath labored.

"She looks—she looks so familiar to me. Her eyes, they remind me of my wife, my Rosa." He faltered. "I lost my family—my wife—during the war. But my little daughter, my Ania, might still—"

Fear engulfed Sophie and she swooned.

In a moment the man was by her side, his arm behind her back, helping her to sit down as he relieved her of the photograph. "Pani Kumiega! Pani Kumiega!"

The door opened and in walked Janek. His presence became smelling salts to Sophie. "Janek!" Relief and need poured out together.

Janek's face changed from one of puzzlement to worry to shock to furious anger. He was across the room and behind the desk in a moment, dragging the man from Sophie, pulling him across the desktop and onto the floor. The photograph crashed to the floor, its glass shattering.

Sophie screamed. She screamed for all the fear of losing Charlotte, for the shame of the lies she'd told to the man who loved her, and for the chaos that had suddenly broken loose.

Janek punched the man in the face once, breaking his glasses. The shock of his violence must have brought him up short, because he pulled the man up by the shirt collar.

A horrified secretary appeared in the doorway. "Mr. Kumiega!"

Janek pulled back, his breath coming short. "Call the constable. Call him now."

Sophie knew her husband fought for control. Those years of fighting and killing and preserving life came at a cost. She'd rarely seen his fury, but she witnessed it now and knew she never wanted it leveled at her.

"No." She struggled to regain her voice. "No, Janek. Let him go."

But Janek was in a rage she could not reach. He did not hit the man again, but pushed him back to the floor. "Get the constable. Now!"

The secretary, wide-eyed and blushing from the scene before her, ran to do as told.

Sophie stood. "Janek, you mustn't—"

"Mustn't what? Mustn't prosecute the man who raped my wife?

I might not be able to prove what he did during wartime, but I can level charges against him now—breaking into my office, threatening and molesting my wife. To the full extent of the law, I will—"

"Rape—molest your wife? What are you talking about?" For the first time the man, crumpled on the floor, spoke, his words garbled behind a loose tooth. "She was going to faint. I helped her to sit down—that is all!" he insisted, his eyes pleading.

A flicker of confusion swept Janek's eyes and they caught Sophie's. Desperately, she shook her head.

"I came because of the photograph—my daughter, maybe, so like the picture!"

Sophie knew she couldn't explain the scene without telling everything. *And when the constable comes . . . Oh, dear God in heaven! What then?* She couldn't confess, not now, not here in front of everyone.

When she stepped round the desk to reach for Janek, broken glass crunched beneath her shoe. She glanced down, and there, in the photograph, in the middle of Charlotte's precious face, the glass had shattered, cutting her daughter's cheek from her nose. It was so like seeing people torn in two by the war—the bombing, the air raids that came without a moment's notice. It was more than Sophie could bear—an omen, a portent of the future.

She swallowed, trying to collect her wits. She would not look again at Janek, would not look in the eyes of the man now sitting on the floor in the corner by the umbrella stand, wiping blood from his lip and trying to reconstruct his glasses. She picked up her purse, wiped her eyes, and whispered, "I beg you, Janek. Leave it alone."

The narrowing of his eyes and the faint uncertainty behind his anger and righteous indignation stole through her soul. Whatever happened, it must happen without her. Quick footsteps echoed down the hallway, growing closer, closer. The constable and secretary stepped into the room.

"What's this, then?" The constable frowned, his fists clenched to his hips.

Sophie slipped out.

"Sophia! Sophia!" Janek's voice called after her in the hallway, but she took the stairs, nearly tripping down them in her heels, and tore into the street. They could not make her talk if they could not find her.

CHAPTER FIFTY-ONE

ITZHAK SPENT THE NEXT SIX HOURS in the police station, answering questions thrust at him from three different investigators. At least he assumed they were investigators. They reminded him of the Gestapo, only they spoke in rapid English, with British accents. Sometimes they spoke slowly and too loudly, assuming he was stupid or could not understand the language.

Itzhak responded slowly, quietly, looking them in the eye as best he could, expecting at any moment another fist to his jaw. After all, that's what bullish men in authority did. That's all he'd known. But for all their sneering at his accent and talking down to him, they knew nothing of the brutality of the Nazis. This did not compare. He'd borne that hellish landscape before. He could bear it again. Only he must not be deported because they hated his Jewishness, or his ethnicity.

He was now more certain than ever that the little girl in the photograph could be his Ania. Why else would Pani Kumiega behave so strangely, so fearfully? Unless she truly had been raped during the war by someone . . . not by him, certainly. *Has she never told her husband what happened? Does he realize the child cannot be his? She looks as Jewish as the tribe of Abraham. She looks like my Rosa. My beautiful Rosa.*

"You're a lucky stiff, Dunovich." The interrogator poked Itzhak's chest hard enough to leave bruising. "We can't press formal charges without Mrs. Kumiega coming in. Apparently you've scared the lady and she's taken off. Mind you, the moment she returns and signs papers, I'll be on your doorstep. Don't sleep too soundly. I late to have to kick in the door." He laughed, and Itzhak knew the man meant to instill the threat of Gestapo raids.

Finally, well after dark, he was turned out of the station without his tools, which they held "as evidence of weaponry," and without the money in his wallet, which no one seemed to know anything about.

It was after ten o'clock when Itzhak, after walking the four miles, reached his boardinghouse. He knew that the constable was not the Gestapo, was not one of the guards from Stutthof, but the interrogation had triggered reactions in his body that he'd thought he'd left far behind. Sweating in his armpits, palpitations in his heart, unbidden trembling in his hands. He inserted the key into the lock of his boardinghouse, dropped it, and scrambling on the ground, found it in the dark. He inserted it again. At least they hadn't taken that. His landlady would not have taken kindly to being awakened at such an hour.

Itzhak washed the crusted blood from his face and gently wiggled the loose tooth in his jaw. It would be easier, cheaper, to pull it than to see about getting it repaired . . . if such a thing could be repaired. He closed his eyes to the mirror. He'd think about it in the morning.

Itzhak sat down hard on his cot and pulled off his shoes. He buried his head in his hands. *What will my supervisor say when I show up with no tools, and no good reason for not returning to work after today's noon break? Can I lie? Say I was robbed and beaten?* He shook his head. *Who will believe that? And if that woman—Pani Kumiega—presses charges, if she lies and says I molested her, what then? Why would she do that? Why didn't Kumiega listen to me? He's Polish. He's not Jewish, but he's Polish. He should know what he's done to me, what this means.*

No, he would not lie. He would tell his supervisor the truth. He'd worked hard and honorably for the man for over a year. He would explain it was a misunderstanding. *Will he believe me?* Itzhak didn't know. But it was all he could think to do.

Still, when he lay back on his cot and stared at the ceiling, reciting the prayer he'd recited each morning and evening since childhood and praying for sleep to come, all he could see was the face of the little girl in the photograph. The eyes of his Rosa. Despite his hours of self-control and practiced stoicism, twin tears escaped the corners of his eyes. Finally, he slept.

◆

Janek had answered the probing questions of the constable as best he could. In the end, without Sophia there to testify against the man, it was his word against that of Itzhak Dunovich. The constable had finally dragged Dunovich off to the station, more because he was a laborer and a Jew, Janek suspected, than because of anything Janek— a Pole—had said.

Janek left the office and headed for the bus stop, wanting to tear out his hair. *Why didn't Sophia stay? The constable came—there was no danger. I'd not let that man—or any other—lay a finger on her.*

Surely there was more to the story than Dunovich claimed—that the photograph of Charlotte reminded him of his daughter. *What did he say her name was? Ania.*

He could have better understood if Charlotte looked like Itzhak Dunovich. He would have hated that, but it would make sense, given Sophia's abject horror of the man and his compulsion to see her, be near her. But Dunovich had denied any pursuit of Sophia—only said that the child in the photograph looked like his wife. *What does it mean? Or is he just a crazy, war-damaged man?*

Janek was so lost in thought that he missed his stop. Rather than wait for another bus to go the other way, he hoofed the two miles, anxious yet dreading to reach home.

Holding his breath, he opened the front door. No hall light. No kitchen light. No light at all . . . only a soft whimper from the front room. He stepped inside and turned on the hallway table lamp.

"Sophia? Charlotte?" It took moments for his eyes to adjust to the dimness of the room beyond. The only light came through the front window, thanks to the lamp in the street, and now a pale glow from the hallway.

Sophia had apparently retrieved Charlotte from the babysitter. He could make out two forms, sitting in the darkened room. Sophia rocked their daughter with an iron grip around her middle and a far-away sadness in her eyes.

Janek removed his hat and coat, forced a reassuring smile for Charlotte, and knelt before the two.

Charlotte reached her arms out to him. "Papa!" she whimpered.

It was all Janek could do not to slap Sophia into awareness. But he gently pried his wife's fingers from their daughter's middle. Sophia gripped all the harder, sudden terror on her face.

"It's all right, Sophia. I have her. I will protect our Charlotte, and I will protect you. You have nothing to fear, my love. Let me take her. I'll get our tea and put Charlotte to bed. You rest. You rest, my love."

Charlotte, trembling in her fright, dove into Janek's arms. "Papa! Something's the matter with Mamu—with Mummy. Something's the matter!"

"Hush, my darling," he crooned into the little girl's ear, hugging her forehead to his shoulder as he carried her from the room. "It will be all right. Everything will be all right." He prayed that was true.

◆ ◆ ◆

An hour later, having fed Charlotte and prepared her for bed, Janek tucked his daughter in. At least tomorrow was Saturday. At least they had the weekend to sleep, to put things right.

Put things right? Janek wondered if that were possible.

He found Sophia in bed, her face turned toward the wall.

"Charlotte's asleep . . . nearly."

She didn't respond.

"Sophia." He sat on the bed beside her, taking her hand in his. She pulled away. "We must talk. You must talk to me, explain to me." He did his best to keep his voice measured, helpful, hopeful, not accusing in any way.

She turned over. "I can't."

"You can't talk to me, or you can't explain? I don't understand. But I want to. Who is this man, this Dunovich, to you?" He held his breath.

"He's nothing. I—I don't know him."

Janek pushed his fingers through his hair, willing himself calm. Finally, he whispered, "What is he to Charlotte?"

He felt Sophia stiffen beneath the covers. "I don't know," she whispered in return.

Janek sat long by her side. Neither spoke.

At last he stood, undressed for bed, and lay down on his back, his arms behind his head. He stared at the ceiling, but all he saw was darkness . . . years and years of darkness and tension. Darkness and tension of the war and separation behind them. Darkness and tension and separation between them now. And what of the future?

"This isn't how it was supposed to be, Sophia. This isn't how it was for us before. Why now? Why, when we have everything, do we have nothing?"

She didn't answer, but he heard her sniffle and knew she was crying.

"If you won't talk to me, talk to Carrie. Perhaps she can help you." Minutes passed and Janek closed his eyes. It was useless. Sophia hadn't seen Carrie in months. She would not confide in her any more than she would confide in him.

"I can't leave now. Charlotte begins school on Monday."

Her voice in the dark startled him. The notion that she'd heard and responded took him off guard. But she had, and it sounded as if she was willing. It cut him that his wife might talk to Carrie but not to him . . . and yet, if she did, if it might help . . . Janek was desperate enough to try anything, even the swallowing of his pride . . . what little pride he had left.

"I will take her to school."

"She comes home for luncheon."

It was a truth, not an objection. Janek considered. "I will arrange for Mrs. Southerly to feed her, send her back to school, and stay with her after school. You could stay the night . . . even a day or two."

Sophia didn't say anything. Janek took that as a good sign. More minutes passed and weariness pulled him down. Sleep beckoned.

"I'll take the bus on Sunday, after church. I'll be back on Monday, in time for tea."

"As you like." He didn't know if that was too quick, or not personal enough. He didn't know if she wanted him to insist she stay away longer or beg her to return as quickly as possible. He didn't know anything. He only prayed that somehow Carrie would be able to help her, to help them. "I'll telephone her in the morning, to say you're coming."

CHAPTER FIFTY-TWO

SOPHIE LIFTED HER OVERNIGHT BAG from the bus seat and stepped gingerly down the stairs. She felt a little light-headed, and as if something was missing . . . as if Charlotte was missing. But Janek was with their daughter today, and tomorrow she'd be in school. Nothing could happen.

Sophie had planned to walk the two miles to the Chamberlin estate, giving herself time to prepare what she'd say to explain to Carrie why she needed to get away, if only for a day. *Janek is smothering me.* She could say that, but it wasn't true. *I'm smothering me. Life is smothering me.* Sophie bit her lip. *The truth is, my lies are smothering me, crowding me into a corner, but I can't tell Carrie that.*

She was not ten steps from the bus stop when she heard her name.

"Sophie! Sophie! Wait!" It was Carrie, hurrying forward, doing her best to catch Sophie.

Sophie's heart sank. She needed more time before facing her friend, the friend she'd put off for months. "Carrie, what are you doing here?"

Breathless, Carrie reached for Sophie's arm. "I'm just back from the vicarage. We had a committee meeting after church. I thought I'd meet your bus."

"You are—I just stepped off. But isn't this a long way to walk?"

"No longer for me than for you. It's good to be in the fresh air. Cold weather will be here soon enough." She beamed, and Sophie smiled in return.

It's been so long—too long—since I've looked outward, since I've cared about anyone other than myself and Charlotte. The realization stung her. Carrie had been her dearest friend, her only friend, growing up. To have neglected someone so important, so generous in her life, was wrong.

Carrie looped her arm through Sophie's. "Is your case heavy?"

"No, not at all—just a few things for overnight." Sophie blinked back threatening tears.

"It will be like old times. You'll have your old room, and in the middle of the night we can steal away to the pantry and devour tomorrow's pudding!"

Sophie laughed in spite of herself. *It's like coming home . . . like being a child and coming home. Perhaps it won't be so bad after all. Perhaps we can just play at remembering the old days and talk of nothing now. Please, God, give me peace today!*

Carrie chattered enough for both of them the two miles home.

As the houses thinned with more space and wide garden lawns between, Sophie's restless heart breathed a little. She'd forgotten the beauty of the English landscape away from the city.

"He maketh me to lie down in green pastures: he leadeth me beside the still waters. He restoreth my soul." The words from the Psalms seeped through her mind, followed just as quickly by condemnation.

I've stolen a child . . . someone else's child. But, dear Father in heaven, she's my child, isn't she? I saved her! She wouldn't be alive but for me. I've raised her from a toddler. Dear God, please don't take her away! A sob escaped Sophie's lips.

Carrie stopped short. "What is it? What's troubling you so?"

The concern in her old friend's eyes nearly undid Sophie. She so wanted to unburden her heart, but she'd lied to Carrie, too. *"Oh, what a tangled web we weave, when first we practice to deceive."* She shook her head, pulling her arm free to swipe at the unbidden tears. "It's nothing. I—I'm tired, that's all. Weary." She tried to laugh and failed. "Bone weary."

The concern in Carrie's eyes assured Sophie that her friend did not suspect the truth. "We're going to get you home, brew a hot pot of tea, put your feet up, and feed you Mrs. Hettie's hot, buttery scones slathered in currant jam and Devonshire cream."

Sophie smiled. "You can't use your ration on me!"

Carrie huffed indignantly. "And why not? Even if Father were here, he'd demand that we butcher the fatted calf!"

"You mean because the prodigal has returned." Sophie looked away, her throat tightening.

"Not the prodigal—my sister. It will just be you and me and a houseful of loving but nosy staff." Carrie moistened her lips.

Sophie knew that meant she had more to say.

"I don't want to pry, Sophie. I want you to relax and truly enjoy this respite. But when you're ready, I hope you'll talk to me. I pray you'll talk to me."

Sophie glanced at her friend, then looked quickly away. *I've lived a lifetime—ten lifetimes—since we were girls, Carrie. You wouldn't understand. Will I make it through this, Lord? How?*

Neither woman said more until they reached Haverford. Though Sophie and Charlotte had spent their first few weeks in England with Carrie, Sophie had nearly forgotten the estate's magnificence—beauty and order she'd almost taken for granted while growing up, always in Carrie's shadow, always second in her father's affections. Sophie knew that was as it should have been, should be.

What no one could understand was that now she was first in

someone's life—in Charlotte's life, and perhaps, if she hadn't utterly ruined it, in Janek's.

By the time Carrie left her in her old room to settle, Sophie was as weary as if she'd wrestled hay bales in the countryside for a day. The inner war stormed, relentless, never breaking for tea or sleep. She buried her face in her hands.

◆

Carrie was true to her word and did not pry, but orchestrated every comfort for Sophie, including her favorite meal of roast beef and Yorkshire pudding, slathered in brown gravy, with browned onions and carrots.

Sophie pushed back from the table. "That was heavenly! I couldn't eat another morsel. Please tell Mrs. Hettie she's outdone herself. I can't even imagine where she found such a feast."

Carrie pushed her chair back decisively. "Into the library. That was always your favorite room. And your favorite old chair is still there—the one with the comfy overstuffing." She smiled, and Sophie felt invited.

"I nearly forgot." Carrie handed Sophie an envelope from the desktop, once they'd reached the library. "This came for you on Saturday. I meant to forward it to you, but when Janek telephoned I thought to hold it until you came."

"It's from Poland." Sophie's heart leaped, and then she realized it wasn't Terri's handwriting, as she'd hoped. Familiar fear thickened her throat. *Dear God, what does this mean?*

"Yes, I suppose whoever it is doesn't have your address. They may have traced public records for you here. Who is it?"

"I've no idea." Sophie worried the seal on the envelope.

"Aren't you going to open it?"

"I—I don't know. Perhaps later."

Carrie stopped, as if undecided. Finally, she frowned. "You look as if you're afraid of something."

"That's ridiculous."

"Well, then."

Sophie tore the seal and pulled the thin paper from its hiding place, feigning bravado. She saw the words . . . in Polish. Her eyes narrowed as she concentrated to translate. She blinked, trying to conjure a memory.

"Well? Who is it?"

Sophie sighed, relieved beyond words that it was not bad news or an inquiry about Charlotte. "It's from a woman I knew in Poland—a woman whose daughter I taught. She says a friend—someone we both knew—is free, and another friend is . . . away—away, but alive. Thank You, God! And she writes about her little girl—a child in my underground school that I had a coat remade for." Sophie remembered how pleased Estera had been with the wooden buttons, how a packet of food she'd stolen from the store had formed a barrier between life and death, just long enough to get the little girl medicine she'd needed. She never knew what had happened to the family after that.

"Underground school? You were busy." Carrie sat down, interested.

"We were all busy. So much happened during the war."

"What does she want?"

"She wants—she needs—food and warm clothing, shoes for her daughter."

"That's a bit forward, isn't it?"

"You don't understand!" Sophie's righteous anger flared as she looked at the fitted comforts of the room, the grand appointments. "They have nothing. During the war they nearly starved—we all did. And now, with the Communists in charge, they still have nothing."

Carrie blinked.

"You don't even know what it's like to be hungry, to be so cold you fear you might freeze to death before morning if you go to sleep—you fear and you hope. And so many died anyway."

"No," Carrie whispered, taken aback. "I don't know. I'm sorry for what I said."

Sophie did her best to regain her composure. "I'm sorry I became angry. It's just—"

"You're not the one to apologize. I live in an ivory tower. I know it. I've known it ever since you first came here as a ten-year-old girl and opened my eyes to the world around me. The work I did during the war was something, a help, but it wasn't anything like what you did."

Sophie shook her head. She had no wish to make Carrie feel as if her work didn't matter. Every life, every bit done for others mattered, and Carrie did more than most.

"Let me help this woman. Please. I have means to help and would love to."

Sophie considered. These were her friends. She wanted to help them, but she knew that she could not send them the supplies Carrie could. She and Janek were making ends meet and could surely spare a little, but Carrie could make a real difference in their lives. At last she nodded. "That would be wonderful. Thank you."

Carrie clapped, resolved. "I'll get everything together at once and mail it within the week. You'll write and tell them it's coming. You must give me their sizes—approximately, anyway—and a list of what you think they'd like. In fact, let's do it now!"

Sophie smiled. *This is my friend*—"Do it now, before the ink goes dry on the page, before the setting of another sun, before another heartbeat." *I love you, dear friend. Thank you.*

They made the list together—far more extensive than Sophie could have imagined or accomplished.

"You mustn't send everything at once. Things don't always get through, you know."

Carrie nodded. "I've heard that sometimes contents are confiscated, that they never reach the addressed recipient."

"Right. Several small packages, with one or two things at a time, will be better. At least some of it's likely to get through."

"Don't worry. I'll keep sending until we're sure they have everything they need. I promise."

Sophie smiled, and Carrie reached for her hand.

"I'm just glad to have something worthwhile to do."

"I happen to know you do many worthwhile things and that you give yourself credit for none of them."

Carrie tipped her head back, as if shooing off a pesky fly.

"I'll write them tomorrow, when I get home, and tell them to expect packages in installments."

"Perfect."

• ◆ •

The afternoon waned. Because a storm picked up, neither woman suggested the ramble through the woods they'd planned. Instead, Carrie called for a roaring fire to be built in the library. "Still a luxury, using all this wood," she admitted. "But every now and then, why not?"

Sophie drew her cardigan around her. "It's hard to believe it's September. The days are shorter, the nights cooler already."

"I suppose Charlotte will begin school soon? She's five now, isn't she?"

"Six. Yes, she starts school tomorrow, in fact. Janek will walk her to school. I'll be home in time for tea."

"How did it go?" Carrie asked, pouring a second cup of tea for them both. Her eyes caught Sophie's and held them. "The meeting between Janek and Charlotte, and ever since. He didn't know he had a daughter, the last I saw him—ages ago. It must have been quite a shock."

"He loves Charlotte," Sophie defended. "We both do."

"Do you still love Janek?"

Indignation and panic warred in Sophie. "With all my heart."

Carrie set down the pot and handed the cup to Sophie. "Then what is the problem? I promised not to pry, but, Sophie, something's not right. Janek's terribly worried."

"What did he say?" Sophie hated that Janek had confided their problems to someone else—anyone else, and particularly her own friend.

Carrie didn't answer that question. "From where I sit you have everything—a home, a child, a husband who loves you like his own breath. It's all you've ever wanted. I don't understand."

Sophie looked away.

"Is there someone else?"

"Someone else?" Sophie drew a blank, but Carrie gave her a knowing look. "No. No! I love Janek. I love Janek, and I love Charlotte—and everything's perfect."

"It's clearly not perfect," Carrie said softly.

"It is! Or it would be if everyone would just leave us alone and stop asking useless, pointless questions that are none of their business!" Sophie couldn't stop the trembling, the fear and fury that suddenly welled inside her, that all-too-familiar storm that protected her from Janek's questions. Would it protect her from Carrie's? *What must Carrie think of me?*

Sophie knew Carrie was waiting. She was like that, had been like that from childhood. She'd always waited out Sophie's storms until the tide came in again, calmer—until Sophie could form her worries and anxieties into comprehensible sentences.

But there was no comprehending this, no sentences to be garnered, to be spoken. Sharing the truth would implode her life, would surely take Charlotte from her.

"I've wondered from the beginning," Carrie began, "from the day you brought Charlotte here."

Sophie held her breath, refusing to look at her friend.

"She's not Janek's, is she? And she's not yours." Carrie spoke the fatal words softly, without judgment.

Sophie wanted to scream. She stood, knocking over the teacup, spilling the amber brew along the carpet. *Another false move! Does it never end?* "I'm sorry—sorry about the tea." She bent to mop it with her napkin.

"Never mind the tea, Sophie. Look at me."

But Sophie would not. She turned away and walked to the floor-to-ceiling window. Pulling back the drape, she looked out into the pouring rain, saw the wind whip tree limbs in a writhing frenzy. Fear clutched her heart, and yet the realization that Carrie suspected—knew—was also a loosening of the life-sucking band encircling her chest.

Sophie let the drape drop. "She's mine."

"Is she?"

"In every way that matters."

"Have you told Janek?"

Sophie didn't answer.

"He suspects. He told me on the phone."

"He what?"

"He's frightened for you. He loves you, Sophie. He doesn't even care if Charlotte's not his daughter."

Sophie laughed, a half-hysterical, ironic laugh.

"I don't mean that he doesn't care—but he loves you and he loves Charlotte. He won't abandon you—either of you. Just tell him. Tell him the truth, whatever that is."

"You don't know what you're saying. You don't know what you're talking about." Sophie turned at last to her friend.

"No, I don't know, because you've not told me. And you don't have to."

"I can handle this on my own. There is nothing I can't handle—just leave me alone."

"We're not meant to handle life alone, Sophie. It's too hard, too unpredictable, too messy and big. There is One who is willing and ready to help, to travel with us, if we let Him."

Sophie stiffened. The image of Jesus offering to share His yoke, to help carry the burden beside her, came to mind.

As if Carrie could read her thoughts, she whispered, "'Come unto me, all ye that labour and are heavy laden, and I will give you rest. Take my yoke upon you, and learn of me; for I am meek and lowly in heart: and ye shall find rest unto your souls. For my yoke is easy, and my burden is light.'"

"Some burdens weren't meant to be shared." Sophie could not imagine her Lord carrying the lie she'd configured.

"Find rest, Sophie. He's standing at the door, knocking, waiting for you to open it. We have only to confess—to turn away from our darkness and confess whatever it is He already knows—and He waits, ready to help. We weren't made to walk alone, to live alone, to grieve alone. He'll carry your burdens—we all will and be glad to do it—but you must let us in . . . at least let Him in."

Sophie shook her head, helplessness about to envelop her.

"Talk to God—to Janek, to me, to somebody—before you crack. You look on the verge. End of sermon."

"Thanks." Sophie meant it wryly.

"You're welcome," Carrie spoke seriously, then reached to refill Sophie's cup. "Drink your tea before it's cold. There's nothing worse than cold tea."

Sophie knew that wasn't true.

◆

Sophie slipped a note beneath Carrie's door just before dawn, thanking her for her friendship, for helping her friends in Poland, for everything, and promising to be in touch. She made her way silently down the grand staircase and out the front door. Gripping her overnight bag, she stepped lively down the lane in the pale light of dawn, to the outskirts of town where she'd catch an early morning bus.

The sun was just breaking over the horizon as the bus jostled her into London. By the time she reached home, Charlotte would be sitting in her classroom and Janek in his office. But she would be there to give Charlotte her luncheon, never mind Mrs. Southerly's kindness.

She couldn't face another of Carrie's questions or sympathetic, concerned looks. She'd all but pulled the truth from Sophie the night before. If anyone deserved the truth, it was Janek first. Later, if and when life resolved itself, she'd explain to Carrie . . . if there were a way to explain.

Sophie unlocked her front door and stood in the dusky hallway of her home. She set down her overnight bag and looked at the clock in the hallway. Ten o'clock. She wondered what Charlotte would be learning now, her first day of school.

It took Sophie less than half an hour to unpack, wash up the morning dishes Janek had left in the sink, and make herself a cup of tea.

She sat by the kitchen window and pulled the crumpled letter from her pocket, the letter from Warsaw. She smoothed the stationery and read it again, translating more slowly this time, trying to make sense of all it said.

Dear Pani Zofia,

Perhaps you will remember me. I am the mother of Estera, the little girl whose life you saved in every way. I want to thank you, from the bottom of my heart. You saved my daughter first from ignorance and fear, when you taught her in the underground school. You saved her from freezing to death in the winters of the war, by giving her a coat with buttons. We've let the seams in that coat out every year as she's grown. Only now is it too small and will go to another child in need. You saved us all from starvation through food packets. I know you risked your life to do this. Thank you, Pani Zofia, and God bless you.

My daughter is all I have left in this world. She is my sunshine and my life—my will to live. My strong husband and beloved son were killed in the uprising. Had you not brought food that day, I do not think my little girl would be alive now.

If you find it possible, please send us food and clothing, and shoes for my Estera. She has no shoes for the winter. I am grateful and keep you in my prayers.

Yesterday I saw Jolanta. Her leg is crippled, but she is well and sends her greetings. She wonders if you still have the package she gave you. She asked me to tell you that your other friend and her husband have relocated north for some years. It's very cold, but they promised to find a way to be with you in time—this is what she said. Pray for them.

Ewa Koblitz

Sophie folded the letter and slid it back into its envelope. She wouldn't have to answer Ewa's question from Irena. Poland was worlds away and not a threat. *But "your other friend" . . . it must be Terri—Terri and Renat, surely.* Sophie swallowed, daring to hope, to believe her friend was alive. *Siberia is the punishment for resisters—"It's very cold. . . . Pray for them." But "for some years" doesn't mean forever. She even said they'd promised to find a way to be with me. It's almost too much to hope—to believe.* Another fantasy, and she could no longer afford to live in fantasies, to hope for things that weren't real. But she would write Ewa—carefully—and ask what she could without putting her at risk.

She must, above all, be glad and grateful Ewa had her daughter . . . her own daughter, the last of all her family who'd been snatched away by that vile war. *That's certain. That's real, and Carrie and I can help her.*

But Ewa's words reminded Sophie that the child she claimed, the child Irena asked about, was not her own. Because of her desperate love for Charlotte, there was a man desperately longing for his daughter, a man who'd lost his wife and all else.

CHAPTER FIFTY-THREE

J ANEK HUNG HIS COAT and hat behind his office door and took his seat. The rumble of the morning tea cart with its one squeaking wheel came down the hallway. He was thankful he'd not missed the young man making his rounds with steaming tea and milk. It had been a busy morning, what with preparing breakfast and getting Charlotte ready for her first day of school, then dropping her off.

Janek smiled at the memory. He'd left her at her classroom door, giving her shoulder a squeeze and saying "Be of good courage" in response to her anxious eyes. He'd kept up the smile until he'd reached the cobbled walkway outside the building, then turned to look back, with a twinge of trepidation for her sake and a mixture of pride and half regret that she was growing up so quickly.

It was a shame that Sophia had missed this first, momentous day of their daughter's foray into the world. Somehow, he didn't think she minded so much. He was quite certain she'd been dreading it far more than Charlotte, this marching forward without her.

It will do them both good to have others in their lives. They have been

*all in all to one another for so long. I'm glad Sophia's with Carrie. It will
do her good . . . perhaps do them both good.*

He prayed the two women had talked, that Sophia had, in some
way, unburdened her heart to her longtime, and too seldom seen,
friend.

Janek had just stirred his tea and taken the first comforting sip
when Iwan Nowak poked his head in the door, a picture of concern.

"Iwan!" Janek was always glad to see his fellow Pole.

"I heard of the row on Friday. Just wanted to know if you and
Pani Kumiega are all right."

"Yes, yes, we're fine. Crazy man terrified my wife, but she's all
right. I sent her away to visit a friend for the weekend, to calm her
nerves. She'll be back today."

Iwan stepped in closer and shut the door behind him. "I need to
apologize."

"Whatever for?" Janek would normally have stood out of respect,
but Iwan's comment caught him off guard.

Iwan motioned to the chair in front of Janek's desk and Janek nodded. Iwan slid into it, his hands intertwined. "I let him in the building.
Said he had a bit to do with the electric and wouldn't be long. It was a
favor, he said. He was on his lunch hour."

Janek blinked. "I don't understand."

"Not sure I do, either. He seemed perturbed, anxious, but I figured he was just in a hurry. Didn't want to be late on his boss's clock."

"He came to my office. My wife was here. When I came in he was
manhandling her."

"Itzhak Dunovich? That doesn't sound like him."

Janek felt his face go red, remembering the man's denials, remembering the punch he'd given him. He straightened a stack of papers that
didn't need straightening. "Well, we never know some people, do we?"

"No, I suppose not." Iwan's frown deepened. "I'm sorry. I should
have asked him further what he planned to do."

"It's not your fault. It's his. He seems to have some sort of strange attraction to my wife."

Iwan shook his head, stood, and turned to go, then stopped. "How do you suppose he knew Pani Kumiega would be here? Did he say? Did she?"

Janek stopped fiddling with papers. *How indeed?* What had Dunovich said? "He said it wasn't my wife he was interested in, but the picture—this picture." He lifted the damaged photo from his desk. "He said it reminded him of his wife and child—in Poland."

"Ah." Nowak nodded. "That makes more sense. The man lost his family in the war."

"We all lost in the war. That doesn't make us crazy."

"He found their bodies—at least his wife's. All he has to remember her by is part of a medallion she wore—a Tree of Life he gave her on their wedding day. He carries it in his pocket."

Janek's breath caught. He didn't want to ask but knew he must. "He lost a child?"

"He never learned what happened to her. That gives him hope she's alive." Iwan hesitated, looked as if he was about to add something, but turned.

"What? What more?"

"He said once that the photograph on your desk, your little girl, reminded him of his wife, that your child has her eyes. He has no picture of his wife or child." Iwan shrugged. "Maybe he's crazy, like you say, thinking his daughter could be here, in England, of all places. Still. Maybe he just wanted to look at the photograph once more, to remember . . . because it's too easy to forget."

◆ ◆ ◆

All afternoon Iwan's story haunted Janek. He couldn't concentrate on his work, or on anything else, but he didn't want to go home. He feigned busyness, closing his door, and asked one of the secretaries to telephone a message home. "Please tell my wife that I need to work late. I'll get tea at the office." He didn't wait for her answer. He had to think, needed to plan.

By seven o'clock the entire building had emptied, but the light still burned in Janek's office. He leaned forward on his desk, elbows on wood, head in his hands.

Lord, have I misjudged this man? Is he simply a haunted man—not dangerous? The scene could have been as he said, and if it was, have I ruined his reputation—his chance to find his own child? If that is so, why is Sophia so frightened? It was the same prayer he'd prayed for hours. And still, there was no answer.

He wasn't certain he could have heard it if there had been. All he could see, hear, feel, smell was the fog of memory creeping into his brain. The moment, after the long, horrific war, when Sophia had opened the apartment door and he'd seen her for the first time in years—thin, pale, malnutrition pulling her skin across her bones, her hair thinning, her eyes still beautiful. And then Charlotte had stepped out from behind her skirts.

He couldn't believe Charlotte was his child—a gift too rare and lovely, a mercy and grace beyond comprehension. *And she was that gift. She is. But is she mine?*

What have you not told me, Sophia? Did you not believe I could love you—that you were enough for me as we were?

At last, because he knew there would be only one more bus to his street that night, he picked up his hat and coat and left the office.

◆ ◆ ◆

Janek dreaded the conversation he knew he must have with his wife. But when he arrived home, after fortifying himself with a pint from the pub on the corner—a habit he'd been very careful to give up after the war—he found her already asleep.

Relieved, he readied himself for bed.

Hours after midnight he woke to hear a whimpering. This time it wasn't from Sophia, who slept soundly beside him, but came from Charlotte's room, down the short hallway, on the far side of the water closet. Quietly, he rose and pushed his arms through his dressing gown and made his way toward his little girl's room. He was half-awake and only remembered that she might not be his little girl, after all, when he pushed open the door.

"Papa! Papa!" Charlotte cried, reaching her arms up for him.

Janek's heart warmed in a rush. "What is it, my little pumpkin? Did you have a bad dream?"

"No, Papa."

"What is it, then?" He pulled her onto his lap and stroked her hair.

"I missed you. You didn't come home for tea."

"I'm sorry, my sweet. I—I'm sorry." He couldn't lie to her. There were too many lies already. "But you had Mummy, yes?"

"Yes." The little girl yawned.

Janek pulled back the covers and laid her down, then pulled the comforter up, over her shoulders, and smoothed her long, dark hair from her face.

"Papa?"

"Yes?"

"Why is Mummy so sad? She cries. She thinks I don't see, but she cries so much."

Janek sighed, a deeper, longer sigh than any he could remember. "I don't know, little one. But I will find out."

"You'll make her better? Make her smile again?"

Janek scooped her into his arms, almost fiercely, and fought back panic at the thought of losing his daughter, his wife.

"Papa! You're hurting me." Charlotte squirmed in his arms.

"I'm sorry, my darling. I'm sorry." There were not enough endearing names in the universe for this precious child, and not enough time to lavish them upon her. He tucked her beneath the covers again, kissed her forehead. "Go back to sleep, Charlotte. Things will look better in the morning." Immediately he regretted the lie.

"You'll fix Mummy's smile?"

"I will do my best."

Janek pulled his daughter's door gently closed and walked into the kitchen. Moonlight filtered through the curtains over the sink. He ran cold water and splashed his face, drying it on his pajama sleeve. Sleep was useless, impossible.

He knew what he needed to do. He had done Itzhak Dunovich a great wrong; they both had. He didn't know if Sophia's time with Carrie had helped in any way, but from what he could decipher of Charlotte's pleas, he did not imagine so.

Janek straightened. He'd best get on with it. If Sophia woke as he dressed, they would talk. If not, he'd go ahead on his own and tell her after. He didn't pray but determined to take her sleeping or waking as a sign of which he should do.

Janek dressed in the dark, not trying to be quiet. By the time he sat on the edge of the bed and tied his shoes, he'd gained courage.

He let himself out the front door, not realizing until he was standing at the bus stop in the predawn drizzle that he'd forgotten his hat, his umbrella, even his overcoat. It didn't matter. Getting wet was nothing compared to all that mattered.

Help me, God. Help us do what is right. Help us not lose everything in the process, not lose each other. Sophia will go mad if Charlotte is taken away. Dunovich is all but mad now. And why not? What would I not do to save or reclaim my wife or child in such a circumstance?

He made it to the office just as a member of the custodial staff unlocked the front door from the inside. Janek went directly downstairs to Iwan Nowak.

"Pan Kumiega! You're here early. Out to catch the worm, are we?" Iwan smiled at his own joke; then, taking in Janek's disheveled appearance, he frowned. "Are you all right? You look as if you haven't slept a wink."

It was all Janek could do to stand. "I need to find Itzhak Dunovich. Is he here? What time does he come in?"

Iwan straightened. "He doesn't work here, remember? He just came by last week when—he doesn't work here, you know, and his contract work here is finished."

"Do you know where he works? How can I reach him?"

Iwan looked away. "I don't know that he's working anywhere. Lost his job, as I understand it."

"What?" Janek felt the blood drain from his face.

"The police kept his tools, so he couldn't work. The foreman didn't want a man—a Pole, or more likely, a Jew—with a smudge against his name."

"But we didn't file formal charges."

Now Iwan looked at Janek hard. "Do you think that matters?"

"I've got to find him."

Iwan's jaw tightened. "Perhaps you've done enough."

"What?"

"I went to his work on Saturday, trying to find him, to see if he was all right. He'd been sacked. I pestered till they gave me his home address, so I went there. His landlady evicted him the moment she learned he'd been hauled into the police station. Said she didn't want criminals in her boardinghouse, that she'd never wanted a Jew any-way. She'd only rented to him because he offered to repair her house's poor wiring since the bombing."

"He has no job, no home. How will I find him?" Janek felt as if he'd been caught trampling over Dunovich's grave.

"I've no idea. Don't know as you can. Like I said, Pan Kumiega, perhaps you've done enough." Iwan Nowak picked up his set of keys and left the room, leaving Janek standing in the small pool of light from the overhead lamp.

CHAPTER FIFTY-FOUR

SOPHIE HAD NOT INTENDED to oversleep. It was Charlotte who woke her up. "Mummy, must I go to school today?"

Sophie batted the sleep from her eyes and squinted at the alarm clock—quarter past eight. "Oh, my darling!" She pushed from the bed and slid into her bedroom slippers. "We're late. Go, find your uniform, and I'll make the tea." She shooed Charlotte from the room and stood blinking. *Where is Janek? Didn't he come home last night?* Panic raced her blood, until she saw his clothes from yesterday across the chair. *I was so exhausted. I must have slept straight through.*

They barely made it to school before the buzzer sounded. Sophie realized, only upon stepping out the school door, that she'd forgotten to remove her apron at home. *Thank heaven I have a coat!* She hurried the five blocks home and closed the door. It was then that she realized Janek had left no dishes in the sink, that he must not have stopped to eat.

She sat at her dressing table, took down her hair that she'd barely combed that morning, and brushed it out. With each stroke she

368

thought of her time with Carrie, of all Carrie had said. She thought of Ewa and Estera, mother and daughter in Warsaw—how Ewa said that she'd saved them. Sophie closed her eyes. *I'm not anybody's savior. I'm a thief, and I'm terrified.*

She fingered the carving on her jewelry box, the box Janek had given her, tracing the rosettes and vines. *Beauty, minus thorns. Not like real life.* She opened the box, took her trinkets from the bottom, then gently pulled the lining from the edge of the box. She felt across the white silk until she found the bump beneath and pulled the gold half medallion from its hiding place, fingering the severed edges of the tree branches.

Sophie felt the breaking of her heart, saw the crack in each of her relationships widening . . . her lies, her deception of Janek . . . her strained relationship with Carrie . . . her keeping of Charlotte from her father, for surely Itzhak Dunovich was her father.

Dear God, I only wanted to keep her, to love and protect her! I lost my babies and You gave her to me, didn't You? Isn't she truly mine now? Shouldn't she be?

Sophie groped her way to the bed and lay down, huddling on her side in a fetal position, holding her pillow, weeping into the coverlet. Suddenly the losses of all the years of war overwhelmed her. Janek leaving to fight. Janek not returning. Mr. Bukowski trying to rescue her picture of her beloved. Mr. Gadomski, who hid her in the library, who hid and helped so many. The Garbinski family—the dead, cold baby she'd carried to the cemetery. Aaron and Judah Bukowski, shot running into each other's arms in the street outside the ghetto. Dr. Korczak and that precious parade of orphaned children, marched to the train bound for Treblinka. Terri—*oh, dear God, what has happened to you, sister of my heart?*

Once the storm started, it could not be assuaged. Sophie screamed, she sobbed, she mourned and keened for all those she'd loved and could not save. And then she mourned for Charlotte, whom she loved with all her heart and would now lose. She wept until the bedding was soaked. She wept until there were no more tears.

How long she lay, Sophie didn't know. Eventually, two things emerged.

I've lost all I have—everyone I have—except Janek and Charlotte, if only I have her a little while longer. My lies, my deceptions push them away, destroy them and the love they—we—so desperately need. I've broken every bond of trust.

Confessing to Janek means losing Charlotte. But I've already lost her. Itzhak Dunovich will take her away, won't he? Will that mean losing Janek, too? Will he forgive me? Can he? Will he ever trust me, love me, again?

Sophie felt she was waking from a dream—half dream and half nightmare of her own making. She closed her eyes, squeezing them tight, then opened them to the room around her. How had she gotten herself in such a mess? *By pretending. By pretending that what I want—Charlotte—is my own and shoving away her past, her truth . . . her truth and mine.*

She'd been brave during the war, jumped in when something needed doing, when someone needed saving. *Now see what I've done to Itzhak Dunovich. He doesn't deserve this. At least I didn't press charges.* She groaned at the ridiculous justification she'd just given herself. *I can't do this! I can't carry this any longer!*

Carrie's words came back to her. *"We have only to confess—to turn away from our darkness and confess whatever it is He already knows— and He waits, ready to help. We weren't made to walk alone, to live alone, to grieve alone. He'll carry your burdens. . . ."*

Please, God. She opened her heart, bare and true and naked for the first time in longer than she could remember. *Please, forgive me. Forgive me for pretending Charlotte is mine, for wishing and hoping that she had no other family to come looking for her.*

Sophie sobbed at the realization of such a wish—to hope for the deaths of fellow human beings so that she might have their child.

Forgive me, Father. Forgive what I've done to Itzhak Dunovich, for what I've withheld from Charlotte, for the lies I've told Janek, for my cruelty and coldness to him, for the lies I've told Carrie. The list felt endless. And yet, as she prayed, as she scraped each dark confession from the hidden places in her mind, her heart, Sophie felt some of the weight lift.

Father, You cared for me, watched over and preserved me through the most horrific times in Poland. Why You saved me, when so many others died, I don't know. But You did. And You saved Charlotte . . . my Charlotte . . . Itzhak Dunovich's daughter. Even after we escaped Poland, You guided us over the mountains. We could have frozen, could have been caught, shot. So often, time after time, You made a way when there was no way, just as Pan Bukowski always said You could.

Please, Father, show me that way now. Show me, and give me the strength to follow You.

Sophie sat up. She dreaded all that lay ahead. She dreaded the outcome. But she felt cleaner, as if the hidden cavities of her heart had been swept bare, replaced by something empty. She knew better than to leave those spaces barren.

What should I do, Lord? Not what do I want, this time, but what should I do? I can't do this alone—and I shouldn't.

Sophie breathed deeply, stood, and looked at the clock—eleven thirty.

Before she could change her mind, she dialed Janek's office.

◆

"Yes?" Janek answered on the second ring. His voice sounded hollow in his own ears.

"Janek, it's me."

"Sophia." Janek felt the beat in his heart, the thud in his stomach.

"I have something to tell you. I need to—" The telephone line crackled. It sounded as if Sophia sobbed.

Despite everything, Janek's heart went out to his wife. "What is it, Sophia? I didn't understand what you said."

"I said, can you come home? For lunch—after lunch—when Charlotte's gone back to school? Can you come for the afternoon, while she's still in school? I need to—we need to talk . . . alone."

Janek pondered. He'd planned to go to Itzhak Dunovich's old boardinghouse . . . beg the landlady to tell him where he'd gone, if she had any idea. He'd offer her money if that would help her memory, or her guess.

"Janek? Are you there? Did you hear me? I need to talk with you about—about Charlotte, about Poland." The voice came tentative, childlike, over the phone.

He moistened his lips. She'd lied to him—repeatedly—and he didn't want to be dissuaded from what he knew he should do. But he should listen to what she had to say before he sought out Dunovich. He'd no idea if he'd even be able to find the man. And Sophia was his wife, after all. He owed her that. And he loved her.

"Yes. Yes, we need to talk. I'll be home." He set down the receiver without awaiting her response. The wheels were set in motion.

◆ ◆ ◆

When Janek walked in the door, Sophia was sitting at the kitchen table, a broken medallion linked to a delicate gold chain spread before her on the table. Janek's throat went dry at the memory of Iwan's words . . . *Something about part of a medallion—a Tree of Life—Dunovich carries in his pocket.*

Sophia didn't look up, just kept twisting the ring on her finger.

Janek sat opposite her. "Talk to me." He was glad, relieved, that his voice came out even—not angry, not solicitous, not commanding, but quiet.

She drew a deep but ragged breath, searching his eyes. "Where to begin . . ."

"Poland. Tell me what happened after I left for Romania. Tell me everything."

Sophia looked as if a knife had been thrust between her ribs, but at last she nodded and began, a slow, nearly mechanical rendition of all that had gone before.

"I was in the library when the Germans came with their planes, their bombs. Their strafing. Explosions—glass, craters, buildings blown apart . . . everywhere. By the time I got home—nearly home—our apartment was blown open, like the front of a doll's house." Sophia looked up as if she'd just thought of something. "Pan Bukowski rescued your picture for me . . . a gift that I lost in the war . . . but he died doing it." She bit her lips. "I lost our baby . . . the third day of the bombing, I think. Pan Gadomski saved me, hid me in the library basement. Terri's father . . ." She broke down.

"Terri is Tereza Gadomski?" Puzzle pieces began to fit. Janek wanted nothing more than to take his wife in his arms. No matter what else had happened, she needed him now. He needed her now. But when she didn't answer, he waited, afraid to stop her flow of words.

Sophia talked and talked, as if recounting a long-ago tale. And it was a tale, a series of horrors and sacrifices and gestures and rescues so intense, so prolonged, he could not believe she'd held it in so long.

By the time Charlotte came through the door, Sophia had given details of life with the Gadomskis, of her friendship with Terri. She'd just reached the death and burned body of Pan Gadomski, the man who'd been godfather to Janek. He knew he must hold himself together, but he, too, would need to grieve for that dear man.

"Wait. Wait, Sophia. I'll take Charlotte to Mrs. Southerly. I'll be back. Just wait."

Sophia didn't answer, but sat very still.

Janek ushered Charlotte across the way, asked Mrs. Southerly to keep her for tea and a few hours into the evening, promising to pay her double, and returned to Sophia, still sitting at the table. He put the kettle on. They both needed a break.

But Sophia continued before he'd measured the tea into the pot. He sensed she was on a mission now, not to be stopped again. Stories poured out of her . . . of Dr. Korczak and the children marched to the train, of helping the Bukowskis, of Judah's love of watercolors, of carrying Pani Garbinski's baby to the cemetery and pleading for a proper Jewish burial. She told of Renat and all the ways he'd helped them—all the risks they'd taken. She told of Terri's love and loss of Piotr, of her love for Renat, of how hopeless a future it seemed, of the day her friend brought the baby—the toddler, whose name was Ania . . . That was all either of them knew, except that she wore a half medallion around her neck.

Sophia fingered the broken piece. "I learned later that it is a Jewish symbol . . . a Tree of Life."

"All its branches severed." It was the thing Janek had thought when Iwan had described it to him, the metaphor he saw now.

"Yes." She looked into his eyes for the first time since she'd begun the story. "I knew nothing of her parents, where she came from, to whom she'd been entrusted . . . nothing. And I never saw Terri again." Sophia's chin began to quiver, the tears running down her cheeks. Janek thought she'd break down, but she didn't. "This letter came . . . from Poland. See what it says? Maybe that's Terri. Maybe she and Renat are together."

"North," Janek read. "Siberia?"

"I think so."

"Then she's not dead. That's good. There's hope."

"Yes, thank God." Sophia swiped the tears from her eyes, nodding. She tried to smile, then stepped back in time, back to Poland and the war. "Every moment after that I feared discovery. I moved, several times, always aided by the underground. My mission was to keep her alive. I named her Karolina while we were in Poland—Charlotte—for my mother, and because it means 'free'—'feminine' and 'free.'"

"But she wasn't yours . . . wasn't ours." Janek desperately needed to keep hold of reality. *What more could she have done? Dear God, see what my Sophia suffered, what she endured!*

"When the man came to lead me out of Poland, I could not leave her. I would not leave her. The ghetto had been emptied—'liquidated,' they called it, and burned. Jolanta, the woman who ran the network to rescue children, had been arrested, and posters said she'd been killed. Terri was gone. I could not leave Charlotte, and I could not leave without her, so I lied. I lied to save her, to keep her . . . and I kept on lying."

"But you lied to *me*, Sophia. You told me she was our child." Janek didn't want to plead, but the tones, soft, barely accusing, crept in.

Sophia sobbed, but caught herself, and he admired the self-control she exhibited. "I was afraid."

"Of me?"

"That you wouldn't want her, that you would make me give her up."

"You think I am so cruel?"

"You wanted a child—our child—and I cannot give you that, Janek. If ever I would have been able, I'm not able now."

"You don't know this."

"I believe this. Look at us. There is no reason to believe otherwise."

"This is why you won't go to the doctor?"

She looked away. "He would realize I hadn't given birth, that Charlotte couldn't be my child—my biological child. The doctor would tell you, and then—then . . ."

"Then I would know, and you'd have to tell the truth."

"I'd lose everything—Charlotte, you, our family."

"You believe so little in me? You trust me so little? Is my love this small to you?" He stood and walked to the sink, bracing his hands against it, squeezing his eyes shut against the pain—Sophia's pain, his pain, how totally incomprehensible this would be to Charlotte. "Did you think I didn't suspect she wasn't mine? Did you think I would never learn the truth?"

Sophia didn't answer.

"How do you think this makes me feel—to learn the family I love, the family I live and work and would die for, is not my own? That our daughter does not belong to me—to us?"

"I'm sorry." He barely heard her whisper. "I was afraid. That's not a reason, I know . . . but I was so afraid."

"You're sorry," he sighed. "You were afraid . . . And what of Itzhak Dunovich? He has the other half of the medallion—Iwan told me he carries it always. He recognized his dead wife's eyes in Charlotte's picture—his Ania. He is her father, Sophia. He has a right to his daughter. What now?"

"I don't know. . . . I believed, when she came as a helpless little tot into my arms, that God gave me this child to raise. Janek, I hoped I would see you again. I hoped I would see you alive, but I didn't know—couldn't know that. All I knew was that I had her—had been given her. I didn't go out seeking her—she was brought to me."

Janek closed his eyes and nodded.

"We can give her a better life than Itzhak Dunovich," she whispered.

"What did you say?"

"I said we can give her a good life. She believes we're her parents. We're a married couple. You have a good job—we have citizenship. What can an electrician, living without a wife, give her? Who would keep her in the day while he works?" She pleaded with Janek, then turned away. "God can't be so cruel as to take her from us . . . can He? It's too much to ask—a sacrifice that can't be borne. It isn't possible . . . is it?"

Janek reached for his wife's trembling hands. They were cold and he enveloped them. "How can we ask that? It's the sacrifice God made—giving His child. Do you remember?" He waited for that to sink in. "And what of Dunovich? He's searched all this time for his daughter—the only family he has left in the world. What does God intend for him? Is he to sacrifice his daughter so we can have her? Is he Abraham? Is there no ram in the thicket for him?"

Sophie leaned her head on their entwined hands, shaking it wearily from side to side. "She has three parents who love her. Who gets the ram?" she whispered. "I'm afraid, Janek. I'm so afraid he will take her."

He squeezed her hands, his own heart breaking. "I'm afraid too. I love Charlotte with all my heart . . . almost as much as I love you." He saw Sophia shudder, felt her tears on his hands. "But we can't withhold a daughter from her father. It wouldn't be fair to Charlotte or right for Dunovich. To keep such a secret will destroy us, Sophia. Look, already, what it has done to us. To go on pretending would eat away our souls. You've no idea the things I imagined."

"I'm sorry. I'm so very sorry."

"God made a way for Abraham and for Isaac. He will make a way for us. I don't know what it is—I don't pretend to know. I don't pretend to believe we will be allowed to keep her, but we can ask. We can try. Already we've hurt Itzhak Dunovich. His police interrogation has cost him his job, and his lodgings."

"What?" She raised her head.

"He lost his job. His landlady evicted him. I don't even know where he lives now."

Sophia pulled her hands away and wiped her eyes. The room had grown dusky. "We have to find him." She sniffled and wiped her nose. "We must help him. We'll tell him the truth and beg his forgiveness. But I don't know how I will survive—if I can survive if he takes her from us."

"We will survive. We will survive together." But Janek didn't know how either.

"Don't tell her—not yet."

"No," he agreed. "I will find him first . . . talk with him." He studied Sophia and knew it was something he must do. Even if Itzhak Dunovich wanted to talk with Sophia about all that had happened in Poland—and surely he would—Janek knew he must be the one to first approach the man, and the first to apologize. "I owe him that. And I'll do all I can to get him reinstated, or to find him another job. My rashness ruined his reputation."

Sophia leaned across the table and stroked his cheek, her eyes speaking gratitude. "No, my love, it was mine. And I am so very sorry—for not being honest, for not reaching out to you, for not trusting you from the beginning. I was wrong."

Gently, Janek pulled her fingers from his face and kissed them. He opened her palm and kissed it, closed her fingers upon it, then wrapped her hands in his and pulled them to his heart.

CHAPTER FIFTY-FIVE

ITZHAK HAD PICKED UP WORK where he could—always day work for laborers, paid on the spot, and sometimes cheated on the spot.

He shared a room, rented by the week, with another laborer, drank weak tea, and ate cheap meat pies from street vendors. He pinched and saved every penny in the hopes that he would be able to one day afford his own tools, gain a steady job once more, and when he found his Ania—if he found her—rent two rooms and a bath.

Each Tuesday, Thursday, and Saturday he asked for his mail at the post office window, praying for word from one of the societies he'd approached for help. Finally, a letter came, the envelope padded, from Poland. He was so excited he nearly missed the slim envelope behind it. He stuffed it inside his jacket pocket and tore open the mail from Poland, then stopped on the post office steps.

He didn't want to open it there, to look at whatever pictures it might hold. He wanted to sit, unobserved, and savor each face from the past.

Itzhak crossed the street, walking down the park's pathway until he found a bench, the seat already warm, drenched in early October sunshine.

Please, Adonai, let there be a photograph of my Rosa—just one. I won't ask for more. He stopped. He couldn't imagine ever asking for another thing in life.

He pulled the packet of photos, wrapped in an extra fold of onionskin paper, from the envelope. A photo of Rosa's mother and father on top. Itzhak swallowed. Beneath it, one of Rosa as a baby, held between her parents, and another of Rosa as a little girl, with her mother. Tears threatened the corners of Itzhak's eyes. The little girl staring out at him looked so much like the one in the picture on Janek Kumiega's desk.

I'm not meshugge, *after all. If they saw this picture, they would understand. Anyone might see—might recognize the resemblance.* It was all he could do not to weep aloud.

He swiped at his eyes with his coat sleeve to better see the next picture and gasped. It was Rosa and him—a picture taken close up, on their wedding day. After the wedding, in the garden outside her parents' home, beneath the linden tree. Sunlight dappled her gown. Slightly shaded, but there they were, smiling, young, not a thought of the war or separation to come. He peered closer still. There, in the hollow of Rosa's throat, lay the Tree of Life medallion he'd clasped round her neck—whole. Itzhak stroked the curve of her neck, the cascade of her hair. The lump in his throat grew ten sizes. He pulled the half medallion from his pocket and set it beside the photo. One and the same.

He forced himself to look at the last picture. Rosa in the same garden, the bump beneath her dress showing—the bump that was Ania. She was standing under the same linden tree, one hand clinging to the lowest branch to steady herself, the other resting on her precious baby. Despite the war, despite the rationing, how radiant, how happy she looked!

He'd forgotten this photograph, taken on a borrowed camera, perhaps a week before they'd left Marya's home for the ghetto. The only picture of Rosa pregnant. The only picture of the promise of Ania.

Itzhak closed his eyes. *Thank You, Adonai! Thank You!*

Itzhak sat on the bench with the loves of his life until the sun set through the trees. Dusk fell swiftly and the cold damp of autumn seeped into his bones. He stood, feeling a stiffness he didn't want to own, and shook his limbs to recirculate the blood. He hadn't realized that his foot had fallen asleep. Rather than catch the bus to his rooming house, he'd walk and save the pence.

Itzhak was nearly back to his room when he remembered the other envelope in his pocket. He pulled it out, but it was too dark to read the return address.

Back in his room he set his precious photographs on the table beside his bed and slit the seal of the other envelope with his thumb.

Dear Pan Dunovich,

    I owe and offer you my sincere apologies. I have learned that your actions in my office when last we met were honorable toward my wife, and I sincerely regret every hardship my calling for the constable has caused you.

    In my determination to reach you I have been to see your former employer and former landlady. While they did not know your immediate whereabouts, I did my best to clear your name with them. I have also recovered and returned your tools to your former employer. He said they belonged to him. I hope that was true. If not, I will do all in my power to help you recover them. I believe he would like to rehire you, now that the truth has been established.

*Please, sir, I would like to speak with you in person. I pray
you will forgive my rash behavior and allow me to meet with
you. There is more I need to say.*

You may reply at the address below.

*I remain your servant,
Janek Kumiega*

Unexpected—astonished—confused were words too small, too
insignificant to express Itzhak's reaction. He sat on the side of the
bed, holding the letter, staring into the lamplight.

*Why would Kumiega seek me out? Why apologize now? What does he
want to speak to me about? He's done all the damage he can . . . everything but see me deported. Is that it? Is he trying to find me to see me out
of the country?*

It had been hard enough for Itzhak to get day labor in London
labeled as a Pole and a Jew. The end of the war had brought an influx
of men needing jobs and women furious to have their jobs taken away
to accommodate those men. Without references, without his own
tools, there were no open doors. It was only his skill in a moment his
former employer had desperately needed someone—that, and the rec-
ommendation by Iwan Nowak—that gave him that first break. *The
break Kumiega made disappear in a moment of misjudgment.* Itzhak
rubbed his jaw. He still felt Kumiega's punch, at least in memory.

No, he didn't trust the man. Why should he? Itzhak balled the
letter and threw it in the trash.

• ◆ •

Monday came and the weather turned bitter cold, the London rain
relentless. Itzhak stood outside the fence for day laborers until his feet
were soaked. Despite edging his way to the front of the queue, he was
not chosen. *Meat pie again . . . only one today.*

The day stretched too long and too cold before him. He decided to walk back to his room. He couldn't say why, but he took the long way and passed Kumiega's office. He'd thought about the letter all weekend and had retrieved it from the dustbin, spreading it out, rereading it. *What does he want?* It was the question Itzhak could not erase from his brain—and still, the photograph on Kumiega's desk haunted him.

One way to test Kumiega's sincerity is to see if he really did go to my boss, if he really did retrieve those tools. Itzhak's pride would not keep him from taking back his job, if Kumiega was truthful.

Itzhak knew he was the best electrician his boss had employed. He also knew the man despised Jews and thought Poles and Lithuanians worth trampling on. *But it is a job.* Itzhak had eaten enough cold and greasy meat pies with precious little meat. If he did find Ania— though those hopes had dwindled with the onslaught of bad luck, injustice, poverty, and hunger—he would need a steady job, able to provide income for a home and someone to care for her during the day.

He was proud, but he was no fool. The war had taught him he must seize opportunity and not look too closely in its face.

Before he could reconsider, Itzhak tramped to his old place of employment. It was time for morning tea break, and his boss usually took his break at the pub across the street, just as they opened for the day.

Inside, Itzhak removed his cap as his eyes adjusted to the dim room, the low ceiling, the chairs and tables crowded into corners and windows that protruded oddly toward the street. He found his old boss alone at the bar, nursing a pint.

Itzhak plopped his coins on the bar, three seats down, not acknowledging the man. "A pint, if you please." His accent would give him away, yet the man didn't look his direction. Could it be that he hadn't heard him? Or that he didn't want to recognize him?

The bartender shoved a mug toward Itzhak with one hand and swept the coins from the bar with the other.

Itzhak took a long drink, steadied the mug on the bar, and waited, but the man said nothing. Itzhak shifted in his seat. This wasn't what he'd hoped. Still, there was no point in coming all this way and playing coy. "Mr. Schlesser? Good morning to you."

Schlesser looked up, his eyes a mite filmy. He stared at Itzhak several moments before he seemed to recognize him. "Dunovich? Itzhak Dunovich?"

"The same." Itzhak felt on surer footing now.

"I fired you. Sacked you. Sent you packing."

"You did."

"A foolhardy thing, that." He turned, taking Itzhak in more fully. "That man—that man said he punched you and called the constable down on you. What's his name?"

"Kumiega."

"Kumiega. Came round, brought your tools, said it was all a misunderstanding and his fault. That true?"

"It is."

Schlesser turned back to his drink. "I suppose you're still Polish or something near."

"And still a Jew."

"Hmmph." Schlesser took a swig. "Can't be helped."

"No." Itzhak tightened his jaw. He wouldn't apologize for who he was.

"Looking for a job, are you?"

"Possibly."

"Possibly?" Schlesser clearly hadn't expected that. "You're the best electrician I had."

"Yes."

"Rather a big head, eh?"

Itzhak didn't say anything.

"Come round in the morning. Your tools will be waiting . . . if you want your job."

"An increase is in order."

Schlesser's neck reddened and Itzhak realized he might have gone too far.

"Half shilling an hour increase, not a penny more."

"Done." Itzhak reached his hand out.

Schlesser acted as if he didn't see, but Itzhak pushed his hand closer, under the man's nose. Schlesser shook it once and let go.

Itzhak retrieved his cap and stepped into the street, his shoulders set straighter than they'd ever been in England.

◆

A week of work on his old job passed before Itzhak believed it would not be jerked from him. At the end of two weeks, when he held his pay in the palm of his hand, he breathed hope. He didn't even stop for tea but rushed back to his rooming house and showed the pay to Rosa's photograph.

"Miracles happen sometimes, my Rosa. Do you see? Do you see?"

He knew she would be proud of him, and pleased. If only he'd been able to do such work, able to receive such pay while she lived! So much he would have been able to buy, to do for her and for their Ania. The realization pierced his heart.

He traced her picture . . . paper, only. What he wouldn't give for the beating heart, the flesh and blood of her before him. Itzhak closed his eyes and lay back on his bed. Some nights he longed for sleep on the off chance he might dream of her, of their days and nights and life together. Other nights, he dreaded sleep—on the off chance he might dream of digging up her body, of unclasping the medallion from her neck.

He pulled the half medallion from his pocket. Rubbing the severed tree limbs reminded him of his severed heart. He sat up, unable to breathe.

He opened the drawer of his bedside table and pulled out Kumiega's letter. Itzhak spread it out, over his knee, and read it again. *What does he want? What could he or his wife say to me that matters now?* But he knew. He knew and he didn't know. He feared and he hoped, and he dared not hope. *Could the girl in the picture be our Ania? Is it possible?*

For weeks Itzhak had pushed the hope, the daring to hope, from his heart. But now that he had a job, now that he could support his daughter if he found her, he was ready to open his mind again.

He pulled out a pen and paper. Writing the letter didn't mean he would have to mail it. It meant only that he *could* mail it. If he wanted Kumiega's cooperation, he must be polite, though he felt anything but polite toward the man.

> *Pan Kumiega,*
>   *I recognize your efforts to restore my reputation.*
>   *If you are serious in your desire to speak with me, meet me in the park outside the post office after four on Saturday afternoon.*
>
>   *Itzhak Dunovich*

CHAPTER FIFTY-SIX

SOPHIA PRESSED THE LETTER into Janek's hands the moment he walked in the door from work. Janek didn't need to ask who it was from. The fear in Sophia's eyes told him everything.

He read it. "To the point."

"Do you think he suspects?"

"I don't know." Janek didn't want to fool himself, didn't want to fool Sophia, to give her false hope. "How can he not?"

It was the hardest few days either he or Sophia had known. Each smile Charlotte gave them tore at their hearts. They feared her smiles for them were numbered, feared her songs and dances about the house, her hugs and good-night kisses were numbered, not in years, but in weeks, or days, or moments.

Still, for the first time, they faced uncertain days together. That, to Janek, made all the difference, and he prayed it would sustain Sophia. She seemed so fragile to him, so likely to break.

◆

Saturday came too soon. They had agreed that Sophia would take Charlotte to the cinema, buy her ice cream, make the day as pleasant and memorable as possible. It would give Janek time to meet with Dunovich and not require Sophia to stare into the eyes of their daughter without crying.

Janek reached the park twenty minutes ahead of time but found Itzhak Dunovich waiting on the bench across from the post office, the bench on which he'd first found Sophia while she'd waited and watched.

"Pan Dunovich." Janek removed his glove, extending his hand, even though it felt cold and shook slightly.

Dunovich hesitated, looked wary, but stood and removed his bare hand from his pocket to give a slight shake in return.

This will be hard. He's angry, and who can blame him? What will he be when he hears? "Shall we walk?"

Dunovich looked as if he might object, but then fell into step beside him.

Janek had rehearsed this moment over and over. Now that it had come, he couldn't begin. They walked a quarter mile, a half mile, and still Janek didn't speak.

Dunovich stopped abruptly. Janek nearly tripped. Dunovich took a packet from his coat's breast pocket, an envelope. From the envelope he drew photographs, which he held before Janek. Janek reached for them, but Dunovich pulled them back abruptly and held them at arm's length.

"Please, I want you only to look."

Uncertain, Janek leaned forward. The first appeared to be an old picture. He saw a child—a little girl with her parents. He realized with a sudden jolt that the girl in the photograph could have been Charlotte's older sister. Janek felt his heart sink. Before he could speak, Dunovich withdrew the photograph and showed another—what appeared to be a wedding photograph. It was a young Dunovich and a woman . . . a beautiful young woman with Charlotte's eyes.

"Look closely. Her eyes. Are they familiar?"

Of course they are! But it wasn't the woman's eyes Janek saw in that moment. It was the medallion. *Branches, trunk, not severed.* He felt the ground become uneven beneath his feet. Dunovich steadied him, then pulled out yet another photograph—the same woman, older, thinner in the face, but clearly pregnant.

"This was taken in the summer of 1940, perhaps a week or two before we entered the ghetto in Warsaw."

Janek was sick . . . sick at heart. He pulled his handkerchief from his pocket and wiped his brow, even though the evening wind tore at his coat.

"Do you need to sit down, Pan Kumiega?"

The familiar Polish expression, the compassion that he knew came hard to this man he'd wronged struck a chord in Janek. He nodded, unable to speak.

Dunovich guided him to the nearest bench.

"Your wife?" It was a silly question.

"Rosa. Our daughter, Ania, was born inside the ghetto."

"Mr. Dunovich—Pan Dunovich . . ."

"Itzhak."

"Itzhak." Janek dreaded to begin. What he would say could not be taken back. It would change everything . . . forever. "What happened? In Poland?"

"I left them. I left my wife and daughter in Warsaw to find my parents. We'd last seen them in Vilna, but there was no word. I thought only to be gone a short time—a month, no more—to bring them to Warsaw."

"Pan Nowak told me your wife was killed."

"Yes."

"You don't know what happened to your daughter." It was a statement of fact, a cutting to the chase.

"No."

Janek marveled at Itzhak's patience, the way he could paint a tremendously painful, life-changing picture in so few words. But it was Janek's turn now. Everything else Itzhak Dunovich might say would be superfluous.

Janek fingered the half medallion in his pocket, half of the one he'd seen in the photograph. At last he pulled it out and held it in his palm.

Itzhak gasped—half sob, half laugh. He didn't reach for the medallion but returned the photographs to the envelope and pocketed them near his heart. He pulled a length of chain from the same pocket and fitted its broken branches and trunk to the one in Janek's hand. "Whole," he whispered. "Shalom."

Janek closed his eyes. There could be no doubt.

"Tell me."

So Janek did. He told Itzhak all that Sophia had told him of the day her friend appeared with a little girl wearing half a medallion around her neck. He told him that the woman who was to reclaim the child never came, that Sophia had taken her underground and fed her, clothed her, saved her. When the ghetto burned, she began to accept the invented story of the child being her daughter. She gave the little girl her mother's name and raised her as her own. When it came time to leave Poland, she brought the girl out with her, claiming she was their child. "She saved Charlotte's life."

"She saved my Ania's life. And I am grateful. This makes my life worth living."

Janek moistened his lips. "Sophia and I—we've not been able to have children. The child she was carrying before the war started was lost to us."

"I'm sorry for you, for Pani Kumiega."

"The thing is, Pan Dunovich—Itzhak—we'd like to adopt Charlotte."

"Her name is Ania."

"Ania . . . believes she is our daughter already. We love her as our own. I believed she was mine. I couldn't love her more if she were. We could make the adoption private—quiet." Janek had been talking so quickly, so earnestly, that he didn't realize when Itzhak stood.

"I have waited and searched and hoped to find my daughter alive all these years. She is all I have left of my family—of my Rosa—in this world. I will not give her up. You are insane and selfish to ask such a thing."

"Think of Char—Ania! Sophia and I love her, can provide for her— a home, a family."

"I am her family!"

"She wouldn't be here if Sophia hadn't saved her. Please, if you won't listen to me, listen to her. All she went through during the war—"

"All she went through? I have no doubt your wife suffered. You could not live in Poland without suffering. But she is not Jewish! She has no idea what it is to watch your family starve, to see your friends shot or sent away in cattle cars, never to return. Her family was not lined up and gunned down, to fall in mass graves! Or made to dig up their bodies and burn their remains. Don't talk to me about the war being a hard time!"

"I'm sorry. I'm sorry. You're right."

"Every day I pray for my daughter's return. I escaped, I have survived, for this hope. She is part of Rosa and part of me. I want my daughter, Kumiega. I want her now."

"Think, Itzhak, I beg of you. How will you care for her? You're not married—a man living alone. You work. You will pull her from the only family she's ever known—at least, the only family she can remember."

"I will make arrangements for an apartment this week. I will come for her next Saturday."

Janek felt the world closing in on him. "Listen, if we can't adopt, please, let us be part of her life. Could you not be an uncle to her?"

"An uncle? You insult me, Kumiega! Would you be an uncle to your child?"

"I'll be anything in the world to Charlotte. Just, please, don't take her out of our lives. Pray about it—that's all I ask—please. We pray to the same God. We worship the same God. Please. Please."

◆

Itzhak left the park in a fury that quickly faded into euphoria at having found Ania, into joy and thanksgiving.

Blessed be Your Name, Adonai. All glory and honor and praise to You. You made a way when there was no way. You parted the Red Sea and brought my Ania to safety.

As he prayed each night that week, Itzhak's anger softened further at the realization that Adonai had worked through this Gentile couple, this Gentile woman who so loved his daughter . . . enough to risk her life for a Jewish child, Rosa's child, his child.

Still, they kept her from me, Adonai! he argued. *She is Jewish—and she must be raised as a Jew to honor You.*

A voice inside his head argued back. *When they realized the truth, the man, Janek, reached out.*

But she is my daughter! My Rosa's flesh, and mine. How can having her be wrong? How could giving her up be right? It would be like Rosa dying all over again. She only gave her away to save her. She meant to find her after the war. Adonai, You see the medallion. Papa was right. It is Rosa's promise to our daughter. I must keep that promise!

The voice in his head spoke again. *These good people love her too. They gave Ania safety and a home when you could not.*

Fear and love and anger and hope threatened to drown him. *You would not bring me such joy to have me give her away. . . . This I know!*

This is true. I love you, Itzhak, with everlasting love. I love Ania. I love Sophia Kumiega, and her husband, Janek.

Love was such a strong bond, such a tender emotion, so easily stolen. Itzhak closed his eyes. *I love you, Ania, my daughter. What is best for you, my Ania? What can I give you that they cannot give tenfold?*

Itzhak wrestled for hours, then for days. In the end he prayed, *Give me wisdom, Adonai. Show me what is best for my precious daughter. Give me wisdom and shalom—wholeness, peace, well-being for her, for me . . . and for the Kumiegas.*

CHAPTER FIFTY-SEVEN

SOPHIE SAW THE WEEK AS a death watch, knowing that Itzhak Dunovich would come on Saturday and change all their lives forever.

All week, as she combed and plaited Charlotte's hair, she did her best to memorize the highlights in each strand. She washed and pressed her school uniform with the care children lavished on newborn kittens.

At night it was almost too much to tuck her daughter in, knowing she wouldn't see her smile again until morning. The nights were excruciatingly long. Mornings, days sped by. Saturday came.

At breakfast, Janek asked their daughter, "Do you remember that I told you we will have a visitor today?"

"Yes, Papa. Someone from Poland—where we are from—you said."

"Yes, that's right. Pan Dunovich. He is your family. He wants to see you, to spend time with you."

"I still don't understand where Poland is." Whether Charlotte willfully ignored Janek's use of the word *family* or not, Sophie didn't know.

"It's very far away, my darling girl."

Sophie looked to her husband, thankful for his presence, thankful she was not alone to face this, and thankful he prepared Charlotte as best he could.

Minutes ticked by. Itzhak Dunovich would come soon to take their Charlotte—his Ania—away. She feared they hadn't prepared her enough. It was not right that they hadn't better prepared her. *But how? How do we tell our daughter that she isn't our daughter without frightening her? Tell her that a stranger will come and take her away?*

All week Sophie had thought wild thoughts, conjured elaborate schemes in her head. *I'll take Charlotte to Scotland, to Wales, to America. We can change our names. I can get a job to support us, perhaps in a library. In time, I'll contact Janek and he will join us. Itzhak Dunovich will never find us. Charlotte will never know that her father came looking for her—that he is anyone other than Janek.*

Just as surely, she knew those were fantasies. She would not leave her husband. She would not deceive him again. And though her heart fought her head, she would not, could not do such a thing to Itzhak Dunovich, or to Charlotte. She'd surrendered Charlotte to God; there was no going back.

When the knock came at the door, Sophie thought she might be sick. But Janek stood, squeezed her shoulder, and disappeared into the hallway. Sophie wrapped her arm around Charlotte's small shoulders. There was so much she wanted to say, needed to say, but the words wouldn't form. And then the man was before them.

Sophie's memory of Itzhak Dunovich had been hazy, denial mingled with a fog of fear. But as he bowed before her, flowers in hand, she saw that he was a handsome man in his own right, a man worn by cares and war, certainly, whose eyes showed that he'd probably slept as little as they had the night before.

"Pani Kumiega." He did not move to kiss her hand, as Polish men were wont, but handed her a large bouquet—a bouquet that must have cost him dearly. Yet his eyes were not on Sophie at all, but on Charlotte—hungry, eager eyes.

"Pan Dunovich," Sophie returned, nodding, a lump in her throat.

"Please, call me Itzhak."

"Itzhak, this is Charlotte." Janek spoke needlessly, Sophie thought, for the man's entire presence was glued to the little girl. He knelt before her, offering a smaller bouquet, reminding her of the day Janek knelt before Charlotte for the first time with just such a gift.

Charlotte looked into Itzhak's eyes, now just at her level. She saw the flowers and smiled. "For me?"

"Yes." He smiled, his eyes welling. "For you, my little princess."

"That's what Papa calls me too."

A shadow crossed Itzhak's eyes, but it disappeared quickly. "Then it must be true, yes?"

Charlotte smiled again, ducking her head into Sophie's side. Sophie's heart lurched.

"Sophia." Janek pulled her from her near despair. "Perhaps you will bring us all coffee and cake." He turned to Itzhak. "You will sit with us, yes?"

"Yes, for a time."

Sophie all but fled to the kitchen, hands trembling as she cut slices of the cake she'd prepared just for this moment. She didn't trust herself to pour the coffee. She must call Janek to carry the tray.

Everything prepared, she stepped back. A little laugh—Charlotte's laugh—came from the sitting room. Sophie groaned inside and tears trickled down her cheeks. She turned to the sink and braced herself. *Oh, Lord, I can't do this. Please. Please, help me. I don't understand—not any of this.*

Unbidden, the thought came to her: *Would you change one moment of your time with Charlotte? Would you go back and refuse to take her, to save her, to bring her to England?*

"No! No, Father!" She swiped at her tears, determined not to show a tearstained face to Charlotte, refusing to imagine that as her darling's last memory of her. "I would not change a moment. Thank You! Thank You for each precious day we've shared. Only, please, help me now. Help me do what is best for Charlotte . . . for Ania. Help me to want to do what is best for her, and for her father."

She wouldn't call for Janek to carry the tray. She would do it herself. It was her offering and she would bring it to the altar.

Sophie lifted the tray and walked as steadily as she could to the sitting room. There, sitting on the sofa, Itzhak leaned close to their little girl, showing her old photographs.

"And this is your mother, before you were born. You see the swelling there? That was you, inside her. You have her eyes, you see?"

Charlotte looked up as Sophie came into the room. "Mummy— come see! A picture of you and Papa on your wedding day, and one before I was born. You look different."

Sophie thought her heart might break. How could she answer? How would Itzhak Dunovich answer?

Sophie set the tea tray on the table, smoothed her skirt, and knelt before Charlotte. "Let me see, sweetheart." Charlotte handed her the pictures. The first was Itzhak and his wife on their wedding day. Sophie nearly gasped. The resemblance between the young woman with dark, laughing eyes and Charlotte was unmistakable. No wonder Itzhak Dunovich had been drawn, like a moth to flame, to the photograph on Janek's desk. She glanced up at Itzhak. His eyes challenged her, then relented. She understood. War upon war inside.

"These are beautiful pictures, my darling. Do you see how the woman looks like you? So pretty . . . the same dark hair, the same smiling eyes?"

Charlotte didn't say anything.

"But they are not pictures of me." Sophie swallowed. "They are pictures of another mother . . . your mother who gave you birth, and your father, Mr. Dunovich." Sophie couldn't speak after that. *Please, Janek, take over!*

But it was Itzhak Dunovich who spoke. "You are a very lucky little girl, you know."

"I am?"

"Indeed you are! You have two mamas, one named Rosa and one named Sophia, and two papas—me, Itzhak, and the other, Janek, here—who have always loved you very much, who will do anything and everything possible to love you, to take care of you, to make certain you are safe and happy."

"Is that true, Mummy?" Charlotte turned to Sophie.

"Yes, my darling. It's very true!" Sophie could hardly speak.

"There is something I must say, my little one." Itzhak took Charlotte's hand. "Families are not always who or what we're born into. . . . Sometimes in life—and in death—things happen that we do not expect, that we cannot control. Sometimes families are what we make them."

Sophie glanced up at Itzhak in wonder. The tender smile he gave her held no recrimination, only appreciation. She smiled in return, fearful, wary, but thankful.

"I don't understand. Nobody has two papas and two mummies," Charlotte insisted.

"No, it is not an easy thing to understand, my daughter," Itzhak continued. "It will take a very long time to explain—to tell you the story of your life, and of all the parents who love you." He shrugged and drew a deep breath that sounded like a sigh. "Perhaps it will take all of your life for us to explain . . . and all of ours." He glanced at Sophie and then at Janek.

Sophie felt her husband's pulse quicken from across the room—a flicker of hope.

"I will come each week to tell you more of your story, and of your grandparents and great-grandparents, and their stories. I will tell you now that your mama's name was Rosa, and that she died in the war . . . but before that she made certain you would be safe, by giving you to your mama Sophia, to care for you until I could return."

Charlotte looked as if it was too much to take in, and Sophie knew it was. *How can it not be?*

"Did Mama Rosa name me Charlotte?" The question surprised each of them.

"No," Itzhak said softly. "She named you Ania. A beautiful name, it means 'grace' and 'bringing goodness.' Your birth, your life, was grace to your mama and me."

"Charlotte Ania," the little girl whispered. "I have two pretty names."

"Yes."

"But I still don't understand."

"No," Itzhak said. "But you will, in time. There is no hurry, is there?" Now he looked at Sophie and then Janek, but Sophie's heart was too full to speak.

"No hurry at all." Janek spoke, his voice broken.

Itzhak nodded and turned again to Charlotte. "One day soon I will take you to the synagogue, where I worship. And when you are grown I will take you, I hope, to Poland to see for yourself where you came from."

"Why can't we go now?" And then Charlotte seemed to back-pedal. "We'll go. All of us."

"It isn't safe . . . not yet. Perhaps one day. One day, yes, perhaps we can all go."

Sophie felt her frozen heart crack, the seeping in of a thaw she hadn't imagined, could not even now comprehend. She looked into Janek's eyes, rounded with love and hope. To think she'd believed there was no way. To think she'd almost given up on this good man.

She looked at Itzhak Dunovich as he pulled two medallion halves on gold chains from his pocket—the medallion she'd believed would be her undoing, the medallion she'd dreaded to see reunited. Pan Bukowski's words came back to her. *"Remember the Red Sea . . . Adonai makes a way when there is no way."*

Itzhak placed a half medallion around Charlotte's neck, the other half around his own. He leaned down and touched the two together, forming a whole. "This, my princess, belonged to your mama Rosa. It is the Tree of Life. It is a symbol of the beginning and the fulfillment of everything—wholeness—of our life forever with Adonai."

Charlotte leaned against him, mesmerized by the intricate tree limbs, perhaps weary from the upending of her known world, and not understanding all the words the grown-ups in the room, in her life, spoke. Itzhak put his arm around her and began to hum, then sing.

Sophie took the seat on the other side of Charlotte, recognizing the words from the Polish lullaby he sang, a lullaby she imagined Rosa had sung to their daughter as a baby. She joined him now.

"Oh, sleep, my darling.
If you'd like a star from the sky, I'll give you one."

Note to Readers

WHILE ON A WRITERS' RETREAT, I received a Facebook message from longtime friend Sandra Lavelle asking if I'd seen a news article. Her link led me to an amazing story—the discovery and unearthing of a WWII escape tunnel in Lithuania by an international team of archaeologists.

Goose bumps ran up my arms as I read. Something about it rang familiar—as if I'd been there before.

I walked into town that morning for a coffee and newspaper to clear the "ghosts" from my brain. While sipping coffee in the outdoor café, I came across the same story in print.

And then I remembered. Years before, while doing Holocaust research, I'd viewed a powerful documentary, *Shoah*, in which Claude Lanzmann, over an eleven-year period, had traveled the world to research and interview surviving concentration camp inmates, SS commandants, and Jewish, German, and Polish eyewitnesses of the "final solution"—Nazi efforts to systematically exterminate human beings. *Shoah* was first presented in French (1985) and later in English (1999).

The documentary includes over nine hours of heart-wrenching, mind-boggling interviews and tours, including the testimony of men who'd been assigned the unthinkable in the Ponary Forest.

When it appeared that the Russians were closing in and would retake Lithuania, Heinrich Himmler, for fear that Nazi wartime atrocities would be discovered, ordered eighty Jewish men to dig up and burn bodies (approximately 70,000 Jewish and 30,000 others) that the SS had shot and dropped into mass graves. Details of the assignment were too horrific to comprehend. Prisoners knew that they, too, would be murdered once their gruesome labor ended so that there would be no witnesses. It was then that the prisoners contrived to dig, by night, a tunnel from their pit of imprisonment to the forest's edge, and escape. They had only their hands, spoons, and a few electricians' tools to do the job.

Until new technology (using radar and radio waves to scan the area) verified the existence of the tunnel in 2016, the story had been relegated to the stuff of myths—an escape tale so fantastic people found it hard to believe.

With the tunnel's discovery, old interviews were resurrected and the children of Holocaust heroes rejoiced that their parents' accounts were confirmed. *Nova* aired a documentary revealing the scientists' search and tunnel discovery in 2017.

Past interviews included the story of a man (Isaac Dogim, sometimes spelled Itzhak Dugin) who, in the process of digging up bodies, found those of his family. Some sources reported he found his mother, three sisters, and their children. Some sources said it was his wife and sisters. According to the story I read, he had identified the partially decomposed bodies of some of his family by their clothing and his wife by the medallion she wore around her neck—a medallion he'd given her on their wedding day.

I remember walking back to the retreat house after reading the story in the newspaper, legs trembling with the realization that this was what I would write next. I didn't know how my fictional story would begin or end, or even the story's purpose; I only knew that I was angry such carnage had ever taken place, that it must not happen again, and that I couldn't get the image of this man's horrific, heart-breaking discovery of his wife out of my mind. By the time I reached the house, I could see and hear some of the characters in my head, and a picture of the medallion had formed clearly in my mind. I walked inside, shared the newspaper story with author friends Terri Gillespie and Carrie Turansky, and said, "This is my next story, and what if the medallion is the Tree of Life?"

As I reread transcripts containing Itzhak Dugin's (or Isaac Dogim's) and other interviews, and began researching details, I asked the Lord to show me the greater purpose of this story—what in this would bring Him glory and what would He teach me through its writing? What would bless and encourage readers?

For several months, my sister, Gloria Delk, and others had sent me links to Irena Sendler's story. Irena was a Polish Catholic social worker who accepted the challenge to develop a network within Żegota (the underground Polish Council to Aid Jews) to rescue children during WWII. Despite terrible risks, they smuggled 2,500 Jewish children from the Warsaw Ghetto and certain death at the hands of the Nazis, then hid them in Polish homes, convents, churches, and hospitals until the end of the war.

For years I've admired Irena Sendler and those who worked with her, as well as the courageous Polish families and others who took in children. I thought how wonderful it would be to tell her story—their story. But it had been done, in numerous books. Best of all is *Life in a Jar*—a nonfiction account of Irena's heroism and the American teens who uncovered her story for the world based on firsthand interviews. I could add nothing to that brilliant work, and yet I couldn't get her story or her lifelong mission and approach to life out of my mind.

Irena's father, a medical doctor, treated impoverished Jewish patients for typhus when no other doctor would risk helping them. While treating his patients, he contracted typhus. As he lay dying, the young Irena asked him why he'd done it. He replied that when someone is drowning, you jump in to save them, whether or not you can swim. It was a principle Irena lived by all her life.

Of the 2,500 Jewish children her network helped to save, approximately 2,000 were found after the war. Though their parents had been murdered (mostly at Treblinka), many were united with extended family, thanks to lists Irena had kept hidden of the children's Jewish names and the new Aryan names and addresses they were assigned. Approximately 400 to 500 children were never found.

Theories abound regarding the whereabouts of those 400 to 500: Perhaps they and their foster families had been discovered and killed by the Nazis or died by other means during the war. Perhaps the foster families had been forced to move away or hide, taking the children, and left no means of contact. Perhaps the foster families had bonded so closely that they wanted to keep the children or the children knew them as their only parents, and they moved away so they wouldn't have to give them up. Young children might never even know they were Jewish.

What became of all those children? What became of one?

I wondered, if I had hidden a child, loved and treated them as my own for several years of war, bonded with them and believed their parents had perished . . . if that were the only child in my life and my only reason to get up in the morning and keep going, if I'd grown to fear the powers that be and what might become of this beloved child if I came forward, would I be able to give up that child at war's end? Would I lie to hide and protect that child—and my family? Would I lie to my family?

Irena Sendler's story and these threads entwined through my heart and mind and joined with the threads of Itzhak Dugin's (or Isaac Dogim's) story to form a whole.

Most of the other characters in this book are creations of my imagination, inspired by stories I've read or composites of interviews I've conducted. Father Stimecki is a composite of priests who gave the names and identities of Polish Catholic dead to Jews to save their lives and to extend medical benefits when those benefits were denied Jews under Nazi occupation. Jan and Antonina Żabiński owned and operated the zoo in Warsaw and hid Jews and others there during the war, including (for a short time) Irena Sendler. Dr. Janusz Korczak was a respected Polish pediatrician and well-known radio personality who advocated for children and authored the beloved children's book *King Matt the First*.

During the war, Dr. Korczak ran an orphanage for Jewish children in the Warsaw Ghetto. Though repeatedly offered opportunities for freedom, he refused to leave the children for whom he cared. Very much as my story portrays, Dr. Korczak marched with the children to the train that would take them all to be killed at Treblinka.

These are the real heroes of this story.

The Medallion is a reminder to help when help is needed, regardless of the cost to ourselves.

It is a reminder that anti-Semitism has run rampant not only through history, but continues in our country and throughout the world today. We must be vigilant, knowing that "never again" can be the outcome only when we all stand for our neighbor and those in need, and when we all stand against hatred and violence.

It is the story of our surrender to the One who loves us with everlasting love and knows best and beyond what we can imagine—even when we're terrified that our losses and letting go will consume us.

As Pan Bukowski taught Sophia, we don't know how the Red Sea parted when Moses and the Israelites, desperate, at their wits' ends and pursued by enemies, stood at the water's edge—only that God made it happen.

In the same way, He can part the Red Seas—the deep and raging waters—of our lives. When we are still enough to watch, to listen, when we lean not on our own understanding but trust in Him, acknowledging Him in all our ways, He will direct our steps. Trusting Him is our path to peace, to the fullness of shalom.

When there seems no way forward, our God who is able can forge paths we never imagined.

God's eternal love and blessings for you,
Cathy Gohlke

Discussion Questions

1. As Irena Sendler's father lay dying of typhus, contracted from the impoverished Jewish patients he treated when no other Gentile doctors would, he reminded her of something she'd heard from him many times before: if you see someone drowning, you must rescue him, even if you cannot swim. Do you agree with this philosophy? How do characters in *The Medallion* live this out?

2. Pan Bukowski retrieved things important to Sophie and others after the initial bombing that damaged their apartment building. In the process, he was killed. Why do you think he took such a risk? Should he have done so?

3. Pan Gadomski was willing to separate himself from the daughter he loved in order to protect her and to further the cause of Polish resistance to Nazi oppression. What do you think of his decisions?

4. For a long while, Terri did all in her power to keep a promise her father had made to Janek, to protect Sophie. Was that fair when she knew Sophie wanted so desperately to help with resistance activities? What would you have done?

5. The Dunovich family struggled with whether or not to hoard food in order to sustain themselves through threatening days ahead. Do you believe they made the right decisions? Why or why not?

6. Believing the Gestapo would soon be at her door, Rosa made the heartbreaking decision to give up her daughter. Can you imagine doing this with your child, or would you have made a different choice?

7. The Żabińskis hid Jews and others in their zoo. Some Polish Catholics hid Jews in convents, and some Poles, both Catholic and Protestant, hid Jews and resisters in their homes. Many worked to feed or clothe or in some way help those whom it was illegal to help under German occupation. Do you think you could have done these things? What do you think led some Polish Gentiles to help Jews and others to refrain from helping?

8. Sophie was so terrified of losing Charlotte that she led Janek to believe Charlotte was their biological daughter. Why do you think she was so afraid? How did you feel about her decisions?

9. Itzhak Dunovich searched long for his daughter and could not wait to claim her. But in the end, he struggled with what was best for Ania. What do you think of his ultimate conclusion?

10. Later in life, Irena Sendler said, "After World War II, it seemed that humanity understood something, and nothing like that would happen again. Humanity has understood nothing. Religious, tribal, national wars continue. The world continues to be in a sea of blood. The world can be better if there's love, tolerance, and humility." Do you agree or disagree? What do you believe is the answer for our world?

About the Author

Three-time Christy and two-time Carol and INSPY Award–winning and bestselling author **CATHY GOHLKE** writes novels steeped with inspirational lessons, speaking of world and life events through the lens of history. She champions the battle against oppression, celebrating the freedom found only in Christ. Cathy has worked as a school librarian, drama director, and director of children's and education ministries. When not traveling to historic sites for research, she, her husband, and their dog, Reilly, divide their time between northern Virginia and the Jersey Shore, enjoying time with their grown children and grandchildren. Visit her website at www.cathygohlke.com and find her on Facebook at CathyGohlkeBooks.

Don't miss more great fiction from
CATHY GOHLKE

When Annie Allen's brother dies with the sinking of the *Titanic*, the last thing she wants is a friendship with a stranger, especially the man her brother died saving.

Driven by a shameful past and a perilous future, Maureen O'Reilly and her sister flee Ireland to New York in search of safety, liberty, and opportunity.

One letter, one request, leads to a truth so dark, Rachel Kramer and Jason Young—an American journalist working in Germany—will risk everything to bring it to light.

CP0756